SKELMERSDALE

A tale of life and love in 18th century
Scotland.
Flight from Revolutionary Paris leads
Walter Paterson to seek his family roots.
But times are changing in Scotland too.
In fast-expanding Glasgow and
Enlightenment Edinburgh, Paterson
discovers adventure.
In Strathblane he finds a future and, in the
hand of the pretty Primrose Moncrieff,
fulfillment.

Helen Lillie grew up in Strathblane. After
graduating from Glasgow University she
went to America to study at the Yale
Drama School. For many years she has
written a Washington letter for *The Herald*
in Glasgow. She and her Scottish husband
live in Washington D.C. She has
published two other novels and many
articles.

HOME TO STRATHBLANE

Walter Paterson, the son of an emigré Jacobite Scot, is forced to flee Revolutionary France. Wounded and confused, he is brought by the rum-running Captain Abernethy to Glasgow and then to the village of Strathblane where contraband is stored and sold.

As he recovers his health, Walter Paterson falls in love not just with Scottish country life, but with the lovely young sister of the local Laird. Unattainable alas! . . . until he puts his life in order.

Caught up in parish politics, Walter Paterson finds that times are turbulent in Scotland too. There's conflict between the conservative Kirk Session and an enlightened and brash new doctor. The local economy is growing, tied to Glasgow's rapidly expanding trade. Attitudes in the local society are changing fast.

Helen Lillie sews a fine thread of accurate period detail as she takes her hero from Strathblane to bustling Glasgow and Enlightenment Edinburgh, then back home to Strathblane and love.

From across the range of eighteenth century Scottish society, Walter Paterson encounters some convincing characters.

Captain Andrew Abernethy fearlessly plies his illegal trade in brandy, wine, rum and tea between France and Scotland. He is warmly encouraged in his challenge to the authorities by wide popular patronage.

Mr Campbell – the Session Clerk of the Kirk and Exciseman, both positions of high authority. An imposing figure and a traditionalist in all matters, he keeps a firm hold on all in the parish.

Alison Graham is the widowed proprietress of Leddie Green estate. A cultured hard-working and practical woman who has designs on the Laird.

Jean MacDougal – the plain-speaking daughter of the farm at Puddock Hole who nurses Walter Paterson back to health and gives wise council.

Henry Moncrieff has fallen into the Lairdship of Kirklands estate through the death in the American War of his elder brother. Wears his responsibility heavily.

Primrose Moncrieff young, pretty, educated and able, keeps house for her brother and can influence the Laird in most things. But her caution in managing the right outcome puts Walter's love at risk.

Douglas Stewart is the new young doctor who brings a disreputable past to his village charge. He does not stand on ceremony and has some radical ideas about medicine and life – passionate and impulsive, a man ahead of his time.

HOME TO STRATHBLANE

HOME TO STRATHBLANE

Helen Lillie

© Helen Lillie

First published 1993
by Argyll Publishing
Glendaruel
Argyll PA22 3AE

06003419 ○

The author has asserted her moral rights.
No part of this book may be reproduced or transmitted in
any form or by any means mechanical or electrical,
including photocopy, without permission in writing,
except by a reviewer in connection with a newspaper,
magazine or broadcast.

Acknowledgement for the use on the cover of part of John
Grassom's Map of Stirlingshire, 1817, is due to Central
Regional Council Archives.

**British Library Cataloguing-in-Publication Data.
A catalogue record for this book is available from
the British Library.**

ISBN 1 874640 40 8

Cover painting and illustrations by Marcia Clark
Typeset and origination by
Cordfall Ltd, Civic Street, Glasgow
Printed and bound in Great Britain by
HarperCollins, Glasgow

Respectfully dedicated
to the memory
of
the late George S Pryde
who as Professor of Scottish History
at Glasgow University
introduced me to the study of
my own community, the Blane valley,
and also to Henry Grey Graham's
Social Life of Scotland in the Eighteenth Century
which eventually inspired this novel

ACKNOWLEDGEMENTS

Many people have helped with this book, either with information or moral support. Here, in alphabetical order, are some of them:

Albert C Capotosto, a former boss on whose time I wrote the first draft; Dr Catherine Gavin, teacher and role model; Audrey Gillon of Georgetown Presbyterian Church; at *The Herald* – Anne Johnston, Arnold Kemp, Betty Kirkpatrick, John Linklater and especially, Edna Robertson; Alladine Bell Hockensmith, encourager since our days at Yale Drama School; Martha Irwin, who coped with the manuscript; my cousin Dr Morag L Insley, who reinforced me on the medical parts; my late mother, Helen B Lillie; Helen M Lowe CA; Mairead Maginnes and the Department of Scottish History at Glasgow University; my longsuffering husband Charles Scott Marwick and his nephew, the late Ewan Marwick; my editor-publisher Derek Rodger; the late P A Spalding, poet and lover of Scotland; Sylvia Sunderlin who had unwavering faith in the book; and my agent, Cathie Thomson, who also had faith in me. To all, mistakes are mine, not yours!

All the characters in this book are fictitious with the exception of the dominie, Mr Benjamin Hepburn, whose deplorable conduct is described in Guthrie Smith's book on The Parish of Strathblane. There never was a Laird of Kirklands though the name recurs in the Parish annals. There was however, a farm called Puddock Hole which I have taken the liberty of moving to the opposite side of the Blane valley.

Helen Lillie Washington D C, July 1993

CONTENTS

PART ONE

FLIGHT FROM TERROR

The appearance of the country is agreeably picturesque; coming from the South, the traveller at first ascends from the fertile fields of New Kilpatrick into what appears to be an extensive heath; but he no sooner enters than he finds it interspersed with cultivated fields, and here and there observes a lake of several acres. Descending into the valley, he is charmed with the verdure of the country, the mildness of the air, and the appearance of cheerfulness and plenty which is displayed around. Several neat villas scattered along the bottom of the hills, here and there a cascade precipitating its torrents from their sides enliven and beautify the scene. In summer the landscape is enlivened and adorned by the luxuriant foliage of the woods with which the hills are skirted and the whole receives an air of grandeur from the abrupt precipices with which the hills terminate.

Description of Strathblane in
The Old Statistical Account, 1795

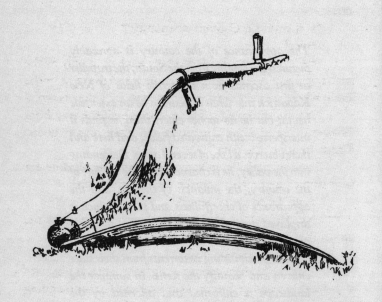

I

THE EQUINOCTIAL GALES had blown so long and hard that, though she had been expecting it all week, the knock on the farm house door took Jean MacDougal by surprise. But even knowing who it might be, she armed herself with a heavy broom before she opened the door a chink.

"Is it yourself, Captain Abernethy?"

"Aye."

She let him into the dark, chilly kitchen lit only by the smoking peat fire and a solitary candle set on the table by the loom where she had been weaving cloth for a new gown.

"It's a terrible night for ye to come all the way from Glasgow. Never mind the muck and glaur on yer boots. Come in out o' the rain."

Tension made her talkative. She had been all alone for several days and nights and she was a sociable girl.

"Is yer faither here, Jean?"

"No. He's at the Hallow Fair. He should be back the morn. But I can help ye wi the crates."

The Captain shook his head.

"They're too heavy for a young lass." He was big, with a seaman's weather-beaten skin and clear, commanding blue eyes. But as he brushed the wet out of them, they did not meet hers and she wondered why.

"Would ye like a hot toddy or a dram before ye start to unload?"

"No, thank ye kindly. I . . . er. . . "

It was so unlike him to be indecisive that she asked,

"Has something gone wrong?"

"Naw. What exciseman would be out on a night like this? But, Jean . . . I've brought a man wi me. He came over from France on my ship."

"A Frenchie?"

"Naw. A Scot like you and me. Wi money. His faither paid me well to get him out o' the country and save him from the guillotine."

Her eyes narrowed.

"Did he ken ye were a smuggler?"

"I carry legal freight too, Jean. It's just the odd keg or barrel, some wine or brandy. And the tea. Ye know that. Can I bring him in out o' the cold?"

"Faither doesnae like me having strange men here when he's awa. Or onytime."

"Jean. Ye dinnae understand. This laddie's sick. . . And yer auntie – the midwife – Mrs Semple, cured that sailor o' mine with the fever last year. . . "

Her brown eyes flashed.

"If ye're plannin' to leave this Frenchie here, ye can think again and think different. I'm all alone – and if my faither came back and found a sick man in yon bed! It's one thing, Andra Abernethy, letting ye rent the back o' the barn for to store yer liquor – and to help ye sell it, but I'm having no more o' yer riffraff in my house!"

"He's no riffraff," the Captain protested. "He's a gentleman. And Jeanie, he cannae go any further. It was a long rough voyage and he was sick to death."

"I'm no wanting no sickness here."

"He's wounded."

"Then I'll see to his hurts and ye can take him back tae Glasgow."

"Ye'll be well paid." He drew a purse from his pocket and emptied it onto the kitchen table. The ugly face of George the Third stared at her from the coins.

"It's no enough for the risk I'd be taking. . . " But there was hesitation in her voice. It was a goodly sum for Scotland in 1792.

"Who'd know he was here?" asked Abernethy.

"The whole valley! It's a gossipy wee parish, Strathblane."

He shrugged this off. "Tell them he's distant kin. We all hae them in Scotland." And then he added, "there's more money that his faither gave me for his passage from Boulogne."

"I thought there was a ferry from there to England."

"Aye, but for that he'd hae needed a passport . . . and there was no time. Jean, this Revolution in France, they're starting to call it a 'Reign o' Terror'. There's a new government every week and this last one – the Tribunal or some such name, I cannae keep up with them – is arresting every rich aristocrat they can lay their hands on, confiscating their property, and then beheading them."

"Ye just telt me this man was a Scot."

"Aye. His faither's a banker in Paris. Paterson's their name. But he's connected with some o' the nobility, or at least his son was involved with one o' them in some politicking trouble."

"And why were these Patersons in France?" asked the young Jean MacDougal whose interest was clearly deepening.

"I didnae ask. Maybe they were Jacobites and went there after the '45. The faither was the right age for that. . . Will ye no take a look at him?"

"Aye," said Jean grudgingly, "and I'll ask him a few questions, too." She took a plaid down from a wall hook and draped it over her head and shoulders. "I'm making no promises. Even with what we get frae the sale o' the tea, it's hard enough, without another mouth to feed."

The cart drawn by two ponderous Clydesdale horses was already sinking into the farmyard mud. An old sail formed a tented enclosure between the crates of contraband and as Abernethy drew it back and held up his lantern, Jean saw a long body curled fetally under a cloak. She stretched out her hand and fingered the material knowingly She drew the collar back from the man's face and gasped. He was young, pitifully young, no older than herself. In health he would be handsome, with regular features and a shock of fine blond hair, but now his skin was drawn and fevered, his eyes shut, his face tense with suffering. Bloodstains smeared his blue jacket and on the hand that emerged from his ruffled shirtcuff – at an odd, unnatural angle – he wore a heavy signet ring. Not one, but two, elegant gold watches dangled from a chain on his waistcoat.

Yet for all these signs of affluence, he reminded her of the little wounded animals she could never turn away from the kitchen door, the lambs, the helpless puppies and kittens she raised every season.

"Weel?" Abernethy challenged, and despite her misgivings, she nodded.

"Take him ben the hoose. I'll hold the lantern for ye."

As the Captain lifted him from the cart, the young man's eyes opened and he cried out but he was too far gone to protest. In the kitchen, they peeled off his wet cloak and between them, hoisted him into the box bed.

"You take off the rest o' his claes, Captain, while I find a nightshirt o' faither's. Should I gie him a toddy?"

"Try a peg o' brandy to bring him around and heat some bricks."

As she gathered up the cloak she asked,

"Whaur's the rest o' the money?"

"Ach, Jeannie, there was no more."

She did not believe him but decided to bide her time. They had had business dealings before and she had never been outsmarted by him. As she bustled about the kitchen, he asked,

"Can ye gie me a drink and some food before I go back

to Glasgow? It's a gey long, hard twelve miles and there's no sign o' the weather improving. I may no be able to get back aboard the *Mary Ann.*"

"Where is she docked?"

"Off the Broomielaw, but I didnae dare bring her close to shore in this weather."

"I've broth all made, and ye can take some bread and cheese to eat on the way."

"Thank ye kindly," Captain Abernethy almost sighed in appreciation.

Having undressed the young man and put the nightshirt on him, Abernethy shambled towards the door and announced,

"I'll be taking the tea and brandy intae the barn . . . what there is of it."

Jean gathered up the discarded garments and went through them carefully. She found some loose French coins in the pockets, a couple of fine linen handkerchiefs, and two gold watches. There was also an official-looking document, some kind of identification paper, in French, and made out to "Walter James Paterson". It was dirty and crumpled and had been much handled. She tidied it with the rest of the small items into a dresser drawer and took the clothing out to the back door, where she dumped them into a bucket of cold water to soak out the blood.

"Louis! Louis!" came a man's voice from the kitchen *"Louis! Depeches-toi! Pour l'amour de Dieu, Depeches toi!"*

She ran back to find the stranger trying to struggle up in bed. He had handsome blue eyes but there was no light of reason in them.

"Here! Bide a wee!"

He caught her wrist with his left hand. *"Maman! Clemmie. . ."* Then, in a crescendo of agony, *"Pierre! Pierre! Non! Non! Laissez!"*

The unbuttoned nightshirt fell open, revealing a soiled bandage around his right shoulder. Alarmed, she started to strip it off and as she did so, he gasped and fainted. When Abernethy returned, she was bending over the bed, a basin of water and some clean rags within reach on the table.

"Captain, have ye seen his wounds?"

He looked and shivered. "Eh, sirs!"

"And his wrist. Is it broke, d'ye think?"

He touched the swelling gingerly. "Aye."

"He'll need the doctor."

It was the Captain's turn to hesitate. "Can ye trust him?"

"He's new to the parish. I'm no acquainted, but my auntie fair likes him."

"Gie him a wide berth, Jean. He could turn us over to the Excise."

"That's no likely but he might tell the Laird who's a justice o' the peace and terrible against the French. . . " The sick man moaned. "But . . . Andra! What'll I do? This laddie might die! He's gey weak!"

"Ach, no. He's young an' strong and he survived a rough voyage. Put a clean bandage on him and let yer auntie break his fever. Maybe I can bring him back to Glasgow on my next trip."

"And when might that be?"

"Ten days or so. I've a big cargo to unload and I need to make anither trip out this way before I sail again. I couldnae make my other deliveries with him in the cart." He picked up his lantern, anxious to go before she changed her mind. "I'll be away then, Jean."

She grabbed the broom again and barred the door. "Whaur's the money? The laddie didnae have it."

"Ye're awfa' hard for sic a young lassie."

"We need it. We make nothin off the farm these days."

"Ye'll promise no to call a doctor 'till I'm well away?"

"Not if ye bring my auntie up here in yer cart!" When he shook his head, she pleaded, "I'm here masel' wi a strange man that's sick to death! Andra', please! Her cottage isnae far down the road. And I'll put up some food for ye to eat, on the return trip!"

"Verra well," the man relented.

"And hand over that money! Whatever they gave you to bring him here."

He tossed another purse at her. She tore it open and her face fell.

"These are French coins!"

"Aye. But they're gold! Ye can change them in Glasgow. What else did ye expect, woman?"

"But, Captain. . . "

"Put them in the plate when ye go to the kirk. And see ye treat Mr Paterson well, you and Mrs Semple."

She glared at him.

"Ye can trust me, Andra Abernethy."

II

Easing back the bed curtain with his uninjured hand, Walter Paterson looked curiously about him. He was in a small kitchen, with pots simmering over a hearth. A grandfather clock ticked erratically in one corner. There was a rough kitchen table with chairs and in a corner a spinning wheel, set up with its wools near a window which opened onto a farmyard. In the background, he glimpsed hills and moorland.

It was a far cry from his beautiful home in France, but it felt safe. Am I really on my native heath at last? he wondered. And how did I get here? He had a confused remembrance of a ship in heavy seas, being taken off it in freezing rain and revived by the rawest whisky he had ever tasted. Then he had been loaded into a cart where pain had knocked him into unconsciousness.

Later, he remembered two women, one a heavy-handed crone who ruthlessly bound a makeshift splint onto his broken wrist, ignoring his agonised cries, and another who was warm, redolent of milk and the clean peaty smell of the country, who had cradled him in her arms like a baby.

Now here he was, his mind clear again, in a pleasant if humble haven, drowsy as though from some potion, with a faint taste of herbs in his mouth.

A man's hat, a blue Scots bonnet, hung from a nail on the wall along with several plaids, and through the half-open door he saw the back of a young woman taking his clothes down from a line. Hens scratched around her feet.

Do I have Rousseau's Noble Savage to wait on me? he mused, and is she beautiful?

Jean came bustling through the kitchen with the basket of laundry, too occupied to glance towards the box bed.

"*Bon jour, mademoiselle* . . . er . . . how do you do?" Did she, he wondered, speak Gaelic? Though he had travelled all over Europe, his ignorance of Scotland was lamentable – if he really was in Scotland.

She swung around. Curly brown hair framed a square, fresh face and her shabby worsted dress showed the frank curves of a solid, well-proportioned body. Her feet were bare and muddy but she had a clean white kerchief around her neck.

Walter appraised her as not beautiful – attractive certainly, though not his type.

"So ye're better!" she exclaimed with a warm smile. "Yer claes are all washed and your money and watches in the drawer." She jerked her head towards a big dresser, her arms occupied with the laundry basket.

"How long have I been here?"

"Twa days. Ye didn't know me afore."

"I don't know you yet, *mademoiselle.*"

"My name is Jean MacDougal and this is my faither's farm of Puddock Hole in Strathblane. Ye can bide here as long as ye want, Mr Paterson . . . but now if ye'll excuse me, I'll be taking in the rest of the wash, for there's another shower blowing up over Loch Lomond."

She moved on into what he supposed was an outhouse, but came back almost at once, stirring something in a pewter mug.

"Auntie said you were to take this when you woke." She eased him up in bed and with the movement, pain flared up in full force.

"*Dieu!* My shoulder!"

"Ye've suffered fair cruel with it." She pressed his left hand. "Auntie says there's a bullet bedded in ye, and ye've all manner of cuts and bruises. Forbye your wrist needs proper setting."

Gently she made him swallow the herbal drink and then touching his forehead, she remarked as if as an afterthought, "I think the fever's well broke. Would you like a fresh nightshirt?"

All he wanted was to lie still.

"No. Thank you. Just let me rest."

"Aye, and maybe now I can leave ye, I should go for the doctor. Auntie's only a howdie – a midwife – she knows naught about surgery."

Walter had already suffered so appallingly at the hands of an inexperienced medical man, he couldn't face the prospect of some unknown country sawbones who might do him more harm than good.

"No. No. I don't want a doctor. . . How far are we from the city?"

"From Glasgow? Twelve miles."

Glasgow. He frowned. "Where exactly are we?"

"In the Blane Valley. That's in Stirlingshire."

"And . . . where is Edinburgh from here?"

"Eh. A long way. . . "

"I must go there."

"Ye're not fit to travel, laddie. . . What's your name? If you don't mind, it's an awfa' mouthful calling you 'Mr Paterson'."

"Walter. And you?"

"Jean."

He raised her hand to his lips with an attempt at gallantry.

"I thank you Jean, for all you have done. And . . . no doctor, please."

She smiled.

"As ye say Walter." She smoothed his fair hair, planted a little kiss of her own on his brow. "Ye have anither wee sleep now."

"Yes. I must build up some strength."

For he had to go to Edinburgh. All the way from Paris to Boulogne, on that terrible journey, with the fear of arrest by the Revolutionary police at every stop. His father had told him, over and over again,

"Go to your Uncle Alexander in Edinburgh. He'll take care of you. You'll find him at the Parliament House. He's an advocate. His wife, your Aunt Janet, was a Miss Hay, and you have four cousins – Betsy, Peter, Susan and Grizel. They live in the Old Town, in the Lawnmarket. . . "

. . . Or was it the Grassmarket? Walter had been so overwhelmed by pain and guilt for the disaster he believed he had brought about that he had not taken it all in, though he did remember his father saying that the Edinburgh Patersons lived near the University where there was a medical college

– one of the finest in Europe.

More recollection surfaced and with them questions. Was Louis de Sincerbeaux alive? Had he gone to Holland or to Coblenz to join the emigre army? Were his parents and his sister Clementina still safe? What had actually happened when he and Louis were evading arrest, trying to get out of Paris, away from the guillotine. . . ?

. . . The Guillotine that they had watched at its bloody work in the Place de La Concorde . . . that fatal morning.

The recollections were too terrible in his weak state. He pushed the whole dreadful experience down in his mind, resolved to concentrate on getting well and continuing on to Edinburgh.

That should not be a long journey, for was not Scotland a small country compared to France?

And what a beautiful one, he reflected as, following the progress of rain clouds across the distant hills, his eyes closed again.

The fever had indeed left him and soon he was out of bed, testing his shaky legs. But he had underestimated the debilitating effect of the pain. It would stab his shoulder unnervingly when he least expected it, and his wrist hurt with maddening insistence. Walter had been reared to be spartan so tried to hide his discomfort, but the effort sapped his small store of energy and by night-time he was thankful to retreat to the hard, narrow box bed, where he could let down his guard and sob into the straw-filled pillows.

But, however hard he tried to muffle the sounds, Jean always heard him and came downstairs to comfort him as she had done in his sickness and he felt no shame revealing his weakness to her.

"Why aren't you married with a dozen children?" he asked her one evening as she fed him a posset of hot milk.

"Who'd look after ma faither if I was gone? And yourself, lambie. . . Forbye I've no tocher."

"What's that?"

"I think the English word is dowry."

"A marriage portion?"

"Aye."

"I'll give you the money. I owe it to you."

"Ach no, laddie. It's our duty to care for the poor."

As the son and heir of a prosperous banker, this thought was novel enough to make him laugh.

"Jean, I'm not poor. Although . . . perhaps for the moment. . . But you turned over a lot of gold to me."

"Aye, and ye'll need it yersel'."

"Only to pay for my journey to Edinburgh. After that my family will take care of me. My uncle's an advocate and they're always rich."

Certainly his relatives would be better off than the MacDougals, for on short strolls around the farm he had observed that their land produced few crops. Most of their ready money must come from housing and selling Captain Abernethy's contraband.

He had been amused, when neighbours stopped in to collect bottles of wine or packets of tea, to be introduced to them by Jean as 'my cousin from Linlithgow'.

"It's as well no to mention that the Captain brought you here," she told him privately. "And I do have an aunt in the East that married well."

The MacDougals, Walter learned, had come down in the world. They had a roomy house furnished with some fine old family heirlooms to prove this. It was primitive however. Though Walter being young and having done a lot of travelling, quickly adjusted to the lack of conveniences and having to wash in cold water, if at all.

Jean was an excellent cook. When she went out she

dressed stylishly in dresses she had made herself out of fabric woven from the wool she spun and dyed. Although she lacked formal education, she was intelligent and had considerable worldly wisdom. She was also a better manager than her father.

Angus MacDougal, the farmer, was a big toothless man in his fifties who though he laboured hard all day, considered himself a landowner. He was, he explained to Walter, a 'kindly tenant' whose forebears had owned the *poffle* or freehold of Puddock Hole for many generations – longer, he was fond of pointing out, than the Moncrieffs, the most substantial family in Strathblane, had owned the estate of Kirklands, which ran adjacent to the farm.

"I'm a heritor in the kirk," Angus stated proudly, though this meant little to Walter. "The minister bows to me every Sunday as he does to the gentry. And I'd be among them masel' if it wasnae for ma legal plea. . . "

Walter soon understood the ramifications of the MacDougals' lawsuit as well as Angus himself, for every evening the old man would talk at length about his case, which concerned a strip of moorland between his ground and that of the Laird of Kirklands, Mr Henry Moncrieff. When the land had been enclosed, some twenty-five years back in the time of Angus's father, its ownership had come into question. The MacDougals had let their cattle graze on the Kirklands fields and the other family had complained – since they had been to the expense of putting up dykes and fences. The Moncrieffs then tried to buy out the MacDougals who, at one particularly destitute moment accepted the bribe.

A few years later, however, the rotation of crops had improved their finances and Angus's father used this very money to start a 'plea' against the Laird of Kirklands which had been draining their resources ever since in a long, wearisome progress through the law courts in Edinburgh.

The Moncrieffs had repeatedly offered to settle, but the MacDougals were stubborn, or at least Angus was, with the rigidity of an unsuccessful man. Walter could not see that there was any case at all, but Angus insisted on it and escorted his somewhat reluctant guest over every debatable field – on which his cows were even then grazing – as he explained dyke by dyke, how much he had been 'diddled' out of by the wealthier family.

Walter could not help remarking, on one of these expeditions, that Moncrieff of Kirklands seemed to be an uncommonly good agriculturist. His ground was clear of bracken and he had fields of oats and barley, whereas MacDougal raised only pasture grasses for hay.

"Hay gies a good return," Angus explained. "Ye can raise it for a couple o' years in succession and sell it at sixpence a stone."

"Doesn't that wear out the soil?"

"Maybe. Aye. But ye can add bit lime afore ye plough it up for oats the third season." He nodded towards the Kirklands fields. "The Laird's what they call an Improver. He has they new-fangled notions. Wheat!" Angus spat. "He e'en tries tae grow wheat!"

"Why shouldn't he? It grows everywhere in Europe."

"We've never done it in Strathblane," said MacDougal as though that closed the matter. He pointed towards his own pastures. "You see yon cows? They're Highland. I fatten them all summer and sell them in Glasgow at the Hallow Fair. I sold a big drove the day you arrived. They new beasts is puny yet, but they're thriving. The Ayrshires are something new. I bought them off a grand farmer up the Blane Valley and I should get six pounds a head for them next year."

Walter was fascinated. He had always been interested in growing things and had often heard his Scottish family talking about relatives who owned estates.

"What kind of man is this Laird of Kirklands, Mr. MacDougal?"

"He's no like his faither. I had my bit o' disagreement wi the auld man, but apart from the plea I admired him. The heir was killed fighting in the American wars. Mr Henry was the second son. So he'd been put into business and didnae grow up to farming."

"What did he do for a living?"

"He worked in Glasgow in the cotton trade. Ach!" Angus spat once more. "They city folk that thinks they know all about the land!"

"But his crops seem to be growing well."

"Wearing out the soil."

"Doesn't he use manures?"

"Aye. Aye. All they new-fangled dungs. Learning from a Society o' Improvers in Glasgow instead o' from experience. And planting trees all the time."

Walter supposed that it was because the Moncrieffs of Kirklands had more capital to invest that their fields looked so much more fertile.

"Forbye," Angus went on, "the auld Laird was a guid customer o' Captain Abernethy's. Mr Henry, he buys his liquor from the stills."

"Stills?"

"Aye. Up in the moors. Of course, we don't take to do with them."

"You mean . . . they make whisky?"

"Aye. We have six public houses in the parish that cannae afford the Captain's prices. And they're close to the Laird, these rascals are! Mr Henry Moncrieff," Angus added humorlessly, "believes in encouraging local industry."

As a banker's son, Walter had been brought up to pay his

way. Jean had turned over to him a pile of French coins but she refused steadfastly to accept any of it for his room and board although he told her she was entitled to it.

"No no, my laddie. As I telt ye before, it's Christian duty and charity."

"Then you must let me help you, if I can. I know I'm not handy, with this wrist crippling my fingers so, I'm afraid to use them. But surely there are things I can do for you around the house?"

She shook her head at him as though he was a presumptuous child.

"You werenae brought up to domestic duties and I didnae need another pair o' hands. Just get well now so you can get your way to your ain folks."

The best way to rebuild his strength Walter felt, was to walk. So walk he did, feebly at first, but with determination. Unfortunately walking alone gave him opportunity to brood on his helplessness and his bad situation. Before the sky had fallen in on his life, Walter had been on a three-year Grand Tour of Europe with his friend Louis, Vicomte de Sincerbeaux, and he was accustomed to exercise his lively curiosity and draw conclusions. So now he studied the land, comparing MacDougal's fields with those of the obviously more affluent Moncrieff of Kirklands.

One day Jean asked him,

"Could ye find yer way on the Boards Road after dark?"

"The Boards Road? That is the one outside the farm, is it not? With that big stone you call the Gowk Stane. Yes. I know it well. Why?"

"Captain Abernethy should be back any day. And we maun make sure the coast is clear for him. The Laird's uncommon harsh agin smuggling and dealing with the French and we're no completely sure o' the Exciseman."

"You have an Exciseman here, in this little village?

"He lives here. Aye. We're on the edge o' a big commercial community for all we look so rural. All the mills and the imports, like. Mr Campbell's an important man in the parish – he's the Session Clerk for the Kirk. And he's ambitious and he tries to stay far ben wi the Laird."

"Does this Mr Campbell know about the Captain and . . . er . . . your dealings with him?"

"In a wee village like Strathblane people know most of whatever goes on. But Mr Campbell would be mighty unpopular if he tried to stop Andra' Abernethy coming here. Naebody – not even the gentry – likes to pay Excise dues. They go down to London to help the English. The only household that doesnae buy liquor from us is Kirklands. Of course, the Laird's a Justice o' the Peace. And . . . ye never know, Walter. So maybe you should patrol the Boards Road and whistle if anyone goes by. That's the clearest way to the farm by road."

"It sounds an ideal job for a cripple."

Glad of something useful to do, he hurried through his supper and left eagerly for the Boards Road, a miserable track that ran along one side of the escarpment and down to the valley. From this vantage he had a magnificent view of the beautiful Campsie Fells, and though country life had not been fashionable among his French friends, despite Queen Marie Antoinette and her *Petit Trianon*, he had always appreciated nature, especially after he discovered poetry and found that both the British and French Romantics paid tribute to its pleasures. He had also read Rousseau.

Trying his own hand not unsuccessfully at verse, he had cultivated the sensitivities and the transition from day to night fascinated him, especially the Scottish dusk. The air on his first evening on patrol was full of melancholy peace which suited his mood and in the distance, up the valley, Ben Lomond towered purple against the sky. Closer by, the

Campsie Fells stood out from a profound shadow of their own making and down in the valley, lights began to flicker in the small townships, which he had still not explored, of Edenkiln and Netherton.

III

He was trying to count the cottages when the girl joined him. Quite simply, he became aware that he was not alone, turned his head, and found her there, by the Gowk Stane. She was gazing across the valley at the darkening hills with a self-absorption as deep as his own. She was young and slim, with long curling brown hair and a delicate face that suggested a cameo.. She wore a green dress, well made though a little shabby and out of style, and a plaid was thrown loosely around her shoulders.

She blended so completely into the surroundings that for a second he thought she must be some creation of his mind.

Then a lively little black dog bounded out of the bracken and approached Walter with a questioning bark. Suddenly aware that someone was there besides herself, the girl turned. She had clear green eyes with black lashes that made an entrancing contrast to her pink and white complexion.

They looked one another over in silence. Then he bowed.

"Good evening," he said – an inadequate greeting, but he was so stunned by her sudden appearance, it was all he could do.

She lowered her pretty lashes modestly.

"Good evening, sir." Suddenly she fluttered them

upward again and asked, "Have I the pleasure of your acquaintance?"

Her speech had none of the rough accents he had become accustomed to at Puddock Hole Farm. She spoke as his parents did, with the merest Scots intonation.

"We have not met, *mademoiselle*. My name is Walter Paterson."

"*Mademoiselle?*"

"I'm sorry. I have just arrived from France and habits of speech are hard to break."

In the soft evening light she appeared to him as the most beautiful creature he had ever seen.

She also was sensitive. Though her eyes looked him over curiously and she seemed to want to ask more questions, she made as though she was as absorbed as he had been in the sunset. She did however, draw a little farther away and motioned the dog to her side.

Walter stood transfixed, watching her as the clouds massed in the bright sky and the mountains darkened in shadow. Then, just as he was summoning up his courage to speak, she forestalled him with a quiet, "Goodnight, sir."

He could not let her go like that. He had to know her name.

"Stay a little please, . . . "

"But I am expected at home."

"Where is 'home'?" When she did not reply but looked surprised, he went on impetuously "You are like. . . " A line from a play flashed into his mind. "*A shadow like an angel with bright hair*. . . Are you real? Do you exist?"

A mischievous smile broke over her heartshaped face which he now noticed had a delightfully uptilted nose.

"Do you really not know who I am, sir?"

"No! How could I? You have not told me!"

She hesitated then tossed her head like a fine lady.

"You must indeed be a stranger to this valley. I am Miss Moncrieff of Kirklands."

She favoured him with a small curtsey, turned, then without looking back walked off in the direction of the mansion house, up the road. The dog bounded after her.

Abernethy delivered several boxes of tea later that night so there was no more reason for Walter to patrol the Board Road. But he bided his time. The following evening when Angus MacDougal started on one of his periodic harangues against the Laird of Kirklands, Walter interjected casually.

"Is Mr Moncrieff married?"

Angus snorted. "Naw. He bides alone."

Jean took him up at once. "He does not, faither! Wee Miss Primrose is keeping house for him the now."

"I thocht she went to Edinburgh to be with her sister, the yin that got married and has all the children."

"Ach, ye're away behind with your news, faither! Miss Primrose has been back in Strathblane these last three months. She was ill in the spring and Miss Catherine – Mrs Hamilton, I should say – sent her back to the country for the summer."

"What was wrong with her?" asked Walter.

Angus gulped the tea he had been drinking.

"She was aye a puny wee creature. She went into a decline."

Jean shook her head.

"Naw. The cook telt Auntie she'd had the influenza. It's unhealthy living in Edinburgh, a' they cramped wee 'lands' in the auld toon. Ye'll hae to watch yersel' Walter, once ye get there."

"I've no intention of going into a decline. Miss . . . er . . . Primrose must be a lot younger than the Laird."

"Aye. She's the baby o' the family. There was Mr Ralph

that died, and Mr Henry – he's Kirklands the now – and the eldest Miss Catherine – and twa brithers that went to India in the Army. And there was anither twa or three that died young. Then Miss Primrose. It was awfa' hard on her, both her parents and her elder brither being taken from her so close thegither."

"They're no hardy stock the Moncrieffs," Angus commented complacently.

"It's yon big hoose," Jean went on. "It must be terrible cold in the winter, though I hear that Mr Henry's new wing is verra elegant."

"I suppose the Laird and his sister do a lot of entertaining?" mused Walter.

"They'll be wantin' to get her married off," remarked Angus. "It's a wonder she didnae catch some man in Edinburgh."

"Possibly she didn't meet anyone she fancied," said Walter.

Jean started to clear away the dishes.

"I heard yon Mr Melville that runs the inkle factory in Netherton was sweet on her. Leastways, they're aye thegither."

"He maun hae a fair amount o' money," ruminated Angus. "Kirklands would like that."

Walter got up irritably, looked out at the door, found it was raining and damned the weather. Jean eyed him sympathetically.

"Is yer arm hurtin', lambie?"

"Not much worse than usual. Let me help you with these plates." He piled them onto a tray with his left hand. Angus stumped off to the byre while Jean commenced her washing up.

"It must," pursued Walter hovering, "be somewhat quiet here for a young lady like Miss Moncrieff."

"She'll hae plenty o' housework to keep her busy."

"Don't they have servants?"

"Aye, but she'll hae to keep a sharp eye on the maids, and there's a' the spinnin' and sewin' and the hens and distilling cordials, a gey lot of work. I'm telt she's a guid housekeeper for all she's so young."

"How old is she?"

"Aweel, she was born the year after William – that was the youngest boy. He died. And he was in the same class at the village school wi ma brither Alec that went to sea. Alec was three years younger than me and I'm near twenty-four. That would mak Miss Primrose nineteen."

Five years younger than I am, thought Walter. Just right.

"They say she's fond o' music. She plays the pianoforte and the harp and she has a lovely singing voice."

"It seems a long time since I heard any music."

Jean opened the back door and threw the slops into the yard. "Aye, we've been ower busy nursing you to have ony music. But if I'd known ye liked it, I'd have had Jock MacLean to come by with his fiddle and play for ye. He's a footman up at Kirklands and a nice laddie." Her eyes lit up unexpectedly. "Maybe now ye're feeling better we can hae a wee party!"

As soon as the weather cleared next day, Walter headed for the road that led past Kirklands House. It was not far from Puddock Hole but he had little luck spying out the land. A forbidding entrance gate barred his way and the avenue was planted with young trees and curved so that he could not see the building. He headed back towards the farm, watching the clouds blowing across the Campsies and, engrossed in trying to express what he saw in poetry, he almost tripped over Primrose Moncrieff.

She was sitting on a knoll just off the miserable excuse

for a road and she was peeling a soaked and muddy stocking from one slim leg. A dainty buckled shoe – also muddied – lay beside her on the turf.

Walter averted his eyes politely from these details as he bowed. "Good-day, Miss Moncrieff."

She pulled down her skirts and looked up with a flash of green eyes. She was even prettier in daylight than in the evening for her cheeks were rosy in the wind.

"I trust you didn't suffer an accident, *mademoiselle*?"

"I slipped!" She flung the words out angrily. "And I put my foot into the bog almost to my. . . " – she stopped herself in time – " . . . over my ankle."

"Would you like to dry yourself at the farm? At Puddock Hole? There's a good fire in the kitchen and I'm sure that Miss MacDougal. . . " He trailed off, remembering the feud.

"Thank you, sir. I am almost at home and I do not feel the cold." Then as if realising she had been ungracious, she gave him a smile that made his heart race. He held out his left hand.

"Allow me to help you up."

As she gripped his fingers and he hoisted her to her feet, she said diffidently,

"I am sorry. . . I know that you told me your name but . . . I don't think that I remember it. . . "

"Walter Paterson."

"Walter Paterson," she repeated as though the sound was magic. She slipped her bare foot into her shoe and as she straightened herself her eyes fell on the makeshift sling that supported his broken wrist. "You must have suffered an accident yourself."

"Of a kind, *mademoiselle*. The fortunes of war. . . "

Their eyes, on the same level, for she was tall, met and held. In that moment he knew she had been wondering as much about him as he her.

"I was born in France but my parents were Scots. My father was out in '45 and went into exile. He has a business in Paris."

Like a good child at a tea-party she inquired,

"And is this your first visit to Scotland?" He nodded. "How do you find it?"

He shrugged. "From the little I've seen, it's more restful than France."

"But surely," – there was lively intelligence in her green eyes – "the last few years must have been very stimulating. So many new ideas and concepts! So much to talk about! In Edinburgh, last season, there was a great deal of philosophical discussion about what was happening in Paris."

"But there, alas, it had gone far beyond ideological talk." Before she could ask anything more, he continued, somewhat to his own surprise. "Do you . . . can anyone? . . . in this beautiful and peaceful place, imagine what is happening just across the English Channel? The terrible forces that are at work? The murdering of a whole society, the undermining of everything that we, the people of education, were brought up to believe in?"

"You do not sympathise with 'Liberty, Fraternity and Equality'?"

"No, I don't. In theory, perhaps. But not when they are an excuse to seize power and misuse it. In Paris now, the innocent and the guilty alike are in constant fear of imprisonment and even death for anything, or nothing, perhaps for merely being rich or from old families. There's no justice left!" He stopped. "I apologise. I don't mean to bore you."

"But I enjoy talking about ideas, sir! I am not just some silly miss who never reads serious books!"

"I never thought you were. And I would like to know you better. Perhaps, for a start, we should talk about ourselves?" When she looked nonplussed, he went on "You are the Laird's sister, are you not?" She nodded. "Are you as interested as he is in improving the land?"

She gave a little chuckle.

"Oh, I'm interested of course. I like to know what's in the kitchen garden. But I'm not like Henry. He is a truly dedicated Improver. You can see the difference in his policies almost month by month. How long will you be staying in Strathblane, Mr Paterson?"

"Only until I'm fit to travel to Edinburgh. I have relatives there."

"So have I. A married sister. It's a beautiful city. You will like it. . . Where did you tell me you were staying?"

"I didn't tell you, but I'm at Puddock Hole Farm."

"Oh." Her face fell, and she went on hesitantly, "You are not like the MacDougals. How did you know them?"

Her brother, he remembered in time, was strongly against smuggling so he must be careful what he said about Abernethy.

"I was wounded in France and very ill and the ship's captain who brought me to Scotland was afraid I would die. So he brought me out here because Miss MacDougal's aunt is . . . is a wise woman and skilled in herbs, as I am sure you know." To change the subject, he continued "But that is a rather long story and you must be cold which is not good for a young lady with delicate health. May I escort you home?"

"Thank you. I can find the way myself." She held out a small slightly muddy hand and he bowed over it.

"Perhaps we can meet here again, Miss Moncrieff?" By her smile he knew this was an acceptable idea. After all, he was good looking and clearly a gentleman. But he must not give her any chance to refuse. "You don't need to tell me. I take the air each afternoon on the Boards Road, unless it rains."

Her little dog which had been chasing a rabbit in the field, now scampered up, jumping at Walter and wagging its tail as though they were old friends.

"You see, Miss Moncrieff? Your protector accepts me. May I hope you will do the same?"

She said nothing and this time it was his turn to break off the encounter.

"Miss Moncrieff, I must insist you go home and get warm! Good-day." He bowed once more in his best continental style and swung off down the track towards the farm.

IV

It rained for several days but Walter, who didn't mind getting wet, went out anyway familiarising himself with the moorland and holding long imaginary conversations with the Laird's sister.

Until that evening at the Gowk Stane, Walter Paterson had not realised how cut off he had been from people of his own kind. Much as he liked and respected the MacDougals, their way of living and their interests were as foreign to him as anything he had experienced on his European travels.

The gently spoken Miss Moncrieff reminded him of his sister Clementina to whom he had always been close. His friend the Vicomte de Sincerbeaux had wanted to marry her and his aristocratic family had prolonged the Grand Tour on which Walter had accompanied him in the hope that time and distance would diminish the attachment. A banker's daughter, though pretty and well-bred, was not the kind of match the heir to an ancient French family was supposed to make.

However, despite plenty of sexual experimentation in

the cities of Europe, Louis had remained determined to wed his childhood sweetheart. And so despite warnings about the changed political climate there, the two young men had returned to Paris. They found the Vicomte's parents had already moved to Amsterdam to escape the Revolution, and what had then happened in Paris had been so disastrous Walter still could not think about it.

He wondered if well-born young Scottish girls had their matrimonial futures arranged at an early age? He suspected not. His parents had married for love and their domestic happiness, despite years of uncertain fortune, was the kind Walter wanted for himself. He had often wondered though, where he would meet a like-minded woman, for he had not done so in Europe.

There was a spot on the moor where he could see the Kirklands House gate and when the weather turned sunny, he stationed himself there. Early one afternoon she tripped down the drive, her dog running before her. On the road, she glanced in both directions but if she saw him, she gave no sign. She headed across the fields in the direction of a clump of trees and Walter followed at a discreet distance.

But the little black dog had his own ideas. He was dashing straight ahead towards an enclosure where there was a bull. Obviously his mistress knew this for she too started to run calling to the dog.

Sprinting across the heather, Walter reached the gate and chased the little animal away before it could wriggle through. But the unaccustomed exertion hurt his arm so badly he had to lean against the dyke to stave off a faint.

"Are you all right, Mr Paterson?" Her voice, at his shoulder, was full of concern.

Sweat broke out on his forehead. He brushed it off with his left sleeve, straightened and turned, doing his best to smile at her.

"Yes thank you, Miss Moncrieff. It was . . . just a momentary weakness. . ."

"You look pale. Perhaps you should sit down?" She was carrying a big rug, which she now handed to him. On her other arm, he noticed there was a block of sketching paper and a bag.

"You are most thoughtful, *mademoiselle*. But . . . thank you . . . I am recovered."

"I was going down to the lochside to complete a picture for my sister. Would you care to accompany me? You could rest on the plaid and," she smiled, "keep an eye on Sandy for me."

Walter called to the dog, held out his left hand to be sniffed at and encouraged the terrier to follow them through the wood. Behind the trees there was a small loch.

"Shall I throw some sticks into the water for him, Miss Moncrieff?"

"No. He prefers to hunt for rabbit holes. He's forgotten about the field." She spread the rug on the little pebbly shore against a clump of rocks where they were able to sit, without getting too close, and rest their backs.

Pain was still pulsing down Walter's arm but he was so happy he found it easy to ignore.

"What a beautiful spot this is!"

"Yes! It's so . . . miniature . . . the little loch, those young fir trees. I come here often. It's so peaceful, so far away. . ."

"It could inspire poems."

The green eyes slanted quickly in his direction. "Do you write poetry?"

"Sometimes."

She had opened up her sketching block and was setting out pencils and crayons.

"Why don't you recite some to me while I'm drawing?"

But Walter too knew how to flirt.

"Oh no, *mademoiselle*. Not until we know each other better. . . I see your picture is already begun?"

"Yes I would have completed it ere now had it not been for the rain." She was moving herself about unselfconsciously, narrowing her eyes, measuring her perspective with a pencil. Walter, who had never been able to draw a line, admired the competent way she went about her work. She had strong, well coordinated little hands and concentrated on her moves like a professional.

"You have studied art, Miss Moncrieff?"

"I take lessons in Edinburgh when I stay with Kate. My sister. Didn't you say you had relatives in the capital, sir?"

"Yes. An uncle. His name is Alexander Paterson and he's a lawyer."

"Oh? What kind?"

"I believe he's an advocate."

"Then my sister's husband may know him. He's a W.S." Noticing his blank look, she explained, "A Writer to the Signet."

Walter was still mystified but, not wanting to confess to such ignorance about Scottish matters, he nodded sagely.

"Do you spend the season in Edinburgh each year?"

"Oh no! I just go there for visits, now and again. I prefer living in the country. Besides, I have to keep house for my brother."

"He does not plan to marry?"

"He does, but not until he has found a suitable bridegroom for me." She giggled. "Though I think he has a lady in mind. For myself," she went on, with a firmness that contrasted attractively with her delicate appearance "I do not intend to be any man's wife until I have found someone I can both love and respect."

"My sentiment on marriage too, Miss Moncrieff."

"But in France, these things are arranged, are they not?"

"Not for Scots. I am still a bachelor."

"Tell me about Paris, Mr Paterson. With this Revolution, it is unlikely that I shall ever go there."

He sighed.

"I'd rather tell you about Florence or Hanover or even Amsterdam."

"You've visited all those places?"

"Yes, and Vienna too." This seemed a safe topic so he enlarged on it, and as though taking the hint that he did not want to talk about his own past, she asked questions about the ancient monuments in Florence and Rome and mentioned the old masters in the art galleries. She was well informed on the history of painting and to his delight shared his love of modern music, particularly his favourite Mozart.

By the time she had completed her picture – which to his uncritical eye was remarkably pleasing – they had both learned a lot about each other's interests and were sufficiently at ease for him to suggest they meet again the following afternoon if it didn't rain.

Primrose did not commit herself. But she did not refuse either and she allowed him to walk as far as the Kirklands gates at the end of the afternoon. She did not however, invite him in to meet her brother as he had hoped.

Next day the sun was still shining and he found her by the lochside, drawing little sketches of leaves and stones, preoccupied and quiet. Walter himself had no need for conversation, content to sit beside her and work out a poem in his mind, while the water lapped gently and there was a soft murmur of animal life in the trees behind them.

Later in the afternoon they did talk but what they said had little significance. It seemed to be part of the harmony between them. They laughed too, at her little dog who chased a water rat into the loch and got unexpectedly wet. A breeze blew Walter's long fair hair out of the back ribbon which usually confined it. He was not able to push it back – Jean usually tied it for him each morning – and in the end Primrose reached over and helped. The touch of her hands seemed known and he longed to kiss her, but didn't dare.

When clouds started massing above the hills, he helped her up off the plaid and her eyes, smiling into his, were more blue than green against the water.

As they walked back towards the road she said, "I have never met anyone like you. I don't think you can be very practical."

"True. But why do you think that?"

"You never talk about money."

"I don't have much of it to talk about at present," he laughed. "Besides, there are more interesting topics of conversation, as we found yesterday."

"I agree. But Henry my brother, if he was here, would be looking at the sky and saying if it didn't rain soon, it would be bad for the crops or else it would spoil his newly dug drains if it did rain too hard. And you haven't once told me how much a head those cows over there will be worth at the next Hallow Fair."

"But I don't know these things. Do you?"

"I know how the people in Strathblane live. I visit them and when they need food or clothing, I see that they get it."

"How the Revolutionaries would hate you! You keep the peasants from being discontented!"

"We don't call them peasants here, and the more you give them, the more they want."

"But they must know that they're well off and that's why you aren't having the troubles we have in France where so many people are starving."

"Henry wouldn't let anyone starve. He is very generous. In fact, Edward says. . ."

"Who's Edward?"

"Edward Melville. He owns a factory in Netherton."

"And for what does he presume to criticise you?"

"He says we are too open-handed. He doesn't believe in spoiling his workers."

"That sounds as though he underpays them."

"He says he pays them what they are worth. They're all Irish or Highland. Some of them don't even speak anything but Gaelic."

"What was it that Shakespeare said about using every man according to his worth and who would escape whipping?"

"That was in *Hamlet*. I must quote it to Edward. He laughs at Henry and his estate, says it's foolish to invest so much capital into something that offers so little return. He believes it would have been better for my brother to remain in the cotton trade where he did very well."

"Maybe he feels there are more things in life than money."

"He likes it, though" said Primrose, so solemnly that he burst out laughing. "Don't you?"

"I've never thought much about it until now. It was always there."

"And what about the future?" she asked directly. "Love and friendship can't exist on air."

They stopped and their eyes met.

And suddenly they were no longer outside on the moor. They were in a small world of their own creating and Walter's heart was pounding wildly. He was about to take her hand when he stopped himself, afraid emotion would take him beyond control. This girl was not only good company, she was desirable, and she had just, innocently, let him know that she wanted their relationship to be a serious one.

And from the way she was tilting her head, he knew she was expecting him to kiss her. There was nothing he would have liked better but he had learned from past experiences that this could quickly lead to other intimacies. And he had not as yet even been introduced to her family.

"Miss Moncrieff . . . Perhaps we had better both go home."

"But it is so pleasant here today. Tomorrow it may rain again."

"I know, but . . . "He risked taking her hand, kissed it quickly, then strode off, trying not to think about the hurt look on her face.

V

This is all very fine and romantic, he fumed to himself many hours later, tossing around in the box bed, stirring up the pain. But now what am I supposed to do? I am to all practical purpose in a foreign country with little money, no prospects of work and no health. It is no time to fall in love.

It was love, not mere physical arousal, that Walter Paterson had felt. The fact was he knew what he wanted. He wanted to spend the rest of his life in Strathblane with Primrose Moncrieff. But how, and in what circumstances? He must take control of his situation. He had procrastinated long enough.

The rain was falling remorselessly and Jean kept going back and forth through the banging back door, feeding the hens and doing her other farmyard chores. She was making a big pot of broth and the atmosphere indoors was heavy with peat smoke and the smell of cooking.

"Have you ink and paper, Jean?"

"Aye, in that drawer in the sideboard. But ye cannae write."

"I can try, with my left hand."

He found the necessary materials and settled himself at the kitchen table. There was no question of holding the pen in his right hand. That would be too painful and stir up too many terrifying memories. So it took a long time to put anything down, but eventually he did.

"Please, Jean will you tell me if this is legible?"

She picked up the paper.

Dear Father,

I am safe in Scotland at a farm called Puddock Hole in Strathblane, outside Glasgow. I have been well cared for by good people. Tomorrow I leave for Edinburgh to seek my uncle. Please write to me in care of him. My love to yourself, mother and Clementina.

Walter.

"Ye're no going' to leave us the morn!"

"Yes. I am."

"Ye're no fit for the trip! Forbye, it's the Sabbath!"

"Then I'll go on Monday or whenever the stage-coach leaves." And then as if to convince himself, "Jean, I have to go some time. I'm getting no better. I need a good surgeon."

"Aye, that's what Auntie telt ye!"

"There must be banks in Glasgow that would change my French money." He wandered restlessly around the room. "Why does it have to rain all the time? Jean, give that letter to Captain Abernethy to deliver when he's next in France. I've written the address on the back of it and the printing is quite clear, I think."

"Abernethy! Walter! I'll gie you all the money I have in the house and I'll get it back from Andra' when he comes here next! I've been waitin' for this chance ever since he stuck me with all those French coins the night he brought you here!"

"I could surely change that money in Glasgow."

"Aye, but you'll need some Scots money too, ma innocent wee lambie."

By afternoon the wind had changed and a pale watery sun was trying to come out. Walter headed for the Boards Road despite Jean's protestations about the cold.

When there was no sign of Primrose by the Gowk Stane, he strode purposefully towards Kirklands House. He would take the bull by the horns and call upon the Laird.

But as he approached the gate, two horses trotted past him. A plump red-faced man with light hair and popping blue eyes was astride the larger. The other rider was Primrose, in a smart blue riding habit and a fashionable hat.

As they came abreast of him, Walter would have greeted her if a rapid flash of her eyes had not warned him against it. Her companion glanced down, and with no attempt to lower his voice, asked as they trotted past,

"Who the devil is that?"

Walter did not hear her reply. All he knew was that she had cut him in public and he was furious. He headed back towards the farm, then finding himself too upset to risk Jean's cross questioning, he stayed on the Boards Road, reminding himself firmly that he was in no position to become emotionally involved. And of course the beautiful young Miss Moncrieff – probably an heiress – would attract other men beside himself. It was simply that he hadn't seen any of them before. The whole situation was ridiculous and he had been insulted.

Feeling the moral superiority of this realisation, he turned his attention to the view. The weather had undergone a characteristic Scottish change, the sun was shining and the shadows of clouds were moving along the range of the

Campsie Fells. The effect was both dramatic and beautiful and Walter began to grow more calm. He had even reached the point of working on a poem in his mind that compared love for women unfavourably with love for Nature when down the road came the sound of horses' hooves again.

"Mr Paterson!" she called and in that instant all his new-found stability was gone.

This was the moment for the light touch but instead he glowered.

"I'm sorry," she gasped "I couldn't . . . that was Edward Melville. He might have told Henry. . ."

"You haven't told your brother about me?"

"No. Please help me dismount." He held out his left hand to her and the momentary nearness of her attractive body stirred up afresh the unruly sexuality he had experienced the day before. This added to his confusion.

"I was on my way to call on you and introduce myself."

"Oh, you mustn't do that! Please! Besides, Henry might not have received you. There's a feud between him and Mr MacDougal."

"I'm not a part of it."

"No, but you live at Puddock Hold Farm and . . . "

"So I can't speak to the Laird of Kirklands."

She flushed.

"It . . . isn't that . . . I'm sure you could, but . . . at this time. . . "

"At this time when I'm wearing an old farmer's clothes and have no money. . . "

"Oh please be reasonable," she shot back, stealing his thunder. "What would my brother say if he knew I had encountered a strange man on the road and . . . and talked to him and met him again, unchaperoned? You have a sister yourself. How would you feel?"

"How do *you* feel?"

She blushed.

"I . . . I know that everything between us has been . . . innocent. And . . . I enjoy your company. . . "

"But I'm not good enough to be introduced to your family."

"You are! But . . . when you've been to Edinburgh and found your relatives, it will be different and. . . "

"And I will have some background and a known income."

"Exactly!" She broke into a smile that fuelled his rage. "Perhaps I can go to Edinburgh too, and we can meet there, properly introduced."

"Meanwhile, I know where I stand, Miss Moncrieff. And it is just as well. For I am indeed going to Edinburgh. At the beginning of next week." He bowed, and with air of certain finality as if making a public announcement, asserted, "So this is goodbye."

He marched off, ignoring her cry of dismay. Let her walk her horse back to Kirklands, he thought. It's not far. . .

But many miles socially, it seemed. In France he had understood all the complicated structure of different classes but he had assumed the Scots were more democratic. Primrose had seemed such an independent young woman, so frank and friendly, it had not occurred to him that she might be inhibited by her family situation.

And there was the nagging knowledge that she might be right, and her brother would indeed be upset by her striking up an acquaintanceship with a young man of unknown background.

It was too late now. Once he left Strathblane, he'd never see her again. Or the mountains and the valley.

Emotions tore at him. He didn't want to leave. There was something here that touched a chord in his nature, something that he had never found before, in all his travels.

He didn't want to go back to a Scottish version of his old life, studying law, working in a city. He wanted to stay in Strathblane and manage a farm, properly and using modern methods, like the Laird of Kirklands.

Moncrieff and I would get along very well, he thought bitterly. If only we could meet. . .

PART TWO

ENTRANCED

There was much murmuring in the Parish against me, as too young, too full of levity and too much addicted to the company of superiors to be fit for so important a charge, together with many doubts about my having the grace of God, an occult quality which the people cannot define.

Autobiography of 'Jupiter' Carlyle

I

ANGUS MACDOUGAL ALWAYS went to church and Jean usually accompanied him. On the morning before Walter planned to leave, she was up earlier than usual, brushing her father's best suit, polishing his boots and ironing one of her 'good' dresses. But there was no sign of making breakfast.

"For what festival are you preparing?" asked Walter from the box bed. He had had a sleepless night and felt exhausted.

She paused in her fussing.

"They're havin' a grand service at the kirk. The minister frae Killearn, Mr McPhail. He's famous. We maun get there early."

"Maybe I should go and hear him too?" To be left alone all morning seemed more than he could bear.

She looked doubtful. "D'ye think ye're able?"

"Able to go to church? I have to be able to make the trip to Edinburgh tomorrow."

"Aye, but Mr McPhail has the Gift," she explained enigmatically. "He fair tears the heart oot o' people. Forbye, it's a long walk to the kirk and ye're easy tired. And if ye've ony sins in yer head. . . "

"So you think I'm a desperado with a guilty conscience? What about all that revenue you jilt your government out of?"

Jean looked surprised, smuggling not apparently being one of the sins she meant. "It's no lang since ye were terrible sick."

"I suppose everyone in the parish will be there?"

"Oh aye. It's crowded out for Mr McPhail."

"Does the Laird attend?"

This time she was shocked. "Of course. And a' his household. This is a guid Presbyterian parish. He'd be fined if he didnae."

"Run away," said Walter. "I want to get dressed. Where's my blue suit? I'm not making my debut before the village in your father's old clothes."

"Ye'll look too grand."

"Don't you want a well-dressed escort?"

She brought them from the cupboard. They had been scrubbed clean and ironed and the torn sleeve of his coat had been patched.

"I'll be gettin' dressed upstairs if you need me, Walter."

It took him a long time to dress and to shave and he was struggling with difficulty into his blue jacket when she called through the ceiling:

"Are ye near ready?"

"Can you take off some of those bandages?"

"No, let them alone."

Walter disregarded this advice. He pulled them as tight as he could bear and found he could just get his wrist with its makeshift splint into the sleeve, although the pressure was far worse than he had anticipated. *"Il faut souffrir pour être beau, ma belle Moncrieff,"* he said softly, hoping the pain would abate.

"Whaur's yer sling?" Jean appeared in the doorway. She wore a wide-skirted woollen dress with a shawl and a modish little hat trimmed with pink feathers that was rather over-elegant for the rest of her outfit.

"I'm not wearing the sling." He put on his gold ring, adding the two fob watches. "Is the pretty bonnet in honour of Mr McPhail?"

"The Captain brought it frae Paris. Faither! It's late. Hurry now."

"Don't we have any breakfast?"

"There's no time. We'll hae a bite at Auntie's after the morning service."

"And how long is that?"

"The last time he preached three hours in the morning, and four in the afternoon, but if he isnae inspired, it's less."

The Strathblane Parish Church was already crowded when they arrived after a long walk down and across the valley. Jean pushed her way determinedly into a front pew and wedged them in between two bulky country women, one of them Mrs Semple, the midwife, whose herbs had broken Walter's fever and whom he had met several times. She gave him an encouraging smile as if, he reflected, he was one of her patients about to go into a lengthy labour.

The building was small and dark and would have been both chilly and dank if the presence of too many hard-working and perspiring bodies had not raised the temperature insalubriously. Walter could not see Primrose or indeed, any well-dressed people.

"Jean, where does the Laird sit?"

"Upstairs in the back gallery. Ye cannae see him from here."

In that case, he thought, why did I come?

It must have been nearly an hour before the service started, but the congregation passed the time gossiping and if there was any religious sentiment or any appreciation of their being in a church rather than a social meeting, Walter did not feel it. He found the waiting extremely tedious, not to say uncomfortable.

Then suddenly a hush fell upon the congregation. A big beetle-browed man with a sallow thin-lipped face and fanatic's eyes swept up into the pulpit. He was an impressive figure, his black Geneva gown billowing around him, and the glance he threw over the assembly caught their attention and froze off all conversation. No sooner was the congregation settled than a weedy, red-haired precentor stood up and intoned,

> *Now Israel may say and that truly,*
> *If that the Lord had not our cause maintained. . .*

The congregation took up the melody somewhat tunelessly and strains of Old Testament bloodlust rocked the little building.

The preacher's opening prayer was long and dull and everyone stood for it. There followed another hymn.

Possibly, thought Walter hopefully, he lacks inspiration, and when the congregation scrambled to their feet for a second prayer, he was irreverently prompted to add a supplication of his own that the Gift might be withheld from Mr McPhail, at least for one service. Not that it made much difference. The minister seemed able to pray interminably even without divine prompting. The atmosphere was becoming oppressive.

Jean nudged Walter as he tried to wriggle himself into a more comfortable position in the crowded pew.

"Keep still."

"My shoulder's killing me."

"Ye shouldnae hae put on yer jacket. I've nae sympathy. I warned ye." She sniffed self-righteously at a sprig of appleringy she had put between the leaves of her Bible.

"It's hurting damnably. . . "

"Shh!"

"Do you think he'll keep it to two hours?" whispered Walter and realised he had spoken just too soon. The minister had thrown back his head and closed his eyes.

"O Lord!" he intoned towards the dark ceiling, pronouncing it 'Lard'. "Look down upon this sinful generation of vipers! Smite it with thy wrath. Purge it wi the fires o' thy divine displeasure, for it has forsook thy ways! Grant us thy light, O Lord, that we may see to what eternal torments we may come, because we hae forsaken the Covenant made 'twixt God and Adam wi the Holy Ghost as Testator thereat."

Walter, who had been brought up to believe in a God of Love, looked up in astonishment. Mr McPhail now turned his attention onto the congregation.

"And ye, ye sinfu' sons o' men, that were conceived in sin and soon to return to the dust from whence ye came," he breathed gustily, "that the loathly worms may devour ye and feed upon yer rotting flesh till it shall all be reunited and resurrected before the awful Throne on the Day o' Judgement – I charge ye that ye come to grips wi Christ and that ye wrestle wi Him ceaselessly in prayer lest ye be damned to everlasting unto everlasting."

Walter glanced covertly at the people of Strathblane. They were straining forward in the pews, their honest weather-beaten faces rapt.

"What must it be to be banished from the Almighty God?" challenged the preacher. "Whither must such men go?" He paused dramatically. "Tae everlasting fires! As heirs o' Hell they shall undergo the punishment of God. They shall be drowned in the deluge and consumed in Sodom by fire and brimstone. They shall be slain wi the sword, dashed against stones and thereafter endure the torment eternal."

A woman at the back burst into noisy tears, opening signal for a rustling of handkerchiefs. *Pour l'amour du bon Dieu!* thought Walter, carried away in spite of himself. Is this the Age of Reason?

"Oh, ma brethren," went on Mr McPhail, "who can endure the everlasting flames that shall never be quenched day or night? The wicked shall be crowded like lice into a fiery furnace and every part of their bodies will bear a part in the woefu' ditty. The eyes shall weep, the hands shall wring, the breasts be beaten and the heads ache wi the woefu' crying." His harsh voice rose to a climax.

She was right, thought Walter. I shouldn't have come. He wondered if the minister knew how accurately he was describing the scene before his eyes. The overcrowded church was unbearably hot. Walter himself was suffering increasingly from the pressure of his coat on his wounded shoulder and with Mr McPhail now obviously inspired, there was no relief in sight. Walter shut his eyes and tried to think of something else but the violent words poured over him in hot streams like the brimstone the minister was so fulsomely describing.

". . . And secondly, ma brethren, if Satan and his legions hath so far taken possession o' yer souls that ye do not enjoy the holy pleasures o' the Sabbath here on earth, how think ye that ye will be in a state o' grace to enjoy that Eternal Sabbath to which only the Elect will come?"

The Philosophers . . . the Encyclopaedists . . . Voltaire . . . even Rouseau . . . where are you now? thought Walter desperately, turning hot and cold and aware of an upheaval in his empty stomach. He was suffocating both mentally and physically. The world had become a nightmare of foul air and the rasping voice from the pulpit.

"And it shall come to pass," declared Mr McPhail, "that on the day that they separate the sheep from the goats, and they that are without sin shall pass into the company o' the Elect, ye . . . whaur will ye be?" He paused, wiped his brow and remarked, more naturally, "For ye cannae hang on tae yer minister's coat-tails on the Day o' Judgement." The Gift came upon him again. "Unless ye come to grips wi Christ and cast oot the sins ye were born wi. . . For if ye cannae control the lusts o' yer own flesh, how then think ye to vanquish the temptations o' yer soul?"

He thumped the big Bible before him with such force that Walter came to himself. Everything was spinning around him. He could hardly breathe.

"Jean, I'll see you outside." He stumbled over Mrs Semple and another fat woman between him and the aisle. Everything was turning black as he headed for where the door should have been. This is the finish, he thought blankly. What will she think of me now, fainting in church like some wench with the vapours?

II

A tall figure materialised at his side. Firm hands gripped him and steered him out of the building. A heavy door slammed and the beautiful silence of the churchyard revived Walter's bruised senses and ringing ears. Someone pushed his head down and held it there until the faintness passed.

The hands drew him upright again. They belonged to a young man of his own generation.

"Better now?" he asked, and his deep, pleasant voice, after Mr McPhail's, was as soothing and bracing as the wind itself. Walter nodded, not trusting his vocal chords.

"Take a deep breath," ordered the stranger. "Get some air into your lungs, and take yer time about it."

Walter did as he was told, leaning against a tombstone.

"You're most kind, *monsieur*. I am sorry to deprive you of the sermon."

The young man threw a contemptuous glance towards the church door.

"Ach," he said shortly, "havers and blethers. And no an original thought in the lot."

It was a relief to be back in 1792. "Then why do you go to hear him?" asked Walter breathily.

"He's a change from Mr Gardner, an awful dry preacher, though a good man. And, as for me, I have a position to maintain in the parish. Keep breathing deeply now."

Walter looked him over curiously. He was at least six feet tall and big boned, with straight, springy, unco-operative dark hair cut short in the French fashion. In a broad homely face, his best features were his sharp, intelligent hazel eyes, set off by black lashes and thick clean-cut eyebrows. He had a wide, aggressive mouth, but a kindly smile, and was dressed in a conservative brown suit of good English broadcloth with the most immaculately clean ruffled shirt Walter had seen in Strathblane.

"If you're over your scunner," said the stranger, whose accent was not the local one, "you'll best come in out o' the cold. Take my arm, and keep up that breathing."

He guided Walter round the building to a door leading into the vestry. Through the wall, they could hear the drone of McPhail's voice.

"Now then sir, sit ye down on that bench while I find some water. It's a pity this is not a Border kirk, where I'm sure I'd find some contraband stashed away. You could do wi a dram."

Walter nodded. Now that the faintness was past, he was again aware of the pain. Slipping off his left sleeve, he considered how to free his other arm. The best thing seemed to be to get it over fast. So he set his teeth and tugged at his right cuff.

Everything whirled about him. He would have fallen if his new friend had not caught him. As he loosened Walter's cravat, their eyes met.

"You damn fool," commented the stranger dispassionately. "You should have let me do that."

Walter, gritting his teeth, couldn't answer.

"Now sit still and give yourself a chance. What's wrong

with your wrist?"

"Let it alone."

"I'll not hurt you if you keep still." As he eased the jacket off, blood began to seep through Walter's shirt. "Mercy on us! You're wounded! You should be in bed. No wonder you couldnae thole Mr McPhail."

"Please," Walter gasped, "Let me alone. I'm not having anyone touch me except a doctor."

The young man looked surprised, then laughed. "Very sensible of you. You'll be a stranger in Strathblane, I'm thinking?" He had found a glass of water, which he now held to Walter's lips. "I noticed you getting restless in the Kirk. Had a fellow feeling, for I was bored too. But when you got up, and near landed in Mrs Semple's lap, I realised there was something wrong."

His fingers, as if from habit, came to rest on the pulse of Walter's left wrist. This gesture, his calm efficiency, as well as his good, clean, conservative clothes, suggested a medical man.

"*Monsieur, par hasard*, are you the 'new' doctor?"

"Aye," answered the other dourly, "that describes me accurately."

"You are not what I expected."

"You mean 'ower young'?"

"*Comment?*"

"That's what they say about me here. My name is Douglas Elliot Stewart. At your service, sir."

"My name is Paterson, Walter Paterson. I stay at Puddock Hole Farm. But I . . . I hope to go to Edinburgh tomorrow, on the coach."

"Edinburgh!" echoed Dr Stewart, as though invoking the name of the Promised Land. "You lucky man!" His clear friendly eyes rested on Walter's arm. "Have you made that trip before?"

"No."

"Aweel, it's a long hard one. At least twelve hours from here. You change to the diligence in Glasgow. It could be hard on you."

"Do you know Edinburgh?"

"I'm next to a native o' the lovely place, studied at the University, and practised there too." He nodded toward the body of the Kirk. "When McPhail gets the length of describing the joys of Heaven, I'm thinking of Edinburgh on a Saturday night."

"You studied there?"

"Aye. And after I qualified, I was assistant to a professor at the Surgeon's Hall. Where do you come from, sir?"

"France. I'm a casualty of their Revolution."

"So am I, in a way. At least, without your troubles over there, I doubt if I'd be here in the West. Another sip of water?"

Walter was trying to get up, and the effort was so exhausting he wondered how he was ever going to climb back up the long brae to Puddock Hole.

"Could you do anything for me, do you think?" The question came out involuntarily.

Dr Stewart smoothed down his long white cuffs.

"If I'm Edinburgh enough for you"

Walter smiled faintly.

"You're as Edinburgh as I can get. I didn't seek you out before because . . . well, I didn't know how medicine might be practised here in Strathblane."

"You showed excellent judgement, Mr Paterson. But, I'll not let you down."

Through the wall, the preacher's voice began building to a climax.

"And thirdly brethren, when you consider the Fourfold State of Man. . . "

"McPhail's good for another couple of hours. He's only starting on 'thirdly'. Come away with me to my house. This would be a good time to examine you undisturbed." He hoisted Walter to his feet and dropped the jacket round his shoulders. "Now, let's unbutton that fancy French waistcoat and see if we can take some weight off your shoulder. What's the splint for?"

"It's . . . I think my wrist's broken."

"Aweel, we'll find out shortly."

They left the vestry and headed down towards the valley, where they walked past a cluster of cottages.

"Is this Strathblane?" Walter asked. It was the first time he had been on the village road.

"No. This is the hamlet of Edenkiln. Strathblane is the name of the Parish. Up yonder is Netherton, where Mr Melville has the inkle factory and a' the Irish workers live. And my house is at the top of the Minister's Brae, which we're on. It's no far, but it's steep. Do you think you can manage?"

"There's nothing wrong with my legs."

"You're lucky. I have a weak foot that protests on the slopes."

"Don't you have a horse? Or a carriage?"

"My friend, you are making the popular assumption that all doctors are rich."

Walter stopped. "Do you . . . would you accept French money for your services? It is all I have."

"It'd be closer to legal tender than the tough old hens and bags o' potatoes some of my patients give me! Amazing to see this place so empty. Everyone, even the bairns, are at the Service the day. So we might as well cut through the Glebe fields. Take my arm."

Panting a little, Walter began to realise that he was now committed to what might be an unpleasant experience and, as though sensing this, Dr Stewart resumed talking in his musical voice.

"I miss Edinburgh, Mr Paterson. I grew up in the Borders but I aye loved cities. I long for the theatres and concerts and colleagues to discuss cases. Here in the country, unless you're socially accepted by the gentry, you only meet people when they're sick. And then they're usually," he shrugged, "uneducated. That's my house stuck on the edge of the brae."

"You must have a wonderful view of the hills."

"Aye, but I get little mental stimulation from looking at scenery. They ca' this place *Blaerisk*, meaning, I'm told, a bleak piece o' waste ground. A name I've seen no reason to change. It was the schoolmaster's residence until Benjy Hepburn, the dominie, moved himself down to the Kirkhouse Inn, the more fool he. My predecessor, Dr McKelvie, of blessed memory in the Parish, had a bonny wee estate up towards Duntreath. Here we are."

The house was small and unpretentious and surrounded by a wilderness of untended garden. Stewart gave the front door a hefty push that eventually opened it.

"This place is in awful bad repair. I've had neither the time nor the money to furnish it properly in the six months I've been here." The hall was dark, with a steep staircase and a passage that led toward kitchen premises. There were doors opening onto two other rooms – one, bleak and carpetless, held only a dining table with a single place-setting and two chairs.

The doctor led the way into the other, a big room that gave the impression its occupant was so used to having his possessions close at hand he had lost the knack of spreading them out. One end held professional paraphernalia – an examining table, rows of bottles, a mortar and pestle, beakers and jars and several instrument cases, all extremely neat, clean and functional. The other side of the room was given over to comfortable confusion, with great musty piles of books stacked against the walls, and a big desk littered with papers. The only decoration was a large diploma hung over the mantelpiece, which as far as Walter could decipher it, announced in tortuous Latin that Douglas Elliot Stewart had a degree in medicine bestowed on him in 1791 by the Royal College of Physicians of the University of Edinburgh.

"Brrr!" exclaimed Stewart. "This place is cold as Hell. Sit ye down by the fire while I warm us up some coffee. I leave a pot by the kitchen fire every Sunday afore I go to the Kirk. It's my reward to myself for regular attendance." He swung off down the passage, returning almost immediately with two fragrantly steaming mugs. "D'you want a dram in this?"

Walter's face lit up. "No thank you, Coffee would be luxury enough. I haven't had anything but tea since I left France." He sipped appreciatively. "This is genuine *cafe au lait.*"

"Aye. The milk's good for your nerves and fills you up. Did you have any breakfast?"

"No."

"Neither did I. My housekeeper was so keen to get to the service." He banked up the fire smouldering in the grate. "If we'd stayed to the end, we'd have been ravenous. And there's not much time for a meal before the afternoon performance . . . if you can call it that . . . and it can go on till dark if McPhail's inspired. Ach, now I've got myself dirty. Excuse me while I wash my hands." He went off again towards the back of the house and Walter heard distant splashings. As he came back, Stewart continued, "I'm lucky to have a housekeeper that's worked for doctors before but she says she never saw such a stickler for cleanliness. I'm suspicious of dirt. I'm sure it breeds disease."

He smiled in happy anticipation as he folded back his

immaculate cuffs. "Now let me see that arm, Mr Paterson. Better take your shirt right off. I'll help you."

When he had freed the shoulder of its bandage, he whistled. "Mon, you must have been in a bonny fight. Did someone try to carve his name on you?"

"No. He was trying to dig out a bullet. He was only a medical student."

"And needed a wee bit more training, I'd say. Is the bullet still there?" Walter nodded. "There's no sense in torturing you huntin' around for it if you know where it is."

Experienced fingers were carefully testing the shoulder's mobility. "And I apologise for hurting you. It's only because I have no knowledge yet of where the damage lies. Once I do know, I promise you the least possible suffering. Now tell me what happened."

"I . . . I . . . " Walter caught his breath, as pain shot through him.

"Sorry, laddie. Look, swear all you want. There's no one here but us."

"Jean . . . Miss MacDougal . . . when she changes the bandages," Walter was starting to sweat, "says I always revert to French."

"Good. I'd like to learn some Continental oaths. Was she the girl in the smart hat sitting next to you?" Walter nodded. "Now I know you were shot, and a friend of yours was practising incisions on you. Tell me the rest of it."

"Must I?"

"It would help."

"We . . . " He burst out, "I can't! I can't talk about it! Please don't ask me."

A quick flicker of understanding crossed Stewart's mobile features. "Laddie, it's nothing to me what kind of mess you were in. I'm not passing on anything to the authorities either."

"I did nothing wrong. I simply cannot talk about it."

"That's natural. But it's good for you to talk it out, just the same." Still delicately exploring the various swellings, he went on in his soothing voice. "I think that I can reconstruct all that I need. You were running away from something . . . or someone. You were shot at, and you fell. Trying to stop yourself, you came down on that wrist and broke it."

"That's what Mrs Semple said."

"Oh, so you know my estimable colleague, the midwife?"

"She's Miss MacDougal's aunt. When first I came here, I had a high fever. She broke it with some herbal drink."

"Aye. Some of these are quite efficacious."

"But . . . none have done much for my pain."

"Don't worry, I've stronger medicines. At what point did you stop using your fingers?"

Walter turned cold. It was, of all the dreadful memories, the one he most avoided. "I . . . don't remember."

"Aweel," said the doctor cheerfully, "we'll find out." He stretched and swung over to the professional part of the room where he collected a big roll of bandages and an instrument case, which he set on the desk and opened. Walter involuntarily started to shiver. There was no sign of any laudanum or the like among these sinister preparations.

"Mon! I might have known there's a good reason for not practising on the Sabbath! Jock's at the Service."

"Who?"

"Jock MacLean. He's a footman at Kirklands House, but he aspires to be a healer like me. So I use him as an assistant when I need one. He's good and strong, if not much else."

Walter clamped down on his imagination, terrified.

"I don't imagine one more day would make any difference to you, Mr Paterson. So maybe I should just give you something to ease the pain and send you home. Jock's off on Monday afternoons and we could come to the farm and operate on you in your own bed. . . " He looked suddenly young and undecided. "Aye, that would probably be best." He started to roll down one sleeve.

I couldn't stand the waiting, thought Walter desperately. Mustering what was left of his courage, he said,

"I'd prefer you took care of me now. Here."

"It's going to be rough, laddie."

"Then please, get it over."

Their eyes met and held for a long appraising minute. Then Stewart grinned boyishly, all the indecision gone.

"Very well. We'll try something." He added ambiguously, "Whiles I forget I'm my own master."

He took two medicine bottles from the shelf and, with a touch of ceremony, measured some of their contents into a glass, stirred it carefully and handed it to Walter. "Drink that slowly, it'll calm your nerves. And make yourself comfortable on that couch by the fire. But face my desk if you please." He sat himself down there, opened a big ledger and continued in his mellifluous voice, "I'm going to wait a wee while. Jock may come by if the Service ever ends, and I'd like him to see what I'm going to do to you. There's not much opportunity here to observe interesting cases like this." He dipped a quill into the inkwell. "And I need a little information for my records. Now what's your full name?"

"Walter James Paterson."

The doctor reverted into broad Scots and asked, "Pa'erson wi twa' ts?"

"One *t*. My father used to . . . to make that joke."

"Is he still alive?"

"He was when I last saw him . . . some days . . . weeks ago."

"And that was?"

"When I was leaving France."

"And your mother?" Walter nodded. "Any brothers or sisters?"

"One sister. Her name is Clementina."

"How old are ye?"

"Twenty-four."

"And have you ever had any serious illnesses before this . . . er . . . accident?"

"Only the usual childhood things."

"And where in France was your home?"

"Near Paris."

"Mon, if it weren't for all the troubles over there, that's the place I'd go for further study." He threw down the pen and picked up a pipe. He didn't light it, but it gave him an air of being, as it were, off duty and Walter found himself relaxing slightly. He wondered in passing what had been in the drink besides peppermint. It hadn't tasted like laudanum.

"Did you ever hear the likes of Mr McPhail in France?"

"No. My family were Episcopalians."

"Jacobites?"

"Yes."

"Aweel, ye're not to judge the Kirk in Scotland by yon auld windbag. He's a spiritual descendant of the Covenanters and interesting to me because I'm a son of the manse myself and know all the arguments. It's a fascinating thing too, as a physician, to observe the response of the congregation. I see them other Sundays and a more phlegmatic collection o' people would be hard to find. I often think," he went on, the volume of his voice increasing as though he were lecturing, "that if McPhail were to use his powers of arousing feelings in a scientific way, for the purpose of healing, he would achieve a great deal. When you were in Paris, Mr Paterson, did you ever hear tell of a Viennese medical man by the name of Franz Anton Mesmer?"

"Mesmer? Wasn't he some kind of quack?"

"Aye, maybe he was. He was disowned by his colleagues but my profession has aye been quick to do that to anyone with a new concept of treatment. I met a man in Edinburgh who'd studied with Mesmer, or at least he'd gone to his meetings and observed his methods."

"Didn't he carry out strange experiments with people holding hands? . . . a *baquet*? . . . going into trances?"

"Aye. He used the body's natural flow of electricity to control consciousness. Animal magnetism he called it in the only book of his that I've been able to find. He did some very strange things according to my friend. And naturally he attracted many hysterical unbalanced people. But what really interested me was that he seemed to have stumbled on a way of resolving the biggest problem in modern surgery . . . the suffering it can cause the patient. I myself find it very hard to take the responsibility of inflicting it, having had my own share of pain. Those people that Dr Mesmer threw into a trance apparently felt little or nothing, or if they did, they forgot about it."

Walter felt a slight quickening of interest.

"They talked about that in Paris, I remember. And when I was in Vienna I did hear that he had made some remarkable cures."

"Did you ever meet him?"

"No."

"Or go to his gatherings?"

"No."

"Did you ever have a tooth pulled?"

"Yes. It was horrible."

Stewart leaned across the desk, opened his mouth wide and indicated a gap towards the back of his lower jaw.

"Would you believe that I never felt that huge molar coming out? That fellow . . . that friend of Mesmer's . . . put me into a trance. The extractor, honest man, could scarce believe it . . . he became one of our converts! A group of us young medical men tried it on one another and I used the procedure on some patients myself."

"Was it successful?"

"Extraordinarily so. I seemed to have the knack, whatever it was. And I was on the point of convincing the professor I worked for, that we should experiment at the Surgeon's Hall, when . . . ," he broke off, "when I moved here from Edinburgh. . . "

"What exactly did you do?"

"Nothing . . . nothing except talk to my patients. The way I'm doing now. Sometimes I did as Mesmer suggested and rubbed their wrists." He got up and moved over to the couch and took Walter's left hand in his. "Like this."

There was no denying it was extremely calming.

"Ye're feeling easier already, are you not?"

"Yes."

"Ye have confidence in me, Paterson. Ye wouldnae be here otherwise. Ye believe what I'm telling you and ye're tired. Ye've had a long and difficult time."

Curious how he changes into Scots the way I lapse into French, Walter thought inconsequentially. He must have trained that voice as hard as any concert singer. . .

"Let go, laddie. Shut yer eyes, ye're powerful sleepy . . . ye're no feeling pain now, and ye won't . . . ye believe that, don't ye?"

"Yes," Walter responded, dazed. "Yes . . . I do . . . " The voice went on and on, but he was no longer listening to the words, only to the sound.

Until Stewart told him quietly, "Open your eyes. Take a look around ye. But dinnae try to move."

Walter blinked and became aware that he was no longer by the fireside. He was stretched out on the examining table with a blanket pulled over him. His right side seemed totally immobile and it hurt. But the pain had changed.

Stewart, his sleeves still rolled up and a voluminous, slightly bloodstained apron protecting his Sunday suit, looked exceedingly pleased with himself.

"Ye're going to be fine, Mr Paterson. The bullet's out. Those cuts are all sewed up and your wrist is properly set. It's going to be awful sore, but that'll pass. Dinnae let it worry ye. D'ye remember anything?"

"No . . . what happened?"

"Ye've been in a trance. Ye're a marvellous subject, yin o' the best I ever had. Ye remember naethin at a'?"

"*Non . . . pas du tout. . .* "

"Good." The grin almost split his face. "Ye may find old-fashioned theology in Scotland, Mr Paterson but ye'll aye get the best and most modern medical care, believe me."

III

The front door rattled and slammed, and Stewart called out towards the passage, "Ye damned auld witch! Be mair quiet. I've a patient in here."

A big red-faced woman stuck her head around the door.

"Do ye no want yer dinner then, doctor?" She shook her head in Walter's direction. "Miss MacDougal was lookin' for him. She's on her way up here now. I telt her he'd be here."

"Then hold off my meal until she's gone." After the woman went out, he produced a dark bottle from his desk drawer and poured a shot into a glass. "Now then. That's genuine Strathblane whisky. Distilled illegally in the parish. It'll make ye feel easier."

Walter sipped and gasped.

"It's st . . . strong."

"Aye. And it's a most efficacious pain reliever."

"Could you . . . could you dilute it?"

"If ye want." There was a kettle by the fire, and he splashed hot water into the cup. "Is that better?"

"*Oui. . .* "

While Walter took another swallow, Stewart removed his apron, tossed it into a corner, then put on his jacket flipping down his long white cuffs.

"Yon bullet's a queer lookin' thing. Do ye want it for a souvenir?"

"*Mais non. . .* "

"Then I'll keep it masel'." He stood over his patient and went on seriously. "Mr Paterson, you're a man of great courage. And also, I am sure, of honour and education. You must be aware of the depth of ignorance of the people here in this village. To them, what I just did to you . . . puttin' you into that trance . . . could smack of witchcraft. Maybe it is . . . I cannae explain it scientifically. But it works. And it's just spared ye a damned nasty experience. So I'm asking you, as a gentleman, to say nothing about it, to anyone."

"*Mais absolument.*"

"I'm going to find Miss MacDougal. By the time we come back, you're to have finished that toddy. Call for Mrs MacGregor if you need anything."

As he went into the hall, Walter heard the housekeeper say, "Doctor, ye'll get yersel' intae trouble wi the Kirk Session. What for did ye no come back tae the service?"

"I suppose I created a sensation, doing my professional duty. I suppose I should just hae let the young man faint."

"I'm warning ye, Dr Stewart, they'll be after ye. Wi McPhail preachin' an a'. . . "

He interrupted theatrically, "At least we'll die wi'

harness on our backs." Again the door slammed.

Mrs MacGregor peeped in at Walter.

"Are ye quite comfy?"

"Yes, thank you."

"I'll be in the kitchen if ye want onythin." She gave him a shrewd appraising look, then added, "Sir."

Walter smiled, for want of anything to say.

"Ye'll hae to excuse us slammin' yon door. The lock's no functuatin'." She left.

Walter eased himself up a little, trying to overcome the strangeness. What had apparently happened was so novel and incomprehensible he could not accept it. He tried another mouthful of the toddy. Whisky always made him drunk quickly. But why not? He couldn't feel more disoriented than he already did. He drained the glass quickly and lay back again, closing his eyes and was starting to float into an even more unreal world when he heard Jean's voice.

"Ma poor wee lambie!" she was saying. "Ma poor wee lambie. . . "

"Jean," he opened his eyes and tried to get her into focus.

"Get up now and I'll take you home."

He half rose, then slipped back helplessly.

"I . . . I can't. I'm drunk. . . " He became aware of Stewart standing beside her. "I drank all the whisky. . . "

"That's fine. He can stay here as long as he wants, Miss MacDougal. I'll tak care o' him for ye."

"But ye'll be wantin tae go tae the afternoon service!"

"Ma first duty is to ma patient," said the doctor virtuously. Walter, some of whose perceptions seemed sharpened by the drink, chuckled weakly. Jean stood up.

"Then I'll be on my way to my auntie's. I'll come back later to see how he is."

"It'll be a pleasure, Miss MacDougal."

She hesitated. "Mr Campbell hasnae been here, has he?"

"No."

"Did Walter hae a bullet in his shoulder?"

"Aye. He had." She lowered her eyes. "I'd be pleased if ye didnae mention it."

"I dinnae talk about my cases, Miss MacDougal."

"I meant nae offence, doctor."

Mrs MacGregor burst in, announcing dramatically, "They're here!"

"Who?" demanded Stewart.

"Mr Campbell and Mr Wishart."

"What do they want?"

"Doctor. They're frae the Kirk Session! I warned ye!"

"I'm busy. I cannae see them the now."

"But, doctor . . . !"

"I hae a patient in here. I'll be looking after him for the next hour."

"But, they'll hae to be back at the Kirk."

"I ken." His face was ugly with indignation. There was a loud knock on the door. "Go and gie them that message. And shut this door after ye."

"What is it?" Walter asked, sensing trouble.

"Nothing for you to worry about, laddie."

Outside, Mrs Macgregor's voice rose. "The doctor cannae be disturbed. He has a young man in there who's very poorly and . . . "

"We was wanting to see him about just that," a man's voice interrupted her rudely. "Go and get him. . . "

Jean swept across the room and threw the door open.

"It's my cousin that's sick, Mr Campbell. He'll no mind ye comin' in."

Two long-faced men in black stood on the threshold. One of them was mountainously built with a malevolence in his huge red face that sent a shiver of fear through Walter. He looked like an executioner.

"Guid day, Mr Campbell . . . Mr Wishart." Jean faced them squarely.

"Guid day, Miss MacDougal. And guid day to ye, doctor." The smaller man, who had a wizened pinched toothless face, advanced into the room, peering around him curiously, though he also looked embarrassed.

The doctor eyed them dourly, his hands in his pockets.

"Guid day," he said shortly.

"Is this the young man?" asked the large sinister personage.

"Walter Paterson," said Jean quickly. "Ma cousin frae Linlithgow, Mr Campbell. Ma Aunt Mamie's boy."

He took her up at once. "She was married on a Mr. Haggart."

"Aye. But he died," retorted Jean.

"We're real sorry ye're so sick, Mr Paterson, but . . . "

"This man's in no state to talk!" snapped Stewart. "Now, what is it ye want?"

"Ye're no tae tak offence, doctor," said the short man peaceably. "We're but doin' our duty."

"I'll talk wi ye the morn, Mr Wishart." Stewart's full lips twisted. "I dinnae do business on Sundays."

"We're thinkin' ye do and that's why we're here," boomed the other.

"Is it lawful to do good on the Sabbath, Mr Campbell? What does the Bible say?"

The elder looked nonplussed momentarily. Then he began to declaim in sing-song tones,

"Ye are a young man and irresponsible. Ye dinnae understand, wi yer city ways, that yer conduct in the Kirk is an example to the weaker vessels. Ye hae walked out in the middle o' the hearin' o' the Holy Word, and no returned."

He threw a glance at Walter's bandages. "Ye hae been lettin' blood on the Sabbath wi no cognisance o' the Commandment that *Six days thou shalt labour and do a' thy work but the seventh . . .* "

"I'm familiar wi the text," Stewart broke in. "Ma faither was a minister so I'm likewise familiar wi' the need tae set a guid example. This man lost enough blood withoot me tapping him for more. The door is right behind ye." He drew one hand from his pocket and shot back his cuff, drawing attention to a powerful wrist.

"We represent the Kirk!" declared Campbell shrilly. "We'll no be intimidate."

"Who's intimidating ye?" asked the doctor. He looked them up and down with a calculating eye. "Just the same, I suggest ye waste no time in takin' yer leave." He hitched back the other ruffle.

"I'm thinking," said Campbell, "that this is a Session matter."

Douglas Stewart swung round on his heel so that he was between them and the couch.

"Whatever kind o' matter it is, this is no the time or place to discuss it. I'll trouble ye to leave my patient in peace." As they left he followed them into the hall, his voice rising. "And mind! It was Miss MacDougal that invited ye into ma surgery, no me. Ye're no to come here again out o' curiosity!"

Wishart's voice, more placating than Campbell's, answered,

"Ye maunae tak offence, doctor. We're appointed by the Session to see that people gang tae the Kirk."

"And stay there!" added Campbell.

"Aye. But yer jurisdiction doesnae come ower ma doorstep! I've warned ye afore! By a' the devils in Hell, this time ye've gone too far! I'm complaining to the minister when he comes back about the abuses ye perpetrate! And as for you, Mr Wishart, I'd like to know what you yersel' would do if yer wife was to be taken wi her pains on the Sabbath?"

Again the front door slammed and he was back in the room. He went straight to Walter, smiling reassuringly, pulling the blanket around him.

"Are ye warm enough, Paterson? And whaur's that ither pillow gone to?" He eased it gently into place.

"Doctor," said Jean. "Yon wasnae the way to handle them."

"Why not?" He turned to her. "I'm no takin' onything frae them even if they did hae my predecessor in their pocket. Ye've no idea, Miss MacDougal, what I've had to put up with from the Session. They ask me about ma cases and which lasses are pregnant, and a', and they're resentful that I'll no tell! This is my house and ma' practice, and I'll run it the way I please."

"Aye, but ye maun be canny aboot it. Ye could harm yersel'," chided Jean gently.

"Canny! I'm no wasting canniness on a pair o' bum bailies. If they dinnae like it, they ken what they can do . . . what I want them to do. Leave me alone."

"That wouldnae do ye any guid in the Parish. Forgi'e me for speakin' plainly but I dinnae want ye in trouble on account o' Walter."

Digging his hands in his pockets again, he looked at her in frank surprise. She met his eyes calmly, and when they strayed towards her Parisian headgear, she smiled. The hardness retreated from his face.

"Ye saved the day, Miss MacDougal," Stewart conceded. "Maybe ye should come here more often."

An unexpected dimple appeared at the corner of Jean's mouth. "Are ye wishin' me sickness, doctor?"

He laughed. "Ye Gods! This even-handed justice!"

"Justice!" echoed Walter, whose mind had gone

wandering down unhappy channels as he tried to understand what was happening around him. "There is no justice! It has all be abolished along with the Bastille. What did they want?"

"Who? The elders? I imagine they'd be satisfied wi ma head."

Walter stared in horror, then struggled up and off the couch. "Where's my shirt? My coat. . . "

Jean caught him. "Lambie, lie down! What's the matter?"

"Give me . . . my coat." It was hung across a chair. "I'm going."

"Where, Walter?"

He steadied himself against the desk. "I'm taking to the heather."

Jean looked at the doctor. "He's gone daft."

"Laddie, do ye want to die of pneumonia?"

Holding himself upright with considerable difficulty, Walter said stubbornly, "I'm getting no-one in trouble. Not again."

"No one's in trouble.

"That's what Louis said but I've seen it all before . . . the spies, the prison, the farcical trial, the . . . the guillotine at the end. Do you have a back door?"

"What is all this about?"

"You've got to believe me. *Pour l'amour de Dieu! C'est vrai ce que je dis . . . Louis. . . "* He floundered towards the door.

Stewart barred his way. "Tak a guid look around ye, Paterson. Whaur dae ye think ye are? Ye're in a civilised country."

"France is . . . was . . . a civilised country. They can all prove their innocence. They can see it for others but not for themselves. . . "

He broke into a torrent of French, then reverted into exasperated English. "Louis. Please, for once don't argue with me. I haven't the strength. But you must get out of Paris. We must all get out of Paris . . . *ce serait fou d'y rester. . .*"

"Calm down," said Stewart quietly. "Lie back. Stop talking about taking to the heather. There are no guillotines in, Scotland."

Coming back to some semblance of reality, Walter gasped.

"But, I'm not getting you into trouble."

"I should hae warned ye about that whisky. It hits ye hard and a' at once."

"The whisky makes no difference. I have caused trouble to you."

"I thrive on trouble. But I'm no in it the now. And ye're no to scare Miss MacDougal."

"I'm no that easy scared." said Jean tartly.

He threw her a brief smile and said,

"Naw, I'm thinking ye'd be hard to scare." He eased Walter down onto the couch close to the fire. Then he asked, with a touch of hesitation, "Miss MacDougal, if ye'd like to stay here a while wi yer . . . cousin . . . I'd be pleased if ye'd share a cold collation wi me."

Her eyes opened with surprise. "I always gang tae ma Auntie's on Sunday."

"Anither o' the laws o' the Medes and Persians for Sabbath observation, is it?" He looked again at her bonnet. "You make me forget I'm no in Edinburgh."

"Ye're very kind, doctor."

"It would hae been a pleasure, Miss MacDougal."

IV

"Mon," said Dr Stewart to his patient after he had seen out Jean, "ye're doing me a real favour gettin me out o' that afternoon sermon o' MacPhail's. Would you like a wee bit o' food?"

"Quelle horreur!"

"Very well. I'll be next door if you want anything." Then turning his head in the direction of the kitchen he shouted, "Mrs MacGregor . . . I've had a busy mornin' and I'm starvin'! Whaur's ma dinner?"

She put her head around the door.

"It's on the table. But I cannae find the kettle."

"The kettle? It's here." As she shut the door, he remarked, "She's bonnie."

Walter, with the housekeeper in mind, looked surprised.

"Miss MacDougal, I mean. She's . . . shapely."

"She's heavy," remarked Walter absently. He felt wretched but, trying to learn more about his condition he asked, "What did you do to me?"

"Plenty. Ye should mak a guid recovery."

"Yes. But, how did you do it?"

"Oh . . . yon . . . "

"It was something to do with Mesmer . . . ?"

Stewart grinned and cleared his throat as if to make a speech, then stopped himself.

"Dinnae start me. . . "

"Please tell me . . . it was so strange. . . "

"Aweel, I put ye tae sleep but I dinnae ken exactly how. . .

"There must be some explanation."

"Aye, but even Dr Mesmer himsel' didnae ken what that was. I'll gie ye his book to read sometime. It's in French."

He swung over towards the window. "Mercy on us! The Kirklands carriage no less! Hey, Mrs MacGregor. . . "

She was already wrestling with the lock.

"It's Jock, doctor."

"Ye're too late, laddie!" Stewart shouted good-naturedly to his assistant as he stepped outside. "Ye missed a' the fun! But ye can come in and tak a look at the patient."

Walter heard a flat young male voice speak ponderously in a strong Strathblane accent, "Miss Moncrieff's compliments to Dr Stewart, and if the young gentleman is still here, she'd be pleased to drive him up to Puddock Hole."

"In her carriage? That's monstrous thoughtful of her. I'll hae him ready in a minute."

But Walter was again trying to struggle up.

"No! No! *C'est impossible! Absolument impossible!* I will not . . . !"

"Why not?"

"I can't!" uttered Walter in panic. "You must tell her I've gone. . . I can't. . . "

"Ye can too. There are two big footmen here to help ye."

"No! I'm drunk!"

"And who's to blame ye?" Stewart was expertly slipping Walter's arm into his shirt sleeve.

"*Mille tonnerres!* I refuse!"

"Now then, laddie, ye didnae panic afore when ye might well have, and ye're no to panic now. What's the matter?"

"She musn't see me like this."

"She isnae there hersel'," interposed the footman. "We drove her back to Kirklands first."

"*Mais pourquoi?* Why. . . "

"Laddie, ye'll never walk up to Puddock Hole the night. Ye can stay here, if ye'd rather, but ye'll no feel too brisk the morn either. It's fair providential to have a carriage to drive ye."

"You . . . are quite sure that she isn't there, herself?"

"I assure ye, and ye dinnae look so bad, even if she were."

"But . . . why?" repeated Walter, wincing as his coat was fastened round him.

"It's no every Sunday that something happens in the Kirk to relieve the monotony. Nor a new face in the Parish. Women are curious." He reached for the whisky bottle. "Here. Anither dram." Walter shook his head. But the doctor relentlessly held the glass to his lips and made him drink it all. The two young men in smart uniforms helped him out of the house, down the path, and into the elegant carriage.

"Doctor, would ye no come wi us and help us at Puddock Hole? We'll bring ye back here."

"A good thought, Jock. Just let me get ma bag. . ."

Walter said to the footmen,

"Kindly tell Miss Moncrieff I appreciate her extraordinary kindness, but I don't see why she should have bothered. . . "

"Ach," said Stewart, jumping in beside him, "ye can wonder about all that the morn."

The vehicle was bumping him about excruciatingly. It seemed to be going over very rocky ground, up a steep hill. The whisky had once more upturned Walter's sense of reality.

"I thought," he muttered to the person beside him, "that the country was flat, north of Paris. . . "

"Ye're a far cry from Paris now, laddie."

"But Louis . . . " Opening his eyes, he looked dizzily round and remembered vaguely where he was and what had happened. But at the same time he seemed to be in another coach, on another journey, and he must not give up yet or they might get him . . . or Louis might change his mind and go back to Paris.

The vehicle shuddered to a stop.

"Tak a guid hold of me now," said a voice from a long distance. "Jock, lift him down if ye will."

"*C'est Boulogne, donc?*" Walter enquired hazily.

"Boulogne? Naw. It's Puddock Hole, and ye're nearly in yer bed."

As they guided him into the farmhouse, another recollection stirred.

"This is the place. This . . ."

"Whaur d'ye sleep, Paterson?"

"In the box bed . . . " The dogs were jumping up and barking.

"Call them off, Paterson."

"Be quiet, Maisie," Walter ordered automatically. They heaved him up onto the bed. Another age passed. He shut his eyes, tried to ignore the humility of being undressed by strange hands. And, goaded by the memories, he tried again.

"Louis, you've got to get out of Paris, Louis . . . "

"Paterson," said a strong voice. "Ye're out of Paris. Ye're in Strathblane. And ye're safe d'ye understand. Perfectly safe."

"Tell her then," he rambled on, "Tell Clementina. . . " Unconsciousness rolled over him.

PART THREE

LOVERS' TRYSTS

My heart thrilled to nature. I had never been in a forest, or any dense solitude, without feeling a tremor, an inner contentment, and a desire never to leave. I looked forward with unmitigated horror to the moment when I should have to part from it and go back to town. . . To end my days I could ask for no more than that modest cottage.

1785 Memoires
Jacques-Pierre Brissot

I

FROM THE BOX BED, Walter heard a smart rat-tat on the farmhouse door and a disconcerted 'Oh!' from Jean, as she opened it.

"Guid morning, Miss MacDougal."

"Guid day, doctor."

"I hope I'm not ower early for ye?"

"No . . . but he's still sleeping."

"I'll come back then. I've another call to make up the hill."

"He's been poorly. He was that sick a' night he couldnae rest."

"I'm sorry to hear that. But he's asleep now?"

"Aye. he dropped off a wee while ago."

"Then dinnae disturb him for onything. I'll come in later."

"No!" called Walter, rallying his strength. "Come in now and get it over!"

Raising his head, he saw Jean trying to hide behind the kitchen door, for she was barefoot and in her shabby worsted dress. Dr Stewart was also less elegant than on the Sabbath, in a well-worn green coat and heavy countryman's boots, incongruous with his snowy linen. He strode purposefully towards the bed, depositing his bag on the kitchen table.

"How are ye the day, Paterson?"

Walter sighed, "*Misérable* . . . "

"What's the trouble?. A lot of pain?" He drew out a tall sandglass, set it up, and his fingers sought Walter's pulse.

"I've been vomiting . . . retching . . . "

"That must have hurt your shoulder."

"It did. Cruelly."

"But . . . why? Surely it wasnae the whisky?" Walter

shook his head. "Miss MacDougal. Kindly fetch a basin of clean water and a bit of soap and towel."

"Aye, doctor." She disappeared towards the back.

"When I left yesterday, you were sleeping soundly. I waited till the MacDougals came back from church and at that time I instructed her to give you a sedative drink, which I mixed up for her, if you were wakeful later on. What happened to that?"

"I spilt it getting up out of bed to . . . to relieve myself. It was dark. I fell . . . I reached to the table for support and knocked it over."

Jean came back with a small ewer of water and Stewart carefully washed his hands.

"What are ye daein that for, doctor?" She was keeping well out of his range, edging towards the staircase.

"It's a protection against dirt, Miss MacDougal."

"Ye'll find nae dirt in my hoose."

"I'm sure there is none. But this is my third call this morning and everyone is not as particular as you are." He dropped the towel casually into the water and started easing his patient up in bed. Walter gritted his teeth. "At ease, laddie. I'll let ye know in good time if it's likely to hurt."

"Everything hurts this morning . . . my head . . . my stomach. . . It was some filthy pigwash she forced down my throat. It made me so nauseous. . . "

"What pigwash? Here, Miss MacDougal!" But she had slipped out of the room. "Well, when she gets back. . . Otherwise, ye're doing fine. Your pulse is strong. Ye've no fever to speak of." He was easing off the dressing and as it came away, a look of pure satisfaction crossed his mobile features. "And no problems with the wounds, thank God."

Walter sighed with relief.

When Jean came back, she was wearing her shoes and had a snood on her well-combed hair. There was also a white kerchief around her neck.

"Come here, Miss MacDougal! Since ye looked after him afore, ye maun hae a strong stomach and ye can appreciate what I've done for him. Is that no a beautiful bit o' surgery?"

Walter noticed that Stewart slipped into the Doric when he spoke with Jean.

Her eyes widened.

"It maun be terrible sore."

"It'll no be sore for long. It's starting to heal already." He pointed with a long finger. "See where I extracted the bullet?" Suddenly he swung round and faced her. "But wi what hae ye been poisoning ma patient?"

"I gi'ed him a guid auld remedy. . . "

"A remedy for what? It's the first time I've heard o' a wound or a fractured wrist being cured out o' a bottle. Though I'd believe onythin in Strathblane. Let me see what you gave him."

As she moved towards the fireplace he eyed her hips appreciatively.

"There it is, doctor."

He held up the bottle to the light, uncorked it, sniffed and made a wry face.

"Ye hae my sympathy, Paterson." He tipped a drop onto one finger and tasted it. "Slaters, ma God! Slaters! In this year of Enlightenment, 1792!"

"It's a guid auld remedy," she repeated.

"Aye. It never killed anyone. Maybe it didnae even scunner them as much as a' the pulverised frogs and things they used to brew up."

"It's in the *Pharmacopoeia*."

"It's no in mine."

She went to the cupboard and drew out a couple of big leather bound books.

"Ye'll no find slaters advocated in the Bible, Miss MacDougal."

"Yon's no the Bible." She handed him a tome. "There ye are!"

He turned over the pages, shaking his head.

"What," asked Walter, swallowing, "are slaters?"

"Woodlice," explained the doctor cheerfully, "baked alive in the oven, or does this edition advise putting them in a linen bag and squeezin' out their juices?" He caught his patient's eye. "It'd be the first thing to come up, laddie. It's a' out yer system by now." He read from the front page. "*The Edinburgh Pharmacopoeia, compiled and edited by Dr William Cullen under the sanction of the College of Physicians of Edinburgh, 1776.* No such a bad book if it werenae twenty years out o' date. I was in Cullen's class in ma first year. He just died a wee while ago. At least it's a more scientific book than *The Poor Man's Physician.*"

"Aye. We hae that too," said Jean proudly. "Ma faither has used these twa books a' his life. Ye'll no find a healthier man onywhere."

"I cannae argue wi that, Miss MacDougal. But I suspect he's been lucky."

"If he's so healthy he should never have needed any medicine," said Walter. Stewart's lip twitched.

"And ye'll find," she pursued, "that it's the same in every house in the Parish. They a' hae at least a *Poor Man's Physician* if they can afford yin. This is ane o' the newest too. It never fashed Dr McKelvie."

"He probably used it himsel'."

"He did that."

"My predecessor, Paterson, whose ghost precedes me on my rounds."

"He was a grand auld man. It was sad that he had to die."

"Did he prescribe slaters?" asked Dr Stewart with interest.

"Aye," Jean retorted. "He had nane o' they newfangled ideas."

"Yer auntie, Mrs Semple, telt me he was apprenticed to an apothecary in Glasgow and that was a' the training he had."

"He had experience," said Jean defiantly.

"And that," said Stewart on a perceptibly sharper note "is what I hear in every house in the Parish. What d'ye suppose I've been doing a' the years I've been studying? And with all due respect, Miss MacDougal, that's the last medicine ye're to give to ony patient o' mine withoot consultin' me first, Dr McKelvie or no Dr McKelvie."

"Ye said yersel' that Walter was doin' well."

"Aye. But look at him. As if that damnably painful arm wasnae enough withoot you gie'in' him a bellyache too. Aweel, it's done noo. I presume ye've a kettle on the fire?"

"What for?"

"The national panacea."

"What's that?"

"Make him a cup o' hot tea."

Walter cleared his throat. "No. I couldn't drink it."

"Ye could too. It'll settle yer stomach, warm ye up. Miss MacDougal, he should also have another blanket and a warm brick for his feet."

"Yin thing at a time, if ye please, doctor." She picked the kettle up and went out to the pump to fill it. Stewart shook his head.

"And they call this the Age of Reason. The 1776 *Pharmacopoeia*. People dosin' themsels wi no thocht o' what they're doin'. Do you wonder I get discouraged?"

He added, in an undertone, "If the elders heard about what I did to ye yesterday, sendin' ye into that trance, they'd dook me in the burn for a warlock."

Jean hung the kettle up to boil and taking down a heavy plaid from behind the kitchen door she bustled over to the bedside. Stewart had finished with Walter's shoulder and was easing him back into Angus's nightshirt.

"Here, lambie, sit up and I'll turn yer pillows for ye."

"Don't fuss over him, Miss MacDougal. Go and make his tea."

"I'm brewing it."

"Oh please, no tea. I couldn't get it down."

"Were ye vomitin' a' night?"

"Towards morning, and before that I had nightmares. What does it matter?" He felt very low.

"Get it off yer chest, laddie. It'll go no further."

For a second, Walter detected an unprofessional sympathy in the other's intelligent eyes.

"I . . . wakened up . . . and began to think about . . . what had happened in France."

"Aye. Reliving every minute. I know what ye mean." He touched Walter's hand briefly. "It's a natural process and it passes. Believe me. But in the meantime, maybe ye'd be better off wi a sleeping draft. Miss MacDougal, never ye mind the tea."

"It's a' made."

"Drink it yersel' then. Bring us a wee glass o' milk."

She picked up a pitcher and poured some into a cup.

Stewart unearthed a bottle from his bag and measured out some of its contents.

"Now then, drink that down. Every drop of it. It'll gie ye some nourishment. And Miss MacDougal, please pay attention. He'll sleep for a few hours, and when he wakens he's to eat something. Broth . . . or brose . . . or porridge . . . whatever he fancies . . . but he maun keep up his strength so no arguments about it. It's only after he's ta'en his supper that ye gie him more medicine. And he may need it because he'll still be in pain."

He measured out another dose. "There, that's for tonight." As he handed it to her, he gave her a faintly mocking smile. "I trust ye agree wi my treatment."

Jean was ruffled, Walter knew. She was tired, worried, and not used to being ordered about in her own house.

"I think, doctor," she said tartly, "that gie'in him yon sleeping draft is the maist sensible thing ye've done since ye came here, for a' yer education."

Stewart's eyes travelled over her white kerchief, then deliberately slid down towards the outline of her full breast against the tight bodice. There was neither admiration nor apology in his cool survey. Jean held her ground, but two spots of colour appeared in her cheeks.

"Thank ye, Miss MacDougal." He gave her a personable smile. "I'm glad to know yer opinion of me."

"If it's ma opinion ye want, doctor . . . " she took a deep breath, "I think ye are the most conceited man I ever met."

Walter noticed that it was Stewart's turn to flush.

"A' right, ma lady." Turning back to his patient, he went on in his usual kindly tones.

"Paterson, that shoulder will be a good deal more comfortable from now on. Ye'll feel like a new man after ye've had some proper rest and there'll be no more nightmares if I can help it." He picked up his bag and shut it.

"Maybe *you'd* like a cup o' tea, doctor?" said Jean with sudden sweetness.

But he was already at the door. "No, thank ye, madam!" he snapped, and left.

II

An autumn storm blew up and Walter followed its progress down the valley from his bed in the brief intervals when he was conscious. Jean made a huge potful of broth and insisted that he take it whenever he was sufficiently awake to do so. He got another strong dose of medicine towards evening and slept heavily through the night.

By Tuesday he was feeling better, for the worst of the pain had receded. Now he needed air. He dragged himself out of bed, put on his clothes with much difficulty and then, despite Jean's protests, he went out, heading for the Gowk Stane.

It was a grey afternoon with rain not far gone, and there was little chance of Primrose Moncrieff being on the moor. Probably, he reflected morbidly, she would think him too decrepit to venture out. He had turned the problem over and over in his mind and still could not make up his mind as to why she had sent the carriage to collect him. If she cared about him why had she not come herself? That he had protested violently that he did not want to see her had completely slipped his mind. He was too confused and upset.

Brooding, he made for the little loch among the trees where it was sheltered, wishing he didn't feel so depressed. It offended his French sense of logic. He had known Primrose such a short time it went against all reason that she should matter so much to him. He had flirted with many girls and done his share of experimenting with women of the town. What he felt for Primrose was something he had never experienced before.

It never occurred to him that much of his depression came from the pains that still coursed down his arm from his wounded shoulder and the steady ache of his wrist. His body had never in the past treated him so roughly. And that too, he could not accept, particularly now he felt that he should be getting better.

He was so lost in his gloomy introspection that she was beside him before he knew it. She had followed him across the moor, the dog at her heels, and she was out of breath.

"Mr Paterson. . . "

Her hair was blowing back from her flushed face. Her eyes were anxious and frightened and to Walter she had never seemed so beautiful. Coming upon her so suddenly, he was at a loss and could only gaze at her, his heart pounding.

"Are you . . . are you. . . "

"I'm still alive."

Her face fell. "Are you still angry?"

"Angry?" he repeated. "Why should I be angry?"

"You were . . . angry with me. I was here yesterday after the rain stopped, but . . . you never came."

"I'm sorry, Miss Moncrieff." His weakness hit him again. "I was in bed all day, and so heavily drugged I couldn't. . . "

Her eyes opened even wider. She looked at the formidable splint under the sling and the plaid. "I didn't realise. Will it . . . is it better now?"

"I hope so. I had a bullet dug out of me."

Her eyes filled with sympathetic tears.

"Don't. It wasn't as bad as it might have been. It was a relief to be finished with it." He noticed that she was shivering. "You're cold," he said increasingly unsure of himself. "Shall we go down to the lochside out of the wind?"

When they reached the rocks she made for their usual seat.

"Let's walk," he said, determined to master his weakness.

But she stopped. "No. Tell me first when you are leaving for Edinburgh."

"Edinburgh?" Then he remembered their last meeting. "Is it important to you, Miss Moncrieff?"

"Yes," said Primrose her tears brimming over. "Yes."

They were back in the vacuum and nothing else mattered, neither convention nor upbringing. He put his left arm around her, drew her awkwardly to him, and kissed her.

She clung to him with a charming lack of inhibition.

"I was so worried about you. You were suffering so, and I couldn't do anything. I . . . I couldn't even come to the door of the farmhouse and ask about you."

"I know. I'm sorry. I can't help it . . . I'm in love with you." He kissed her hair and when she lifted up her face, he kissed her lips.

"Miss Moncrieff . . . Primrose . . . *ma chère petite Primrose . . .* "

"W . . . Walter . . . "

"There are little tears running down your cheeks. If I can't wipe them off, I have to kiss them instead."

"Walter . . . oh, Walter . . . "

"I love you. I mean it. I . . . " Both a little taken aback, they drew apart and looked at one another in amazement. Then suddenly he began to laugh from pure youthful joy.

"*Pour l'amour de Dieu!* You'll have to learn French. I can't court you properly in English!"

She smiled radiantly. "But . . . I've studied French! I can understand it! You just never asked me before!"

III

"Hey, Miss MacDougal!" Douglas Stewart strode through the open kitchen door. "Whaur's ma patient gone to?"

The box bed was empty, covered by a patchwork quilt.

"What hae ye done wi him, woman?"

Jean was sitting by the fire sewing and this time she was in her good dress and shoes.

"He went out. He said he needed some fresh air. I wrapped him up well in a plaid and he'll no catch cold. Sit ye down and I'll call him."

"Wait." He caught her arm lightly as she made for the door. "He'll be back soon. It's turning chilly and I'll wager he's no feeling too spry." And then, as if getting to the point of his visit – "Yesterday Miss MacDougal, ye offered me tea. I hurried through ma calls this afternoon so that I'd hae time to accept yer kind invitation."

"Well!" gasped Jean. "Well, of a' the . . . "

"Of a' the conceit o' the man!" he finished, towering over her. "Ye gied me a reputation to live up to."

"So I see." She moved over to the fire out of his vicinity. "I suppose I cannae violate the laws o' hospitality."

"Good." He took off his greatcoat. "I like ma tea strong wi plenty o' sugar."

She put the kettle on while he sat down at the kitchen table, much at his ease. One of the puppies scrambled out of its box and waddled towards him. He picked it up and fondled it.

"Doctor . . . " she hesitated. "Will Walter's hand aye be crippled?"

He looked her full in the face, sizing her up.

"I set his wrist to the best o' ma ability, which is considerable and I'm actin' on the assumption that it'll heal. But human beings are unpredictable and no responsible physician is going to promise anything." He grinned at her. "That's a' ye're getting oot o' me at the present. I didnae come here to talk shop." His eyes slid involuntarily towards her tight bodice.

"I maun set the table," said Jean agreeably disconcerted. As she laid out the cups he enquired,

"How have you escaped matrimony?"

"Ach, I hae to look after ma faither. I'm the only yin left here."

"What happened to the others?"

"Ma brithers went to sea, and my twa sisters went to work in the mills in Glasgow. Ain o' them got married. She has three bairns. And the ither died. Whaur does your family hail frae, doctor?"

"Ma faither's the minister o' a wee parish in the Borders, if he's still alive. I've had nae word frae hame this six years."

"Mercy! What for no?"

"We quarrelled. He wanted me to follow in his footsteps up into the pulpit. But I've aye been more concerned with the ills o' the flesh than those o' the spirit . . . although maybe they're a' part and parcel o' the same thing. He couldnae see that." Stewart ran his long hands through his dark hair. "There was a lot o' plain speaking."

"So, ye ran away frae hame?"

"Naw. I'd been away to Edinburgh University. I simply wanted to change the direction o' my studies. Ma faither had been prepared to finance me till I was in the saddle bags. Instead, he cut me off wi a shilling."

"And how did ye live?"

"Borderers are nae sae easy killed. I apprenticed masel' to yin o' the Professors at the Surgeon's Hall. He was real guid tae me for he believed in ma abilities. He let me attend his classes free and helped me find employment, for the rest o' ma tuition." He shrugged. "So I managed. By the time I left Edinburgh I was assistant to a physician who had some o' the maist influential patients in Scotland."

"Then what for did ye move and come to a wee place like Strathblane?

He looked at her oddly. "Miss MacDougal, in the six

months I've been here, you're the first person to ask me that."
He hesitated. "It was for ma health."

She eyed him covertly. He was lean, but there was
nothing delicate about him.

"Ye cannae," he added as if picking up the thought,
"live on oatmeal and small beer indefinitely."

"Hae anither scone doctor, to build up yer strength."

He grinned. "Ma mither's family had a farm near
Melrose the like o' this one."

"Stewart isnae a Border name, is it?"

"No. Ma faither was frae Edinburgh. But I favour ma
mither's side o' the house. She was an Elliot."

"Do ye no miss yer folks?"

"I miss my young brithers. But I live for ma work."

"Ye mean you've still got yer wild oats to sow?"

"Yon's anither story. This is mighty tasty tea, Miss
MacDougal. Whaur do you get it?"

She gave him a quick meaningful look.

"I . . . could find some for ye." Their eyes met.

"From the same place that Mr Wishart gets ma whisky?"

She refilled his cup. "It's gey raw spirits made up in the
hills".

"But where else can I get liquor withoot ruinin' masel'
paying excise duties?"

"It can be done, doctor. And the best French brandy
too." She added shrewdly, "and for less than ye're paying
Wishart."

He smiled. "You should be in trade."

Jean's face was enigmatic. "Maybe I am."

When Walter strolled in, they were still sitting over the
teacups, deep in conversation. The puppy had gone to sleep
on Stewart's lap and Jean looked animated and pretty.

"Oh, I'm sorry, doctor. I didn't expect you this early."

Stewart leaned back, tilting his chair precariously. "Who the Devil said you could get up and go oot? Have ye gotten over yer scunner?" His eyes took in Walter's face. "Preserve us! Why did ye try to shave wi yer left hand? Ye've scraped your face to ribbons. Grow a beard."

"Is that what you'd do?" Jean asked.

"Oh Miss MacDougal, ye should see me wi whiskers! I look like a wild Cameronian! Maybe I *should* grow a beard and the people o' Strathblane would think I looked old enough to attend to them."

Walter was slipping off his coat.

"Ach, sit down and hae some tea, laddie. I'm in no hurry. How's the arm?"

"Better . . . but I've no strength in my legs." He slumped into a chair, picked up one of the remaining scones and ate it with relish.

"Ye'll soon get it back. Oh. That reminds me, Miss MacDougal. So ye can legitimately indulge in yer fondness for dosing people, I've made him up a tonic. It's mair effective than slaters and easier to take."

"I don't need any tonic."

"It'll do ye no harm and think how happy ye'll make her . . . measurin' it out for ye three times a day." He set down the puppy and leaned over to open his bag. There was a tall dark bottle on the top which he removed, briefly.

"You been doing some business, Jean?" asked Walter slyly.

"Jean!" echoed Stewart triumphantly. "That's yer name! Of course!"

"Ach. Ye'd never hae guessed it yersel'," she joked.

"Ye've still to guess mine. I gied ye a guid hint. . . "

"The court o' King Robert the Bruce. What do I ken about history? I didnae gang to Edinburgh University. Ask Walter. He's educated."

"Verra well, Paterson. Tell her ma name. It's singularly appropriate."

Concentrating, trying hard to remember the exact wording on the diploma, Walter said, "Douglas . . . Elliot . . . Stewart."

Jean sang mockingly,

Hush ye, hush ye, Dinnae fret ye!
The Black Douglas willnae get ye!

"Aye – also *Ma name is little Jock Elliot, and wha' daur meddle wi me?* – Ach, ye're ower observant, Paterson! I'd have had her guessing for anither hour and had an excuse to waste ma time."

"*Eh bien*, I haven't had my tea. . . " Walter had his own reasons for being in good humour. "Jean, are there any more scones?"

"Aye, and bring some more for me too Jean," called the doctor.

"There's only enough left for Walter and I'll hae ye know, Dr Douglas Stewart, that for all you feel yersel' tae be such a privileged character, ye didn't bring me intae the world."

"Naw. That's one event for which I'll admit I'm ower young. If I hae been presumptuous madam, I make ma apologies."

"Away wi ye, and attend to yer patient. . . "

"He's still havin his tea. And I'm glad to see he's got his appetite back. Yer stomach's back to normal again, Paterson?"

"Yes. And there seems to be nothing left to eat. No scones, anyway."

"Well, what was it your French queen said? If there are no scones, eat cake?"

"I don't believe she ever said it but it's a good suggestion and Jean's bannocks are excellent. Tell me, were there any repercussions?"

Stewart's black eyebrows shot up. "What kind o' repercussions?

"Did you have any trouble from the men from the Church over my . . . er . . . "

"Naw. I didnae hear another word, and I dinnae expect to."

Jean collected his teacup and asked, "How soon does Mrs Wishart expect to be brought tae bed?"

"Miss MacDougal, ye ken everything! D'ye suppose a'body in the Parish. . . ?"

"She maun be four months on the way at least. It's obvious. . . "

"What is?" asked Walter.

She cleared the rest of the dishes onto a tray. "Ma auntie's elderly and doesnae want difficult cases and there's nae anither doctor for five miles. And he's old, too."

"He shouldnae find that ony disadvantage. Come Paterson, let's see ye. Tak yer coat off and lie down."

"I'm up and I'm staying up."

"Ye can get up again after I leave. In the meantime, I want you up there, stretched out and wi yer shirt off too."

Jean had gone into the back and produced a basin of water and a towel. "Here ye are. To wash yer hands."

"So ye remembered that, eh?"

"Aye, it was that unexpected!"

She disappeared out to the back. As she returned Stewart was saying,

"I wish I had mair patients the like of you. In the first place, ye're an interesting case. And in the second, yer system behaves the way the books say it should."

"Is he making progress, doctor?"

"Aye, he's much, much better the day." Stewart gave Walter a slightly curious look. "And particularly in his state of mind."

"How can you tell that by poking at my shoulder?"

"Ye'd be surprised. Would it be convenient for you to assist me, Miss MacDougal? I'll no can get up here every day and you might hae tae change his dressing yersel'."

"Forbye," Jean added, "ye like to hae somebody tae order around."

He laughed. "Maybe I do. And I love to teach people. I've been training young Jock MacLean."

"How long will it take," Walter asked," before I'm fully recovered?"

"A couple o' months if all goes well."

"*Mille tonnerres!*"

"Did I hurt you? Sorry."

"No. Yes. Damnation! I had no idea it would take so long."

"And to think," said Jean in a knowing way, "ye'll be in and out o' here a' that time, doctor!"

"Mon! I hadnae thought o' that." This time there was enough lechery in his smile to send her scurrying outside again.

"It was a bad break Paterson, and ye didnae hae it properly set at the time. A' right, to encourage ye, I'll say maybe six weeks."

"But . . . I'm so anxious to go to Edinburgh. . . "

"Aweel, ye'll be able to travel as soon as that shoulder's healed, which'll be soon. But, as I warned ye, it's a long hard trip and it could set back your recovery." He glanced around the warm kitchen and asked, "What for are ye in such a hurry to leave here? I'm sure ye're accustomed to more luxurious surroundings but what more can you really want than what's here?"

The Laird's sister in bed with me, thought Walter and that could never happen at Puddock Hole.

"I need to talk to you, doctor. Let's go down the road."

"Better lie still for a wee while, laddie."

"But I want to ask you some questions." He slid back on the pillow. Not only did his shoulder hurt but he was exhausted. Stewart considered him dispassionately.

"It'll do you no good to lie there and worry." He looked around for an excuse to put off time. "Just gie me a few minutes to explain to her about the medicine."

He repacked his bag quickly and followed Jean out to the back. He stayed away for several minutes. On his return, he pushed the door shut.

"A'right, Paterson. We can talk freely. She's busy in the byre. Are ye resting more comfortably now?"

"Yes, thank you. Look, I don't want to bother you with my problems but . . . this was something of a shock."

"There's no need to apologise." He drew his pipe from his coat pocket and lit it. "Don't ye know there's nothing gives more pleasure than handing out advice? What is it specifically that's troubling you?"

"I'm no relation to the MacDougals. They took me in out of pure kindness. I can't live off them for two months, or even a month. I can't repay them."

"Ye've no kin in Scotland?"

"In Edinburgh, though I don't even know where they live."

"Aweel Paterson, as I said before, it's a difficult trip and ye'd run the risk o' startin' up anither fever from overtiring yersel'. Ye need time to build up yer strength. Maybe it won't be too long."

Walter lifted his hand and dropped it again with one of his foreign gestures. "I must have been crazy to think of making that journey."

"Forgive me for asking, but hae ye ony money?"

"French money."

"Ye could change that in Glasgow. It's better than

nothing."

"I can't write," said Walter deliberately. "For anything I know how to do I have to be able to write. I don't suppose I'm fit for anything." And then after a moment's thought, "Or do you know anyone here who might like language lessons? Or could I perhaps teach in the village school?"

"Mon! That's a solemn thought! The Strathblane bairns talkin' French!" He puffed on the pipe. "Look laddie, God forbid I should preach but ye maun be patient. Ye've had a bad nervous shock and quite apart from your injuries, it's ma opinion ye need rest and quiet to recover yersel'. Miss MacDougal says it's nae bother to her if ye stay on here. Ye can repay her eventually. So try not to worry. Have ye ony plans for the future, once ye get to Edinburgh?"

Walter looked gloomy. "No, I suppose I'll have to be guided by the family. My father wanted me to study law."

"Ye could do that in Edinburgh."

"I hate the idea. But . . . " He shrugged.

The back door creaked open. "May I come in to ma ain kitchen?" Jean asked.

"Oh aye, seein' ye're here," said Stewart. "Man, Paterson, d'ye know what kept me so long out in the byre? She wanted me to prescribe for an ailing cow!"

"You should feel complimented!"

"Dr MacKelvie," said Jean, "kent an awfa' lot about the beasts."

"So far, I'm no that versatile." Stewart drew on his greatcoat. "But I was thinking Miss MacDougal, hae ye tried feedin' her on neeps?"

"Faither disnae hold wi they new-fangled crops."

"Ma uncle in the Borders was growin' them for his cattle ten years ago, if that isnae too recent."

Jean seemed about to make some retort then changed her mind.

"I'll bring ye some," Stewart continued. "There are families in this parish that pay for their medical care exclusively in neeps. I ken they're guid for ye but there are also whiles I cannae stomach the sight o' anither yin."

She smiled. "I'll trade ye yin o' the puppies for them. If ye'd like."

"That would be grand, Miss MacDougal. Maybe the wee bitch that seems to fancy me?"

"The very one I had in mind for ye, doctor."

IV

Captain Abernethy on his next visit with a consignment of wines and spirits assured Walter that his letter was on its way to his father. The seaman also promised to get in touch with the Paterson family, although he warned that communications and travel were bad due to the increasing unrest in France.

So having done all he could, Walter resigned himself to staying in the Blane Valley, at least for a while. This he did not find hard to do, since he was seeing Primrose Moncrieff several times a week. They took the air in the afternoon on the Boards Road and talked endlessly in meetings that seemed to exist neither in time nor space, but to be independent of the world around them. The daily life of a young Scottish girl of good family was very different from that of her French counterparts he found. He was indeed quite impressed by the amount of hard work that Primrose put in, keeping house for her brother, whom she still refused to let him meet.

"You don't understand," she told him. "He hates the French."

"But I'm not a Frenchman."

"I know, but you grew up there. He's heard about you, of course . . . everyone has in Strathblane . . . and he's very suspicious about why you're here."

"Then why shouldn't I meet him and explain?"

"No. Please, Walter. He might forbid my seeing you."

"But my dear girl, my attentions are entirely honourable. I would like to marry you."

"How do you know that on such short acquaintance?"

"I don't know. But I do. I've never felt so at home . . . in any place or with any other young woman." He looked across the valley at the Campsie Hills. "I would like to stay here for ever and manage an estate like your brother's."

"The MacDougals wouldn't like that. There is a feud between them and Henry, as I'm sure you know."

"The plea, yes. I've heard all about it many times."

"Henry would like to settle but Mr MacDougal won't. It's one of those tiresome matters that goes on and on . . . and it's one reason Henry would be suspicious of you . . . that you live at Puddock Hole."

With the touch of practicality that Walter found so unexpectedly charming she added,

"And you have no money. You don't know what your prospects are. Henry is anxious for me to make a good marriage. How could he accept you as my suitor?"

"Once I'm fit enough to go to Edinburgh and find my family I'll soon settle that question! My father isn't poor. He's been successful in banking. I'll wager he's already moved his assets out of France, if he hasn't already gone himself. He's always told me that he'd provide for me well. The law was just something I was to study because in this unsettled world, you never know. I might have to earn my living. He did, after the '45. But I would prefer the country life."

It was into this engaging and for the most part peaceful environment that there materialised one day at the end of October Jean's cousin, Willie MacDougal from Glasgow. His arrival was heralded by a laboriously penned letter announcing that on Thursday he would alight from the coach from Glasgow and drink tea with his relatives at Puddock Hole prior to spending the night with his Aunt Semple. On the following day, he would be visiting Mr Melville on business at the inkle factory in Netherton.

"What's an inkle factory and what does Willie do?" Walter asked.

"Mr Melville manufactures cloth and Willie's in the cotton trade, the same as the Laird afore he came oot here tae live. Willie imports and exports to America. He has a fair ability for business. Started oot just himsel' and now he has six men working for him. Self-made," added Jean proudly.

"Does he often come to visit you?"

"Not since Effie died . . . that was his wife." Suddenly her eyes gleamed. "Walter, ye ken why he's comin'? He must have heard aboot ye." This business wi Melville they could do in the town."

"What does he know about me?"

"Ach away wi ye, Walter! Willie was aye sweet on me afore Effie caught him." She went on, "Ye're to wear yer ain bonnie blue suit. And yer twa watches. And yer signet ring."

"Willingly. What about the doctor? Should we ask him to come in the morning?"

She tossed her head. "Naw. I'll be havin' a special baking for Willie."

Slightly mystified, Walter observed her preparations. She did an extensive housecleaning, scouring out the kitchen. She polished the furniture in the parlour and shone up her silver teapot. On Thursday she baked all morning, then dressed herself in her best Paisley muslin and seated herself primly in the front room while Walter and Angus shared a bucket of warmed water in the kitchen. She even prevailed on her father to put on his Sunday clothes, despite his protests.

Such an occasion had been made of the visit that Walter found Willie an anti-climax. He was large and fat, possessing all the solid virtues save eloquence. After Jean had entrenched him on the sofa, he sat there for a long time without uttering anything more constructive than long drawn-out sounds – "Aye . . . eh . . . mmm . . . uh, huh . . . mmm." It was only after she had started to serve a mountainous tea that he roused himself to talk.

"Ye'll be a friend o' Captain Abernethy's then, Mr Paterson? Aye . . . mm. And how much will ye be makin' on yer cows this year, Uncle Angus? Did ye get a guid price for yer hay? Aye . . . eh . . . mmm. And how's Aunt Semple's rheumatics? A peety. Aye . . . Ye still hae the same minister, Mr Gardner is it not? Aye . . . "

Walter's boredom became so insupportable that he began to think if Stewart walked in and suggested the immediate resetting of his wrist, he would welcome it as a diversion. He had eaten too much, and a heavy late afternoon pall had settled on the room. Possibly Willie was a victim of his own monotony. It must have been gruesome to live with.

Only Jean's vitality seemed unflagging, perhaps because she had been too busy to eat. She was not only unusually animated but she also struck Walter as slightly on her guard. And when Angus got up to see to the cows and Walter offered to go with him, she cut him short.

"Naw, laddie. You stay here, in case the doctor comes." She turned her company smile on Willie. "We hae a new doctor, a very brilliant young man frae Edinburgh. He taught at the College. He's been unco obligin', comin' here to care for Walter. But of course, he's single and his time's his own."

"Aye," said Willie lugubriously. "Aye, it makes a difference no havin' a wife." A pious sorrow settled over his face. As for Jean, she looked as if she had said more than she intended.

"Effie hasnae been dead long, Willie."

"A year, Jeannie. A year and three months. I can begin to look round me again."

She reached for the teapot as though for protection. "Some mair tea?" She armed herself with a plate of scones, "And anither o' these. . . "

He shook his head. "Naw, I dinnae enjoy ma food the way I used to do." He turned to Walter. "Ye maun be a help to Uncle Angus. A man can do mair around a farm nor a woman."

Walter sighed. "Not as yet I'm afraid."

"Aweel," said Willie comfortably, "yer airm will mend."

Jean said brightly, "We'll miss Walter when he goes."

But it seemed as though Willie's mind was hovering towards an idea.

"Jeannie, while he's still here could ye no come to Glasgow for a wee visit wi Flora and her bairns?"

"Oh no, Willie. No while he's still sae crippled."

Her cousin looked like a sick cow. "It's been a lang time Jeannie, since ye came to ma hoose."

"No since Effie died."

"Naw. And there's been nae ither woman across the doorstep since. Bar the girl that cleans," he added truthfully.

It was at this juncture that the collies set up a welcoming bark.

"That maun be the doctor." Jean jumped up and opened the parlour door. As usual, he had come into the kitchen without knocking. "We're in here!"

Douglas had scooped up his favourite puppy and the little dog was licking his face.

"Miss MacDougal, ye're a sight for sore eyes in that dress." He saw Willie. "Oh, I beg pardon. I didnae realise ye had company."

Jean made the introductions and offered the doctor tea. Stewart sat down heavily, stretching out one leg carefully. He looked tired to the point of exhaustion.

"I really shouldnae take the time but . . . thank ye, Miss MacDougal."

Willie considered him.

"I kent yer predecessor here. His name was McKelvie. He was a grand auld man."

"So I've heard."

"He gied me some pills for ma stomach . . . ye mind Jeannie, yon awfa' stomach I had the last time I was here? I hae some o' them yet. They were very guid, very guid indeed."

"I'm glad to hear it." Stewart sipped his tea. "Are they havin' much influenza in Glasgow?"

"Aye. Aye. There's a wheen sickness. I havenae had it masel'."

"You've been lucky. It's taking its toll in Strathblane. Though not as much as the measles." He set down his cup "One child just died."

"Whose was it?" asked Jean.

"His father works at the inkle factory. Irish. A big family and a' the young ones ailing." He pushed back his hair firmly and looked at her. "I was wondering Miss MacDougal, if ye could gie me a wee bit o' advice. How do I get the school closed for a few weeks until the infection has died down among the children?"

"It's a matter for the Kirk Session, doctor. They run the school."

"Aye. And ye know what Mr Campbell thinks o' me." He smiled wanly. "I'm ower young to hae ony judgement.

The bairn's dying is an act o' God!"

"Have ye talked to the minister?"

"He's on ma side. And he doesn't lay the blame on the Almighty either. But I cannae expect him to go agin Campbell. He owes his livelihood to the Session."

"Maybe ye could take it to the Presbytery in Dumbarton."

"That would take time . . . and a lot o' bairns could sicken."

It was at this moment that Angus returned. Douglas rose politely to greet him. Then, as if struck by an idea, he said,

"Mr MacDougal, ye're a heritor o' the Kirk, are ye no'?"

"Aye, that's right, young man."

"Then maybe you can help me. I want the school closed until this measles epidemic has died down. Mr Campbell is agin it but. . . "

Angus interrupted him abruptly. "If he's agin it, then I'm agin it too."

"But . . . it's takin' a fair toll o' the children's health and surely that's important."

"Mr Campbell's the Session Clerk, doctor. Naebody questions his decisions."

Douglas inhaled sharply. "I'm questioning this one. As a physician I consider it my duty to recommend measures that improve the well-being of the parish."

"Aweel, ye've made yer recommendation and Campbell's turned it doon. Ye've no jurisdiction ower the Kirk. And Dr McKelvie never pushed himsel' forward like that."

"I'm no pushing masel'. I'm thinkin' o' the bairns. Surely they have the right. . . "

"Rights! Rights!" echoed Angus. "There's ower much

talk o' rights these days. That's what caused all the trouble in France. Was it no, Walter? People wantin their rights."

Before Stewart could interpose, Jean responded quickly. "If ye've finished yer tea doctor, maybe you should be seein' to Walter. Gang intae the kitchen . . . it's warm in there. And I'll join ye shortly."

The two young men rose. Douglas bowed to Willie and also to Angus and followed his patient into the hall, limping a little and not even trying to hide his discouragement.

Walter felt for him. He slapped him on the back.

"Mon cher ami! How glad I am to see you!"

"Stop acting like a damn Frenchie."

"But . . . *Mon Dieu!* I thought I would expire from boredom! *Affreux!* That great ox in there! Have another cup of tea. There must be some in the big pot. You look awfully tired."

"Maybe I will hae anither cup. I'd little enough sleep last night. Who is he?"

"Mr MacDougal's nephew. A cotton importer . . . a self-made man. He may look stupid but Jean says he's making a lot of money. How does he do it?"

"Mon, if I knew how to make money, I'd tell ye. Which reminds me, Paterson. I must ask ye a few questions. First of all, apart from yer boredom, how are ye feeling these days?"

Trying to cheer him up, Walter grinned.

"Much improved. And let me save you the trouble of interrogating me. Am I sleeping better? Yes. Do I still need opiates? Only now and again. Do I eat properly? Like a pig. You must give me some pills for my indigestion after that tea party. Do I have as much pain in my wrist? It doesn't seem so bad. Do my bowels move? Yes. Anything else?"

Stewart laughed.

"Aye. Have ye had the measles?"

"What? Oh . . . yes. I think so. When I was small. We

all had it . . . Louis, Clementina and the little Sincerbeaux girls."

"And do ye like children?"

"Indeed, yes. I'm very fond of them."

"Good. Then maybe ye'll have heard Miss MacDougal speak o' Mrs Graham of Leddrie Green House?"

Walter had heard of her, though not at the farm. "The widow who has that pretty place on the other side of the valley?"

"The verra same. She has a son, Bobby. He's nine. The only child she didnae lose in infancy, I'm told. And he's delicate. It was for his health that she moved oot o' Glasgow after her husband died. She's had the laddie at the village school and he was yin o' the first to come down wi measles. Had it unco badly too, I feared I'd lose him. But he recovered. Now she wants to keep him at home for a while. Hepburn the dominie is a clever man, but he's also a drinker. And he's unpredictable . . . no for nervous children. Mrs Graham was asking me yesterday if I knew o' onyone hereabouts who could instruct Bobby, or at least keep him occupied. I told her about you. . . "

"Did you tell her. . . " He looked down at his arm which, while they had been talking, he had been freeing from his coat sleeve.

"Paterson, ye're fitter than the boy. And ye'll be using that hand shortly. Hae ye been exercising it, the way I telt ye?"

Walter shook his head.

"Why not?"

"I . . . I don't believe I can."

Stewart took his patient's right hand in his own and bent each finger carefully. "Ye've got mobility there."

"But . . . no power . . . "

"Because ye've no been trying."

"I can't, I tell you. . . "

"I think ye can, but there's something in yer mind holdin' ye back." He sighed wearily. "Whatever it is, I cannae deal wi it the day and maybe nor can you. In any case, it doesnae matter because this boy can write, so a' ye need to do is . . . well . . . tutor him. He has books. He knows what he has to learn to keep up wi his classmates. And Mrs Graham wouldnae want ye there every day or even all day at first. It's a fair walk over to her house but the exercise will do ye good. And if the weather's stormy or ye hae a bad night wi a bout o' pain, she'll understand if ye stay hame."

He went to the basin, washed his hands, then came back and removed the bandage from Walter's shoulder. He nodded approvingly.

"Just as I expected. These wounds are healed up and ye dinnae even need anither dressing. The next time I see ye, I'll show ye some exercises that will help ye regain the strength in yer muscles. And afore ye go over to Graham's, I'll put ye into anither trance. I've aye longed to do that again, to prove some matters to masel'. And it'll save ye some discomfort."

"I have no objections to that. Tell me about Mrs Graham."

"She's a nice lady. I'm surprised that she hasnae married again. I understand her husband was a lot older than she was. If she was a few years younger, I might be tempted to court her masel' and make an advantageous match."

"You could make a *mariage de convenance* and keep a mistress."

"In Strathblane? Are ye daft?"

Jean called from the other side of the door, "Let me in, please!" She was carrying a tray of dishes. When she had set it down on the table, she went over to Stewart, touching his arm gently.

"I didnae want to say more in there doctor, but I ken ye felt bad about losin' that bairn."

He shrugged. "I suppose it's something I maun get used to. I did a' I could for him but . . . the wee soul was half-starved. He couldnae muster enough strength to fight the fever. Melville doesnae pay his workers a living wage."

"Aye. That's why they're so discontented and radical. Last winter there were eight or ten bairns died o' the measles and they were a' frae Netherton. And . . . ye're right, doctor. In Killearn they kept the bairns home for near a month last winter and they didnae have half as much sickness as here."

"Then, if ye'll forgive me asking this, Miss MacDougal . . . why won't your father help me? Or Mr Wishart who has a child on the way?"

She smiled and shook her head. "Neither o' them dares cross Mr Campbell. He's the Exciseman."

"What has that to do wi it?"

"Do ye no mind whaur the brandy came frae that I gi'ed ye for attendin' to Walter? And Mr Wishart has a still that's unco profitable, I'm telt. And if it isnae contraband, it's some ither thing that's the secret o' his hold ower the Kirk."

"Isn't there anything I can do then?"

"Aye there is," Jean answered, "but dinnae ever tell ma faither I suggested it. What ye maun do is talk to Mr Moncrieff. He's a fair-minded man and as the Laird, he has authority over the Kirk. His father appointed Mr Gardner and naebody raised any question o' patronage the way they often do. And Campbell's unco anxious to stay in Kirkland's good graces. If he says he wants the school closed, it'll be done."

"Would he listen to me, do you think?"

"What for no? You go up to his house a' the time."

"Aye, I bleed him regularly and prescribe for him too."

She smiled up at him. "Ye're half way to Kirklands the now. Gang straight there when ye're finished wi Walter and tell Mr Moncrieff about the bairn dyin' just as ye telt it to us. But can I make yin suggestion?"

"I asked ye for yer advice, Miss MacDougal."

"Just remember when ye're with him that ye're no there as his physician. I mean, ye're no telling him what to do. Ye're asking him for help in a matter that concerns the Parish."

Stewart smiled ruefully. "Excellent counsel. I'll keep ma temper in check." He flipped down his long white cuffs and closed his bag. "Thank ye. May I stop on my way home and tell ye what happened?"

"If ye can spare the time."

"I'll make the time." As he was drawing on his greatcoat, he remarked, "Ma housekeeper aye makes me change into ma Sunday clothes to gang up to Kirklands but maybe for once it'll no matter how I look."

"That's a very well-cut suit you're wearing," Walter reassured him.

"And doctor," added Jean, "you look as though you hadnae slept. It's guid the Laird should see that ye came to him straight away." And then almost as an afterthought she asked, "What is it that's wrang wi yer leg?"

"Nothing. At least, nothing new. I've a weakness in it and when I'm as tired as I am the day, I forget to control it. Was I limping?"

"Aye. And dinnae try to hide that frae the Laird either. He feels fatherly aboot the people o' Strathblane, even those Irish workers doon at the factory. But dinnae say onythin' against Mr Melville, for they're friends."

"I'll remember."

She pulled a sprig of white heather from a bunch of dried flowers on the window ledge and stuck it in his button-hole. "That's for guid luck."

He took both her hands in his, raised them to his lips and kissed them respectfully. Walter noticed with surprise that Jean was blushing. And she stood at the door and watched as the doctor started up the Boards Road towards the big house.

V

The Laird agreed to overrule the Kirk Session and the village school was closed the next day. Moncrieff also told the elders that it was to remain that way until the doctor considered the measles epidemic had run its course.

And Walter, a couple of days after Willie MacDougal had come and gone, called upon Mrs Graham of Leddrie Green House, wearing his own blue suit and with his wrist less conspicuously strapped up. He found the widow charming. There had been a bad moment, as he walked across the valley, when he had wondered if she would treat him like an inferior or even as a servant, but she greeted him warmly, offered him a glass of wine and, after they had talked a little about Paris which she had once visited, and he had told her about his family and education, she had introduced him to her son, Bobby.

He was a frail-looking little boy and he seemed curious about Walter's carrying one arm in a sling.

"Can you toss a ball, Mr Paterson?" he asked wistfully.

"Yes, of course," Walter reassured him. "But you'll find it tricky catching it. I throw with my left hand. However, I can kick with both feet, so we can play football, if your mother agrees."

The remuneration Mrs Graham offered him was generous, according to Jean.

"It's all going to you," Walter told her.

"Naw, naw. It's for yer trip to Edinburgh." But after he insisted, she agreed to take half of it. "Put the rest in the drawer o' the sideboard laddie, along wi yer watches and yer ring and that French money the Captain left. Ye'll need change to put in the plate on Sunday. If ye're able to work, ye're able to gang to the kirk," she added firmly.

So at the end of the week, Walter found himself once again in the cramped old Strathblane church. Mr Gardner, the parish minister, was in the pulpit and he generated a lot less emotion than Mr McPhail. The congregation sat back and listened with varying degrees of attention to a dull but scholarly dissertation which lasted one hour. A few curious glances came Walter's way, but he had a feeling most of the villagers knew who he was and this gave him a pleasant sense of belonging. He also knew the Laird's household sat in the gallery but he was able to identify some of the local personalities, notably the grim Mr Campbell and his friend Mr Wishart, who was accompanied by a mousy little woman draped in a voluminous cape, presumably to hide her condition.

Angus MacDougal, Walter also observed, got a bow from the minister, as was his right as a property owner and an important member of the community.

Moving down the aisle at Jean's heels after the service, Walter felt a light touch on his arm, and Stewart's voice said softly,

"Ye didnae spare me the sermon the day, but at least I got a nap."

"I'm sure you needed it."

As they emerged into the wintery sunlight, a short well-dressed man passed them quickly and the doctor swept him a low bow.

"Good morning, Mr Moncrieff. A fine day, is it not?"

The other acknowledged the greeting with a perfunctory nod and hastened on towards one of the carriages standing by the gate.

"Is that the Laird?" asked Walter.

"Aye. Hae ye never seen him afore?"

Primrose's brother resembled her though he had none of her good looks. His hair was a dull brown, his features good if undistinguished. He gave the impression of a busy man who found life hard and full of problems.

Stewart now greeted Jean.

"Where's yer Auntie, Miss MacDougal?"

"She maun be poorly. Her legs are bad in this kind o' weather. I'm going to see her now."

"May I escort ye as far as her cottage?"

"Thank ye, doctor." She took the arm he offered her. "I'm glad to see ye're no limpin'."

"I never limp," Stewart replied with obvious pleasure, "when I'm squiring a pretty woman."

Walter lingered behind in hopes of a glimpse of Primrose. Between them, Jean and the doctor seemed to know most of the village people, for they both stopped and greeted little groups of parishioners standing around the churchyard talking.

Walter had just finished saying good morning to Mrs Graham and Bobby when Angus MacDougal joined him looking annoyed.

"Laddie, gang after Jean and walk wi her! I cannae move that fast, and she shouldnae be traipsin' off like that wi the doctor! Makin' a public spectacle o' hersel'!" he fumed.

Walter sprinted after the couple.

"Your father says I'm to chaperone you," he explained to them merrily. Jean glowered.

"Who was leading the singing?" Walter asked Stewart by way of conversation.

"Benjy Hepburn, the schoolmaster."

"He's a good musician, but he seemed a little uncertain at times."

"Too much drink last night," commented the doctor dourly. "There are Sundays he can scarcely stand upright. I hope he doesnae spend his free time this week in the pub. But I fear he will."

"Ye maun be popular wi the bairns, keepin' them oot o' school," Jean put in.

"Aye, but if I fulfil anither ambition they won't like me. There are cases of smallpox in Glasgow and I've heard there's some ways ye can protect people against it. Engrafting, they call it. It comes from Turkey. The wife o' the British ambassador there had it performed on hersel' and her children. I've written to a medical friend in Edinburgh, asking if he knows how it was done. I'd like to try it here and forestall an epidemic."

"And who would pay for that?"

"That's the problem, Miss MacDougal. The Kirk Session isnae likely to make an offer and I'd have to do a lot o' persuading to get Kirklands to loosen his purse strings."

"Have ye mentioned the idea to Mrs Graham?"

He smiled. "Aye. As a matter o' fact, I have. I'm learning."

"Isn't the Laird supposed to be sweet on my employer?" asked Walter.

Jean gave him a surprised look. "And how did ye ever hear that, lambie?"

Since Primrose was the source of his information, Walter was at a loss to reply. Fortunately, Stewart came back into the conversation with a query about what Mrs Semple did for her bad legs.

"She takes yin o' her herb potions," Jean told him. "Is there nothing ye can do for the rheumatics?"

"If I could cure the rheumatics," declared Stewart, "I'd make a fortune. Believe me, I keep thinking about it and reading a' I can on the subject."

"Do you ever think o' onythin' besides yer work?" she asked glancing up at him with a touch of coyness.

"What else is there to think about in Strathblane?"

"Women," Walter suggested.

"Speak for yersel', Paterson." They had reached the doctor's gate. "Aweel, Miss MacDougal, I'll leave ye here. Remember me to yer Auntie and tell her I'll drop by and see her the morn. I've a great regard for her as I think she kens, and maybe I can help her a little." He smiled at them both and leaving him to wrestle with his front door, they continued along the road to Mrs Semple's cottage which was only a short distance away.

Walter hung around outside and by the time Jean emerged, Angus had caught up with them.

"We're going home for our meal, faither. Auntie's in her bed." She took Walter's arm and marched briskly ahead. At the farm, she laid out a platter of cold mutton and a loaf of bread in stormy silence. Walter was hungry, and so, evidently was Angus but Jean ate nothing. When they had finished and she was starting to clear the table, the old man suddenly barked at her to sit down and pay attention to him. She did, glaring.

"Ye're a disgrace," he told her severely.

"I've done nothing wrong, faither."

"Ye made yersel' unco free wi that young doctor, in front o' a' the Parish . . . walking off wi him in public."

"He saw me up the Brae. What's wrang wi that? There was nae . . . impropriety. . . "

"It's no impropriety I'm worried aboot, Jeannie. Ye hae mair sense than that. But it's no wise to show how far ben ye are wi that Stewart. Mr Campbell's fair furious wi him over the school closin'. He didnae like the Laird comin' into the Session meeting and layin' doon the law. And I ken fine it was your idea."

"And what if it was, faither? It was sensible. They kept the bairns home in Killearn last winter when the measles came and there werenae sae many o' them died."

"Aye, but this is Strathblane. And now the whole parish'll ken it was you put the doctor up to bringing the Laird into it and putting doon Campbell." She said nothing. "Jeannie," implored her father, "d'ye no see the danger to us? Campbell's the Exciseman."

"He'll no be telling Mr Moncrieff about the Captain," said Jean.

"Oh but he might just, to keep himsel' in the Laird's guid graces. That's mair important to him than the odd bottle we gie him. I've aye been careful to support Campbell, as a heritor, in whatever he proposes in the Session. And now ye've challenged him. It's dangerous, I'm telling ye."

"He cannae prove a thing."

"Is proof ever needed in this valley? We've been walking a tightrope for years, Jeannie. And now wi the Laird so suspicious o' foreigners, it's worse. I'm telt he's gettin curious aboot whaur a' the French brandy's coming from, that's on his friend's tables."

"Wi the big tips Campbell gets frae Mr Wishart to keep away frae a' the stills, he's no in a verra guid position to tell on the likes o' us. We could pass on a few things about a' the local whisky distilling if we were so minded."

"Jeannie, the Laird doesnae mind aboot the stills. It's onything that comes frae France. . . "

"Maybe I'm a danger to you too, Mr MacDougal," said Walter in a state of mounting concern.

"Naw, naw, laddie." But the farmer went on, "It was just a peety that when the parish had gotten used to seeing you . . . and maybe even believing Jean's story that ye're a distant cousin . . . that she had to go and make hersel' conspicuous wi Campbell's enemy, the doctor."

"That's enough, faither!" She jumped up angrily. "It's aye the same! Every time a man looks ma way, ye find some ither thing wrang wi him! Every man except yon fat Willie! And that's why I'm twenty-four and still a tocherless spinster." She burst into tears. Walter would have gone to her but Angus stopped him.

"Leave her alane, laddie. Gie her time to think. She'll see that I'm right. It's dangerous to cross a man like Campbell And that's what she's done, encouraging the doctor."

"Faither, you leave the doctor oot o' this. He'd never ever heard o' the Captain until I gied him that bottle for taking care o' Walter. And . . . he's got enough trouble, the puir laddie."

She fled upstairs to her bedroom, slamming the door.

Angus got up. "I'd best be on ma way to the afternoon service. Are ye coming wi me, laddie?"

Walter shook his head. He felt he had had enough of the undercurrents of Strathblane society for one day. And he was disturbed about Angus's remark about the Laird's xenophobia. It didn't bode well for his own future plans.

VI

Towards the end of his first week at Leddrie Green, Mrs Graham invited Walter to join her in a glass of wine before going home.

"Mr Paterson," she said, "I hope you know that I'm very happy with the way you're tutoring Bobby. It's good for him to have a man to discipline him. And I'm so relieved he won't fall behind with his studies. It won't be long now before he goes to the university in Glasgow."

"He seems very young for that?" queried Walter.

"He could go when he's twelve but a lot depends on his health as well as on how much he learns next year. But that isn't what I wanted to talk to you about!" She hesitated. "I am sure sir, that you left France in much too much of a hurry to pack any luggage."

"True," Walter smiled ruefully.

"That blue jacket is very smart," said Mrs Graham, "but soon it will be too thin for our Scottish weather. It is quite usual here for a family to supply their employees with clothing and I have several good suits of my husband's that I kept for Bobby. But he will not be tall enough to wear them for some time and I think that little would need to be done to make them fit you. Iain was about your build. Would you accept them?"

"I'd . . . I'd be honoured to wear them, *Madame* . . . it is most thoughtful of you. . . ."

"Then go upstairs to the back bedroom where I've laid them out. Pick whatever you think you need, and I'll have the Edenkiln tailor come up here to fit them on you. There are shirts also."

"Miss MacDougal could alter those."

"Then take them home with you today. Another glass of wine?"

"No, thank you." He got up and kissed her hand. "You're very good to me, Mrs Graham."

"Mr Paterson. I'm so delighted to have found you!"

There were three suits with smart waistcoats, a handsome overcoat, a beaver hat, some shirts and several pairs of strong walking shoes, which Walter found comfortable if roomy. All the clothes fitted him reasonably well, though the late Mr Graham must have enjoyed the pleasures of the dinner table for the waistlines were wide.

His elegant friend, the Vicomte de Sincerbeaux, might have criticised the cut of the clothing as out of style but

Walter was delighted with everything. He had hated wearing Angus MacDougal's rough smelly garments, much too big for him anyway, and to have something of his own again was satisfying. Jean sewed some tucks into the shirts and the village tailor did a credible job of altering the other garments.

Mrs Graham's whole mode of life made Walter feel at home. It was so similar to that of his family back in the country outside Paris. Leddrie Green was the kind of house his father would have had in Scotland, if the '45 had not condemned him to exile. The widow herself reminded him a little of his mother, though of course she was much younger, and less of a woman of the world. In her thirties, sonsy of face, a little untidy perhaps in her dress, she was passionately fond of her home and of her extensive garden. Even though she had a troop of estate workers available, she could often be found on her hands and knees around some special rock plant, grubbing happily in the soil and letting the winds and sunshine take their toll of her fair skin. She also loved to play chess, a game Walter was good at, and one that he had started to teach to Bobby when it was too wet to go out for walks.

"Do I have your permission to show him some grown up card games too, *Madame*?" Walter had asked.

"Why, of course." Her prominent blue eyes narrowed speculatively. "Do you play whist, Mr Paterson?"

"Indeed I do."

"Then perhaps you can make up a table with me with the two ladies at Balaggan. They love whist and I can seldom find a fourth partner. The doctor's fond of cards, but he's too busy and besides, with all these confinements he's unreliable."

"What about Miss Moncrieff?" asked Walter greatly daring. "Doesn't she play?"

"The dear child lives so far away. I don't like to invite her without her brother, and of course he has a great deal to do. I really can't ask her to walk over here and the Laird doesn't like to use the carriage for one person. Besides, she should be among young people, not a bunch of old hens like the Miss Rutherfords and me." She beamed maternally at him. "I hope you don't mind, Mr Paterson."

"No, not at all, *Madame*. I'm extremely fond of whist."

So, one afternoon as he was about to leave, Walter was requested to stay on and drink a cup of tea with two well-dressed spinsters, elderly ladies who began by patronising him slightly, but quickly succumbed to his charm and good looks. They also liked his way with cards when, after the refreshment, they sat down to a rubber of whist.

Walter enjoyed himself. But since it was a sunny afternoon, he feared that Primrose might be looking for him on the Boards Road. They had worked out a pleasant routine of foregathering there, when he was on his way back to Puddock Hole. Their time together was brief for the days were short now. But at least they could meet and he would walk with her to the Kirklands gate after kissing her behind the Gowk Stane.

On the day of the first whist party, the ladies did not play for long. He suspected the little gathering had been set up to find out how well he fitted into the group and, once that was established, the objective of the little social event was accomplished. Evidently, they accepted him as a gentleman for they offered to drive him part of the way home.

"We are going to supper at Ardunan House, Mr Paterson," cooed the elder sister, "and we could drop you off at the Minister's Brae, near the doctor's house, and that would save you a climb up the hill."

So he was not too late for his tryst. When there was no sign of Primrose close to Puddock Hole, he continued up the track towards Kirklands. Suddenly her little dog appeared wagging its tail and he caught sight of her up ahead. He whistled loudly and she turned, though with apparent reluctance.

"*Chérie*, I'm sorry. I couldn't help being so late." He made to kiss her but she drew back haughtily.

"It's chilly and I'm going home. What happened to you?"

"I was playing whist at Leddrie Green."

She pouted.

"You might have told me you had . . . another engagement."

"But I didn't know until this afternoon. And how could I send you a message? I'm sorry, Primrose. I came as fast as I could. Fortunately I got a ride in a nice carriage part of the way."

Curiosity got the better of her.

"Who were you playing cards with?"

"A couple of old biddies, friends of Mrs Graham's."

Her green eyes widened.

"Surely not Miss Rutherford and Miss Alice?"

"The very same."

"Walter, they are extremely well-connected! They're related to the Edmundstons who own Duntreath Castle. I'm surprised they'd associate with . . . with . . . "

"With a mere tutor? Ah, but I play a mean game of whist!" Again he tried to kiss her and again she drew back.

"But you had no business leaving me in the lurch."

"Primrose, as you just pointed out indelicately, I'm a dependent of Mrs Graham's. If she asks me to stay and entertain her guests, I must do so. Besides," he added, taking the chance, "it's your own fault. If you'd let me be open about our friendship, I could have told her and she would have let me leave. As it was, I had no excuse."

"You musn't ever say anything about me! She'd pass it on to Henry. He goes to see her all the time. He says it's to help her with her trees and all her planting. Don't you see him there?"

"He comes in the morning when Bobby and I are busy with *Julius Caesar* or the theorems of Pythagoras, shut up in the library. So we haven't met." Privately, he suspected that Mrs Graham mightn't have told the Laird that she had a young man coming to the house every weekday. He might not approve.

"Primrose, why doesn't your brother marry her? I think she's very lonely without a husband."

"He says he can't marry until I'm off his hands."

"Well, I'm ready to take you any time! I know I have no money but at least I now have employment and, if you would only be frank with your family about me, your sister in Edinburgh might be able to trace my uncle who lives there."

"Walter, you don't know my brother! He's so determined I'll make an advantageous match."

"Like the rich Mr Melville?"

"You know I wouldn't have *him*."

"How do I know? And is it up to you to decide? It wouldn't be in France. You're a woman and you're not even of age. And you see Melville all the time. I know you do and it worries me, Primrose. It would be much better. . . "

"No. Walter, you can't or won't understand! Henry is absolutely unreasonable about anything to do with France or the French! He thinks they're all dangerous revolutionaries over there."

"I agree with him. We would get along very well."

"But, don't you see? The way you came here and living at Puddock Hole, he wouldn't consider you. He'd think you were up to no good."

"But surely now that I'm working for Mrs Graham, I'm respectable at least. *Chérie,* I hate subterfuge. And I'd tell him I didn't expect to make you my wife until I was able to support you properly. But at least he'd know why I was here and my circumstances, and he'd understand. . ."

"But, he mightn't understand! Walter, if he didn't he might lock me up like that Highland lady on the island . . . Lord Lovat's wife, who was kept shut away from society for years!"

Mr Moncrieff, from the little Walter had seen of him, seemed the last person likely to do any such thing. "Why are you afraid of him, *Chérie*?"

"Oh, he . . ." She nibbled on her lip. "It's just that Henry wasn't brought up to be the head of the family. The responsibility for me and my future fell on him when our elder brother was killed in the American Wars. So he's overly protective of me. It's the same in the parish business. He's not sure of how to act, either as Laird or as the justice of the peace. At least he worries endlessly about what he should do. And he gets dreadfully upset if anything goes wrong. He blames himself."

"But he listens to people," Walter retorted, thinking of the closing of the school.

"He listens to far too many! He can't make up his mind sometimes about who is right and who is wrong. He lacks confidence in himself and when he gets all tied up in knots he gets terrible indigestion."

Walter burst out laughing.

"It isn't funny! It makes him hard to live with! And . . . and to plan meals, because he thinks I'm not feeding him the kind of food that soothes his stomach. But when the doctor tried to put him on a bland diet, he wouldn't have it because he was denied all his favourite drinks and dishes." She gave a housewifely sigh.

"Darling Primrose, the last thing I want to do is upset your brother's digestion, but as your fiancé, don't I have rights too?"

"Maybe . . . but . . . as a woman, I am entitled to my own life and to make my own decisions!"

"You said that like a . . . revolutionary."

"Because I expect to be treated with consideration?" She tossed her head and, calling to her dog, raced off towards Kirklands.

VII

Though annoyed and upset, Walter had accomplished more than he realised. Several days went by and Primrose did not reappear by the Gowk Stane. The weather was bad, so he did not really expect her. But he worried. Then at the end of that week, just as he and Bobby were getting ready to go out for their afternoon walk, the parlourmaid came and told them that Mrs Graham wanted to see them. A carriage had drawn up outside the house earlier and they had heard people alighting. The boy had been curious, so now he rushed ahead of his tutor and into his mother's drawing room which seemed full of visitors.

The widow, in her Sunday outdoor clothes, met them near the door.

"Bobby, go and put on your warm jacket and your outdoor shoes. We're going to see around Mr Melville's inkle factory. But first you must say 'how do you do' to Miss Moncrieff and the Laird. They are going with us. You too, Mr Paterson."

But Walter had frozen in his tracks. Primrose was sitting on the sofa, a small glass of claret on the side table. She wore a fashionable blue velvet dress and a big hat trimmed with ostrich plumes. A fur scarf with an appealing little muff to match lay close by.

Her brother was studying the garden through the

window. Bobby swept the company an exact replica of his tutor's elegant French bow, then kissed Primrose's hand as he had seen Walter do when greeting his mother.

"Well, well!" said Henry Moncrieff with the heartiness of someone unused to children. "You're becoming quite a courtier, young sir."

"Run along, child, and make yourself ready. Mr Melville will be here soon," instructed his mother. "Mr Paterson, please help yourself to some claret."

"Can't I have some too, Mama?"

"Certainly not!"

Walter took his charge by the arm and swung him around towards the door.

"*Robert, écoute ta Maman. Allons-y!* . . . " He was about to make his own escape with the child when Mrs Graham called him back.

"Let him put his own coat on, Mr Paterson. I want you to join us in a glass of wine." She poured some and handed it to him. "Henry, this is Mr Paterson, who is tutoring Bobby. Mr Moncrieff farms the Kirklands, Mr Paterson. All those beautiful fields you've so often remarked on."

The two men bowed, eyeing each other like wary cats in a disputable territory. Since Walter's right arm was still in a sling, there was no question of their shaking hands.

"And of course, I don't need to tell you *monsieur*, who this lovely young lady is," went on the widow, beaming. Walter turned scarlet. So did Primrose who, after one flash of her green eyes, lowered them and sat very still.

"I think perhaps you had better introduce us, *Madame*." His social training in Europe had been quite rigorous enough to cover most situations but never one quite like this.

"Why Mr Paterson, this is Miss Moncrieff, who sent her carriage to take you home from the doctor's that Sunday you were taken ill in church!"

"What carriage? What Sunday?" asked the Laird. He glared at his sister. "Nobody ever tells me anything."

To Walter's surprise and delight, she rose to the occasion. Meeting her brother's eyes, she said calmly,

"It was when you were in Moffat, Henry, taking the goat's milk cure for your dyspepsia."

Mrs Graham, aware that somehow she had created an embarrassing situation, put her hand on the Laird's arm.

"Now, don't be cross with her, Henry. It was one of the sweetest gestures imaginable. Mr Paterson was near to collapse . . . that awful old MacPhail was preaching interminably . . . and Dr Stewart took him out and up to his house. This thoughtful child, when the service was out, sent her carriage to take him back up the hill. You would have done the same I'm sure, had you been there."

Walter took a deep breath.

"I . . . I am happy at last to be able to express my gratitude in person Miss Moncrieff, although I trust your footman passed on my thanks." As he bowed to her, he contrived to catch her eye, and there was a teasing twinkle in his own.

"I perceive that you're not entirely recovered from whatever . . . er . . . ailed you," said Kirkland eyeing the sling.

"No sir, it may be some time yet. . . " He plunged on quickly. "I am greatly interested in your agriculture, Mr Moncrieff. I have been admiring and studying your fine fields and the way you are cultivating new crops. Your planting. . . "

Unluckily, this promising start was cut off by the arrival of Edward Melville. He was nattily turned out in dark blue broadcloth and looked both business-like and successful.

"Ah, dear Mr Melville!" fussed Mrs Graham. "We are all ready for you. Do you have time for a mouthful of claret before we leave on our excursion?"

"Thank you, thank you, Mrs Graham. There is no

hurry. I am at your disposal for the rest of the day." With a familiarity that riled Walter, he sat himself down beside Primrose on the sofa, then addressed her brother.

"Henry, when I was in Glasgow yesterday, I picked up the latest issue of *The Advertiser* and I brought it with me. There's bad news from France."

Walter involuntarily started to ask what it might be, then stopped himself. Mrs Graham drew him forward.

"Mr Melville, Mr Paterson."

Not bothering to rise, the businessman looked him over as if taking in the old-fashioned hand-me-down suit and remarked,

"Haven't I seen you before somewhere?"

"You have passed me on your horse on the Boards Road sir."

"Where do you live . . . up that way?"

"At Puddock Hole Farm."

Melville's eyebrows rose.

"Mr Paterson is tutoring Bobby," Mrs Graham quickly explained. "And doing it so well I'm not about to send him back to the parish school as long as that Hepburn is dominie. Henry, you've really got to do something about him! He's perpetually drunk I'm told and all the parents who really want their children to receive some education are complaining."

The Laird puffed out his chest.

"My dear Alison, I'm happy to be able to tell you that only last night the Kirk Session met and informed Mr Hepburn that he must seek other employment. Mr Campbell came to see me this morning and gave me a very full account of the meeting."

"And when will Mr Hepburn depart?"

"Soon, I am told. And then of course, we will need to find another schoolmaster."

"Perhaps you could use Mr Paterson?" said Mrs Graham excitedly.

"Oh no, *Madame!* I wouldn't be capable. . . " Walter protested.

"But you're a wonderful teacher! Why, you have Bobby speaking French as though it were his second nature."

"That's not hard, *Madame*. He's a most intelligent boy and children pick up languages so easily. I myself grew up bilingual without thinking about it and so did some of my French friends."

"You grew up in France?" asked Melville.

"Yes sir. I also speak and write German and have some Italian that I learned from my Grand Tour. But I couldn't cope with the scholastic requirements of a parish school, though I would be glad to help, if needed."

"Are you a stickit minister?" inquired Melville.

Walter, a little mystified, shook his head.

"He's much too handsome for the ministry!" Mrs Graham fluttered her eyelashes which, Walter noticed, disturbed the Laird who retaliated by changing the subject.

"Those saplings, Alison . . ." he gestured towards the window " . . . are they the ones I ordered for you from McAuslin's?"

"They are Henry, and I don't think they're growing very well."

"How long have they been in the ground?"

"Nearly six months and they're so puny."

"At least they're alive. But do you want me to take up their lack of progress with the firm the next time I'm in town?"

"Henry, I hate to be a nuisance to you. . . "

"You are never a nuisance Alison and I will be only too delighted."

"When you were in Glasgow, were you able to do

anything about the rye grass?"

"Yes. I lodged a complaint with the Farmer's Society. They'll buy us more seed."

"Really Henry. I don't know what this parish would be like without you! You set us all such an example!"

"Oh, come now Alison," protested the Laird clearly flattered. "It did very well before I got here." He turned to Melville. "What was the news from France?"

"As bad as could be. Those Revolutionaries are preparing for war. They've threatened to declare the River Scheldt open to trade. That would infringe our treaty with the Dutch, imperil our interests in Europe. We would have to go in."

"They can't do that!" exclaimed Moncrieff. "It would be a breach of international law."

"This present government in France, *monsieur*, has very little respect for the status quo," interposed Walter quietly.

Both men turned on him.

"You believe they would follow a policy unacceptable to Britain, Mr . . . er?" said Melville.

Walter shrugged, "Why not?"

"Even when Mr Pitt, as he assuredly will do, sends a note of protest?"

"Why should that upset them?"

"Mr Pitt," said Moncrieff belligerently, has always believed in peace."

"So whoever holds the power in Paris at this moment is justified in believing that he will not sanction a war," replied Walter.

"You mean those Frenchies would think so slightly of a British Prime Minister?"

Walter nodded.

"They have little respect for their own rulers and they put little stock in words."

"Words? You call the pronouncements of our House of Commons *words*? Are you a Radical?"

"Not to my knowledge, Mr Moncrieff. I know very little of British politics. But I am, perforce, a realist because of what I have seen happening in France. And I am very pessimistic."

Primrose stood up.

"Perhaps, as we have all finished our wine Alison, we should start on our excursion?"

"Yes my dear. Yes of course. Mr Paterson, would you like to come with us? I'm sure Mr Melville would not mind."

From the chilly glances he was getting, both from the factory owner and the Laird, Walter knew better.

"Thank you *madame*, but . . . I am to see the doctor this afternoon."

"Oh, then you're excused. Would you like to drive part of the way with us?"

"*Madame*, before I leave, I must arrange some homework for Robert. And now I must see where he is and . . . " He bowed quickly to the company and fled down the corridor, where for once he showed little patience with his pupil, ordering him crisply to hurry and join his mother. He then disappeared into the library, where he stayed until the sound of carriage wheels was well in the distance.

PART FOUR

RADICAL DEPARTURES

O God! I could be bounded in a nutshell,
And count myself a King of infinite space,
Were it not that I have bad dreams.

Hamlet
William Sheakespeare

I

WALTER HAD SPENT a disturbing hour at the doctor's earlier that week. Stewart had sent him into a trance and when he had come out of it, the last of the supports were gone from his wrist and he was told he could start using his hand freely. He had no intention of doing something which he considered so problematic and asked,

"Why did you make me unconscious? Removing the supports can't have hurt."

His friend, for once, was evasive. "Ach, it makes it easier for me. I cannae enjoy ma work wi ma patients squawking."

"I never squawk!" said Walter indignantly.

"Naw, ye dinnae. I apologise, Paterson. There's never been a peep oot o' ye, even when ye must hae been in the most ungodly pain."

"Then why the trance?"

"Look laddie. I get little enough opportunity to practise such esoteric procedures. No sense in giving Campbell and the Kirk Session grounds for adding witchcraft to their case against me. Forbye, ye're an ideal subject. The best I ever had." And with that, he changed the subject so deliberately he left his patient uneasy.

Now, as Walter made his way home from Leddrie Green, with no prospect of meeting Primrose that day, he decided to stop off at the doctor's house after all. When no-one answered his knock he wandered around to the back green where he had noticed that the housekeeper was taking an impressive washing of white shirts off the clothes line.

"Is the doctor expected in this afternoon, Mrs MacGregor?"

"He's there the now. But he's busy wi a patient. Do ye hae an appointment?"

"No . . . but do you think I could wait until he's free?"

She considered this, folding a garment neatly. "If ye wish." She gave him an appraising look. "Ye're a lot better these days, Mr Paterson."

"Yes thank you, I am."

"Ma auld master, Dr Tait, aye used to say to me, Mrs MacGregor, yon Dougie – that's what he ca'ed him – is gaun far. It was a pity he had to leave Edinburgh but the professor telt him it would be guid experience, here on his own."

She picked up the basket of clean clothes and started towards the house. "A change o' linen every morn! Dr Stewart's an easy man to work for but he makes a gey lot o' laundry. Wait in the ither room, Mr Paterson. I'll see when he'll be free."

As she pushed open the consulting room door, Walter heard a reedy male voice intoning monotonously.

> . . . *Now o'er the one half world,*
> *Nature seemed dead, and wicked dreams abuse*
> *The curtained sleep. Witchcraft celebrates*
> *Pale Hecate's offerings;*
> *And withered murder. . .*

"Breathe!" interrupted Stewart's voice. "Breathe! Afore ye choke yersel'." He came to the door. "How now, ye secret, black and midnight hag! What d'ye want?"

"Mr Paterson's here, doctor."

"Oh, tell him I won't be long. Go on, Jamie."

Though she shut it, the door creaked open wide enough for Walter to see an insignificant looking and miserably self-conscious young man in dark clothes, from whose lips the cadences of Macbeth flowed oddly.

> . . . *And withered murder,*

Alarmed by his sentinel, the wolf,
Whose howls his watch, thus with his stealthy
pace,
With Tarquin's ravishing strides, towards his
design
Moves like a ghost . . .

"Breath!"

"Ye telt me to take it on one breath last week."

"But breath laddie," Stewart explained, "is not a mere mechanical convenience, it's yin o' the greatest dramatic pointers ever invented. Don't they learn ye how to deliver yer sermons at Glasgow University? Now tak the speech again."

Jamie resumed.

. . . Is this a dagger which I see before me,
The handle towards my hand? . . .

When the ordeal was over, Stewart got up from his desk and drew his patient over to the window.

"Now then, let me look at yer throat." There was a brief spluttering gag. "Good! No redness at a'. Do ye feel ony soreness?"

"Naw," said Jamie in some surprise.

"Ye see? Do ye believe me now when I tell ye there's nothing organically wrong?"

"Aye, I suppose so. . . "

"Then go and sin no more. And practise those breathing exercises. Every day."

"Aye. . . "

"For next time, try Macbeth's speech in the first act –
If it were done when 'tis done, then 't were well 't were done quickly.
That takes a lot o' breath."

"Doctor! I've missed an awfa' lot o' classes. If I'm

better, could I no go back to Glasgow?"

"Oh, aye. Of course, Ye're discharged. And I wish ye luck, Jamie."

He slapped the young man on the back. "I could mak a guid speaker oot o' ye, if we had the time. Cultivate it. It's a useful attribute in your intended profession. And if ye've any more trouble, let me know. Dinnae be lettin' they Glasgow physicians mak' money off yer throat."

As they headed towards the door, Jamie asked,

"Are ye no gien me a bottle, doctor?"

"A bottle? For what?"

"For fear I lose ma' voice again."

"Listen, laddie, if ye use yer speaking equipment properly . . . yer lungs and yer diaphragm full o' air a' the time . . . ye' ll no hae any more hoarseness."

The puppy danced out from the kitchen as he shut the front door on his patient.

"Sadie, ye limb o' Satan, ye're no allowed in here during the working day! Come in, Paterson! It'll be guid to see somebody wi a bit o' sense. That was the minister's son," he explained. "He's gaun intae the church himsel'. Did you ever hear a worse murderin' o' Macbeth? I saw the great Sarah Siddons in it in Edinburgh. It was an actress in her troop who taught me to use my voice."

"Other things too, I hope."

"Oh, aye. . ." He did not seem surprised to see Walter. "Now pull your chair up and let me massage that wrist while we're talking."

"My employer thinks you're a better doctor than your predecessor," volunteered Walter by way of conversation.

"It's about time somebody in Strathblane found that out and if it's gossip we're passing on I've heard from Miss Flora Rutherford that you are an excellent whist player. It was wonderful the way you managed your cards with one hand, she said."

"Mrs Graham seems to want me to socialise."

"Dinnae be making the Laird jealous, Paterson. It could upset his digestion which I've just about got under control."

"She introduced me to the Laird this afternoon. He was there with his sister. . . "

"A very pretty little lady."

"Beautiful."

"She'd be more your type than mine. When I see her in church, I fancy she looks like yin o' they French fashion dolls. Am I hurting you?"

"No," snapped Walter who had gone tense.

"Is it a case of *chercher la femme?*

That was coming too close to the truth. Walter shook his head and to change the subject, indicated the doctor's right leg, resting unobtrusively on a small stool under the desk.

"What's wrong with your foot?"

"It's partially paralysed from a childhood sickness."

When he offered no further explanation, Walter asked,

"When can I leave here Stewart, and go off to Edinburgh?"

"Any time laddie, but ye'd be better off if ye waited until ye had the full use o' yer hand."

His patient sighed.

"Is there no way," the doctor asked, "I can make ye content to stay here and recover at a proper pace? I thought once ye'd found something to occupy yer time, ye'd be happy."

"Is nursemaiding a little boy any life for a grown man?"

"But ye've also been a disabled man."

"*Mille tonneres de diable!* Do you think I don't realise that?"

"Maybe," mused Stewart, "ye're better than ye think. Take a grip on that pen o' mine, dip it in the ink and write yer name."

Brought face to face with the fear that most haunted him Walter began to shake. "I . . . couldn't."

"Ye havenae tried."

"No. . ."

"Laddie, if ye've some old business in yer mind . . . forget it, or talk about it. What's upset ye?"

"It's nothing," Walter blurted out, "that you can do anything about."

He had found Primrose was right. It was going to be hard getting to know her brother.

"A' right. Though I'm wondering what really brought ye in here if ye believed that?" He leaned back in his chair, clasping his hands behind his head, his clear hazel eyes resting meditatively on his patient. The clock on the mantelpiece ticked noisily and through the window Walter could see Mrs MacGregor taking in the last of the laundry, for the shadows were lengthening at the end of the short winter day. They sat in silence for so long that Walter was moved to say, a shade uncomfortably,

"Don't try any of your Mesmer tricks on me."

"Mesmer? I was thinking of exercises for yer fingers. And since ye dinnae want to talk," he went on, "let me tell you about ma foot." He stretched out his hand again and resumed his gentle massaging of the wrist. It was as relaxing as his voice. "The doctor who attended me in that childhood illness was an elder in ma faither's kirk. He could do nothing, and after the paralysis hit, he telt me I'd be lame and walk wi a stick a' ma life. And nae mair playing games. But it was an act o' God . . . oh aye, and I should praise the Almighty for laying a cross on me. Ma faither agreed. That's why I was so angry wi the Strathblane Kirk Session when they used that same hoary auld argument to keep the school open and let the children infect each ither wi measles."

"But what could you do?" asked Walter his interest mildly aroused. "You were just a child."

"I was seven and as stubborn as I am the day. There was anither doctor in the village, an Episcopalian wi a practice among the huntin' fraternity. They swore by him for he patched them up when they fell off their nags. My parents of course, refused to call him in but one day, in desperation, I stumped over to his house on my wee crutches and I waited till he came back frae his rounds. And then, Paterson," he smiled reminiscently, "I was introduced to medical ethics. He refused to see me because I was the ither man's patient."

"Mon Dieu!"

"But he also couldnae have a child screamin' wi rage and despair on his doorstep, so in the end he let me into his surgery . . . a great big beautiful room full o' books and sunshine . . . and he examined me and made the same diagnosis as his colleague. My foot would aye be useless." His fingers quickened a little as he went on.

"But just as I was openin' ma mouth to start bawling again, he telt me that though the art o' medicine couldnae cure me, there was much that could be done if I could do it masel'. And with that, he brought out a skeleton . . . imagine how that intrigued a wee lad! . . . and gied me ma first anatomy lesson. He showed me which o' ma bones were affected and why I couldnae use them. And then he set before me a big book o' drawings of the muscles and tendons and explained those too.

"I was fascinated. And the doctor himsel' was so different from that auld windbag who, as I look back on it, talked about predestination because he wouldnae help me. This ither man took the time to consider ma case and he telt me that since I was still growing, I might train ma healthy muscles to take over some o' the work o' the useless ones.

"And he taught me a set o' exercises, warning me they'd be hard. They were gruelling. And whiles, it was terrible discouraging for I never did recover any movement in those withered muscles. But I built up ma strength in the rest o' them and soon enough I was running as fast as the ither boys.

"He also explained to my father that I had been very sensible and had sought a second medical opinion. And before they could say anything about paying him, he informed them that I was doing it masel'. I would reimburse him by weeding his flowerbeds, which I could do on my hands and knees. So there was nothing ma faither could do to stop me. I mind every minute o' that day, Paterson. It was the turning point o' ma life."

"I'll wager it's what made you a doctor."

"Aye, maybe so."

"So maybe your sickness *was* an act of God?"

"Tell it not in Strathblane. Tell it not even to Miss MacDougal. I'm an atheist. If I do believe in anything, it's that God . . . if there is such a Being . . . helps those who help themselves."

Walter laughed. "And you can trip up hill and down dale."

"Aye, but I'm pretty sore by the end o' the day. Once I get free o' debt, I'm buying a horse."

"I've often wondered," asked Walter, "why you left Edinburgh?"

"That's a lang story, laddie. Let's leave it for anither time. Forbye, ye didnae come here to talk about me, but about yersel'."

"What is there to talk about?" Walter's face fell. "You know it all."

"I know what happened to you, but not why."

"I suppose I was just caught up in history being made."

Stewart picked up his pipe, lit it with a taper from the fire and sat down again at his desk, smoking quietly.

"Tell me about Paris," he suggested.

"I haven't spent much time there in the last few years," Walter replied with a shrug.

"Why not? Because of the Revolution?"

"Partly. I was on the Grand Tour, to Vienna and Rome with my friend, Louis de Sincerbeaux. His family were my father's chief clients at his bank. He managed their estate after Monsieur le Marquis and his wife and the younger children packed up and joined the emigrés in Amsterdam. Life was becoming so difficult for aristocratic families. Louis the Vicomte was my age. We'd grown up together but I wasn't such a spendthrift as his other friends. My parents were canny Scots. So on the tour, I handled all the arrangements and my father impressed on me that I was responsible for keeping us out of trouble."

"And did you?"

"Of course not! We were in all kinds of scrapes." Walter chuckled, his usual reluctance to talk about the past in abeyance, perhaps because his hand felt unusually easy and the atmosphere in the room was relaxing.

"Girls?"

"Girls. And gambling. But mostly it was new ideas. We were studying after all. It was stimulating in those days to be able to investigate matters we'd never been allowed to talk about at home. The prospect of a new kind of world where people would be able to have more opportunity. . . "

"Aye, we had the same interests too in Edinburgh."

"It was all especially liberating to Louis. He'd been brought up to believe he'd have to spend his life at Court and make a *mariage de convenance*. He'd always been in love with my sister and she with him."

"And I suppose a banker's daughter wasn't good enough for a French aristocrat."

"It was more than that. It was a tradition for the Sincerbeaux to wed with certain old families. They thought the world of Clementina. And of me too. They felt we were a good influence on Louis. When we left Rome, we went to Amsterdam to visit them. And Louis made it plain that now he was of age and had inherited his own money . . . and it was plenty . . . he was going back to France to marry my sister. It seemed reasonably safe. The family had never been unpopular and you must remember, we didn't realise how the temper of the times had changed."

"Did your father no see what was happening"

"He did! He wrote to Amsterdam telling us to stay there but we had already left. And . . . once we reached my parents' house out in the country, nothing would stop us from going into Paris to see the changes there. Louis was determined to meet Madame Roland and when he did he was completely smitten by her and her ideas. But his going to her salon attracted attention. There were spies who were always looking for aristocrats to arrest." He stopped. It was all coming back again as it had in the nightmares.

"Aweel . . . what happened?" Stewart prompted quietly.

"We . . . we had been to visit Pierre, the medical student and were walking about the streets. We were shocked at the way people looked at us in our good clothes and . . . what our friends told us. . . " He stopped, swallowing.

"Go on. Talk about it, talk it out. That's what Dr Tait aye telt me."

"Some of the people we had known were in prison but they were all far richer and more important than the Sincerbeaux. And as for us Scottish Patersons, no one had anything against us. My father was on good terms with many men in power. He'd always been generous with loans.

"We were leaving for home that day. We had hired a carriage and it was already at the Sincerbeaux *palais*, their townhouse. Pierre said before we left we must see the guillotine in action. Have you ever seen an execution, Stewart?"

"Aye, hangings. I went to them a' when I was a student. That was where we got our cadavers for the anatomy classes."

"Did they give you nightmares?"

"Aye. Especially later . . . when it came close to home. Go on, keep talking laddie."

"We . . . we turned a corner into our street. And there were soldiers hammering on the door. We panicked. Remember we'd just come from the Place de la Concorde, seen the tumbrils. We turned and started to run. And they ordered us to stop. And when we didn't, they shot at us and . . . hit me. I fell. . . "

"And broke yer wrist."

"Yes. Louis hauled me up, dragged me away. We knew the neighbourhood better than the soldiers, so we lost them. Pierre tried to . . . to dig out the bullet. Louis was arguing, saying why shouldn't he let himself be arrested? He'd done nothing wrong. He favoured the Revolution. Those damned political theorists!"

"Aye, I know the type."

"But . . . I knew! They could claim all his family estates if they executed him! My father had told us that! And Pierre agreed. There was only one thing to do . . . get out of the city as fast as possible. Pierre was a smart Parisian, even if he wasn't much of a surgeon. He knew the safest places where the guards were most lax. He strapped up my wrist as best he could, got me into my coat and threw a cloak over me. Then he splashed some red wine over us. I changed identification papers with Louis just in case and we took off in the carriage.

All the time Louis was arguing and I was frantic with fear for him. It was such a nightmare. I was terrified I would collapse and he'd have second thoughts. We were almost at the gates when Pierre asked me if I could sign Louis' name if I had to. And . . . and . . . "

"And the very thought was too much wi all the pain ye were in."

Walter nodded trying to fight down his emotion.

"Did you actually have to write?" asked the doctor.

He shook his head. "They . . . were too busy to bother about three drunken students, let us through without any argument."

"So . . . ye didnae fail yer friend."

"No . . . but I could have ruined everything. I think about it all the time. The very thought. . . "

"What happened once ye were clear o' the city?"

"We drove hell for leather to my father's house. I . . . I don't remember much. I think I was delirious. Louis left for Amsterdam at once on the fleetest of horses. And my father loaded me into his own carriage and we headed for the coast."

"Where you were turned over to the old rum runner."

Walter was shaking uncontrollably and tears were running down his cheeks. He covered his face with both hands.

"Stop blaming yersel', Paterson. And stop punishing yersel' for something that never happened. Ye were, just as ye said, a part o' history. And it's past, so let it go. Let everything go."

Walter laid down his head on the desk. He had no idea how long it was before he was calm again and the sense of horror was gone, even the last of the pain. He dug a handkerchief from his pocket with his left hand and wiped his face.

"I beg your pardon Stewart, I'm sorry. . . "

"Laddie, I expected something like this." The doctor puffed calmly on his pipe. "And now for a wee bit o' encouragement." He pulled open a drawer in his desk, drew out a sheaf of loose papers covered in inky handwriting. "Tak a look at that."

Walter James Paterson – the name was scrawled across the page many times. At first it was barely legible but gradually it took the form of the writer's own characteristic signature. On the next page were some lines from Ronsard in French, which he had often whispered to Primrose.

> *Quand tu serais bien vielle,*
> *Au soir, a la chandelle. . .*

Walter stared at the papers not daring to believe the evidence of his own eyes. It seemed too good to be true. Stewart's voice brought him back to reality.

"Yin o' the most important things I learnt from ma auld friend in the Borders Paterson, was that no matter how good a physician might be, in the end the patient's own mind has a good deal to do wi any cure. I knew that wrist of yours was properly set. I did it by the book. But you would never use your fingers. You always tightened up when I suggested it. Frankly I hadnae the courage to insist in case there was some physical failure. So I put ye into a trance to find out. You were used to actin' on ma suggestions. The very first time ye were here, I made sure ye were really in a trance by tellin' ye to walk over to that table and lie down. And ye went like a lamb to the slaughter."

Nervous reaction setting in, Walter gave a little laugh. "An unfortunate way to put it," he said.

"Aye, but true in a way. Last Monday I telt ye to write something and ye did. Ye talked a lot too but all in French."

As Walter once again struggled with emotion, Stewart intoned,

> *Canst thou not minister to a mind diseased,*
> *Pluck from the memory a rooted sorrow,*
> *Raze out the written troubles of the brain,*
> *And with some sweet oblivious antidote*
> *Cleanse the stuffed bosom of that perilous stuff*
> *Which weighs upon the heart?*

He dipped the pen in ink, handed it across the desk.

"*Therein the patient must minister to himself.* Write something. Anything ye can. The evidence is before ye. And dinnae stop to think about it."

Walter gripped the quill with his stiff fingers and produced a slightly less shaky signature than the one above it.

"And the next line o' Macbeth laddie, is *Throw physic to the dogs; I'll none of it.*" He strode out of the room and returned with a bottle and two short glasses.

"For medicinal purposes Paterson, though this isnae the brandy I customarily use on patients." He poured two liberal drinks. "But we've both earned a dram. Now pick that up wi yer right hand like a proper gentleman. Dinnae spill a drop and drink to the bonnie lass o' Puddock Hole. D'ye realise Paterson, that without you I might never have got to know her?"

II

When Walter, a little drunk from the brandy, charged into the farmhouse and demonstrated how he could use his hand, Jean burst into tears and threw her arms round his neck.

"Lambie, I've been praying so hard ye'd be cured. I was scared ye would be crippled. But now ye'll be leaving us!"

"Not yet, unless you throw me out. I've got a lot of hard work to do, rebuilding the strength in my fingers. Stewart's given me some exercises. When I can write legibly, I'll send a long letter to my family in France and tell them where I am and how well you're looking after me."

"I'd miss ye terribly if ye went," said Jean. "It's so lonesome here wi just faither and me."

"*Eh bien*, I don't feel so badly about staying now that I'm contributing a little money to your household. And I can help with the farm work too."

"Naw, naw, laddie! That's no for a gentleman to do."

"But I want to learn all about farming. At least teach me to milk the cows. It would be good exercise for my fingers."

Mrs Graham the next morning was also delighted to see him in such perceptibly lighter spirits.

"But please Mr Paterson," she urged, "don't leave us now. Wait till spring at least."

"I certainly won't go until I have some word from my parents in France."

"That is wise. And meanwhile, would you like to make a trip to Glasgow on Friday? Before it grows any colder, Bobby needs some winter clothing. And perhaps you could take him to have his hair cut?"

"Willingly *Madame*. I could use a barber's services myself."

The next day, looking forward to his outing on Friday, Walter left Leddrie Green early, for Dr Stewart had been summoned to check over his young patient and make sure he did not require the services of a dentist or other specialist in the city. The weather was cold but pleasantly sunny and Walter hoped Primrose would be walking her dog somewhere near Kirklands. He couldn't wait to tell her his good news and also find out about her visit to Melville's inkle factory.

Although he wasn't sure if she would come at all – she had been so distant to him – he found her by the Gowk Stane and he threw both arms around her. Then he took her right hand in his and squeezed it hard.

"Walter! You're fully recovered?"

"Almost."

Like Jean, she began to cry.

"Stop please, Primrose. Your tears unnerve me. Look, now that I'm a whole man, I want to give you this."

He drew off his signet ring. "It's old-fashioned but my father gave it to me when I was twenty-one. It has the Paterson crest on it. I'd like it to be our troth but since we can't pledge that openly, call it a Christmas present."

She showed more signs of tears but brushed them off.

"I'll call it our troth, Walter."

"*Chérie!*"

"But . . . I can't wear it! Henry would be curious. Will it be all right if I put it on a chain round my neck?"

"It's a little big for you anyway."

She tried it and it was, although she managed to keep it on her middle finger.

"But lots of girls wear rings on chains, Walter. When . . . when their betrothal is private, like ours."

"What did your brother think of me?"

"Oh dear!" she laughed ruefully. "My lovely plans to have you acquainted went sadly wrong! He was so upset and annoyed about my sending you home in the carriage. Not because I had sent it, but because I had never told him."

"You see. You would be far better off being frank with him."

"It's too late now. . . And then you shouldn't have talked to him about France. Now he suspects you are a Radical."

"I told him I wasn't."

"And Edward didn't like your having claret with us. I think he's jealous of you . . . you're much handsomer than he is."

"Thank you," said Walter with a mocking bow.

"But . . . Henry's a little worried too about your being so 'far ben' with Alison."

"That's ridiculous. I like her, but only as an employer . . . so I'm no further ahead? Do you think, now that I've been introduced, that I could ask him to show me over some of his fields? I really want to find out why his land is so much more productive than MacDougal's. And I want to learn about agriculture. He might be able to lend me some books."

"Why don't you let Alison borrow some of them for you, and pass them on?"

"A good suggestion. She'd do it for me, I'm sure."

"Yes, she likes you a lot, too," said Primrose dubiously.

He kissed her. "Now don't *you* start being jealous! The doctor's already warned me not to upset your brother's stomach, worrying about Mrs Graham and me! Why doesn't he marry her? He can afford it. She's a sweet lady Primrose, but she's much too old for me. Besides, you're the one I love, the only one. I want to marry you. Can we now consider ourselves engaged?"

"Oh yes! If you're sure. But . . . I'm so afraid Walter, that when you go away to Edinburgh and find your family and resume your old life, you'll forget all about me because I'm a country girl."

"I'm a country boy myself. I think I always was. I prefer fields and mountains to streets . . . and fresh air."

She shivered. "You'll get plenty of that here. And it's becoming far too cold to meet outdoors. There's an empty cottage below our kitchen garden. It's full of old furniture that we discarded when Henry decided to rebuild the house and had it decorated by Mr Adam."

"And pray, how is the *chatelaine* of the Kirklands going to explain this . . . love nest?"

"I have to sort through a lot of boxes and decide what we should throw away. I would have done it in the spring, but I had the flu, and then I was in Edinburgh most of the summer, with my sister Catherine. Walter, I can light a little fire in the grate and we can be very comfortable. I've never liked meeting out here on the Boards Road. There are too many prying eyes."

"There's never a soul in sight!"

"Village people don't need to be in sight to know what's going on."

III

The day before the Glasgow excursion – and after the doctor's visit to Leddrie Green – Mrs Graham asked Walter if he ever played the piano.

"No. I never learned, *Madame*. My sister did but the only musical instrument I ever studied was guitar. I bought a beautiful one in Rome, but of course. . . " He shrugged regretfully.

"I have a guitar up in the attic, Mr Paterson. I used to play it before I owned the pianoforte. I'll find it for you. It would be good for your fingers."

"And more interesting than the doctor's exercises. I could teach it to Bobby."

"An excellent thought!"

So they took the guitar with them to Glasgow to have it restrung. Walter had hoped that on the trip he would see something of the road into the city but Bobby, a gregarious and lonely child, was so delighted to have his tutor's company without the interruption of lessons that he chattered constantly and asked questions throughout the long twelve mile journey. Mrs Graham too seemed anxious to hear about Walter's European tour and now that he was overcoming his reluctance to talk about the past, he enjoyed himself, giving them amusing and considerably expurgated accounts of the scrapes he and Louis had got into in Rome and Vienna.

"Did you hear a lot of music there, Mr Paterson?" asked the widow.

"Yes. Concerts, oratorios . . . but we liked the operas best."

"And who is the foremost composer?"

"Herr Mozart. But he died a couple of years ago. His operas are full of ideas as well as melodies. Once the guitar is repaired, I'll sing you some of his arias."

"And we'll see if we can find any scores of his operas. Would you like to show Mr Paterson the University, Bobby?"

"No!" Her son made a face. "I want to buy things."

"But all the stores are close by each other. Do you need to do any shopping for yourself, Mr Paterson?"

"No thank you, *Madame*. You have already outfitted me well. But when I have changed some French money, I'd like to buy some trinket for Miss MacDougal. She loves pretty things but she's so frugal she won't even buy ribbons from the packmen who come to the farm door selling them." He grinned. "I bought some for her though, with the money that you gave me."

"I'm so glad! She's an attractive young woman and has a lot of style, I've noticed. I'd like to meet her sometime. Perhaps after church one Sunday?"

They were now travelling along cobbled streets between tall buildings in rows upon rows, and there seemed to be a great number of people about.

"There's the University, Mr Paterson. Isn't it handsome! And here we are at the Trongate. Let us down here, Jamie!" she called to the coachman, "and be here outside the Tontine Cafe at four to pick us up. We'll go to the bank first, Mr Paterson."

He was surprised at how much Scottish money he got for his French coins.

"You're rich, *monsieur*!" exclaimed Bobby.

"Rich enough for a little gift, anyway."

"Why don't you take us for some hot chocolate at the cafe before we leave for home?" suggested Mrs Graham.

They dropped the guitar off at a music shop and were promised it would be in good repair by the afternoon. They also browsed in a bookstore where Walter picked out some educational material for his pupil and invested in an English-French dictionary, to help with translation work of a book by Mesmer he'd promised to do for Douglas Stewart.

Then they headed for the clothing emporiums, where Bobby was fitted out with woollen vests and underwear and measured for a little suit by the tailor, who promised it would be sent out on the public coach and left at the Kirkhouse Inn in Strathblane.

"Mr Paterson, you must have some warm gloves."

"I'll buy them myself *Madame*, I insist." It was a small sign of his new feeling of independence.

Mrs Graham then disappeared into a mantua maker's leaving her son and his tutor at the barber's. There, with relief, Walter had himself shorn of the long hair that had grown since he left France, and which he had been tying back in a old-fashioned way. While Bobby's hair was being trimmed, Walter thumbed through some recent copies of *The Glasgow Advertiser* and caught up on the foreign news.

It was bad. There was a lengthy account of the trial of Louis XVI, and news that two French frigates had sailed up the River Scheldt in flagrant violation of international law. Scottish xenophobia and conservatism were rising, he noted with foreboding. In particular, there was much complaint about the paper money the French government was printing up. The Attorney General had just brought in a bill to Parliament prohibiting its circulation in Britain. How lucky Walter reflected, that his father had given him coins rather than *assignats*. Perhaps as a banker he had foreseen how these would lose their value.

There were also rumblings about the pernicious influence of Thomas Paine and his ideas which, according to the *Advertiser*, were causing "unrest and most serious alarm among the country gentlemen in Scotland." France was held up as an example of the dire results of "giving more power to the people". Walter was inclined to agree, though he felt that to describe the planting of a Tree of Liberty in Dundee as "an insurrection" was editorial zeal.

Amidst the gloomy news, Walter's eye was caught by an advertisement for ladies' furs, newly arrived from America and on sale in a shop in the Trongate. This was close by and he and Bobby found it without any trouble. There, an eager merchant brought out for their inspection a number of muffs and tippets, many in strange pelts that he had never seen in Paris, such as lynx and racoon.

While Walter was trying to decide which fur would look best on Jean, Bobby spotted his mother passing the shop and called her in to join them.

"*Madame*, I need a woman's advice. Do I buy Miss MacDougal a muff or some kind of wrap? And in which type of skin?"

Mrs Graham examined the workmanship knowledgeably, then modelled the tippets for him. In the end they settled for a red fox muff, roomy enough to hold a purse or warmed stones to keep the cold away from the hands.

"Miss MacDougal can wear that with anything," the widow pointed out. "The capes might not fit. Besides," she added as they left the shop, "they were ridiculously overpriced. That was the only reasonable item in the place."

"Now let me treat you to a good meal before we leave for home," suggested Walter.

"Goody," cried the boy. "I'm hungry! Can I really have hot chocolate, Mr Paterson?"

"If you promise not to get sick in the carriage."

"I won't. I'm healthy! The doctor said so. I don't even have any bad teeth."

"And long may that last," sighed his mother. "What do you think of our city, Mr Paterson? Is it very provincial compared with Paris?"

"No indeed, *Madame*. I'm pleasantly surprised. It is so busy and prosperous and the people are most pleasant, though I confess I find them hard to understand."

"That's the Glasgow accent!" said Bobby. "I used to speak that way when we lived here."

"No you didn't, dear. But the Strathblane villagers do have less of a burr. It's because they're closer to the Highlands. where even the most humble speak good English, if they have any at all besides the Gaelic."

"Do you know where the coach for Edinburgh leaves, *Madame*? I might as well find out when I'm here."

"In the square, by the inn. It goes every day in the morning. And you needn't worry now about being able to afford it."

It was growing dark as they left Glasgow and Bobby was so curious about the guitar that Walter spent the return trip explaining the fingering to him. Though it kept the boy amused, it again hindered observation of the route. Walter's chief impression was that they passed through several small townships, then climbed a steep hill that brought them up to a broad plateau studded with lochs. A breathtaking view of the Campsie Hills was outlined in the strong moonlight, with the distant Ben Lomond barely perceptible.

"There's going to be a heavy frost," Mrs Graham remarked. "And someone in Glasgow told me this winter is likely to be a record one for bad weather."

"Yes, I read something about that in the paper."

"Well, we must expect it. This is December after all."

The cold hit Walter when he climbed down from Mrs Graham's comfortable little carriage at the end of the road leading to Puddock Hole. Going past the doctor's house, he saw a light and, on an impulse, knocked on the door. Mrs MacGregor, enveloped in a heavy knitted shawl, opened it.

"The doctor's out at a confinement in Edenkiln, Mr Paterson. He'll no be home for a while, I'm feared."

"Don't worry, Mrs MacGregor. I just stopped by to tell him I'd got myself a good French dictionary. Will you give him that message?"

"Aye." She shook her head. "Maybe it'll encourage him, the poor young man. He's been workin' terrible hard. I only hope he doesnae tak sick himsel'."

IV

On December 31st – Hogmanay – the MacDougals had a party. There was a hint of snow in the air, but it held off and nearly twenty guests turned up at Puddock Hole late in the evening. They were mostly farming people from farther up the valley and Walter had met some of them briefly, after church. The prettiest of the girls was Primrose's maid, Mamie who was wearing a pale green silk dress, a hand-me-down he suspected, from her mistress. She came with Jock MacLean who, because he aspired to be a medical man, turned out in a dark suit copied by the local tailor, line for line, from Dr Stewart's Sunday outfit. The young man also spoke with great precision and in the accents of the gentry – at least, when he remembered – but for all that, he was full of fun and an excellent fiddler. Walter had brought the guitar back with him and between them they played for the dancing, which took place in the parlour, cleared for all its furniture for the evening and offering an unexpected amount of floorspace.

Walter had always loved to dance. His mother had taught him the basic Scottish steps as a child. With his parents and his sister, he had often performed foursome reels and strathspeys. So with a little preparatory coaching from Bobby and with Jean for a partner, he had no difficulty joining in the fun. Soon he was having such a good time he almost forgot that Primrose was undoubtedly the belle of Melville's ball.

"Oh my, she looked lovely!" Mamie had exclaimed upon her arrival. "A new gown her sister sent from Edinburgh . . . the sheerest of blue silk, and trimmed with silver! And a sable cape frae her brither. Ye should hae seen her, Mr Paterson. She was as elegant as any French lady in Paris!"

"I'm sure she was," he agreed, jealousy gnawing at him.

"But she'll no' eat any better than we're daein' here," said a pretty young farmer's wife, extremely pregnant. She edged towards the kitchen table where Jean had set out the sumptuous buffet.

"Help yersel'. Ye're eatin' fer two." Jean glanced towards the front door as she had already done several times that evening, then inquired of Jock if the doctor was busy with a confinement.

Mrs Semple ensconced in the armchair by the kitchen fire answered knowledgeably, "There's nae lassie likely tae be brought tae bed this week, unless it's yersel' Effie, wi' all that dancin'."

"Then, whatever's keeping him? Everyone else is here. Are ye sure ye invited him, Walter?"

"You invited him yourself. I heard you."

"There's aye a lot o' accidents on Hogmanay," Jock pointed out, "And the night's young yet."

By midnight the party was going fast and furious and Walter was demonstrating some French ballroom dancing with Mamie when Angus shouted from the kitchen that the clock showed 1793 was upon them.

Everyone applauded. There was much toasting in whisky and kissing and, in the midst of the happy babble, came a loud knock on the front door. "Someone's first footin' ye Jean!" said Mrs Semple.

"Let's hope it's a tall dark man," someone answered. It was.

"Combustibles and comestibles!" announced Douglas Stewart, striding over the threshold, his arms full of bundles. "Tobacco for Mr MacDougal and oranges for my hostess."

"Watch out, doctor! Ye're smack under the mistletoe!" warned Jock.

"Am I?" His head was grazing it. "In that case . . . " He handed the bigger package to Jean then put both arms round her and kissed her without apology. Shedding his topcoat and beaver hat, he moved into the kitchen to greet Angus and Mrs Semple.

He was wearing such a smart evening suit he put the rest of the company to sartorial shame.

"*Espèce de sans-culotte!*" Walter jeered, indicating the modish long trousers.

"I suspect that's an insult, Citizen Paterson. And what about your Revolutionary haircut?"

"We are both very much *à la mode, mon brave!* A happy New Year to you!"

"And to you too, laddie. Miss MacDougal . . . Jean, I apologise for bein' so late. I had to go home and change. There was a big stramash at the Kirkhouse Inn and much blood flowed. Whaur were ye Jock, when I needed ye?"

"Hae ye met everyone, doctor?" Jean inquired.

"And how would I ever meet a healthy bunch like yon? Present me if you please. Ah, but here's one lady I know." He kissed the pregnant girl's hand which made her giggle.

"A dram first," suggested Angus.

"Thank you. A guid New Year tae you, Mr MacDougal." Jean took him by the arm and introduced him to the rest of the company who were, Walter noticed, a little overawed by his elegance, though they warmed to his friendliness.

"What happened at the Kirkhouse Inn?" asked Mrs Semple, who thrived on gossip.

"I didnae arrive until it was over but seemingly Benjy Hepburn, the dominie, was the one who started it. Drunk, as usual."

"Is the schoolmaster no gone?" asked one of the farmers. "I thought the Kirk Session gied him the push last month, after we complained."

"Ye're no' quit o' him yet! Nor like to be. He was flourishin' a paper signed by Mr Campbell, sayin' he was a guid, well-qualified instructor and a man ony school would be lucky to employ!"

There was a gasp of astonishment.

"And how did he ever get a testimonial like that?" someone asked.

"If we're to believe what he said in his cups the night . . . before half the men in the village . . . it was his price for offering his resignation."

"Mercy on us!" exclaimed one woman. "Does that mean he's no goin' to leave after all?"

"Why should he? Wi such a glowin' character and the

Session Clerk's name at the bottom of it, why should Strathblane lose his valuable services?"

"Mr MacDougal!" exclaimed the pregnant girl's husband, "Ye're yin o' the heritors. D'ye ken onythin o' this?"

Angus looked embarrassed.

"I kent Hepburn had asked for a recommendation. He said he'd never find employment withoot yin. So I suppose they wrote it."

"And now the chickens are comin' home tae roost!"

Douglas downed his drink. "Man! I wish Campbell had been in the pub the night! Benjy was in full flight, sayin' he didnae gie a damn for him, or for the minister or . . . if ye'll excuse me ladies . . . 'the hail bluidy lot o' them!' That was when yin o' the ither drunks – he has five children at the school – took a poke at the dominie and the fur started flyin'. Or at least," he added quickly, "that's how I heard it. I was just leaving home tae come to this party when they summoned me to bind up the wounds. By that time, they were a' passin' oot, or cryin' for help and I had to cart Hepburn upstairs to his bed on ma back, for no one else would do it, an' he was that fu' he couldnae walk,"

"My, my! This is goin' to set the tongues waggin'!" chuckled Mrs Semple.

"And Mr Campbell's goin' tae be in trouble when the Laird hears o' it," added one of the farmers.

"Serve the auld gauger right for sendin' the price o' whisky sae high we maun break the law tae get it," growled another, filling his glass from the nearest bottle.

Jock ran a satirical trill on his fiddle and Douglas, who, Walter suspected, had already had a few drinks, went into a lopsided little hornpipe and started to sing.

The de'il's awa, the de'il's awa,

The de'il's awa, wi' the Exciseman,
He's danced awa, he's danced awa,
He's danced awa wi the Excisemen.

There was a round of applause, though Angus MacDougal looked troubled. Jean patted his shoulder. "Cheer up, faither. Campbell's trouble wi' the Laird will be naithin' to do wi' us! Anither song, doctor?"

"Here's what they were singin' down at the pub. . .

For a' that and a' that,
It's comin' yet for a' that,
That man tae man, the world o'er,
Shall brithers be for a' that.

Though this went down well with the younger guests, the elders shook their heads and Angus muttered that "Yon was downright subversive."

"Gie us an Edinburgh love song," suggested Jock and Douglas, clearing his throat, sang out,

There's nought but care on every han',
In every hour that passes, O,
What signifies the life o' man,
An 'twere na for the lasses, O.

"Now, everyone, join me in the chorus.

Green grow the rashes, O,
Green grow the rashes, O,
The sweetest hours that e'er I spent,
Are spent among the lasses, O!

"Ye'll be leadin' the singin in the Kirk when the dominie

goes," commented Mrs Semple. Walter followed Stewart with some Jacobite songs, reassured by Angus that the Pretender was long dead. Everyone joined in.

"It's gettin unco late," someone said eventually, "and we maun be on our way."

"We'd best be leavin' too, Jock," said Mamie. "I maun be back at Kirklands in time to help Miss Primrose after the ball."

As the party began breaking up, the couple from Milndavie farm offered to escort Mrs Semple to her cottage. But the old lady, starting a fresh drink, shook her head, "Naw naw, the doctor can see me hame." But Stewart it seemed, had other plans and threw Walter a pleading look.

"*Chere Madame Semple*, when you are ready to leave, please give me the pleasure of accompanying you down the hill."

"Aye aye, Walter lambie, and ye can first foot me too."

They ambled down the Boards Road with the rest of the company and at her cottage she invited Walter to join her in a nightcap. He felt he already had far too much to drink and the elderberry cordial she poured him was so strong that he wished she had given him that instead of one of her herb potions when he had been in pain. He took a few sips, then made his escape from her garrulous reminiscences. The morning light was starting to show above the hills, and at Puddock Hole the candles were out in the parlour though all the company had not departed. There was a soft murmur of voices male and female, and Walter observed the shape of two bodies amorously entwined on the floor in front of the fire. In the kitchen, Angus was slumped in his chair, snoring loudly.

Walter roused him gently. "I'm back, Mr MacDougal. You can go to bed now."

The farmer snorted and opened his bleary eyes. "Hae

they a' gone? Yon young doctor. . . ?"

"I don't see his coat in the hall." It was far too dark for that.

"Then I suppose I maun go to my bed. . . " The old man stretched and staggered a little. On the pretext of helping, Walter eased him up quickly through the vestibule and up the stair.

As Walter came back down again, he pulled the parlour door shut. Then he threw himself fully clothed, onto his bed acutely envious of his friend. Fortunately, he had had so much to drink that he fell asleep quickly. By the time he wakened, thirsty and hungover, the morning was half gone. Angus was out in the fields and Jean was half-heartedly tidying up the house, humming to herself and with a new dreamy look in her eyes.

PART FIVE

OLD WAYS; NEW WORLDS

And now good-morrow to our waking souls,
Which watch not one another out of fear;
For love, all love of other sights controls,
And makes one little room an everywhere.

The Good-Morrow
John Donne

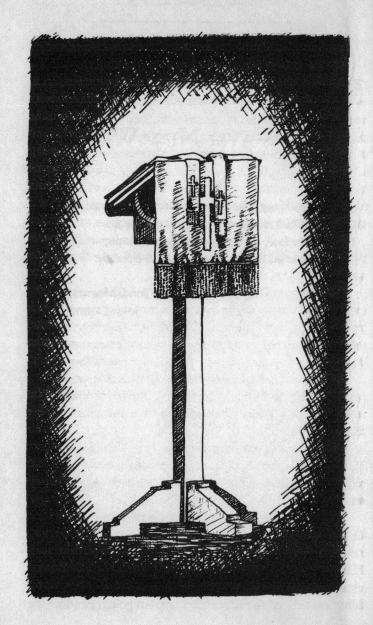

I

IN JANUARY THE WEATHER took a turn for the worse, and Walter suffered acutely from the cold which swirled across the bare floor of the farm kitchen and through the cracks in the walls. Even piling more plaids on the bed did not keep him warm and he thought with longing of his family's comfortable home in France. Jean came down with a chill and was so unwell that she had to let him help with some of the chores, chopping wood, feeding the hens, and even milking. She flatly refused to have the doctor.

"There's nae a thing he can do," she reiterated between sneezes, "And I dinnae want him to see me like this, wi ma nose a' swollen and red."

But when Walter succumbed to the infection and took to bed wheezing, she insisted on summoning Stewart who prescribed mustard plasters. "Keep him in till he's completely well," he ordered. "I've had several cases of pneumonia. And that's a disease that can take strapping young fellows."

Jean nodded sympathetically. There had been a farmer up the valley who had succumbed, leaving a widow and several little children. The Laird had bought up his land to help the family.

Fortunately Walter recovered quickly but he and Primrose abandoned their late afternoon trysts at the cottage because he was afraid she would catch something and she in turn, wanted him to stay out of the cold.

When he was able to return to Leddrie Green, he found himself running a small school for some of the children from nearby estates were no longer going to the one in the village. The deplorable Hepburn had departed perforce, after his outburst at Hogmanay and an old retired dominie was doing his best to keep the educational system going, pending the appointment of a new teacher.

Walter liked having more pupils. It reminded him of how he and his sister had shared their lessons with the young Sincerbeaux. He trained his pupils to talk to one another in French and Italian, flattering himself that though they might not be comprehensively grounded in Caesar's Gallic War and the theories of Euclid, at least they would be able to communicate should they ever travel on the Continent.

One afternoon, on his return from Leddrie Green, Walter found a strange horse tethered in the garden. The kitchen was full of pipe smoke, for Captain Abernethy was sitting by the fire with Angus and the now convalescent Jean.

"I've news for ye, laddie! I seen yer faither in France and he sent ye something." He handed over a heavy purse full of gold coins. Walter promptly passed it to Jean who shook her head.

"Naw, it's yours."

"I'm putting it in the drawer and we'll argue about it later. Captain, how are my parents? What is happening over there?"

"It's bad . . . awfa' bad. Worse a' the time. They've beheaded the King and there's a new government every week. Yer family is gettin' set to move. They were busy packing up the day I was out to their house. I'd gone to yer faither's bank in Paris. It was closed but the concierge telt me whaur he lived and I stopped off there on ma way tae the coast."

"That was very kind of you, Captain."

"Ach, I was feared he never received yon letter ye gied me for him. And he hadnae. They fed me a guid dinner," Abernethy went on. "Yer mither was unco glad tae hear ye were alive and well."

"Did you see my sister too?"

"Naw. She'd gone to England they said."

"With . . . her fiancé, the Vicomte de Sincerbeaux?" Walter asked eagerly.

"I dinnae ken. Maybe she went to look for you. He's a shrewd man, yer faither. I'm thinkin' he was letting' her tak a load o' baubles, jewellery and the like for a young lady goin' abroad would be less suspicious. He and yer mither were planning on travellin' light and yer mither was sair vexed aboot leaving all her beautiful furniture."

"They would be. They're going to Edinburgh?"

"Aye. But he wasnae sure how long it would tak them, findin' a ship. So he asked me to tell ye to stay here till ye hear from them. I assured him that onythin' addressed tae Puddock Hole Farm, Strathblane would surely find ye."

"Captain, this is wonderful news. Isn't it Jean?"

"Aye it is indeed, lambie."

"Do you think Captain, that they will be able to take their money with them?"

"A guid deal o' it, if they're canny, and I'm thinkin' yer faither is."

"Indeed yes. You don't know anything about the Sincerbeaux?"

Abernethy shook his head.

"Naw. But ony yin that's frae an auld family is daein' their best to leave France now, the guillotine's that busy. And wi the war, too. The French maun gie the people some victories if they want to stay in power. It's a bad, bad business." He shook his grizzled head. "And that's why, Mr MacDougal, I've nay a thing for ye this trip. But I've found anither supplier to tak the place o' the man who was executed. And if his prices are acceptable, I'll ship ye some wine and brandy next month. The seas are rough but there's aye a period in February when there's a break in the winter. Ye think ye can sell that tea, Jean? It's near double what it used to cost."

"I can aye sell tea here."

"Guid. I'll let ye ken when I dock. I'll hae a lot o' deliveries to mak so I'll send a messenger ahead o' me and ye can get the barn cleared.

"Ca' canny, man," Angus warned. "We're no wantin' strangers around for the Exciseman to notice. He used to look the other way and of course we gied him somethin'. But now I'm no sure we can trust him."

"What happened? Mr Campbell's aye been yin o' the most compliant in the West."

"Aye. But he's been in trouble wi the Laird. He's the Session Clerk ye ken and there was a misunderstandin' aboot the dominie leavin'. Campbell wrote a letter o' recommendation for him that fair angered Moncrieff. He's turned agin Campbell and if he were to find out how he'd condoned smugglin' French liquor these many years, he'd tak it up wi' the authorities and Campbell could lose his livelihood. The Laird's unco agin the French. He doesnae mind people savin' a few pence on revenue buying whisky frae stills, but onythin' that comes frae overseas is different. And anither thing . . . " Angus paused and looked at his daughter. "This parish is changin'. There's new people comin' intae it and they're no daein' Campbell's biddin'. He's been losin' some o' his power so he's worried. He maun curry favour wi' the Laird. I'm feared he'll be daein' it by tellin' him when yer next delivery arrives."

"I thought you and Campbell were guid friends."

"Well, we tolerated each ither. But," again his eyes were on Jean, "now he thinks I've gone ower to the enemy camp and he'll no speak tae me."

She bristled. "Because o' the doctor, I suppose." Walter nudged her to keep quiet.

"Then I'd best be careful," Abernethy was saying. "I'll come by wi a small consignment first, maybe just the tea . . .

to make sure the coast is clear."

"Would that be wise?" Jean asked. "Would it no tip Campbell off? People ken whenever a cart like yours go by at night. And they talk. Ye're well kent in these parts Captain, don't forget that."

"I'll tak ma chances, lassie. I've taken plenty afore. And I'm no feared ony yin'll tell Campbell."

But both Jean and her father looked troubled.

II

Walter went to church every Sunday now like a proper resident of the parish, and after sitting through another visit from Mr MacPhail, he knew he was fully recovered. Mr Gardner's sermons were unconscionably long and dreary and members of the congregation coped with this in a number of ways. Dr Stewart made no attempt to disguise the fact that he sat in the back pew so that he could nap. He also used the time, he confided to his friend, to review his cases. Walter studied the villagers, many of whom he now knew by name. Also, from listening to Jean and her aunt, he had learned a good deal about a lot of people, possibly more than they knew themselves.

Country life, he had quickly discovered, wasn't any bucolic paradise. Marriages were unhappy and spouses unfaithful as frequently as in sophisticated circles.

The power structure of the parish also fascinated him. At the centre was the Laird who, as the biggest landowner and a justice of the peace, was the only person able to overrule the all-powerful Kirk Session. It in turn, was controlled by the Exciseman.

"Why are people so afraid of Mr Campbell?" Walter had once asked the doctor.

"He's a bully," Stewart said. " And like a' bullies ye have to keep remindin' him that ye're no' scared o' him. Once he finds a person's weakness, he exploits it for a' he's worth. And he's no above a bit o' blackmail. I hope he never gets ony hint o' why I left Edinburgh."

"Well, why did you?"

"Ye'll find out soon enough when ye go to the city and meet ma auld colleagues there."

The week after Captain Abernethy's meeting Walter, looking around him before the service started, noticed that the mousy little Mrs Wishart was not present. He hoped nothing had happened to her, for he had perforce, overheard plenty about her problems with past pregnancies from Mrs Semple.

"The doctor's goin' to hae his hands full wi her," the midwife had told Jean. "He gied me a real cross-questionin' on what happened wi all her miscarriages . . . two o' them . . . and a still birth, the puir soul. He's fair determined she's goin' to hae a healthy baby this time."

"D'ye think she will, Auntie?"

"Ye can never tell. He's keepin' a gey close eye on her, goes up there every week to examine her."

Jean had sniffed, "I thought it was her sister Aggie that was the attraction. . . "

But that Sunday it wasn't Mrs Wishart's condition that intrigued the MacDougals.

"See yon creepie stool!" whispered Jean to Walter, as they settled themselves beside Mrs Semple.

"What's that?"

"For some lassie caught in the act. D'ye ken who it might be, Auntie?"

The midwife shook her head. "Maybe anither o' Melville's workers."

Since Dominie Hepburn's abrupt departure, a skinny

young man with an off-key rasping voice had been acting as precentor. He was about to lead off for the first hymn when Mr Gardner from the pulpit, motioned the congregation to remain seated.

Out of the vestry, in a formal body, came the members of the Kirk Session led by Campbell, who was dragging with him a tiny girl, little more than a child, but perceptibly pregnant. A great shock of frizzy red hair made her face look pitifully white but she was pretty in an immature way. Her shabby clothing looked too thin for the chilly church and she was shivering from cold and fear.

The Exciseman pushed her roughly down onto the little three-legged stool set in front of the pulpit. There she huddled, snivelling and covering her face with her hands.

The grim elders grouped themselves around her and, at a sign from Mr Campbell, the minister, looking acutely embarrassed, addressed the congregation.

"Brethern, this year has commenced no as a year o' grace but alas o' disgrace here in Strathblane. There is lust and sin among us, and to remind us o' the straight and narrow road, the Kirk Session has decreed that as an example, we bring out the stool o' repentance, which as ye know, we have not used these many years."

He paused briefly.

"The young lassie ye see before ye, Mary Kennedy, is unwed but great with child. So, according to ancient practice, she must appear before us through this service to remind us o' the wages o' sin."

He leaned forward in the pulpit and addressed her directly.

"Stand up, Mary Kennedy, and face the body o' the congregation." Trembling and twisting the fingers of her hand round the fringes of a tartan shawl that did little to camouflage her condition, she rose. "Mary," he intoned, "I charge that you name your partner in sin, the father o' your child."

The girl looked up at him. Her startled eyes then flickered quickly back towards the gallery, where the gentry sat. Surely not the Laird, wondered Walter.

"Who is he, Mary?"

But she lowered her head again.

"I'm no sayin', sir. . . " The words were barely intelligible.

"Speak louder if you please."

"I'm . . . no . . . sayin'. . . "

"Then," he continued ponderously, "I can but ask of the man, if he is here present, that he let his conscience be his guide. And may it bring him to contrition and true repentance. May it also bring him to understand his responsibility towards this poor victim of his lust. Is he here?" he asked directly, his eyes sweeping over the assembly.

There was not a sound or movement in the church. The people of Strathblane were as rapt as when Mr MacPhail addressed them.

"The subject o' our service the day," continued Mr Gardner, "is appropriately the Seventh Commandment – *Thou shalt not commit adultery*. But lest we forget that it is but one of the vices the Lord condemned through the mouth o' Moses his prophet, we will commence by reading that part o' the Book o' Exodus that describes the rest."

As he began his first lesson the elders seated themselves in the front pew. Before he sat down, Campbell pulled the girl to her feet, and she rocked back and forth as though she had scarcely the strength to stand, her eyes downcast and her little mouth working.

After the Bible reading, Mr Gardner launched into a lengthy prayer, which brought the congregation to its feet and then there was a psalm with many verses. At its close,

Walter for one was glad to sit down again. The tension in the church reminded him unpleasantly of the crowds around the guillotine. The people of Strathblane were watching Mary Kennedy as avidly as the Parisians had observed the aristocrats on their way to execution.

During the singing, the girl had sunk down onto the creepie stool, still covering her face with her hands. But as the congregation settled themselves for the New Testament lesson, Campbell moved up the steps and taking her roughly by the arm, pulled her to her feet.

"Ye maun stay standin', wuman!"

She protested faintly, "Eh sir, is the wee stool no' there to be sat upon?"

A ripple of nervous laughter went through the congregation.

"Ye are here as an example, lassie! Ye'll stand, the better for a' tae see yer shame."

He spun her round and pushed back the shawl from her protruding waistline. She shut her eyes again and stood swaying throughout the reading, which the minister kept mercifully short, and during another lengthy prayer and hymn. Moisture trickled down her cheek – either tears or sweat – and her face was now ashen. As Mr Gardner rose to preach, she suddenly clutched at her bulging waistline and, with a small scream, crumpled to the ground and lay there, moaning.

"Get up," ordered Campbell. But she stayed huddled on the stone flags, rolling back and forth as if in pain. "Wuman!" repeated the Session Clerk towering over her and grabbing her by the arm. "Dae as ye're telt!"

The minister, distressed, leaned forward in the pulpit and was about to speak when he was drowned out by a voice from the back of the kirk – the doctor at full volume. "This is barbaric! Do you seek to kill both mother and child?"

Down the aisle he strode, the skirts of his greatcoat flapping wide.

"Get away from her!" he barked at Campbell, who retreated back to his pew. "Keep yer hands off her!" Kneeling beside the girl, his huge frame protecting her from all the curious eyes, he laid his fingers gently on her belly. For the first time, Walter noticed metal bands that reinforced the sole of one boot. His voice, gentle now and reassuring, travelled clearly through the building. "Easy, lassie. Easy. Take a deep breath and relax." Her eyes fluttered up to his face as though for a moment she did not know who he was. Then, recognising him, she screamed again dramatically.

"Now, now . . . there's naught to worry about."

She burst into noisy tears.

Douglas's back stiffened and he braced his foot. "Put yer arms around me an' hold tight. I'm goin' to carry ye out o' here." She flung herself on him and balancing carefully, he gathered her up. He stepped back and with the girl clinging to him, he faced the congregation.

"May I remind ye," he said, "of the words used by the founder of yer faith when they brought to him a woman caught in adultery? In the very act. The scripture says – *He that is without sin amongst you, let him cast the first stone.*" His eyes raked the church including the gallery, then came to rest on Campbell. "The Gospel according to John, chapter eight, verse seven."

The girl wailed again and hid her face in his shoulder. "Wheest wheest, lassie. Once ye've got yer feet up ye'll feel fine." He looked up at the pulpit and said politely, "My apologies for interrupting the service, Mr Gardner. By your leave, I'm taking this young woman home."

All his attention focussed on the girl, he started slowly down the aisle. "Whaur d'ye live, Mary?" She pulled herself up on her skinny little arms and whispered in his ear.

"Netherton, eh?" he repeated loudly, with emphasis on the place name. "It's guid it's no further afield, for ye're unco heavy. Someone open the door, if you please."

When a man in the back jumped up and lifted the latch, Stewart kicked it wide with his left foot. Nor did he make any effort to close it behind him and it slammed shut with a reverberation that echoed through the silence.

After a few moments, Mr Gardner raised his black-draped arms.

"Let us rise and pray. . . O Lord," he began with more feeling in his voice than Walter had ever heard, "Forgive us, for we know not what we do. And give us charity. For if we have not charity we are as nothing. In the name o' the Father, the Son and the Holy Ghost. Amen."

The surprises of the service were not yet over. Mr Gardner had scarcely pronounced the benediction when there was a clatter of steps down from the gallery and Jock MacLean in his smart Kirklands livery pushed his way through the crowded aisle and called out,

"The Laird wants to see all the heritors in the vestry."

Angus MacDougal moved over to join the members of the Session while Jean and her aunt exchanged apprehensive glances. Since they sat so far forward, they were among the last to leave the church. But Douglas was back waiting for them by the door, doing his best to be inconspicuous.

Mrs Semple approached him like a ship in full sail. "Will she miscarry, think ye, doctor?" she asked loudly. The people who had gone out before her turned expectantly and eavesdropped without apology.

He shook his head. "No, but it could hae been a gey close call." Lowering his voice he went on close to her ear, "I'm thinking there's not a thing wrong at a'. She was just," he glanced towards the building, "playing to the gallery. And who's to blame her?"

"Ower near her time for that kind o' public castigation."

"My opinion exactly, Mrs Semple. D'ye hae the Gaelic?"

"Aye. A wee bittie. Enough to get by."

"Then please do me a good turn. Stop by and see the lassie and reassure her there's not a thing wrang. I'd a hard time getting through to her, she was that upset." He added darkly, "And dinnae offer her ony o' yer herbal drinks. She wants the child."

"She's ower far along for ony interference," the midwife responded without any rancour. "Just tell me whaur she lives doctor, and I'll go there the morn."

"It's the third house on the Killearn Road, a terrible rundown shack. She stays wi a sister I gather, and they're both employed at the inkle factory. Or were. I telt her she maun stop working and keep off her feet but I'm no sure she understood."

"Has she enough to eat, think ye?"

"Aye. She seems to be provided for." His eyes on the back of Edward Melville who was stepping into his carriage, Stewart added, "I'll wager the baby'll have bulging blue eyes in a red face."

"And it'll no be the first," commented Mrs Semple shaking her head.

Then as if to make lighter conversation, the doctor turned to address Miss MacDougal.

"Is your cold better, Jean?" he asked.

"Aye it is, thank ye Douglas."

So they were now on first name terms, Walter noticed. And no wonder after Hogmanay.

"I'm glad to see ye're learning. You came back for the end of the service this time," Jean remarked.

Douglas Stewart grinned. "Only because I'd left ma hat behind. My best beaver. But it's lucky I did for Jock says the Laird wants a word wi me after he's finished wi the Session.

How was the sermon, Paterson?"

"'*Hélas*, he cannot even make adultery interesting!"

"No personal experience of it," commented Stewart, "though there's plenty o' it in the village."

"Aye, and what I dinnae understand," ruminated Mrs Semple, "is why the Session ordered the creepie stool for yon puir wee craitur when it's no been in use for a' the lassies we've had in trouble this mony years."

"It's yin o' Campbell's ploys to show the Laird what a guid public servant he is," Jean said. "Improving the morals o' the parish, and a' that. . . "

"Aye, after his double dealing ower Benjy Hepburn," muttered Douglas. He looked about him and asked, "Is there naebody seeking free medical advice the day? Usually they're a' after me to prescribe for their ailments when I'm coming oot o' the kirk."

"Aye, and I ken Jean and I are waiting for Angus but who are a' these folk waiting for?" asked Mrs Semple. For although it was a damp and chilly day, the whole village was lingering, scattered around the churchyard in small silent groups and making no move to go.

They're waiting for the heads to start rolling, thought Walter. But he kept this idea to himself for he noticed that Douglas was uncharacteristically tense and Jean too was quiet. Walter was looking for something funny to point out to distract them, when round the side of the building came Mrs Graham.

"My dear Dr Stewart!" she bustled impetuously up to them. "How gallant of you! Is the girl all right?"

"Yes she is, thank you. And . . . " he threw a quick triumphant glance at Walter, "before my friend Paterson beats me to it, may I present to you Miss MacDougal of Puddock Hole?"

The two women curtsied politely. Jean's clothes were

not as rich in fabric as the widow's but she looked, Walter thought, far more stylish in her feathered hat and carrying her new fur piece.

"Miss MacDougal, I am so happy to make your acquaintance. I hear so much about you."

Jean turned slightly pink and responded in a little rush of words, "Walter telt me how you picked out ma muff. . . "

"I hope you like it."

"Aye, I do. I thank ye, ma'am. . . "

"Mr Paterson. Whatever has become of Bobby? He ran off with some other boys and I can't find him?"

"I think I see him playing hide and seek among the tombstones. *Robèrt!*" he called out, "*Viens vite!*"

"*Oui, oui monsieur.*" His charge materialised smiling innocently. "Here I am, *Maman.*"

She took his hand, shaking a fond head. "You're incorrigible. You pay no attention to me at all. You need a man to keep you in order."

As if on cue, the Laird emerged from the church, followed by the minister who looked relieved. Behind them came the elders and heritors, a formidable phalanx of dark-coated men whose faces, Walter observed, were extremely solemn. They looked not unlike schoolchildren he thought, who had just received a severe dressing down. Behind them, with even longer faces, came little Mr Wishart and a glowering Campbell.

The various heritors joined their families but still the congregation made no move to depart, unabashedly waiting to see where the power was now lying.

Douglas Stewart, in an unusually sycophantic gesture, swept off his handsome Sunday hat and bowed low. "Your servant, Mr Moncrieff."

"Ah, there you are doctor." The Laird paused in front of the Puddock Hole group and Walter experienced the same gloating anticipation in the crowd that he had sensed in the Place de la Concorde as the knifehead of the guillotine was poised to descend.

But if the Strathblane people expected to see Stewart's blood spurt, they were disappointed.

"How is the young woman?" Moncrieff was asking solicitously. "I trust your prompt action spared her the worst?"

Douglas took his time about replying and when he did, it was in his best professional style and accent.

"With rest and care she should avoid a miscarriage, sir. However," his eyes swivelled towards Campbell, "should she be subjected to any further emotional upset, it could be dangerous both to her own health and that of her unborn child. Even further interrogation would be detrimental."

"There will be none," said the Laird. Although the tall physician and the swarthy exciseman both towered over him, he contrived to dominate the scene through sheer force of character. He was not an impressive looking man but he had an earnest sincerity that commanded attention and respect. Now he turned to the villagers.

"We must move with the times," he announced. "We live in an enlightened age and the creepie stool is a relic of the past. I am not condoning immorality but I am strongly opposed to methods of discipline that seem to gloat over weakness. Salacious gloating at that. Mr Gardner agrees with me and the heritors and Session have now voted to abolish a practice that Dr Stewart has aptly called barbaric. We must strive in all ways to be merciful."

He bowed to Mrs Graham. Then ignoring everyone else, he walked briskly to the gate, entered his waiting carriage and rode off.

Campbell, his face dark with fury, stalked through the churchyard alone, avoiding the interested eyes that followed his progress down the hill towards Edenkiln.

"Game and set to you, *mon brave*," Walter murmured to Stewart who raised an enquiring eyebrow. "You don't play tennis? I mean you have won the day."

"Aye but now they'll be looking for anither rope to hang me," warned Douglas. But he let out his breath with a little gush of relief and clapped his hat back onto his head. He turned to Angus and smiled.

"Mr MacDougal, since I would now appear to be respectable, I hope ye'll no object to my escorting yer daughter up the brae?"

But Jean, with the whole village watching, had already taken his arm.

PART SIX

CAMPBELL'S REVENGE

The stait of man dois change and vary,
Now sound, now seik, now blith now sary,
Now dansand mery, now like to dee;
Timor mortis conturbat me

> **Lament for the makaris**
> **William Dunbar**

PART SIX

Caregiver's Burden?

I

THE BLOW, WHEN IT CAME, fell fast and unexpectedly. As Abernethy had forecast, there came a break in the wintry weather in mid-February and the captain turned up with a consignment of tea which he stored in the back of the barn.

"I've found some guid brandy," he told the family at Puddock Hole. "I could deliver by the end of this week if you think it's politic."

"Make it Thursday," Walter suggested. "The Laird is having guests that evening to dinner so he'll be occupied."

"And how d'ye ken that, laddie?" asked MacDougal.

"Mrs Graham has been invited."

"So Thursday be it," said the Captain. "We'll come as soon as it's dark for there's cases to stack. Be sure ye clear a corner for us, Angus."

This Walter and Angus did. They cleared bundles of hay outside and with the cows well tethered in their stalls, there was plenty of floorspace in readiness.

"It's turning cold again," Walter remarked as they were completing the task.

"Aye, the winter's coming back. Ye maun bundle up the night when ye're on patrol." For it was still Walter's assignment, once the rum-runner arrived with his horse-drawn cart, to keep an eye on the road leading up from Edenkiln past the Milndavie farm and Mrs Semple's cottage. That way assuredly, the Exciseman would come, possibly making a detour if he required reinforcement from Mr Wishart.

On the far side of Puddock Hole, bleak lonely fields and rough land stretched out until the impressive entrance to Kirklands House marked the intersection of the Boards Road and other tracks leading towards Mugdock and the highway to Glasgow. Walter was by now familiar with the nocturnal sounds made by rabbits and hares and all the other small wild creatures that made the moor their home. He knew the track well and the darkness did not hinder him. He was sure he would have no trouble picking up the approach of anything bulkier than a deer.

So his mind was free to roam as he passed briskly up and down past the Gowk Stane and he found himself considering the Laird's party. It had been described to him by Primrose as a strategy to bring her brother and the widow Graham together. Seeing her at Kirklands, from the head of the table in his fine new Adam dining room, might encourage him to ask for her hand.

He remembered her words, "And then, Walter dear, Henry will be glad to have me married too."

"Who else will be at the party?" he had asked jealously, and she had looked a little embarrassed.

"Edward Melville. . . "

"Is your brother still trying to make a match between you?"

"Oh no," she had responded a shade too fast. "I've told him I don't care for him."

"Well, I'll be thinking about you, entertaining him while I'm up on the Boards Road. I do that every evening," he added quickly. "I like to take a breath of fresh air before I go to bed."

On this Thursday evening, his mind was not completely at rest about his beloved. In France he had seen the pressures put on young girls to marry men who were distasteful to them. He had suffered too with his friend Louis through a period when his family were trying to arrange a match with a well-born young lady whom the Vicomte could not stand. So Walter was not confident that Primrose could stand up to her powerful brother if he decided she should be the bride of his wealthy friend.

It was a cold clear night with little wind and sounds travelled. But those he suddenly heard were not what he expected, nor were the running feet coming from the anticipated direction. They were approaching from the Kirklands side and someone was calling his name.

"Walter! Walter!"

"Primrose!" He hurried up the track and caught her in his arms. Under her big cloak the moonlight picked out the diaphanous layers of silk skirts that she had gathered unceremoniously in both hands, revealing flimsy evening slippers, unsuitable for the rough road.

"Oh Walter! Thank God! Thank God!" She was sobbing with relief.

"*Chérie*, what's happened?"

She clung to him fiercely. "Mr Campbell . . . he came for Henry while we were at table . . . and they're going to the farm."

"*Mille tonnerres!* When?"

"Now! Henry was gathering servants together when I left. You told me you walked here . . . so I knew . . . " she was panting, "you . . . must be . . . keeping watch."

"I am. And Primrose, let me go! I have to warn them!"

"No ! No! You must save yourself!" She was trying to drag him back up the road towards Kirklands. "Alison has her carriage. She'll meet you at the gate and take you to Leddrie Green. You can hide there and escape to Glasgow tomorrow."

"*Chérie*, how are they going to the farm? I heard nothing."

"They're crossing the fields, past the hall. That's the quietest way, Mr Campbell says. He . . . he," she was sobbing, "He had it all worked out, the horrible man. He knew you'd be watching the road."

Walter was trying frantically to loosen her clinging hands.

"Let me go Primrose, please. I must warn them!"

"It's too late! Save yourself! Please Walter!"

"I can't. I won't! Don't you see, that's why I'm here?"

"I know. That's why I came! I . . . "

"Abernethy and Jean . . . they saved my life. . . "

"Then they'd want you to save it now!"

"No Primrose, I can't desert them." He pulled her towards him in a strong swift embrace that loosened her clutching hands. When he broke away, she staggered and fell with a scream. He hoisted her quickly to her feet, swung her round towards Kirklands, then ran before she had time to get another grip on him. She wasn't hurt, he was sure, and he might just get there in time.

Down the road he rushed, cursing himself for not having covered the back approach to Puddock Hole. All seemed quiet there . . . ominously so. He tried the farmhouse door and found it locked. But a window flew open and Jean's voice hissed,

"If ye tak anither step, ye thouless loon, I'll shoot ye!"

"*C'est moi! C'est moi!*"

She let him in.

"Jean, Campbell . . . and men from Kirklands . . . they're coming across the fields."

"Aye, faither thought he heard something and they stopped working. Keep quiet. Wheest now. . . " They moved to the back and peered out the window. The farmyard was dark and still.

"Where's Abernethy?"

"Hiding wi the cabin boy by the wall. Trying to keep the horse quiet."

"And your father?"

"He's oot by the gate." She was clutching a big old

pistol in shaking hands.

"Do you know how to use that?" Walter asked. She nodded.

"D'ye want it?"

"No. You might need it. Any other weapons?"

"Ma grandfaither's broadsword. On the table."

He tiptoed back, slipping off his topcoat and tried to pick up the huge blade.

"*Diable*, it weighs a ton!" His mind now working at top speed, threw up the memory of bandits he and Louis had encountered in Tuscany. "Where are the butcher knives?"

"In the back . . . but lambie!" She too was clinging to him. "Save yersel'! Run for it! Ye cannae dae ony guid! Hide out on the road till they're gone. If they come . . . "

"No! What do you take me for? A molly-coddle? I'll do what I can. Find those knives for me. Quick!"

She slipped into the lean-to behind the kitchen and came back with two formidable meat cleavers. He took one in each hand, balancing them experimentally as she let him quietly out the back door where he stood poised in the shadow.

Suddenly a ring of torches flared, encircling the farmyard, picking out Abernethy and his cabin boy with their horse and cart by the barn. Through the gate came Campbell, dragging Angus MacDougal. Behind him were the Laird and Edward Melville, both of them, Walter noticed, in evening clothes under their cloaks. A clutch of liveried servants carrying improvised weapons followed them.

"Yon's the man!" roared Campbell, triumphantly pointing at the Captain. "And yon's his contraband!"

The footmen made a rush for the cart . . . to be stopped by Abernethy, brandishing a formidable cutlass.

"This is ma lawful property. Ye'll leave it alane."

Moncrieff, with as much aplomb as a general with an

army behind him, strode forward. "You will permit a search. If there is nothing illegal here, you have nothing to fear."

Melville freed his right arm from his cloak. He had a business-like duelling pistol in his hand and now cocked it.

"No, Edward." ordered the Laird. "We are making a peaceable arrest."

But this was not to be. At a sign from Abernethy, the cabin boy jumped into the cart, flogged the horse into action and headed for the gate, the rum-runner covering his track. There was a sudden wild shouting, for a group of estate workers armed with pitchforks and clubs, were in the way. Surrounding the vehicle, they stopped the lunging, rearing and now terrified animal and dragged the boy down. He too was armed, and Walter had just time to see him start to hack defiantly at his opponents when the Captain shouted.

"Help Angus, Paterson!"

The farmer was struggling in Campbell's grip and crying out in anguish, "Mind the hay wi' they torches! The hay . . . "

Jettisoning one knife, Walter hurled himself at the Exciseman, delivering a wild punch that doubled the big man up and sent him sprawling. MacDougal broke loose and rushed towards the barn, spreadeagling himself against the bales.

"Keep awa'! Keep awa' wi they lights! Ma beasts are a' in that byre!"

It was too late. In the confusion, and as more reinforcements crowded into the small farmyard, a spark from a torch ignited the hay. With an anguished shout, Angus threw himself on the flames to smother them.

"Water!" barked the Laird. "In the trough!"

There was a disorganised scramble as servants aimed the contents of two leaky buckets at the conflagration. The farmer, beside himself, slipped in the mud and went down, straight into the flames. There was an anguished scream as his clothing caught fire and he reared back to his feet staggering, a living torch.

Moncrieff, to his credit, pulled off his heavy cloak, and tried to throw it over him while Walter struggled in the grip of two hefty ploughmen.

Above the noise came Melville's voice. "Henry! Stand back!"

A shot rang out and Angus, with a choking yell, collapsed, blood pouring from his chest.

With the added strength of rage, Walter broke free, ran to his side heedless of the danger from the fire. But one glance showed the man had passed help.

"*Assassin! Espèce d'assassin!*" Berserk with fury, Walter rushed at Melville, knocked the pistol from his hand and slashed with the butcher's knife, aiming straight for his rival's crotch. He missed, but the sharp blade plunged deep into a fat hip and there was a satisfactory roar of pain as blood spurted down the white satin breeches.

Rough hands hauled Walter off before he could do more damage. Sheer numbers overpowered him and brought him to the ground.

"Sock him, Geordie!" someone panted.

"You dirty peasants! Keep your hands off me!" He aimed his fist at a footman's face and connected even as a club came down on his own head, shattering his senses in a burst of stars.

II

"Eh mon. Ye're a guid one to hae in a fight, Paterson," came Abernethy's voice from a long distance. "Yon was a fair lickin' ye gied them. Ca' canny now. Lie still."

Walter opened one eye and shut it again quickly. Water was dribbling over his face. As consciousness returned, so did a pain down one side of his head. And when he touched his head, his fingers came away sticky with blood.

"Wh . . . where are we?"

"In the big hoose."

"In Kirklands?" When he took this in, he laughed shakily. "*Mais ça, c'est formidable.*"

"Ye were pretty formidable yersel' back at the farm."

"Th . . . thank you Captain." He sat up carefully. "Why is it so dark? They should give us more light."

"Prisoners are lucky to hae yin candle, laddie."

"Prisoners . . . we're prisoners?"

"Aye."

He distinguished another shape huddled at a small table. "Who else is here?"

"Just Willie . . . ma cabin boy."

Recollection was coming back.

"Was he dead, Captain?"

"MacDougal? Aye."

"And . . . Jean . . . ?"

"They didnae search the hoose. They found the cases in the cart and wi the auld man deid, the Laird had mair than he'd bargained for . . . mair than enough for yin night, I'm thinkin'. Are ye hurt bad?"

"I . . . don't know." He tested his limbs, starting with his right hand which, to his relief, responded normally. "Just my head."

"Aye, ye got a fair dunt and ye're bleeding a wee bit. D'ye want a drink o' water?"

"No, thanks . . . " A tightness in the pit of his stomach boded ill for keeping anything down. "What will happen to us now?"

"We'll be turned over to the Sheriff."

"And . . . then?"

A rough, scared young voice came out of the gloom. "And then we'll a' be hangit."

"Wheesht, Willie. Would ye hae a handkerchief, Mr Paterson? His hand's cut bad."

Walter found one in his pocket. "Does it hurt?"

"Aye, but no' as much as hanging."

The guillotine might have been quicker, Walter reflected in passing, but he kept this thought to himself.

"Are we really *en route* to the gallows, Captain?"

Abernethy spat.

"Naw. We're caught red-handed but first we'll hae a trial. That means they'll hae tae lock us up in the Tolbooth in Glasgow and I've weaselled oot o' that jail afore."

Thinking of the Bastille and the Conciergerie, Walter asked, "How?"

"There's aye a turnkey that can use a few bottles of free grog for leavin' doors unlocked." He slapped his pocket. "It's lucky I hae money on me. And ma pipe. But nae baccy, mair's the pity. Do ye smoke, laddie?"

Walter shook his head, privately thankful that his stomach would not have to cope with the smell of tobacco in the cramped room.

"Naebody in Scotland . . . save the Laird o' Kirklands, which is our bad luck . . . has ony use for paying Excise duty to the English. There's plenty of public sympathy for the likes o' us, and this'll no' be the first time that I've been turned over to justice and made ma escape. And when I go, so do you, for I didnae save ye frae the Frenchies to swing on a Scottish gallows."

"Would they hang me? I'm not a smuggler."

"Naw. Ye're no one o' ma' crew like Willie here, but ye're a disturber o' the peace. Ye attacked yon gentleman and wounded him bad and that could mak it hard for ye."

"I wish I'd killed him . . . the way he killed Mr MacDougal." Tears started in Walter's eyes.

"Laddie, Angus was mortal burned. That shootin' saved him terrible pain."

"Yes, but . . . that damnable Melville is a murderer! Why isn't he locked up in here with us?"

"Be glad he isnae, laddie. He's the Laird's friend. He's the gentry. And so are you, so maybe Moncrieff will stretch a point with you."

"I doubt that. And Jean? What will happen to her?"

"She has her auntie. And a sister in Glasgow. And a bit o' siller put by, I'll warrant. Forbye, the whole parish will come to her aid. They're guid people in Strathblane and they'll be fair angered. It's yin thing to arrest the likes o' me but it's anither to shoot an auld man like MacDougal whose only crime was makin' a few pence from distributin' tea and brandy."

Walter remembered thankfully the money in the kitchen dresser. Surely now she would use it.

"Ye dinnae need to sit on the floor, laddie. There's anither chair."

"Thank you. I think I'll stay here." He lay down flat again, trying to fight down an unpleasant chain of physical sensations. He swallowed, breathed deeply, tried to ignore it, but he couldn't.

"Captain, open that window, please. . . "

"Is it no' cauld enough?"

"I'm going to be sick," Walter gasped, trying to choke back the sour bile until he could release it outside. With Abernethy's help he managed to pull apart the heavy window shutters in time and leaning over the sill, he vomited up everything in his stomach. The fresh air revived him but it also extinguished the candle.

"I'm sorry Captain, someone must have kicked me in

the belly."

"Aye, those Kirklands servants were none too gentle with ye. Here, rinse yer mouth oot wi' the water, and spit it out. Then shut that window, for the draught's fair killin'."

"Forgive me, Captain." As he was closing the shutters, he looked and saw they were on the attic floor with a wide roof not far below them.

"Did you ever escape from Kirklands?"

"Naw. I was never held here afore."

"It might be possible. We're not far from the ground up here."

"Ach, it's easier in Glasgow. I've friends near by and ma ship's anchored fair close to whaur the jail is."

"How long will they keep us?"

"Here? Who can say? It's the end of the week, so maybe Moncrieff will no want to mak a trip to town afore the Sabbath is past. Forbye, he's gaun to hae a power o' explanation to do, in the parish, the people'll be that angry aboot MacDougal."

"So, we could be here until Monday?" Abernethy nodded. "I hope they give us some blankets."

"We're lucky tae be in such a shipshape place, laddie."

"I suppose so."

Hugging himself against the cold, Walter sat down on the floor again, his back against the wall. He thought longingly of the warm overcoat he had jettisoned at the farm when the fighting started. And he wondered about Jean. . . From there his mind wandered unhappily to Primrose, somewhere under the same roof. He was deeply touched that she had tried to save him but despite his fears, he was glad he had not let her guide him to Mrs Graham's carriage.

He did not know what to think about his own situation. He had little knowledge of Scottish legal procedure but he suspected that if he got in touch with his uncle in Edinburgh, he might be saved from . . . what? It promised to be a long disturbing night.

The Captain dosed off and the sound of his monotonous snoring added to Walter's nervous tension, as did some tearful snuffling from the cabin boy. To keep warm, Walter got up and started pacing around the room. He was by the door when he heard sounds in the corridor. People were approaching. Someone was turning the key in the lock. . .

Abernethy and the boy woke up and all three captives tensed. Two figures slipped into the room, closing up quickly behind them. One carried a lantern and Walter scarcely had time to wonder if they were going to be taken out and shot, when a familiar voice whispered,

"Is anyone hurt in here?"

"Stewart!"

"Wheesht!" Jock MacLean, who carried the light turned on him sharply. "Wheesht! The Laird thinks the doctor's gone hame but he heard some yin was hurt, and he insisted. . . "

Stewart's eyes travelled swiftly around the room and came to rest on Walter.

"No, it's the cabin boy."

The footman set the lantern on the table and made a move towards Willie who, unprepared, jumped up screaming.

"I'll no be hangit the noo!"

"Wheesht, wheesht!" Jock grabbed him, clamped a hand over his mouth and dragged him back to the table, struggling.

Douglas's voice, low and deathly weary, cut through the fracas. "Let him alane."

Willie, still terrified, slumped back into his chair. Stewart set his bag down on the table. "I'm a doctor, laddie," he said "Ma business is healin'. Not hangin' . . . Jock, gie him a dram while I see to Paterson."

He limped over to Walter and his fingers went straight to the right wrist.

"Your handiwork's safe."

"Aye. But there's blood on yer face." He produced a sponge and, as the doctor dabbed his friend's cheek, he asked softly, "What can I do?"

"Jean. Take care of her."

"Aye. For sure. But . . . for you?

Walter gave a hopeless shrug. Stewart gripped his shoulder. "I was in a waur spot, and here I am."

He turned back to the cabin boy, his movements brittle with tension, and Walter noticed inconsequentially that he was in his shirtsleeves, his cuffs rolled back from his brawny forearms, and his Sunday waistcoat, though protected by a large apron, had not been saved from spattered bloodstains.

"Now then laddie, what's yer name?"

"Willie sir, Willie Lamont."

"Aweel Willie Lamont, let's see what's wrang wi' ye . . . some yin hold up the light, if ye please. I may need Jock to assist me." Walter reached for it. But his hands shook involuntarily when Stewart eased off the grimy handkerchief and uncovered the gaping wound. "Shut yer eyes, Paterson, I cannae hae ye gettin' sick the now."

"Here, I'll haud it." The Captain stepped forward and Walter thankfully beat a retreat.

While Jock laid out the bandages and scissors, Douglas asked in his soothing voice,

"Ye'll be Mr Abernethy, sir?"

"Aye."

"I've enjoyed yer brandy. Miss MacDougal gied me a bottle o' it for operatin' on Mr Paterson here." He coughed and cleared his throat. "That's an unco nasty cut ye've got Willie, but it's no serious I think. And it'll no tak me long tae stitch it up." Jock was threading an unpleasant needle for him. "And I'd appreciate it laddie, if ye'll do yer best to keep quiet and keep as still as you can. We're no wantin' to alert the household to our presence here. It could cost Jock his employment if ony yin knew he'd brought me to attend you."

"Willie'll be quiet. He's a guid lad and a grand fighter," said the Captain.

"Aye. I've just come from patching up one of his victims. Mr Melville among them."

"*He* was mine," Walter interposed with satisfaction.

"Guid for you, Paterson. Now Willie, tak a deep breath and haud tight."

Walter shut his eyes. The cabin boy gave one sharp gasp then Stewart's voice, quiet but resonant, took over, dominating through sheer will power the tension and fear in the room. "When I was at the Medical College in Edinburgh Willie, I won a prize for surgery, I was that quick and ma patients recovered sae fast. And ye will too if ye keep that cut clean. Dinnae let ony yin touch it unless they've washed their hands. That's important. D'ye understand?"

"I'll see to it," said Abernethy. "I've a man on ma ship that's guid wi wounds."

If the doctor wondered how they'd get back aboard, he gave no sign but just remarked, "Guid . . . and Willie, that's the worst over, and no that bad, I hope. I congratulate ye. Ye've mair courage than yer so-called betters. Would ye like another dram?"

The cabin boy, his eyes streaming, nodded and Jock held the bottle to his mouth. "Maybe you would like some whisky too, Captain?"

"Aye. Thank ye kindly, doctor." Abernethy took a long drink of it, then drew out his pipe and put it in his mouth, chewing the stem.

"Are ye out o' tobacco?" asked Stewart as he finished

bandaging Willie's hand.

"Aye. It's in the coat that I left at the farm."

The doctor dug a shabby pouch out of his own pocket. "Help yersel' and keep it. I've a raw throat and shouldnae be smoking."

"Ye're thoughtful."

"It's little enough I can do . . . Jock, pass the whisky bottle to Mr Paterson, if you please."

"*Non!* I'd be sick!"

"Doctor's orders, laddie. It's a cauld night."

Holding his breath, Walter managed to swallow some of the raw, fiery liquid.

The dressing completed, Stewart straightened himself, stretched, then stood as though loathe to leave. "I'd let ye hae the bottle but I may need it later. . . This night I've delivered twa bairns and treated yin, twa, three, four and now five wounded men. And that's only the start." He paused then added grimly, "I'm on my way to Puddock Hole."

Walter tried to speak and couldn't. Abernethy grunted. The doctor's weary eyes travelled over the room.

"Jock, when we've cleaned up here I suggest ye find a chamberpot for these gentlemen. and if ye can sneak ony pillows and plaids in tae them, I'm sure they'd be grateful." He rolled down his sleeves, untied the soiled apron. "Willie, rest easy. That hand'll be fine and they'll no hang ye for a while yet." He gave the cabin boy a reassuring slap on the back and held out his hand, first to Abernethy and then to Walter. "If ye think o' onythin' I can do, Jock can aye get a message tae me."

"There's nae a thing, doctor but we thank ye just the same."

"Aweel . . . Guid night gentlemen, and guid luck."

Picking up his bag, he left with Jock at his heels. The key grated in the lock.

"Yon's a guid man," pronounced the Captain, lighting up his pipe.

III

When the morning eventually came, two Kirklands servants brought in a pot of porridge and some ale. Walter had a dull headache. He had thrashed his situation around so many times that he could barely collect his thoughts and not even the hot heavy food quieted his churning stomach. There was no water for shaving so he felt grubby and unwashed.

Willie's hand hurt and he was again vocal on the prospect of being hanged. Abernethy smoked stolidly and did his best to be nonchalant. But Walter suspected he was not as confident as he tried to appear.

In midmorning three footmen arrived with ropes. One was Jock, who wrapped a dark napkin carefully over Willie's bandage to hide it then secured his hands behind his back. One of the other men, who sported a big patch over one eye, did the same to Walter, dragging the bonds tight with considerable relish.

Walter protested but Abernethy hushed him.

"Keep cool, Paterson. Ye're in no position to argue." As they hustled out into the corridor he added, "And say as little as ye can. A' they're entitled to hear is yer name and whaur ye live."

After being escorted down a series of back stairs, they came through a door into a different world – the living quarters of Kirklands House – and Walter's curiosity revived despite his apprehension. At last he was seeing Primrose's home and it charmed him. It was a beautiful house, as fine as any he had seen in France and decorated in the fashionable

Adam style. As they shuffled down a long hall hung with portraits, he glimpsed an elegant dining room and a pretty little parlour that made him achingly conscious of the Laird's sister. He wondered where she was? Upstairs presumably, unless she had gone to Mrs Graham's.

In a handsome library, Henry Moncrieff sat behind an impressive walnut desk facing long French windows that opened onto a formal garden. A vase of dried flowers and leaves stood beside his china ink-pot – also a tray with a carafé and several pill-boxes. He looked pale and almost as tense as his captives. When they were lined up before him he looked them over, then poured himself some water.

"You are doubtless wondering whether you will be taken to Stirling or to Glasgow," he said. "I have discussed the matter with the Sheriff and he agrees with me that it would be better if I delivered you to the jail in the city. Because of the nature of your offences."

His eyes lingered briefly on Walter. "Since we have no jail in Strathblane, you will remain here until the beginning of the week. I will then have you transported to Glasgow and you will be held in the Tolbooth there until you go to Edinburgh for your trial."

He looked at the Captain. "Your name, if you please."

"Andrew Abernethy."

"And your . . . occupation?"

"I'm the owner and skipper o' a ship ca'ed the *Mary Ann*."

"And where is it berthed?"

The seaman smiled. "I'm no exactly sure o' the name o' the slip."

"That is not an answer. Be more specific."

"I anchored off the Broomielaw three nights ago. I presume she's still lying close by. And ma papers were a' in order, sir. I had a legitimate cargo. It went through the customs at the Port o' Glasgow and ye can find it recorded there."

The Laird dipped a quill in the ink and made notes. "From the nature of the goods in your cart, which the Exciseman and I found last night at Puddock Hole, I deduce that you also carried illegal freight."

"I'm no admittin' onythin', Kirklands. Ye maun prove that whatever ye found wasnae declared afore ye can charge me."

"That will be the business of the legal authorities in Glasgow. Where do you take on cargo?"

"Boulogne mostly, though I use several French ports."

"Are both these men members of your crew?"

"Only this one, sir. His name's Willie Lamont."

The cabin boy was staring with as much dread as though there were gallows above the Laird's chair. "Are we tae be hangit?" he blurted out.

"Should you be hanged?" enquired Moncrieff. "What have you done to deserve it?"

"He's done naught except obey ma orders," said Abernethy. "I tak full responsibility for him."

"Why is he so scared?"

"He's never been in the hands of the law afore, Kirklands. He's young and he's led a clean life, or as clean as ony seaman can."

"And . . . " Moncrieff's eyes travelled to Walter, though he continued to address the Captain. "Who is this man here? And what is his connection with you?"

"I brought him here from France last October and that's a' we have in common."

Moncrieff asked formally. "What is your real name?"

"Paterson *is* my real name, sir. I was christened Walter James."

"And how did you . . . I mean under what circumstances . . . did you meet Captain Abernethy?"

"He could tell you better than I, sir. At the time, I was in the grip of fever and painful injuries, and . . . not clear in my head."

"It was anither gentleman sir," interposed Abernethy "that asked me to tak him to Scotland. His faither, he said he was."

"And did he give you a reason for wanting his son out of the country?"

"Ach, they're a' trying to leave France the now, Kirklands. There's a Revolution goin' on there and war's breakin' out."

"Were you paid for transporting him?"

"Aye, it was a business arrangement. I'd never seen either o' the gentlemen afore."

"And why did you bring this man to Strathblane?"

"He was unco sick, sir. I was feared he'd die if he didnae get proper care. And wi' Miss MacDougal's auntie bein' a midwife, I kent he'd be well nursed at Puddock Hole."

"Do you have any identification papers, Paterson?"

Walter forced his exhausted mind to concentrate. "I have a *laisser-passer* at the farm. It's all but illegible from my blood, but . . . you can see it's in French."

"But you have a Scottish name?"

"Yes, sir. My father was out in '45, but by the time his pardon came through, he had established himself in France."

"So he chose to remain there?"

"Yes, sir."

"What was he doing?"

"He owns a financial house."

"And you? Do you give allegiance to the Pretender?"

"He's long gone, sir. I suppose I was a subject of King Louis, but . . . he's dead too. I don't know who my king is," he said wearily.

"You consider yourself a Frenchman?"

"No! My parents are Scots and though I was born in France and grew up there, this is my country!"

"Then I presume you have relatives here. Where, may I ask?"

"In Edinburgh. My uncle, Alexander Paterson, is a lawyer. I'm sorry, I do not have his name and address."

"Paterson is a common enough name. Do you have anything to prove that you have simply not assumed it?"

Walter thought of his signet ring with the family crest on it, somewhere in that very house, on a chain round Primrose's neck.

"I . . . have two watches Mr Moncrieff, with my initials and the Paterson coat-of-arms engraved on their backs. But they're also at Puddock Hole."

"You have been in Strathblane for a number of months. Why, when you were recovered from your injuries, did you not seek out your relatives? That would surely have been the obvious thing to do."

Walter had an irrational urge to say, "Because I fell in love with your sister." Instead he replied, "By the time I was fully recovered, I had a position sir, tutoring Bobby Graham at Leddrie Green House."

"Yes, Mrs Graham has told me that you also show a great deal of curiosity about her horticultural pursuits."

"Yes, sir!" This seemed a more promising tack, so he continued eagerly, "I have always been fascinated by growing things. I love the country. My ambition is to farm, as you are doing, using modern methods."

"In an estate like Leddrie Green presumably, with your activity financed by a widow who is comfortably off."

"Sir! I am not a fortune hunter! Mrs Graham is a charming lady but my affections are already engaged. . . "
To someone in Kirklands who, for all he knew, might be

listening at the door.

But the damage was done, Moncrieff was scribbling notes. When he finished, he gave Walter a chilly look.

"I will have your papers picked up from Puddock Hole and passed along to the authorities in Glasgow. At that time, I will also suggest that they interrogate you as to your real intention in this country. I have already voiced my suspicions to the Sheriff here and that is one reason I am not delivering you to him. Treason is a matter for the higher courts."

"Treason!" cried Walter. "I'm no kind of traitor! My intentions are simply to . . . live here and observe the land and ultimately. . . "

"And ultimately to sell your knowledge to the French government, with which we are at war. I suggest that you are a spy, Paterson. I've thought that ever since I learnt how you arrived here and your actions have done nothing to change my mind."

Walter was so shocked, his English deserted him completely, and without thinking of the Laird's reaction, he reverted to French. *"Mais ça . . . c'est impensable! C'est ridicule! C'est. . . c'est. . .* What could I spy on in Strathblane?"

"We are geographically close to a large industrial city, . . . one with as much overseas trade as any in the kingdom. Glasgow and its surroundings would be a logical place for a hostile power to introduce a courtier or saboteur."

"But I know nothing of sabotage! And I hate the regime in Paris! I . . . I think I would feel safer in a Scottish jail than anywhere in France today!"

Moncrieff gave him a wintry smile. "You'll have the opportunity to put that belief to the test on Monday Paterson, when you are taken to the Tolbooth in Glasgow. Take them back to their room, Geordie."

"Monsieur, I beg you to listen to me. . . "

"You can tell your cock and bull stories in Glasgow,"

barked the Laird, his hands beginning to shake. Walter's only satisfaction was seeing his interrogator reach for his pills as the prisoners were hustled from the room.

IV

"He doesnae like the cut o' yer jib, laddie," pronounced Abernethy. "Hates a' foreigners, that yin. But they're no' that way in Glasgow. Dinnae be sae low. Things could be much worse. We could hae been incarcerated in some miserable wee local jail instead o' stayin' here where at least it's clean and no' drafty. Forbye, we dinnae hae to pay for oor victuals."

"And it's guid food," contributed Willie, his mouth full. With the prospect of hanging postponed, he was feeling better.

"Aye. Sit doon and eat yer supper, Paterson. Ye maun keep up yer strength."

"True." Walter picked half-heartedly at his evening meal, a stew that was mostly turnips with some tough bits of meat for flavour.

"Aye, we'll no' eat as well until we get back aboard the *Mary Ann*."

"Do you really believe you can escape from the jail?"

"I've done it afore," replied Abernethy. And then as if to accentuate his confidence, he added in his matter-of-fact way, "Ach, that young doctor smokes terrible tobacco."

"It's probably all he can afford," said Walter.

"I maun bring him some decent stuff. I hope the Laird doesnae haud it against him that he cam' here to help us last night."

"The Laird didn't know."

"He'll find out. Yin o' the servants'll talk."

Walter got up, started pacing again.

"I'm angry with myself, Captain. I shouldn't have said some of the things I did."

"I warned ye to say as little as possible."

"And you were right." Walter rubbed his bruised forehead. "I felt so stupid I couldn't think clearly. I just said what came into my mind."

"Aye. That's why I told ye to stay stum. And keep still, laddie. It makes me tired just watching ye."

Walter paused by the window. The prospect of another night lying on the cold unsympathetic floor, to say nothing of two days confined in such a small place with the overpowering smell of tobacco mixed insalubriously with that of human excrement seemed more than he could stand.

Moreover, he had spent the long afternoon thinking constantly of Primrose wondering where she was in the house and what she was doing. And the irony of the situation was unbearable. Guarding his private unhappiness he had tried to occupy his mind by studying the flat roof down below and speculating what lay under it. She had often described the layout of the house to him and because their trysting cottage lay close to the back premises, he had learned a good deal.

Their prison, he suspected, was a servant's garret built over the outlying pantries, sculleries and wash-houses which the Laird had added on to the kitchen. The direction of certain cooking odours, which he had sniffed whenever he could persuade Abernethy to let him open the window, bore this out. If he was right, they were close to the Boards Road.

"Captain, I'm going to escape from here . . . tonight. I . . ."

"Wheesht! They're at the door."

Two servants came in and removed the tray. When the key had turned in the lock, Walter opened the shutters and inhaled the chilly night air.

"Give me a leg up."

"Bide a wee. They might come back. They forgot to empty the chanty."

"I doubt if they're so solicitous for our comfort. Captain, please take a look. Is that too long a drop for me?"

Abernethy lumbered over and studied the terrain. "Naw. But . . . what then? Ye'll no be on the ground."

"There are trees, creepers, rone pipes. I'll take a chance on a good climb."

"Whaur are ye goin'?"

"To Puddock Hole first to make sure that Jean is safe, and then to Glasgow I suppose. And then to Edinburgh."

"Ye're a wanted man now, ye ken."

"Yes, but no one outside Strathblane knows what I look like and surely once I find my uncle he'll be able to clear me of . . . of the ridiculous spying charge."

"Aye. Maybe. But in the meantime, if ye need any help, gang to the Cross Keys in Greenock and ask for Davie MacKenzie. He'll tell ye whaur to find the ship."

"I can't go back to France."

"There are English ports."

"Yes, I . . . suppose so . . . but . . . I want to stay here. If you run into my father, tell him I'm heading for Edinburgh. And . . . good luck to you too, Willie."

"Tak care o' yersel', Mr Paterson. We'll haud ye till ye're ready to mak the drop."

Walter clambered cautiously onto the window ledge and swung himself over it, Abernethy and the boy clutching his wrists. There was a scary moment when he felt his legs dangling in space. Then they lowered him down and after a quick look, loosened their grip.

Forcing himself to go limp, he dropped and hit the rooftop which was not as far as he had feared. He lay for a second, checking his body to make sure he was unhurt, then scrambled up and signalled to Abernethy that he was safe. Then he made a careful reconnaissance, studying the land below. Faint light glimmered from one side of the building. The rest lay in darkness and leaning over the parapet, he distinguished the outline of a window on one wall. It appeared to have a deep ledge and was halfway to the ground.

Trying to think himself back into his boyhood, when he and Louis had spent their summers climbing trees and playing around the outbuildings of the Sincerbeaux estates, he turned his back, took a firm grip on the parapet and carefully swung a leg over it. After some nerve-wracking groping, his toe touched the sill. Holding his breath and saying a quick prayer, he manoeuvred his other leg off the roof, throwing his weight forward and clinging as hard as he could. There was an ominous spasm in his right wrist but his fingers held.

Somehow he moved first one hand and then the other down the rough wall and, as he had expected, found bars on the aperture. A quick look downward showed he was nearly where he wanted to be. He took another breath then let his body fall backwards into a crouch, a trick he mastered as a child. The ground was further away this time and he hit paving stones. But after another physical assessment, he found he was only bruised, though cold seeped through a long tear in his jacket.

But so far, so good. He crawled around the building, trying to get his bearings. There were trees not far away, among them the solid mass of the cottage where he and Primrose had so often met. He crept carefully past a stable and the outbuildings and – after some scratchy encounters with whins and bushes – reached a stone dyke. Once over it, he was on familiar territory and shivering with reaction from the bitter night air, he headed towards the farm.

There were lights in several windows and some kind of horse-drawn vehicle stood in the yard.

Then the dogs ran out, growling.

"Hush, Maisie! Hush, Dandy!"

Now they were jumping around him in welcome, wagging their long plumey tails, but quietly as though they understood. He patted them fondly before they returned to their night quarters in the barn, which he noticed was standing open and empty. Lifting the backdoor latch carefully, he reconoitered the kitchen.

A woman he had often seen in church was filling up the big teapot from the kettle and candles on the kitchen table lit up ashets of pies and bannocks.

As he watched from the shadows, Jean came in to pick up a platter. She wore a black dress that he had never seen before and there were mourning ribbons in her cap. He yearned to call for her but didn't dare.

"Gang back tae yer friends, dearie. I'll bring the food in," said the friend.

As both women headed back to the front room, he willed Jean to look his way but she didn't. It was heart-rending, frustrating. He could not bear to leave Puddock Hole like this, without any word of comfort to her or farewell. But he heard male voices coming from the parlour and dared not stay.

He moved fast to shut the kitchen door to the hall. It was easy to find his other jacket, his topcoat, hat and muffler. Picking up a candle and setting it on the chest of drawers, he went through his few possessions, pocketing his French coins and a small sum in Scottish money . . . enough, he estimated to get him to Glasgow, where he could change the rest. There was still plenty left for Jean. His two watches he linked on to his waistcoat and, as an afterthought, folded up his French identification papers and put them in his pocket.

Then, since his clothes would be of no use to anyone else, he bundled up his shirts and smalls in one of Angus's plaids and stuffed his torn jacket out of sight in a drawer. Not knowing when he might be able to find food, he helped himself to a slice of bannock and a meat pie. Slipping out the back door, he murmured a farewell to the dogs who eyed him from the empty barn.

There was a lump in his throat. At the Gowk Stane, he had to stop to wipe the tears from his eyes and trying to calm himself, he turned for a last view up the Blane Valley.

He beheld an unforgettable sight. A full moon was up and the whole range of distant mountains was as clear as by day, for each one was covered in snow. He could distinguish the massive outline of Ben Lomond with the Grampians behind, and the nearby Campsie Fells with little Dumgoyne at one end were also glittering in the frosty night.

Some day I'll come back here, he promised himself. I'll build a house like Kirklands and be a bonnet laird and write poetry as I dig the ditches and plant the trees.

Primrose had once told him that anyone who slid down the Gowk Stane became 'a native of Strathblane' and they had done this in fun. Now the huge boulder was sticky with frost and as he patted it in farewell, he realised he had left his warm gloves back at the farm. He considered going back for them, making another effort to see Jean, but it was too risky.

V

He had planned to put as much distance as he could between himself and Kirklands before morning but the cold was penetrating and it was slippery underfoot. Besides, he could not leave without finding out what was happening to Jean and there was only one person in the parish that he dared to approach.

So it was with relief that he saw a light coming from the doctor's surgery window and knew he was not out on a confinement. But though Walter knocked long and hard on the front door, there was no response. Finally he pushed through the overgrown spiky shrubbery surrounding the house and rapped persistently on the windowpanes.

A roar came from within and the casement flew open.

"Come back the morn! I'm goin' no place the night! I need ma rest!" This announcement was followed immediately by another shout, "Wait! Ye're no frae Wishart's are ye?"

"*C'est moi! C'est moi!*"

The window slammed shut and seconds later, the door opened and a huge hand hauled him inside.

"Strike me pink! The desperado himsel'! Did they let you go?"

"No! I escaped!"

"How?"

"Climbed out of the window and jumped off the roof."

"Eh, mon! There's no holdin' ye!" They burst into emotional laughter, slapping one another's backs. The young collie, sleeping by the fire, got up and sniffed groggily at Walter's shoes.

"What's the matter with Sadie? She looks drunk."

"She is! I spilt some whisky and she lapped it up. That's why she never barked." Swaying a little, he reached for the black bottle on his desk. "Here! Hae a drink yersel'!"

"Stewart, I can't stand the Devil's brew. Haven't you any brandy left?"

"Aye. A mouthful." He swung over towards a corner cupboard, shabby carpet slippers doing nothing to curb his limp and, as he wrenched open the door, a skeleton swung out.

Walter gasped in horror. *"Dieu! Qu'est que c'est que ça?"*

"Ma auld mentor." Pushing back the rattling bones, Douglas unearthed a flask. Unshaven and in an old seaman's jersey unravelling at the cuffs and neck, he was a far cry from his usual tidy self. He gave off a pungent odour of alcohol and sour sweat. Handing over the brandy, he collapsed into his desk chair and reached for a half-filled tumbler.

"Tak' off yer coat, sit close to the fire. Bottoms up. 'Here's tae us, wha's like us? Damn few and they're a' deid' . . . like puir auld MacDougal."

Walter took a long swallow of brandy.

"He was really dead?"

"Aye. And just as weel for his ain sake." Stewart drained his glass. "He never liked me, Paterson. But . . . if I were a Papist, I'd say God rest his soul. . . Hae ye been to the farm?"

"Yes, but there were people there."

"Aye, the kistin'."

"What's that?"

"Puttin' him in the coffin. Yin o' our barbarous country customs. I should hae attended but . . . I couldnae face it."

"I didn't dare try to talk to Jean. I just took my money and my things and came here. What happened when you were there last night?"

Tears gushed from Douglas's eyes. He wiped them off on his sleeve. "I'm sorry Paterson. I'm awfa tired, and sickenin' for somethin'. Forbye, I'm fu'. . . "

"Any more brandy and I'll be the same. What happened?"

He coughed, clearing his throat. "By the time I got there, she'd dragged her faither ben the hoose. She was keenin' ower him like a banshee, beside hersel'. . . And when she saw me. . . Michty! She was that relieved! But there was naethin' I could do. He was cauld. His chest was half shot away. His hands were a' burnt."

Walter drank again quickly.

"I got whisky doon her, wrapped her in a plaid and took her to her auntie's. I had to near carry her most of the way and she's a big, heavy lassie. The auld lady was fair upset about her brother, but she's a trooper. She made up the kitchen bed, warmed bricks, but . . . " He shook his head. "Paterson, she doesnae think o' me as a man! I'm just, ye ken, the doctor . . . auld McKelvie's successor. I'm no age. I dinnae hae human feelings. Forbye, she thinks o' Jean as a wee girl." He struggled for control. "We undressed her and she fell asleep in ma airms. And then I had to . . . to leave her there . . . in bed, alane."

He banged the desk with both fists. "Me that hasnae had a decent night wi' a woman since I came here, barrin' Hogmanay! I came hame and started drinkin' and how I lived through this day I'll never know." He buried his head in his hands.

"You're in love with her, aren't you?"

"Aye."

"Then why don't you marry her? It would settle everything."

Douglas looked up, his bloodshot eyes as naive and pleading as a lovesick schoolboy's.

"Would she hae me?"

It seemed to Walter that all Jean's actions throughout the winter had indicated as much but it might not be politic to point this out.

"Why shouldn't she? You're . . . *un bon parti* . . . you're very well embarked on a good career!"

"But I've no money, Paterson!" He shoved the ledger angrily onto the floor. "I've been tryin' a' night to balance ma books. Everyone in the parish owes me. Kirklands and Leddrie Green are the only houses that pay my bills wi cash. The rest unload their auld hens and braxie mutton on me. . .

Wi' neeps and tatties for minor ailments."

"Stewart, I left Jean enough money to tide her over. And . . . she has the farm. It must be worth something! But it's a man she needs now, and I daren't stay!"

"Aye. Ye're right . . . " But again he crashed his fist violently down on the desk. "What kind o' prospect am I for any woman in her right senses? After . . . what happened to me last year." He declaimed suddenly, "*I have no spur to prick the sides o' ma intent, but only vaultin' ambition.* Are ye ony good wi figures?"

"No. Stewart, you can still ask her. She can only refuse."

"Aye, and that would kill me."

To distract him from this possibility, Walter said, "You can tell me now. Why did you ever leave Edinburgh?"

"Naw, naw, laddie! Dinnae start on that yin! I left to escape calumny and . . . and shame . . . " He had a fit of coughing. "Tell me aboot the fight. I've heard Jock's version and I've seen the results o' the mayhem, but . . . I dinnae ken exactly how it came about."

Walter took another pull from the flask then told him, hedging only on how he had got the alarm. Douglas listened with drunken concentration, puffing on his insalubrious pipe and coughing again harshly, off and on. By the time Walter had reached the description of his cross-examination by the Laird, his chills had given way to hot anger.

"Moncrieff thinks I'm a spy for the French!" he finally spat out.

"That's ridiculous. Why?"

"Because of the way I came here . . . and because I chose to stay after I'd recovered from my wounds."

"And what were you spying on among the Campsie Fells? Lassies cleekin' lads in the heather?"

"*Je ne sais pas* . . . but he was going to turn me over to

the authorities in Glasgow as a dangerous saboteur."

"He's found a guid excuse for gettin' ye out o' the Blane Valley, Paterson. Ye're ower braw a lad to be in his ladylove's house every day. I might hae kent."

Walter swore vigorously in French.

"Ach, weel . . . ye can aye come back when ye've found yer family."

"I will! I promise you!"

"Tell me the rest o' it. How ye got away."

Walter did so, winding up with his visit to Puddock Hole. "Stewart, do you have a valise I could borrow, for my clothes?"

"Aye . . . an auld one I used as a student." He rose again, staggered towards a pile of books, pushed them over, dragged forward a shabby carrying bag and tipped its contents, also books, onto the floor.

Walter stuffed his shirts and socks into it.

"Can I stay here for the night?" he asked.

"Aye, if ye think it's safe."

"What was that about Wishart coming by?"

"Wishart . . . that's a lang story."

"Tell me."

"Ach. Whaur would I begin?" Douglas pushed back his shock of hair. "I'd been unco depressed . . . maybe I'd some premonition. So I'd gone to Glasgow hopin' a guid meal at the Ordinary and a haircut, even just a stroll around the town, would lift my spirits. Forbye, I needed leeches."

"Leeches!" Walter shuddered.

"Aye." He gestured towards a covered jar on the cabinet. "Useful creatures, though unappetising. But Paterson, I should hae known better. It aye happens that way. I thought for sure Mrs Wishart wouldnae start her pains for anither week but I was scarce down frae the diligence when her husband met me wi the news that she'd been in labour many hours. I rushed in here, dumped ma packages, grabbed ma bag and hirpled up yon hill faster that I ever went . . . and arrived no a moment too soon!

"It was terrible. She'd half the women in the parish there . . . a' except Mrs Semple who might hae done some guid. And she was fair beside hersel' wi pain and the fear that she'd lose yet anither bairn. And damn it! I'd worked that hard to reassure her everthin' was goin' to be fine this time! And now I'd scarce a moment to wash ma hands and chase oot every yin o' them, save her sister Aggie . . . when she started the maist fearsome skirling and there was the first o' her wee sons makin' his way into this vale o' tears."

"The first?"

"Aye, she had twins. And by some miracle, both alive."

"Did you know she was going to have twins?"

"I'd suspected it but I didnae want to alarm her. But . . . God! I never seen ony woman suffer as she did. And for what?" he cried bitterly. "So she can continue to satisfy Wishart's cantin' hypocritical lust and die the next time she conceives!"

"Maybe she won't. . . "

"She'd an unco close call this time. I'm no pattin' masel' on the back but . . . if I hadnae been well trained in obstetrics, I'd hae lost her. And every time there's a knock at the door when I'm tryin' to sleep, I think maybe there wis ae thing I should hae done that I forgot . . . I'd scarce done wi the aftercare and Wishart was just pouring us both a dram in celebration when Jock found me and raxed me up to Kirklands to attend to Mr Melville and the injured servants."

"Did I castrate Melville?"

"Unfortunately no. But wi a' ma stitches in his backside, he'll no be in ony mood for copulation for a while! He's a miserable coward, yon! he hollered so much, it fair unnerved me. No like yon cabin boy. How was he, by the way?"

"Not complaining."

"Guid. He'll be nane the waur. . . It was as I was leavin' Jock said yin o' the prisoners was bleedin' badly. And it came to me that you might be among them."

"You're a true friend, *mon vieux*."

"Ach . . . so now ye're goin' to Edinburgh." He emptied the last of the whisky bottle into his glass and drank.

"Finding my uncle the lawyer may be my only hope."

"So ye maun do it fast. Gang to ma auld chief, Dr Tait. He kens every yin in the town. And . . . he'll help ye as he helped me."

"How do I find him?"

"Ask at the Medical College . . . they a' ken him. He's a professor."

"Will there be a coach going to Glasgow tomorrow?"

Douglas narrowed his eyes, trying to concentrate. He was extremely drunk. "The morn's Saturday. There's nane till Monday."

"And I'd best be away from Strathblane before that."

"Aye . . . first thing in the mornin'. I'll . . . I'll mak ye up a bed."

"No, I'll find everything! You go to bed, Stewart. You're exhausted."

"Aye. And I'm sick too. The influenza, I suspect. And a terrible congestion in my bronchial tubes." He could barely articulate the words. "Ach, I hate to see ye go Paterson. Ye're ma only friend in the place! It's been terrible lonely here."

"You have Jean. Propose to her!"

"Aye . . . aye . . . maybe. Write me a letter from Edinburgh. Let me know. . . " He stumbled towards the stairs.

Picking up a candle, Walter guided him up the steep little steps and through the only open door into a small bleak room, furnished solely with a chair and a truckle bed. The doctor's suits hung on nails on the wall and his clean shirts and underclothing were piled neatly on top of a shabby trunk. The poverty of it shocked Walter.

Douglas threw himself down on the bed, slid off his breeches and pulled up the covers. He held out a hand, his eyes bleary.

"Goodbye laddie. Guid luck."

"Au revoir, mon brave. Bon courage!"

Downstairs the consulting room was warm and fuggy from pipe smoke and whisky. Walter finished his brandy, laid the flask carefully on the desk, wrapped himself in the blanket and stretched out on the couch. Then perhaps because he was used to relaxing there, he fell immediately into a deep sleep.

PART SEVEN

TO THE SARACEN'S HEAD

Cold's the wind and wet's the rain,
Saint Hugh be our good speed!
Ill is the weather that bringeth no gain,
Nor helps good hearts in need.

The Shoemakers' Holiday
Thomas Dekker

I

THE BIRDS IN THEIR dawn chorus wakened the dog who pattered downstairs and nudged Walter to let her out. As he did so, he sniffed the air and found it even chillier than the night before. Nor did Sadie linger long.

He managed to light the candle from embers in the fireplace and tiptoed into the dark kitchen premises, where there was a pot hung over the smouldering fire. The porridge was lumpy and tasteless compared to Jean's but it was warm and filling at least. And after he had a bowl of it, he looked about him and found bread, cheese and oranges.

He helped himself to some of each for the journey, then washed in a bowl of icy water, wishing he knew where the doctor kept his razors. There was no sign of toilet articles downstairs and he did not want to disturb his friend whose heavy snores emanated rhythmically from the bedroom.

After he had added the food to the other contents in the valise, he folded the blanket tidily on the couch and looked around to be sure he had forgotten nothing. It was another wrenching moment. Seeing the papers and quills scattered across the desk, he sat down and after a moment's thought he wrote,

> *Take care of yourself and of J.*
> *I'll write from Edinburgh.*

Then he sat pen in hand, remembering another piece of unfinished business. He did not know how to broach the subject, believing he had kept it a secret. But now he had to send some message to Primrose and he must do it in a way that would not compromise her with her brother. Surely the doctor with Jock's help could get a word to her. He added to the note,

> *Tell P M I'll always love her and I'll come back*
> *and marry her as soon as I can.*

Stewart might be surprised but surely he would understand. Walter blotted the writing and folded the paper over the last phrase. Then impulsively he unhooked one of his gold timepieces from his watch chain and laid it on the note in the centre of the desk adding,

> *From your always grateful patient.*

Then before emotion could gain the upper hand again, he donned his topcoat and picked up the valise, wishing he had asked for the loan of some gloves. He could keep one hand in his pocket but the other would soon feel cold.

From the dimness of the sky, he guessed it was still early. Nor were there any sounds of activity from the adjacent farms.

He headed briskly up the Glasgow road but could not maintain a steady pace for he had to pick his way over a stony track glistening with frost. Fording a small ice-edged burn in one gulley, he slipped and water seeped into his boots. He passed several lochs – one as he remembered known as the Deil's Craig – then found himself on empty moorland. His walks had always taken him in the opposite direction but he knew approximately where he was. He was approaching the village of Mugdock. And since he had learned in the past six months that any stranger attracted notice in the country, he left the road to avoid passing houses. There was no sense in advertising his route should Moncrieff's men come after him.

But his progress across the fields was not easy, nor was it simple to keep his bearings in the dim light of a winter dawn. After passing what he presumed was Mugdock Castle, he found himself going down an escarpment that he did not remember from his previous trip to Glasgow. The road also took a sharp bend – he was going the wrong way. Probably he would eventually reach the city but it would be better to keep to familiar topography.

Retracing his steps for about a quarter of a mile, he came on a crossing he had missed earlier. A road turned left, running parallel with the Campsie Fells, whose solid mass he could now distinguish on the opposite side of the valley.

Visibility was bad, the world around him a study in greys and blacks and he had become enough of a countryman to know a storm was brewing, probably snow. He had to keep changing the valise from one hand to the other to keep the circulation flowing in his fingers. And his boots squelched. Though walking usually raised his spirits and started his ideas flowing, now he could not suppress unhappy thoughts. He was a wanted man, alone in an unfamiliar country. He had left behind the only friends he had – one of them he feared, in bad physical shape. Who ministered to a sick doctor, he wondered?

There were practical problems too. If he could reach Mrs Graham's bank before the news of his being a fugitive reached Glasgow, he could change his French money. But as Douglas had reminded him, the Sabbath was approaching and he did not know whether the financial houses were open on a Saturday.

He had heard that there was a diligence that ran daily to the city from a town called Milngavie but he had no idea where it was or how to reach it. It was probably safer in any case, to keep moving. If the Laird sent out a search party, he had a good start and would certainly hear the sound of horses' hooves in time to duck down behind a dyke or drop out of sight into a ditch.

So he kept on walking, nibbling on the cheese and Jean's bannock. If he had listened to Primrose, he reflected wryly, he would have been in Glasgow by now, spirited away there in Mrs Graham's comfortable carriage. But he did not regret having stayed and thrown in his luck or lack of it with Abernethy.

Soon he came on a stretch of road that he recognised. It was a brae that was far less steep than the Mugdock one and he remembered it because Mrs Graham had told him it was called Craigmaddie and well-known to travellers, as it was where the weather often changed. Strathblane was within the radius of the Loch Lomond showers, hence its dampness. But the valley he was now approaching had the same climate as Glasgow. This boded ill because sleety snow was starting to fall and when he had skittered down the icy road, he was not reassured to find another intersection with two equally well-developed tracks disappearing in opposite directions.

With a vague recollection of the Graham carriage having made a left turn, Walter went that way and soon came on a cluster of cottages with several larger houses standing in their own grounds. In hopes of finding an inn, he traversed the full length of the little village, meeting no one in the unpleasant weather. He must ask directions and felt that the home of some well-to-do person, who might travel regularly to Glasgow, might be better to approach than a cottage. He was also attracted to a pretty grey stone house set back from the road close to an old graveyard where it looked as if a new church was in the process of being built.

Walter paused, set down his valise and did his best to civilise his appearance, slipping the plaid off his shoulder and folding it over one arm. He straightened his hat and cravat and not for the first time, thanked God for the late Mr

Graham's respectable though by now well-worn clothes.

As he was opening the gate, a full-throated pleasant voice boomed,

"Good morning, young sir."

A tall elderly man in clerical black and wearing an old-fashioned bob wig, stood in his path.

"Were you looking for the manse?" he inquired civilly.

"I was looking for someone who might direct me to Glasgow, sir. I have lost my bearings."

"Are you on foot or on horseback?" the stranger asked.

"On foot."

"Well, you're a fair distance from the city but you're on the right road." He held out his hand and Walter shook it. "I am David Haddow, the minister here in Baldernock and always glad to be of help to travellers. You look half frozen. Have you had breakfast?"

"Thank you. I have some food . . . cheese, bread."

"Not too sustaining in this weather. My wife and I are about to sit down to a plate of soup. Will you join us?"

"Thank you, that is most kind, sir. But . . . perhaps I had better press on. The snow . . . "

"The snow is all the more reason for you to have some hot food in your belly."

"Sir," Walter swallowed . . . "I should tell you first that I am a fugitive from justice. I do not want to involve any innocent household in my troubles."

Shrewd humorous blue eyes bored into him.

"Would you be that dangerous Frenchman who escaped from Kirklands House last night? I see from your face that you are."

"I am neither dangerous nor a Frenchman but . . . yes . . . "

"Ah well. There's no need to look so surprised. News travels fast in the country. One of Mr Moncrieff's servants was here not an hour ago searching for you. He has now galloped off to Milngavie and will then most likely turn and go home by way of Mugdock. So you are quite safe." He took Walter's arm. "The church has traditionally offered sanctuary, has it not? Our kirk here is being rebuilt but the manse can offer you asylum. You don't look like one of Captain Abernethy's men," he added raising a bushy eyebrow.

"I'm not. But . . . I was living at a place where . . . how much have you heard, sir?"

"I heard that a poor old farmer who had made a little extra money housing Abernethy's supplies was killed in a raid by the Exciseman. I do not condone smuggling you understand, but I have sympathy with those who do not care to pay the exorbitant duties imposed on us from London. And I know Captain Abernethy. He is in many respects a worthy man." They were now walking up the path to the house. "You'll be quite safe here, young sir. I'll warn the servant to say nothing of your presence if she goes down to the village."

"You are so kind. I . . . don't know what to say."

"Then say nothing . . . except tell me your name."

"My name is Paterson. Walter Paterson. I grew up in France but my family are Scots."

"Kirsty!" called Mr Haddow. "We have a visitor. Set another place at the table and come here and meet him."

A pretty woman with greying hair and a youthful pink and white complexion scurried into the hall. As she whisked off an apron, she bobbed a curtsy.

"This, my dear, is Mr Paterson. My wife Christine, sir."

Walter treated her to his best continental bow and kissed the hastily dried hand she extended.

"La, sir. You are most gallant!" she giggled. "But you're frozen. Come to the fire."

The minister invited Walter to change his wet things

and nothing loathe, he perched on a hall chair and eased his chilled feet out of his footwear. There were several pairs of muddy boots on a mat by the front door. Walter added his sopping ones to the collection, changed his socks, removed his topcoat and pattered into the minister's study feeling very strange.

"I think a little brandy would be in order," said Mr Haddow as he took a bottle from a cabinet and filled a glass. "Here, Mr Paterson."

The aroma and smooth taste were familiar.

"There's a fire in the dining room," he continued, "for we like to warm the house before the Sabbath."

The broth was excellent and Walter shamelessly consumed several platefuls of it, for it was the best food he had tasted since leaving the farm. Mr Haddow tactfully kept up a stream of small talk that called for no response. It was mostly about the weather, now perceptibly worsening with snow coming down so fast it covered the window panes.

"We're in for a storm, Mr Paterson. I think you had best abandon your plans to walk to Glasgow this day. I doubt if this fall will lie long but tomorrow is Sunday when no good Christian should be travelling. So resign yourself to staying here with us until the beginning of the week."

"You are most generous, sir . . . *Madame*. Thank you."

"Our hospitality may not be quite what you are accustomed to for I perceive you are a man of breeding."

"Sir, I have been living at a farm in comfort but in less handsome surroundings than here. You have a beautiful home, *Madame*." As he ate, he had been admiring a walnut tallboy. The dining table was of the same fine wood as were the chairs and the curtains and covers were in floral pastels. The silverware was heavy and glistening, the china good modern Wedgewood. Mr Haddow, Walter reflected, must have some private means besides his church stipend.

"You see Kirsty, my dear? Your efforts to spruce up my old manse are being appreciated! We are not long married, Mr Paterson. I was a widower for many years but now . . . " He smiled fondly at his wife. As they rose from the table Mrs Haddow said,

"Let me show you to your room, Mr Paterson. It will not yet be warmed up for Jessie just lit the fire. But you might like to unpack your portmanteau."

"Would it be an imposition *Madame*, to ask you for some hot water? And . . . if your husband could lend me a razor? I feel so unkempt."

"Of course . . . of course."

The couple bustled around him, showing him to an airy room with a massive four-poster bed. A strapping housemaid brought him up a big pitcher of hot water and a basin then left him to shave, clean himself up and change into his other shirt.

Feeling considerably better, Walter returned downstairs where the minister was dosing over a book and Mrs Haddow was stitching on a pile of colourful cotton.

"Now, sit down and tell us about yourself, young Paterson. There is something familiar about you. Have we met before?"

"I doubt it sir, unless you have been in Strathblane kirk."

"I do occasionally exchange pulpits with Mr Gardner, but have not done so recently. And somehow it is not in that context that I see you. Why did Moncrieff's man describe you as a Frenchman?"

"I grew up in France."

"Well, I've been to Paris but not for many a long year. And now the whole of society there is in a state of flux. Is the city itself much changed?"

"That would be hard for me to judge, sir. I wasn't there

during the changes of government. I was off in Rome and Hanover and such places, on a Grand Tour. But yes, you would certainly find the atmosphere very different."

"Invigorating I would imagine."

That, Walter reflected, was what Primrose had said when they first met.

"It is not invigorating to everyone, sir. It is . . . terrifying. In the name of liberty, there is a worse tyranny than ever before. With men unused to power at the helm, you can never tell what may happen next."

"Then you are not in sympathy with the Revolution?"

"No! I admit there was a need for change . . . for many changes but surely there is a difference between representative government and mob rule."

"Have you read Burke? He remarks, and I think I am quoting correctly, that 'whenever there is separation between liberty and justice, neither is safe.' Are you any relation to Adam Paterson who went out in '45?"

"My father's name is Adam!"

"It must be the same man for you look just like him! Now that you have freshened your appearance, I see the resemblance clearly. He was big, handsome, fairhaired, with blue eyes like your own. Is he still alive?"

"He was in September." He wondered if it would be discreet to mention Captain Abernethy. "I'm told that he is trying to leave France. How did you know him, sir?"

"We were young blades around the town together when we were attending the University in Edinburgh. He was studying law. Does he still practise?"

"No. There was no demand for the Scottish variety in Paris, so he went into commerce and banking."

"What a tragedy! He could have had a distinguished career at the bar if it hadn't been for that misbegotten Prince Charlie."

"He wanted to make a lawyer out of me, too."

"And from your tone of voice, I fancy you have other ideas. Well it's your life young man, and far be it that I should come between you and your family. But there's ower much wasted talent in Scotland these days because of what the older generation wants." He sighed. "But perhaps you'll not have been brought up in such a confining atmosphere as we have here. . . Did you have a sister they named Clementina after the Old Pretender's wife?"

"Yes!"

"Ah, it's a small world, is it not?"

"Do you know my relatives in Edinburgh, Mr Haddow?"

"You mean your uncle, the advocate? It's been some years since we met, not since I was at a General Assembly in 1790."

"Do you know where he lives? Is it in the Lawnmarket or the Grassmarket?"

"Neither, he has moved to a fine new house in the New Town. But you'll find him any day at the Parliament House."

Relief flooded through Walter. He smiled, a little misty-eyed at his host and hostess.

"So now I know where I'm going."

"You didn't before?"

He shook his head. "To tell the truth – I didn't want to leave Strathblane. I was very happy there and made good friends."

"You'd have a lassie, I don't doubt."

"Yes."

"Did you ever think of settling down there?"

"Yes! Yes, indeed! I prefer the country life to cities, although. . . " He looked around the bookshelves. "I perceive you are a scholar. Do you not find it very solitary in the country?"

"Studies are by nature solitary, Mr Paterson. I lead a

busy life as the minister here, and although many of my parishioners do not share my education, they are thinkers and philosophers in their own way, and great debaters! I do not lack for intellectual stimulus, I assure you. Not these days with newspapers like *The Advertiser* making people aware of the issues at stake."

"No, I don't suppose so. And I imagine you go to Glasgow frequently?"

"As little as I can. It's becoming such a big, bustling city, with all this overseas trade on the Clyde. Have you been there?"

"Yes. Once with my employer."

"Ah! You were working?"

Walter told him about Mrs Graham and Bobby, and from there they progressed to more talk of France and his departure from his home. Mr Haddow was well up on the latest news, and pointing to a pile of newspapers by the hearth, he told Walter he could read them the next day while the household were at church.

"I do not think it would be advisable for you to show yourself at the service, Mr Paterson. People would be curious as to whom you might be and word travels, as you know. On Monday I'll direct you to the Old Roman Road that now leads into the centre of Glasgow. The snow should be no hindrance by then. Although," he added with a smile, "it could make travel difficult from Strathblane, where undoubtedly it has been much heavier. Are we going to have tea, my dear?"

Mrs Haddow laid down her sewing and left the room. Once she was out of earshot, the minister said softly,

"I see you think highly of Strathblane's new physician, Mr Paterson. You mentioned his skill several times. Do you think he would come here and prescribe for Kirsty? I'm worried about her chest."

"It's quite a long way and he has no horse."

"He could come on the diligence and I would be glad to drive him home in my trap. And I'm prepared to pay him well. She is my second wife, Mr Paterson. The mother of my seven children died two years ago and left me inconsolable, until Kirsty came into my life. She is not strong and gets bad coughs each winter that linger on. But I hesitate to put her through lengthy examinations in Glasgow by physicians whom I know little about. You are not the first to speak well of this Dr Stewart and he attends the Laird of Kirklands, does he not?" Walter nodded. "Well, Mr Moncrieff can afford the best. He used to go to Glasgow for his medical advice when they had that old man MacKelvie who died."

"You know a lot about Strathblane, sir."

"In certain ways. In others, not at all. Communication is a very uncertain process, even in these days of improved transport. I hear for instance, that this Dr Stewart is not at all orthodox in his methods of treatment, but that they are nonetheless extremely effective."

"That is so, sir. And . . . your wife will like him."

"Then, I'll send him a letter and ask him to arrange a visit once the weather improves. Sssssh!" he cautioned, for the door was opening, and Mrs Haddow and the maid were bringing in the tea trolley.

"Jessie's washed your clothes, Mr Paterson," the minister's wife announced. "and she'll iron them the night if they're dry. And I'll mend that tear in yer shirt for ye. We cannae do these things on the Sabbath but today is young yet."

"You overwhelm me with your kindness, *Madame*."

She dimpled. "It's just . . . the Scottish hospitality, sir. . . "

Later in the day, they had another meal, with some good red wine which, Walter suspected, also came from

Abernethy. They went off to bed early, for the minister had to be up in good time on Sunday. But Walter found a fire in his bedroom grate, a stock of candles and some books set out beside the four-poster. With its feather bolsters and soft matress, it was far more comfortable than the box-bed at Puddock Hole. But although the wine lulled him into quick slumber, he wakened up in the small hours and lay sleepless until dawn was beginning to break.

Then he dropped off and when he woke in mid-morning, the household were in church. However there was washing water in a canister, the fire was banked, and on the bedside table he found a plate of scones and a glass of milk.

Outside the snow lay thickly on the ground, but a faint sun was thawing it and the driveway was already clear. Walter was not especially religious but he looked around the house for a crucifix or some other sign of devotion. He found none but in the minister's study he went down on his knees and thanked God for his good fortune and safety. It seemed appropriate in the manse.

II

Back in Strathblane, later in the morning of Walter's departure, Douglas Stewart was dragged out of his sick heavy slumber by his housekeeper's voice.

"Doctor! Wake up! There's folks downstairs, Mr Campbell and Mr Wishart."

"Wishart . . . Wishart . . . " He shot up in bed as if a nerve had been touched. "Oh, God in heaven . . . what now? Tell him I'll be there immediately." He stumbled out of bed reaching for clean clothing, scarce able to breathe for the congestion in his chest. He could only hope it would loosen as he moved around. He clattered downstairs tying his cravat as he went, pushed past the two elders standing woodenly by his desk and reached for his bag.

"What's the matter, Mr Wishart? Has she fever?"

"Naw doctor. Nae fever. . . "

"Thank God for that." Forcing his exhausted mind into action he asked, "Is she bleeding?"

"Naw. . . "

"Then . . . is it one of the bairns?"

"It's no the Wishart family we're here concerning," barked Mr Campbell. "It's yersel' we're needin' to interrogate."

Douglas stopped in his tracks then snapped the bag shut and slumped down into his chair, glowering.

Campbell bristled with importance. But Wishart, looking embarrassed, was studying the floor.

"Yon Frenchie . . . Paterson . . . escaped oot o' Kirklands Hoose last night. Is he here?" demanded the Exciseman.

So that was it. He let the silence draw out while his foggy brain groped for the best approach. Righteous indignation would be better than anger and less physically taxing. When he spoke eventually his voice was at its deepest.

"Ye wakened me oot o' the first guid sleep I've had in forty-eight hours to ask me a damn fool question like that?"

"It isnae a damn fool question, doctor!" retorted Campbell. "You and he were far ben."

"He was a patient o' mine."

"Aye . . . and after that. Whaur is he?"

"I dinnae ken," said Douglas truthfully.

"I dinnae believe ye!"

"Do you accuse me o' lying, Mr Campbell?"

"I do. We are here on the Laird's orders."

"I'll tak that up wi the Laird in due course. Meanwhile what d'ye want? To search ma house? Ye'll no find onything."

"Was he here last night?"

Mrs MacGregor, who had been hovering in the doorway, stepped forward.

"There was naebody here last night." She ambled up to the desk, straightened the inkwell and made as if to dust off various small objects with the corner of her apron.

"Ye could hae been asleep when he came," Campbell snorted.

"Aye, but I'd hae heard the doggie barkin' if ony yin had come tae the door."

"Was the doctor hame?"

"Aye. A' evening."

What he had been doing was all too obvious. At least there was only one glass in evidence and Douglas noted with relief that Walter had smoothed out the couch and folded the blanket.

"Ye'll swear to all ye're sayin', woman?"

She bunched up her apron, regarding him with her usual massive placidity.

"I can swear wi the truth that I hae seen naebody, Mr Campbell." Douglas started to cough and she turned towards him solicitously. "I'll fetch ye a glass o' water, doctor."

"He'd maybe do better wi a hair o' the dog," snarled the Exciseman. Wishart made a move to speak then shut his mouth. The doctor gasped for breath and when she came back with a tumbler of water, he gulped it down.

For what seemed like some minutes, his wheezing was the only sound in the room. Then with his respiratory passages cleared he lashed out.

"Verra weel! Why d'ye wait? Search ma hoose, damn ye! Search everywhere! And tell the Laird ye've done as much. Much guid may it do ye!"

Campbell looked smug. "Fine," he said. He turned towards the big doors of the corner cupboard, large enough to hide a man and pulled them open. The skeleton swung out, its bones rattling. Thoroughly startled, he stepped back involuntarily.

Douglas smiled.

"Would ye like to see ma ither anatomical specimens, gentlemen? In that box . . . down below the microscope there's a bairn wi twa heids. It was stillborn and I preserved it in spirits as a curiosity." He caught his housekeeper's eye and was again overcome by coughing.

Wishart paled. Campbell slammed the cupboard door and surveyed the rest of the room, his eyes trying to avoid the instrument cases and bottles.

"And be careful ye dinnae disturb the leeches," Douglas advised. Campbell turned his back on the medical paraphernalia and tried to compose himself.

"Mr Wishart, we maun search the upstairs rooms. They would be logical places to hide."

Mrs MacGregor made a protesting movement.

"Whit's wrang, woman? Are ye feared we'll catch him up there?"

"Naw, for he isnae there. But I dinnae care to hae strangers stravaigin' through a house that hasnae been redd up for the day. The doctor's bed's no made."

"It's no the condition o' the beds," retorted Campbell, "it's wha might hae slept in them last night that interests us."

"Alas, sir," Douglas croaked. "I must disappoint you. I lead perforce, a celibate life since the barter system in Strathblane doesnae extend to amorous favours and I dinnae hae enough siller for whores."

"There's nae call for impudence wi me, young man!" snorted Campbell, clearly affronted as he headed for the hall.

To Douglas's surprise, Mr Wishart moved even faster and barred the Exciseman's way to the stairs.

"It'll no do to be officious, Mr Campbell. The Laird telt us to use oor discretion. For ma ain part, I'll tak Dr Stewart at his word that there's naebody hidin' up there."

The big man stopped in his tracks and Douglas, now fully awake, became aware of a subtle change in the balance of power between the two men. The final authority had passed to Mr Wishart.

Campbell, blustering, fell back on a show of efficiency.

"Then if we're finished here, we maun be on our way. We cannae let the grass grow under oor feet." He started to wrestle with the front door.

"I thank ye, Mr Wishart," said Douglas, "Yer confidence in me isnae misplaced."

"I ken that, doctor. And . . . ma apologies for disturbin' yer well-earned rest. Ye maun be weary." He lingered as if to keep contact but didn't know what else to say.

"How is your wife this morn?" Douglas asked, to ease the embarrassment.

A great toothless smile spread over Wishart's wizened face.

"Fine. She's that happy wi the bairns! She was feedin' them at the breast when I left home. A bonnie sight and yin that I never expected to see." There were tears in his eyes.

"Did you find that wet nurse I recommended . . . the little Irish girl? . . . in case her milk dries up."

"I did. But so far so good."

"Be sure she has plenty o' rest. She had a bad time."

When a quick glance showed that Campbell was now out of earshot, Wishart still on the doorstep, lowered his voice and said,

"I'll send doon here wi anither bottle o' whisky for ye. And . . . meantimes . . . " he jerked his head towards his fellow member of the Session, "ye maun excuse him. He's a wee bittie upset. The Laird was unco angered about . . . MacDougal."

"And so he should be."

"Campbell's feared he'll lose his occupation."

"The Laird cannae send him away. Excisemen are appointed by the Crown."

"Aye, but Mr Moncrieff has influential friends. Like Mr Henry Dundas. He visited him once here in Strathblane."

Douglas was impressed. "Did he now?"

"Aye. And Mr Dundas is the maist powerful man in Scotland, is he no?"

"That's what they said in Edinburgh."

Watching Wishart and Campbell depart, from the window, Mrs MacGregor commented amiably,

"I'm fair ashamed o' ye, doctor. I hae a bone to pick wi ye." She held out her hand. In it lay Walter's gold watch, the initials 'W J P' plainly engraved on the case.

"Hell and damnation! Whaur was that?"

"Lyin' on yer desk, plain as a pikestaff. If I hadnae picked it up. . . And a paper too wi his writing on it." She shuffled through a pile of loose pages and handed one to him.

"*Tell P M*," he read aloud, "*that I'll always love her and I'll come back to marry her as soon as I can.*" He frowned. "Who's P M?"

The housekeeper thought, then pronounced,

"Primrose Moncrieff."

He stared at her trying to take it in. She beamed back maternally.

"I dinnae ken what ye learned at the College o' Medicine doctor, but it couldnae hae been common sense. A handsome braw laddie like Mr Paterson and such a bonnie young lady!"

III

"Tak that damned boiled mutton away, "he growled at her later in the day when after his morning rounds, she set a big plate of greasy food before him. "Dinnae serve it up to me again. Gie it to ma dog."

"Shoemaker's bairns are aye the worst shod. Ye've ta'en nae solid food for the last twa days. If ye dinnae eat, ye'll be sick."

"Then bring me an orange."

As he peeled the fruit neatly and sucked the segment, she muttered,

"Ain night withoot ony rest and anither as drunk as a Lord o' Session and nae proper nourishment. . ."

"Mak me more coffee and put milk in it. And be quiet! Ma head's fit tae burst withoot yer clatterings! And I beg yer pardon for ma ill humour, Mrs MacGregor." The tart juice was burning his raw throat. He left the table and she followed him through to the consulting room.

"Ye could never haud yer liquor. . ."

"Haud ma liquor! Woman, can ye no see I'm a sick man! I've been sickenin' these last twa days. I must hae caught it in Glasgow."

"And what's the matter wi ye?"

"Influenza. A full blown case. Ma limbs hurt, ma head's poundin' so hard I can scarcely think. And I know it's not from the whisky either. I've a fever too." He pushed back his shock of hair. "I've seen a'body in the Parish that really needs me and now I'm going' to do what I've been tellin' ma patients . . . go to bed and try and sweat it out. Heat some bricks and mak me a guid strong toddy wi plenty o' lemon juice, if ye please."

"Aye, I'll do that for ye, doctor. And . . . I'm sorry."

There was a loud knock on the front door.

"Oh no. . . " he groaned. "Ask if it can wait till tomorrow. And shut this door."

But she came back agog with excitement.

"That was Mamie from Kirklands! It's urgent she said."

"Kirklands? Why? The two servants were much better. Forbye Jock's doing their dressings. I just bled the Laird last week and left him wi a whole Pharmacopia o' pills for his stomach. . . "

"It's no the Laird, it's his sister! She never sent for ye afore!"

"Naw, she was sick when I first came here and they brought out some quack from Glasgow to treat her." He slumped down at his desk. "Aw, Mrs MacGregor! The very thought o' that Boards Road makes ma leg ache. And it's goin' to snow. I can feel it in the air. What do they think I am?" he protested. "A servant who's at their beck and call? I'm still angry about that intrusion this morning."

"Doctor! That wasnae the young lady's fault! Mamie said she's been lying in her bed cryin' her eyes out these last twa days and the Laird's fair beside himself about her." She went on quickly, "I've got yer guid suit all pressed for the kirk the morn and a clean shirt. And I've water heatin'. Ye aye feel better when ye've had a nice wash. Ye need a shave too." She patted his shoulder. "And I'll hae yer bed warmed up for yer return. It'll no tak long and the snow hasnae started yet. Doctor, ye ken well yersel', Kirklands is yin place ye maun go when they ask ye."

He nodded, ruefully.

He did feel more like himself once he'd cleaned up and changed into his good clothes. When he came back downstairs, she had his coffee ready and he used it to wash down a couple of pills.

"Ye're a guid auld wife, Mrs MacGregor. I apologise for ventin' ma temper on ye."

She sighed. "We a' find it hard, here in the country."

"Ye dinnae like Strathblane?"

"It's ower quiet, after Edinburgh. But I promised Dr Tait that I'd bide wi ye as lang as ye needed me, and I will."

A thought Walter had planted the night before came into his head. Her wages were pitifully small. Even so, if he didn't have to pay them, he would have a little more ready cash. He quoted meditatively, *"That which hath made them drunk hath made me bold.* Maybe I'll mak another call when I'm up the Boards Road." Trying to use his anger to stimulate energy for the trip, he continued, "If I didnae mak masel' so available, the Laird would hae sent for Dr Ogilvy frae Killearn. It would tak him half a day to get here and he'd charge accordingly. Mr Moncrieff's goin' to get a piece o' ma mind about this mornin'."

Rummaging in his desk drawer, he unearthed a small piece of metal and put it in his waistcoat pocket. Then impulsively, he unhitched his big plain watch from its chain and substituted Walter's elegant gold one.

"Doctor, ye shouldnae do that, it's tempting Providence!"

"Why not? He smiled at her boldly. "Wish me luck, Mrs MacGregor."

"You can tell my brother," Primrose told Mamie in a firm voice, "that Dr Stewart will see him on his way out. Meanwhile, we are to be left alone. Sit down, please, sir."

Douglas, his mind foggy, found the bedroom pleasantly dark. He could scarcely see his patient in her enormous four-poster bed.

"I hope I came promptly enough, Miss Moncrieff."

"Oh, there was no hurry. I trust I didn't bring you too

far out of your way?"

"No place is out of my way if I'm needed," said Douglas, setting up his sand-glass on the bedside table. He had never met her, except briefly after church. So as he took her pulse, he make a covert survey. Her eyes were tearstained, the lids puffy and red, and her long fair hair hung unattended around her face. Over a voluminous cotton nightgown, she had a heavy woollen shawl that was more functional than attractive.

Pretty, he noted. Very pretty. Not at all robust and with something so heavy on her mind that she doesn't care how she looks.

"What did you wish to consult me about, Miss Moncrieff?"

She hesitated.

"I haven't been sleeping at all well. . . "

"For some time?"

"The last three nights." She went on in a nervous rush. "I usually sleep so soundly, it worried me. It was so strange."

"Occasional insomnia is nothing to worry about. This has been an upsetting time here in Strathblane. No wonder you were wakeful." He gave her his most reassuring smile. She might be the lady of the manor but she was still a woman. "Had you any other symptoms?"

She shook her head. Dr Tait had always told his students that the most effective way to discourage malingerers was to call their bluff, take them seriously, give them a full examination, then suggest some unpleasant treatment. She had dragged Douglas up a long hill in bad weather and he wasn't about to let her off easily.

"Well, let's see what we can find." He opened his bag, and tucked back his white cuffs, drawing attention to his fine hands.

"Oh, no, I . . . "

"Open your mouth. Wider, if you please. I want to see your throat first. There's a lot of influenza about."

"I've . . . I've had the influenza."

"Then you know it's not a disease to be taken lightly."

There was nothing wrong with her throat and she gagged so mightily he thought she would vomit. When he sounded her chest through the nightgown, he wished heartily that his own was as clear. Mrs MacGregor should see me now, he thought – beside manner, Edinburgh accent and not an idea in my head.

"Have you had any gastric disturbances in these past few days, Miss Moncrieff? Any indigestion? Or nausea perhaps?"

She answered tartly. "No, I have a better stomach than my brother."

No morning sickness, then. "Have you . . . er . . . had any female irregularities?"

"No." She gave him a quizzical little smile.

But there wasn't any doubt about her being in a state of extreme tension. The devil take these gently nurtured females, he ruminated. Why can't they bring their problems out into the open? "Do you have any unusual swelling or lumps? On your breast for example?" She shook her head. "And you have no sign of fever at present, but was there any last night or this morning?" Again she indicated there were none. He decided to try the direct approach.

"Miss Moncrieff, I can find nothing wrong with you. But since you cannot sleep, there must be something on your mind. It might relieve you to talk about it." She was silent, avoiding his eyes. "And whatever you tell me is of course, in the strictest professional confidence. I mean . . . I'm not about to tell your brother."

He sat back in the bedside chair and waited.

Her fingers twisted the fringe of the ugly shawl.

"I . . . I . . . Would you like a dish of tea, doctor?"

"If you would like to have one with me."

She stretched out her hand for a bell on the table and as she did so, the nightgown's long sleeve fell back. Her hand and arm was badly scratched and bruised.

"Miss Moncrieff! You have injured yourself!"

"No. It's nothing." She tried to cover herself again but Douglas, thankful for something tangible, had a firm grip on her wrist.

"The skin is broken. You need a dressing."

"No. My brother would notice. It's . . . much better. It . . . "

"Let me at least clean these cuts up and put some healing salve on them." He was groping in his bag with his free hand. "How did you come to scrape yourself like that?"

"I fell. On the Boards Road. It was at night and I tripped."

"And what were you doing out there after dark, my fair lady?" he thought.

"You should take that heavy ring off your finger. It's grazing your palm."

"No!" she said defiantly, coming to life.

"Then wear it on your other hand for a few days."

Suddenly she held it out, as if for his inspection. "Do you not recognise this ring, doctor?" she asked breathlessly. "You must have seen it."

He had, and it was a man's. But beyond that his mind was blank. He cursed the pills he had taken before leaving home. They had done nothing for his headache, simply made him stupid. This was a fine way for a former instructor at the Edinburgh Medical School to behave. But even as he castigated himself, an impression clicked methodically into place and in his mind's eye he saw the ring on Walter Paterson's short, scholarly fingers.

Tell P.M . . .

Deliberately he drew the watch from his waistcoat pocket, held it up so she could see the crest which matched her ring.

She was sitting up in bed. "Where is he? I thought you would know if anyone did! He must have come to you!"

"Are we talking about the gentleman you had driven home from my house in your carriage?"

"Yes! Yes! Walter Paterson. Oh, Dr Stewart! Is he safe?"

"He's safely away from Strathblane."

"Where is he?"

"Quite honestly, I don't know. In Glasgow maybe by now. I doubt if the stage-coach to Edinburgh leaves on a Saturday, so he'll have to bide there till the beginning of the week."

She sighed with relief, then her eyes clouded again. "Did he . . . did he have any money? He is so impractical."

"He stopped by the farm and collected some after he escaped from here. He took some clothing too."

"When did you see him?"

"Late last night. And don't be telling *that* to your brother, if you please. He sent men to search my house this morning.

"Oh. Oh. Henry is so . . . so unreasonable about anyone connected with France. Mr Paterson and I are secretly betrothed," she announced with a small, tearful smile. "My brother doesn't know. . . "

Many small unconnected incidents that had previously puzzled him fell into place. He took her hand.

"I suspected there was someone. But I never guessed who it was. Your first name is Primrose, is it not?" She nodded. "He slept at my house, left early before I was up. But he left a message on my desk. He wrote, *Tell P.M. I love her and I'll come back to marry her as soon as I can."*

It was probably good for her to cry.

"And . . . and he had a warm plaid and topcoat. He's in good condition, Miss Moncrieff. He's used to walking and it's but twelve miles to the city. Here! Where's the bell? I'll have Mamie bring you some tea."

"No, I don't want any." She was dabbing her eyes with a lacy handkerchief. "They . . . they didn't hurt him, did they?"

Douglas laughed. "No. The boot was on the other foot. Have you seen Geordie's black eye? I think it did Paterson good to find he could defend himself so well."

"He . . . he was going to Edinburgh, he said?"

"Yes. He's on his way." Now he understood why his patient had procrastinated so long.

"Doctor, will you tell my brother I have to go there too? That I need a change? That I should go and visit my sister?"

"Willingly."

"But . . . how will I find him?"

"It's not a big town. Go to my old chief Dr Tait, at the University. I told Paterson to get in touch with him."

"Then write his address down for me, please." She motioned him toward a little writing desk. Douglas, while his back was turned, took the chance to cough up some phlegm. Now that the situation was under control, he was again aware of his own condition. The headache was worse than ever and so was the congestion in his bronchial tubes.

Primrose was chattering happily about Walter and herself. "You musn't breath a word to Henry, he's so ridiculously suspicious. We met on the Boards Road. And . . . we fell in love, almost at first sight."

His thoughts wandered hazily back over the case. "So that's why he rose from his bed so fast and went out. I thought I'd pulled him round unco' quickly but maybe the credit should be yours."

"Oh no, Dr Stewart! You were wonderful to him! Won't you stay and have a cup of tea with me? Or . . . is there something else you would prefer?"

She was beaming at him now – a lovely girl – and for a second he was acutely envious of his friend. "Miss Moncrieff, I would like to be the first to wish you and Paterson joy."

"Oh thank you. And thank you for coming to see me. I wouldn't have asked you in such bad weather but . . . I was desperate."

"I understand. And since your brother will want to know if I've given you any medicine, I'm leaving you a sleeping draft." He found a tumbler, measured some liquid from one of his bottles. "Take that in milk, at night."

"I don't need it now!"

"You do, Miss Moncrieff. You've been upset. And now you're all excited." He smiled at her. "I'll tell the Laird you need a change of air."

"Oh." A worried little frown creased her pretty forehead. "What will you tell Henry? He's been so upset about me, he's been bothering me to find out what's wrong. . . "

Douglas, now on his feet, looked down at her, cogitated for a minute, then said solemnly,

"Since you are so much in love Miss Moncrieff, it would be entirely correct for me to tell your brother you are suffering from a disorder of the nerves."

Her face lit up impishly. "Yes, of course! And that means, I suppose, that I can stay in my bed . . . or at least in my room . . . for as long as I like?"

"Certainly, if it makes you feel better."

"I don't want to see Edward. Mr Melville. Henry wants to make a match between us."

God forbid, thought Douglas. "Miss Moncrieff, I'm prescribing rest and quietness for you."

"But . . . I'd like to see Mrs Graham . . . Alison. She knows all about us."

"I'll suggest to your brother that she spend a few days here with you at Kirklands." That might give the Laird matrimonial ideas too.

"You're so understanding, Dr Stewart. Thank you again for coming to see me. And if you hear from Walter . . . any word at all . . . please will you let me know at once?"

"I certainly will."

She gave a reminiscent little giggle. "And you needn't worry. I'm not pregnant by him."

"I didn't think you were, Miss Moncrieff. Your responses weren't consistent with such a diagnosis. But I had to know for sure. If you want to see me again, or if I can do anything, let Jock know and I'll come at once."

She held out her hand, composed and gracious. "And when I return from Edinburgh, you must come to dinner."

That would be social advancement indeed, though he could think of no worse punishment than sitting at a table, watching his most fractious patient, her brother, overloading his digestion.

"I thank you, Miss Moncrieff. Perhaps when my friend Paterson returns. As he will."

He bowed himself out of her room with an aplomb no Edinburgh physician could have bettered.

Jock was hovering in the corridor. "The Laird wants ye, in the library."

"Aye. But gie me a minute. . . " Douglas let loose the coughing spell that had been building up. Jock steered him into a small butler's pantry and poured him some water.

"Do ye hae that syrup ye gie the bairns wi croup?" Douglas nodded. His assistant found it in the bag and measured out a dose, remarking, "Ye should be in yer bed."

"I'm headin' in that direction."

"And what's wrang wi her little ladyship? Mamie's never seen her that upset."

Douglas remembered just in time that Jock was sweet on Primrose's maid. "She's no upset any more."

"Was she feared she was in the family way?"

"Naw. So ye can scotch any rumours. But, that's a' I'm tellin' ye. Remember ye work here, laddie. Do I look human?"

"There's a mirror behind ye."

Douglas smoothed down his unruly hair, twitched at his cravat, and pulled his waistcoat straight. "Gie me a minute to draw around me the mantle o' medical science, then show me into the library."

He was annoyed to find Edward Melville there. He was also surprised. The factory owner had been sent home and told to stay in bed but here he was, up and dressed, though with his wounded hip carefully cradled on a chair. He looked less ruddy than usual and it must have taken considerable effort for him to sit up. And whatever the topic of conversation had been between the two men, it had clearly not been happy for there was a tenseness in the room and Douglas could tell from long experience that the Laird's stomach was in turmoil.

"How is my sister? What's the matter?" Moncrieff asked. "You were with her a long time."

"You cannot hurry a diagnosis, sir. She was very nervous and distressed." He hesitated, his eyes on Melville. "Do you wish me to make my report to you now, Mr Moncrieff? There is no urgency about the illness and you may prefer to discuss it in private?"

"I am anxious to know immediately." The Laird's tone implied that the other's presence was unimportant. "Is it serious?"

"It is potentially serious. Though not at present."

"What is it? Is it curable?"

"Miss Moncrieff is suffering from a disorder of the nervous system, one that is very prevalent among young ladies. Usually it is a self-limiting condition and often of short duration. But in some instances it lasts a lifetime . . . and in that form it is usually benign." There was no use in scaring the Laird into a full-blown gastric attack. "You should have little to worry about sir, if you follow my recommendation, which is that she should have a change of scene. She tells me she has a sister in Edinburgh and if she goes there, she could also consult Professor Tait at the Medical College. I know him well. I was his assistant and I believe he could resolve her problem."

"Good God! Her condition must be serious indeed!"

"Not at present sir, but I do think you should send her to Edinburgh as soon as the weather permits."

"Certainly. I'll write to Catherine and make arrangements. But . . . I apologise for constantly repeating the question doctor, but . . . will she recover? I'm . . . very fond of my sister. . . " The Laird's voice shook.

"She'll recover sir, and quickly if you do as I suggest."

"I will indeed, doctor."

"And for the moment, she should have quiet and the company of her own sex. Perhaps Mrs Graham . . . whom she is fond of . . . could come over here for a few days to be with her?" The Laird nodded, the idea obviously appealing to him. "And once the snow has passed and the roads are sufficiently clear, Miss Moncrieff should go to Edinburgh. The diversions and stimulation of city life will improve her spirits."

"Diversion? Stimulation? For a nervous disorder?" echoed Melville incredulously.

"For this particular type, sir."

"But . . . to give up the benefit of country air? I'm not disputing your diagnosis doctor, but general health is important, is it not? Or am I wrong?"

"In this case you are," said Douglas flatly.

But instead of recognising the voice of authority, the businessman raised his eyebrows and remarked in his Anglified accent, "Oh really?"

It was enough to make any large man feel like a clodhopper.

"It depends on the nature of the nervous complaint, sir." Turning pointedly to the Laird, Douglas added, "I assure you sir, that there is little cause for alarm."

"What precipitated the illness? My sister was unwell last year but since then she has had excellent health. She goes out in all weathers, walking on the moors."

Yes indeed, thought Douglas. Taking the easiest way out to respond to the Laird he said significantly,

"Young females. . . "

"Oh, oh yes . . . " Moncrieff looked embarrassed. "I'll send her to her sister's as soon as I can. And I'll have Mrs Graham come over here."

"The recent events here in Strathblane," went on Douglas sternly, "have distressed Miss Moncrieff and exacerbated her condition."

"They have been very disturbing for all of us. Tragic indeed. I should have thanked you ere this, doctor for coming here so promptly the other night."

"It was no trouble. I was already half way here at Mr Wishart's house."

"Yes, of course. You must be extremely busy these days."

"There's a lot of sickness in the valley with the winter weather."

"Yes and now it is starting to snow, so we must not

detain you any longer."

He was being dismissed but he wasn't ready to go as yet.

"I . . . " He ran his hand through his hair and coughed, conscious of Melville's critical eye appraising his much laundered shirt and the heavy boots which detracted from the smart cut of his breeches. "I think it would be well if I saw your sister again in a few days."

"Certainly doctor, any time when you feel it is necessary."

Maybe he could bring up his complaint against Campbell when he was feeling better and had the Laird alone. With a small bow, he started toward the door.

"Just a minute, doctor," said Edward Melville.

Douglas turned on his heel. "Yes, sir?"

"While you are here, there are a few matters that we would like to clear up."

"Such as?"

The Laird looked embarrassed. "It's just a formality, doctor. Because I am a justice of the peace I must question everyone. As you have doubtless heard, one of our prisoners escaped last night and is still at liberty."

"The Frenchman who lived at the farm," finished Melville.

Douglas cleared his throat non-committally.

"You . . . er . . . don't know anything about his whereabouts, I don't suppose?" asked the Laird.

Douglas inhaled as deeply as he could. "Mr Moncrieff. I have already been interrogated on that score and in a most offensive manner. Mr Campbell, claiming he acted on your instructions, came to my house early this morning, waked me up from much needed sleep, and refused to accept my word that Mr Paterson was not with me. Only the intervention of Mr Wishart stopped his searching my every room." He forced more air into his lungs. "I am tired of Mr Campbell trying to interfere in my affairs, sir. He insults and denigrates me at every turn. And now he is claiming he has your authority to do so."

Before Moncrieff could answer, Melville spoke up.

"It was perfectly right for the Exciseman to search your house, doctor. This fellow was a patient of yours. You were probably in his confidence. And you were in touch with him while he was captive here."

Douglas was having trouble with his breathing again.

"I don't follow you, sir."

"The night of the raid. You came here to attend to me and to the Kirklands wounded. You then visited the prisoners on your own authority and without telling Mr Moncrieff."

"That was my duty as a physician. I asked if there were any more who had been hurt and was told one man was bleeding badly. I then insisted upon seeing him. Jock MacLean," he added quickly, "had nothing to do with my decision."

"So you did see this Paterson?"

"Yes, for all the prisoners were lodged together."

"And you talked with him?"

"I asked if he was hurt . . . a legitimate question . . . there was blood on his face."

"Of course," interjected the Laird, "of course."

"I cleaned up a bruise on his brow and then attended to the cabin boy's hand."

"And did Paterson tell you he planned to escape?"

"No."

"What do you know about the man?" The question came like a pistol shot and Melville was drumming on the table with his heavy fingers.

A pig, thought Douglas. That's what he looks like, one of MacDougal's pigs. And suddenly his Border blood rebelled. What right did these two men have to patronise and bully him? He was no longer the eldest son of a poverty stricken minister whose livelihood depended on the great ones of the parish. He was a member of a profession far more highly esteemed in Edinburgh than the cotton trade.

He drew himself up to his full height which he seldom did around the small-built Laird and looked down on them, noting in passing that Melville was physically uncomfortable, probably in pain.

"Gentlemen," Douglas intoned in his best lecture room style. "I have had enough. I came here on this nasty night, and sick myself, because I was sent for to attend to Miss Moncrieff. I did not come here to submit to an uncalled-for interrogation. However," he cleared his throat, "since you seek to know more about my patient Mr Walter Paterson, I'll be glad to enlighten you. He is a gentleman of good Scottish family who, through the violence of social change in Europe, has fallen on evil days. If he went over-vigorously to the defence of Mr MacDougal, it was because the family at Puddock Hole had saved his life, taking him in when he was sorely wounded. He was grateful to them and to Captain Abernethy who brought him out of France and away from the Revolutionaries and the guillotine."

"But . . . but he could be a French spy!" exclaimed the Laird. "In the interests of justice . . . "

"Justice!" echoed Douglas, "If it's justice you want to see done, here's one piece of evidence for the defence."

He plunged a hand into his pocket and drew out a small object which rattled down the table. "Since you're familiar with firearms Mr Melville, maybe you can tell me if that is a French bullet or not."

They both examined it curiously.

"Where did you get this?" asked Moncrieff.

"It came to Strathblane in Mr Paterson's shoulder. I dug it out of him. Would the French be shooting at their own spies?" He glared at the factory owner. "And fer what dae ye mean, handin' down opinions on matters ye ken sae little aboot?" His Edinburgh accent was gone and he didn't care.

"I never . . ." Melville's eyes narrowed. "You must have talked with Paterson after his escape."

"Aye. I did. He slept at ma house last night. But where he is now, I don't know, in truth. Far from Strathblane I hope. I mak nae apology for sheltering him, he was my patient and later my friend. I admire him greatly and wish him well."

A fit of coughing spoilt this peroration. It was so severe that when it abated he found both men eyeing him with various degrees of concern.

"Doctor, Mr Melville was about to leave when you arrived. He can take you home in his carriage. You go right past his house, do you not, Edward?"

Douglas drew a difficult breath. "No, thank ye, sir. It's monstrous kind of ye, but I hae anither call to make."

"I can take you wherever you wish to go," said Melville.

"It would no be appropriate. Since I was unable to be at her father's funeral, I maun call on Miss MacDougal at Puddock Hole."

Melville looked at him as though he had committed the height of social error. The Laird said quietly,

"If she needs anything doctor, I trust you will let me know."

"I will, sir." He picked up his bag. Then set it down again and drew out a bottle. "Mr Melville. Ye are at liberty to disregard ma medical advice but when ye do, ye maun tak the consequences. I telt ye to stay off that hip. Ye're a heavy man and it'll no heal if ye put weight on it."

"I had to come up here . . . on a pressing matter."

How to gloss over the murder of Angus MacDougal doubtless, thought Douglas.

"Aye. But ye're goin' to hae a nasty pain the night.

There's enough laudanum in that bottle to last ye till Monday. That's the best I can dae for ye."

"Thank you," said Melville, surprised almost into gratitude. "That is most considerate of you."

"It's masel' I'm considering. I've nae desire to be disturbed and raxed oot o' ma bed once I'm home. Goodnight, Mr Moncrieff and dinnae worry about your sister."

Usually the Laird acknowledged his leaving with a nod. But this time he got up, followed the doctor to the front door and opened it for him. After remarking on the bad state of the weather, he then offered his hand as one gentleman to another.

Douglas plodded down the drive, singing inside himself, *A man's a man for a' that. . .*

IV

At Puddock Hole, he found the parlour full of women. Jean's sister Flora from Glasgow, Mrs Semple, and several neighbours were gathered round the fire, chattering with post-funeral high spirits. There was a plateful of bannock on the table, and tea was being handed round.

"Eh, it's the doctor!" Mrs Semple greeted him, all smiles. She took his coat while he stamped the snow off his boots.

He went straight to Jean, silent in her father's chair, her face pale and tense above a tight unbecoming black dress.

"I'm sorry I wasnae able to attend the burial, Miss MacDougal."

She nodded stiffly. "Ye maun be busy these days. . . "

He took her hand. His own was cold and damp and she looked up at him in sudden concern.

"You're sick," she exclaimed softly.

"Naw," said Douglas embarrassed. They were both quivering.

"A cup o' tea, doctor? And a bit scone?" Mrs Semple was making him at home. "Ye'll hae met Mrs McLardy and ma niece Flora, Jean's sister. And Mrs Curtis. And Mrs Murray."

He bowed to the group.

"My, it was real good of ye to come sae far out o' yer way."

"It wasnae so far," he said awkwardly, accepting a cup.

"Ye'd be up at Wishart's, I suppose."

"No, there was no need."

"My, ye covered yersel' wi' glory there, doctor. Two wee boys and both o' them alive and kickin'."

"I wish you'd been there, Mrs Semple. I could hae used yer experience."

"Ach, I'm past they difficult confinements. Though they did send for me, when they found ye'd gone tae Glasgow. But I kent ye'd be back in guid time and so ye were."

"Only just . . ." He smiled at her. "Some time I'll come by yer cottage and gie ye all the gory details."

"Ach, that puir soul," sighed Mrs Curtis. "I've had five, but nane o' them twins. There isnae ony ither hoose up this way, is there doctor?"

"There's Kirklands."

Interested glances were exchanged among the local women. "Indeed, and who's sick up there?" asked one.

Jean said sharply, "The doctor never discusses his cases." She turned to him, "Hae they recaptured Walter?"

He shook his head. Holding her eyes, he drew the watch from his pocket, looked at it briefly, then put it away again. She nodded imperceptibly.

"I dinnae believe ye need to worry about him, Miss

MacDougal." Before anyone could ask another question, he inquired, "Are ye keepin' on the farm?"

She lowered her eyes. "No."

"It was grand!" exclaimed Mrs Semple. "She sold it! To the Laird!"

Douglas set down his cup so abruptly it rattled in its saucer. "And what are ye goin' to do then?"

"I'm going to live with Flora and her family in Glasgow."

For once in his life he could think of nothing to say.

"She'll be a real help wi the bairns," burbled her sister. "I've aye telt her she should come and live wi me."

"And maybe find hersel' a nice young man in town," said Mrs Murray.

"Aye, Jeannie, ye'll hae to watch oot for yer cousin Willie noo!"

"Maybe she can do better than him."

"Aye, but that bonnie house he built. . . "

"And a' that money he's makin'!"

"Flora, that's nae kind o' talk for a time like this," cut in Jean.

"Ye maun be practical, Miss MacDougal," said Douglas, trying for a sardonic tone that was ruined by a fit of coughing.

"Mon, doctor, that's a terrible hoast ye've got. Hae ye tried slippery elm for it?" asked the midwife.

He was gasping for breath but summoned the energy to reply, "I've no tried onything yet, Mrs Semple. Nae a thing that helped, that is."

"I'll bring ye some drops the morn. That is if I can get out wi a' the snow."

"Aye. It's gettin' thick." One of the women rose and looked out the window. "And we've a lang trip back tae Edenkiln."

"Ye're no goin' yet, Eliza," said Mrs Semple. "Another cup o' tea?"

"Ach weel . . . maybe yin . . . afore I start on ma way."

With murder in his heart, he watched them settle to another round of food and drink. Only Jean ate nothing. She was twisting her fingers nervously in a manner that was unlike her.

Douglas stood up.

"Mrs Semple, hae I yer permission to talk to yer niece in private?"

"Oh aye, doctor. Gang into the kitchen. It's warm in there." He held out both hands, hoisted Jean to her feet, steered her across the hall, then shut the kitchen door firmly behind them.

She turned on him.

"Ye've a fair nerve! What'll they think?"

"I dinnae gie a damn. I couldnae stand they auld hens cacklin' anither minute and neither could you. Jean, I . . . I . . . what can I say?"

Her face hardened and she struggled with emotion.

"I'm sorry if I was rude the now." He tried to take her hands.

"Ye never had ony manners to spare."

That was better. "Ye can insult me all you want if it'll mak ye feel better." He wondered in passing how much she remembered of the night when he had undressed her and put her to bed.

She tore her hands free and covered her eyes with them. "What for did ye hae to come here the now?"

He put his arms around her and drew her close. "As a physician," he said hollowly, "I'd advise ye to hae a guid cry and get it over with."

She stiffened. "Not until they're gone."

"To hell wi them."

He stroked her hair. Jean started to sob, clinging to him desperately and he held her tightly until the worst of the storm had passed. Then he asked, attempting lightness,

"Do you need a handkerchief, afore I'm soaked to the skin?"

She fumbled in her dress, but he had already produced the fine clean one that Mrs MacGregor always put in the pocket of his best suit. He tilted back her head and dried her eyes carefully.

"D'ye never blow yer nose on the Sabbath, Douglas?"

"This is no the Sabbath."

"Naw, but ye're wearing yer Sunday claes." She smoothed his ruffled shirt front. He put the handkerchief away. One arm was still around her waist. She lifted up her face to be kissed.

For once in his life, Douglas was beyond acting. Making no attempt to cover his confusion, he let her go.

"Sit down," he said abruptly, "I hae to talk to ye."

She looked about her. "The chairs is a' in the ither room."

"Then we'll hae to sit on the box bed."

"That would no be nice."

"I would beg to disagree wi ye. But I'm no yieldin' to temptation until I've had ma say."

They climbed up onto the bed. Jean curled herself up against the pillows while he sat with his long legs dangling over the side, the light from the kitchen fire flickering earily on him. He was again at a loss for words.

"Weel?" she asked. "What is it?"

He spread out his hands, studied each one of his long fingers in turn. Finally, he pushed back his hair roughly and turned to her.

"I dinnae ken how to start. I've been that drunk the last twa nights. I cannae think." She was silent. "I'm tellin' ye the worst o' ma faults, or near it. I only drink now and again."

"What about yer conceit o' yersel'?"

"Ma conceit . . . " He paused. "Maybe ye're right. Maybe I am conceited."

"Ach, ye're young enough to grow out of it."

"I'm twenty-six, and I hae a guid future ahead o' me. Or should have." He jumped down, started prowling nervously around the room. "Ach Jean, I dinnae ken how to tell ye."

"Tak yer time."

"I telt ye I left Edinburgh for ma health. That wasnae strictly true."

"I know." He stared at her. "I jaloused ye ran into trouble."

"Aye, ye were right. I near killed a man. I near swung for it."

She was silent then said, "That's what would happen to Melville if he werenae the gentry."

"Ye're right. But it wasnae like that. . . "

"How was it then?"

"Ye maybe heard o' the riots they had last year in Edinburgh? It was caused by yon Muir fellow and that Society o' his, the Friends of the People."

"Aye, the Radicals. They're a' ower Stirlingshire too."

"Feelin' was runnin' unco high in the town. Ye'll hae heard o' Lord Braxfield? The Hangin' Judge, they ca'd him. Ony yin that came afore him . . . if they werenae for the established order . . . he ordered them hung or sent them to the Colonies. And quite right too."

"Ye're no a Radical then?"

"Naw. I'd been workin' awfa' hard. I was preparin' lectures over and above a' ma work at the Infirmary and for Dr Tait. I was takin' a class for him. God, Jean, when I think o' a' that opportunity. . . "

"There's as guid fish in the sea."

"Wait till I tell ye the rest. When I'm tired, liquor goes

to ma head. And I was down at Lucky Ferguson's . . . that's a pub . . . wi the rest of the lads frae the Medical College, havin' a night out. Yin o' them had aye been jealous o' me. He didnae hae ma ability but he was well connected. His father was a doctor and he thought he'd get that job as Tait's assistant and be on his way. And then it went to me and he was angry about it. I should never hae got in an argument wi him, especially not on politics. I started defendin' Muir and the rest o' them, sayin they had some guid ideas. The next thing, we were out on the street, wi our coats off, fightin' it out. I'm a big fellow. I hit him, and down he went. And . . . and the Town Guard were on to us. The next thing I knew I was in the Tolbooth, wi a' the pickpockets and whores and dirty people."

He covered his face with his hands, shivering at the memory. "And ma enemy telt auld Braxfield I was a dangerous Radical. The best way to hae me hangit!"

"And . . . how did ye get off?"

"Dr Tait's a powerful man in Edinburgh. He pulled strings wi the proper people. He even talked to the judge in private. In the end, they let me go and it was a' hushed up. They gied me a floggin' wi a cat o' nine tails, on principle, to be sure I didnae escape unpunished. Ye can still see the scars on ma back."

"Oh, Dougie. . . "

"And, the worst o' it was . . . after I'd recovered at Dr Tait's house, where I was taken after the beating, I had to leave Edinburgh. Nae two ways about that. He'd heard the doctor here had died, so he lent me the money to get started. And that's how I wound up in Strathblane." He made a fierce gesture towards the window. "Wi' measles and rheumatism . . . rheumatism and measles! Once in a while, a difficult confinement for variety. And consumption for which there is no cure. The Laird's indigestion, wi a' its ramifications. Ma ain health goin' to bits and pieces wi overwork and the damnable climate. And no money," he wound up bitterly.

"Dr McKelvie did well enough."

"I'd like to know how he did it. And that's why a' this is no the way I'd hae liked it, Jean. I'm deep in debt, though Tait's gi'en me a' the time I want to repay him. And Mrs MacGregor would like to gang back to Edinburgh. I'd planned to wait a few months. But I cannae risk ye goin' to Glasgow, beyond ma ken."

She sat very still. "What are ye talkin' aboot?"

"I would think I had made masel' plain. If ye dinnae mind doin' yer own housework for a while. . . "

"Housework? I'm no takin' on work as a servant!"

"Hell and damnation woman, hae ye never had a proposal afore?"

"A proposal?"

"Aye. A proposal." He went formally down on one knee before her. "Miss Jean MacDougal o' Puddock Hole, I, Douglas Elliot Stewart, physician and surgeon, hae the honour to ask ye to be ma wife. I canna dress ye in silk attire but I can promise to keep a roof over yer head and . . . and I promise to love ye wi a' ma heart. For I already do!"

Tears ran down her cheeks. But, when she spoke, her words took him completely by surprise. She said triumphantly,

"I'm gettin' a guid price for the farm."

"Jean, are ye turnin' me down?"

"Naw! I mean I'm no comin' tae ye tocherless!"

"Lassie, it's you I want, no yer tocher!"

"Just the same, it'll come in handy. It'll pay off yer debts. Oh Dougie. . . " She gathered him, nothing loathe into her arms.

V

"A merry heart doeth good like a medicine," Mrs Semple had told him comfortably as he left the farm, a big muffler of Angus MacDougal's round his throat, and full of tea and bannock.

By the time he and Jean had returned to the parlour, the local women had gone, but Flora and her aunt had been ready to celebrate. They had wanted him to spend the night, but Douglas was determined to see the minister and make arrangements for the marriage to take place as soon as possible. He stopped at his house, left his bag, and wakened Mrs MacGregor with the good news. She too, tried to dissuade him from going out again, but he assured her a little more exposure could do him no harm.

But, slithering down the brae, he reflected that it was only happiness that propelled him through the deepening snow. It was by now coming down so thickly he could scarcely find the road or even push open the manse gate. Having lost all sense of time, he only realised how late it must be when the minister's wife, rather than the servant, opened the door wearing a big wool peignoir and a nightcap. She was a pretty woman, with a round sonsy face, and he had always liked her.

"Mrs Gardner, I crave your pardon for disturbing you so late but . . . can I hae a word wi yer husband?"

"Aye. Of course, doctor. Come in." He tried to stamp the worst of the snow off his boots, but she motioned him into the hall.

"Never mind the floor. But gie me your coat and hat. Eh! It's a terrible night to be out. Your business must be important."

"Aye, it is." She led him into the study, where the

minister was seated by a peat fire, reading. The dark, dignified room with its plain furniture and well-stocked bookcases reminded Douglas of the home where he had grown up.

"Why, Dr Stewart! Come in and sit down and get warm. It's unco late for ye to be out, is it not?"

"Aye. I apologise for botherin' you, but if ye're anything like ma father, you don't appreciate having announcements thrown at you just before the service, and this is Saturday night." He cleared his throat. "I'm gettin' married, Mr Gardner. I want ye to cry the banns for me the morn."

"Well! well! This is unexpected . . . and good news! One of our Strathblane lassies?"

"Miss Jean MacDougal of Puddock Hole."

There was a surprised pause. Then Mrs Gardner delivered judgement.

"A nice sensible girl. You've made a good choice, young man."

"Thank you." Though he had told himself that he didn't care what people thought, it was a relief to know that this was the way the parish would react. The village women took their lead from the minister's wife on matters like this.

"How soon can ye marry us, sir?"

"As soon as the banns have been cried. But tomorrow I was supposed to exchange pulpits with Mr McPhail."

Douglas's face must have been a study, for Mrs Gardner was quick to reassure him,

"He could still cry the banns. And with this storm, we don't expect him. My husband's not going to Killearn, that's for sure," she added firmly, as she laid a plump hand on Douglas's sleeve. "I was heatin' up a nightcap, doctor, for the minister. I'll make one up for you too."

"And put a guid dram in it, so we can drink his health,"

[285]

said her husband as she disappeared towards the back of the house.

"You're very kind, sir." Douglas slumped into a chair, exhausted.

"There is one point to consider before ye set a date for the marriage," said Mr Gardner. "The young lady has just been bereaved. Would it no' be fitting to postpone the ceremony for a wee while?"

"Had her bereavement been due to normal circumstances, sir, perhaps. But, as it is, I'm thinkin' that it is now she needs a husband at her side. And neither one of us wants any fancy penny wedding. We simply desire . . . to be joined so she can move herself and her bits o' furniture over to my house. The Laird's bought the farm off her."

"Aye, so I heard. And I was glad of it. It shows Kirklands recognises his responsibility in the matter and wishes to make amends. Is he settling the lawsuit, too?"

"They're going to do that, but it's fair complicated."

Mrs Gardner returned with two steaming tumblers redolent of lemon and spice. The tartness started Douglas coughing again.

"Doctor, ye shouldnae be out on a night like this with a terrible hoost like that!"

"I was out anyway . . . and she just accepted me. . . " He was gasping for breath.

"Aye, a young man who's in love can do next to anything!" chuckled the minister. As his wife once more drifted out of the room, he raised his glass, "Health and happiness to you. Did you tell me once that your father had a church in the Borders?"

"Aye. In Darnick."

"He must be very proud of you."

Douglas choked on his toddy. He hated hypocrisy and the way people glossed over bad family situations. His atheism he considered his own business, but he could not let Mr Gardner believe an untruth about his relations with his parents.

"I . . . havenae been in touch with my family for six years, sir. My father disowned me when I abandoned Divinity and went to the Surgeon's Hall."

Mr Gardner shook his head. "I find that very sad." Then he chuckled again. "So your father doesn't know how well you profited from your ecclesiastical studies! The way you flummoxed Mr Campbell in the Kirk! *John, chapter eight, verse seven.* You know your New Testament."

"It aye made more sense to me than the Old one."

"That is true, for many people. And when you came to that Session meeting with the Laird . . . when you wanted the school closed . . . I think you quoted the scripture at Campbell on that occasion also. Aye, your father would have been proud."

His father would more likely have agreed with the Exciseman that a measles epidemic was the Will of God. Douglas was silent, easing his weak foot into a more comfortable position and thinking of the past, which he seldom did.

"Young man, you are at liberty to tell me that this is none of my business, but, since I am about to conduct your marriage ceremony, it would be fitting for me to write a letter to your father. I would tell him how much you are respected in Strathblane and what a fine, dedicated young healer you turned out to be. It might reopen the paths of communication between you."

At least his mother would know he had made a good marriage.

"If . . . if you wish, sir. It would be kind of you. . . " He finished his drink and stood up. "And now I must leave you in peace to go to your bed. It's late and. . . "

"And you'll never make your way up the brae the night," completed Mrs Gardner, reappearing. "The snow's too deep and it's still coming down. My son's bed is aye kept aired, and I've just put some hot bricks into it. I've laid out one of his nightshirts too, and I only hope it's big enough for you. You're biding here."

"No, Mrs Gardner. It's monstrous kind and thoughtful of you, but no. I cannae impose. I . . . I'm a sick man and, once I take to bed, I'm like to stay there a while. Thank you . . . but. no."

"I'm taking no argument from you, young man. I've raised four children and I can see you're sick. You haven't the strength to climb up that steep hill. Forbye, you could easily slip and not rise again. You look that exhausted you'd fall asleep."

"Sleep!" echoed Douglas, light-headed between the strong drink, the heat of the room, and his mounting fever. "*Sleep that knits up the ravelled sleeve of care. . .* "

The worst storm of coughing yet overwhelmed him. When it let up, he found himself slumped on a chair, his eyes streaming. The minister was standing beside him, his kindly face full of concern.

"Now, my mannie, you do as my wife says and go upstairs to bed. She's a grand nurse."

"Aye. And what do you think I should do for you, doctor? What would you prescribe?"

Douglas turned his attention inward and tried to take stock of his physical condition. It had deteriorated sharply, and the weight on his chest was now so ominous he had a flash of the kind of panic he had often experienced as a young medical student when introduced to some dire disease. Now his self-diagnosis was based on experience. He was heading for pneumonia, like the young farmer up the valley, who had died. . .

"A poultice maybe? Or a mustard plaster?" she asked, and he even started to reply, briskly, that the plaster would be better, when he stopped himself.

"I dinnae ken, Mrs Gardner . . . I dinnae ken." The Edinburgh accent went the way of his professional aplomb. Trying to salvage a thread of pride, he said, "The congestion's in ma bronchial tubes. And ma bones ache. But what to do for it all . . . If I'm no' better by morning, ask Jock MacLean. He kens how I handle these cases, for what it's worth."

"I think I'll try a linseed poultice first, doctor. One on your chest and another on your back."

She would see the scars given by the lash. He no longer cared.

"Do whatever ye think best, Mrs Gardner. I'll no' dispute yer treatment. . . " He turned to the minister. "We think we know it a' . . . but . . . we dinnae. . . "

"And that is the beginning of wisdom," boomed Mr Gardner.

His wife put maternal arms around Douglas' drooping shoulders and guided him gently up the stair.

VI

The snow was still lying on Monday and Walter let himself be talked into spending another night at the Baldernock manse. He suspected the Haddows found his company a novel break in their quiet lives. They seemed genuinely sorry to see him go on the Tuesday as he set off after a good hearty breakfast and with some tasty meat pies put up by his hostess to eat on the way.

"After you find your family, young Paterson," said the minister, "please write and tell me about them. And if your father and mother return to Scotland, bring them to see us."

He walked Walter to the gate. "Now you follow this road to the Allander Toll. And when you reach Glasgow, look for the Saracen's Head hostelry in the Gallowgate. Anyone can direct you there. It's where the stage-coach leaves. And on your way to Edinburgh be sure to observe the new Forth and Clyde canal. It's one of the engineering wonders of the day."

Walter clasped the old man in his arms.

"I cannot tell you how much it has meant, being with you and your wife. I feel it has bridged my two lives."

"We'll see you again. And I will be discreet. But if I do go to Strathblane to preach and I meet your little Miss Moncrieff, I'll let her know I am in your confidence." For Walter by the previous evening, had told his new friends all about Primrose.

The roads were wet but clear and he felt more able to withstand the clammy cold. Glasgow moreover, was but a short six miles away. He had no difficulty finding the Allander Toll and the inn but was disappointed to learn he had missed the morning stage-coach to Edinburgh.

However, since he now had plenty of time, he headed for the Royal Bank, where the manager made him welcome, changed his French money for him without any argument and asked at length about Mrs Graham. Walter concocted a story about being on holiday, sure she would not mind. Then he strolled around the city's side streets fascinated, after the long months of country living, by the tall symmetrical buildings and the bustle of the pavements. Glasgow was both prosperous and cosmopolitan he observed, and there were many fine ships in the Clyde.

He wondered how far he was from Greenock and Abernethy's friend there, and it also occurred to him that Jean's cousin Willie would probably help him. All Walter knew of him was that he was in the import and export business, so presumably had quarters near the waterfront. But, the prospect of Willie's company was not enticing. Heading back towards the inn, Walter passed a tall grim building with a tower – obviously the Tolbooth – and he shivered, wondering if Abernethy and his cabin boy were incarcerated there by now.

In the courtyard of the Saracen's Head, a slimly built phaeton with four beautifully groomed horses and a couple of smart footmen stood awaiting passengers. Remembering the roads he had just crossed, Walter hoped its owners did not plan to use it for outlying travel, for it looked designed for speed rather than rough going. It reminded him of a similar vehicle that the Vicomte de Sincerbeaux had bought in Rome, during their Grand Tour. It had fallen apart in the Alps.

Thoughts of Louis made Walter conscious of his plain and now rather dirty clothes, and he wondered what kind of impression the late Mr Graham's cast-offs would make on his Edinburgh cousins. He might not even look smart enough for the Saracen's Head because he had observed that Glaswegians were smart dressers. He could at least get his hair trimmed and sought out the barber he had visited with Bobby. As he headed back towards the hostelry, he felt better groomed and ready for a good hot meal with a glass of wine, which he felt sure he could afford.

The carriage was still there, the footmen lounging near by, bored and chilly. Even their livery looked French, though this could have been a trick of the imagination. He toyed with the idea of waiting to see what the owners of the vehicle were like, but there was a nip in the air so he continued on indoors.

A cheerful fire blazed on the hearth in the saloon and several people were standing around, warming themselves and drinking. Keeping a tight hold on his valise, for Mr Haddow had warned him about pickpockets, Walter looked around him. He saw a staircase leading to a dark upper floor and wondered how much it might cost to spend the night there. There was only one way to find out. He approached an aproned individual standing behind the bar, laid down some coins and, for an opening, requested a mug of ale. He had scarcely sampled it when a huge hand fell on his shoulder and a triumphant Strathblane voice announced,

"So here ye are, Paterson! As large as life!"

Walter swung round, spilling his drink, and found himself staring into Geordie's baleful black eye.

"Just in time tae join yer cronies in the jail! Come alang, ma mannie!"

Fury exploded in Walter. He was not about to be recaptured now. He tossed the tankard of ale full in the man's face and ran.

Bounding up the staircase three steps at a time, he collided with a smartly topcoated gentleman on the way down.

"*Allons! Allons!*" he exclaimed in surprise. "*Qu'est-ce qui arrive?*"

"*On me chasse,*" Walter flung back, brushing past him and he was half way down the corridor before he realised they had been speaking French.

At a corner on the upper landing, the passage separated in two directions. Praying he would find a back stair, he veered desperately. There were running footsteps behind him, and blocking his path was a lady in a voluminous fur cape, who was just emerging from her bedroom, a maid at her heels.

"*Madame!*" he cried desperately, trying to avoid them, "*Laissez passer, je vous en prie!* Let me past!"

She screamed, first in astonishment, then with joy. And instead of drawing back, threw herself on him!

"*Petit frère!*"

He was staring into blue eyes the mirror image of his own.

"*Clementina!*"

Brother and sister fell on each others' necks as the young man seen on the stair caught up with them.

"*Mais . . . C'est toi!*"

"*Louis!*"

The Kirklands' servant came on the scene to find all three, with Gallic abandon, hugging, kissing, weeping with joy. Doors flew open, the waiting maid screamed. Geordie grabbed at Walter and just escaped being kissed too.

"Paterson! Ye're under arrest! Get away from him, sir!"

The Vicomte de Sincerbeaux, unused to such treatment, drew back, and ordered:

"*Allez-vous en!* Go away!"

"We maun tak him tae the jail!"

"Oh no!" cried Clementina, clinging to her brother.

"*Walter, qu'est-ce qui arrive?*"

"*Je suis fugitive et il faut parler anglais avec ces gensla.*"

But Louis' means of communication was more effective than language. He drew a handful of coins from his pocket and tossed them at the lackies.

"Leave us! Go drink our health! *En bas!* Downstairs."

The Scottish footmen, who had probably never seen such lavish tipping, drew back, leaving the decision up to Geordie, who hesitated.

"Sir, I maun tak this man to the Laird."

Walter extricated himself from his sister's arms. "Yes! Where is the Laird?"

"He's here, takin' a bit o' food, and then he's goin' tae talk wi the Sheriff."

"Bring him up! At once! I will be here, I promise! You can leave a . . . a guard if you like! Tell Mr Moncrieff that. . . " – the possibilities of the situation began to dawn –

"that I am closeted with a nobleman from France, *Monsieur le Vicomte de Sincerbeaux*, and my sister. . . "

"*Madame la Vicomtesse*," chimed in Louis. "Now go away! Here! Drink our health!"

A gold coin landed at Geordie's feet, giving the *coup de grâce* to his sense of duty. He touched his forelock, picked up the largesse and started backing off down the corridor, gesturing to his fellow servants to do the same. "Yes sir," he was mumbling, bowing low. "Oh, yes, sir."

"Geordie, you bring the Laird back here!" Walter called after him.

"*Ici!*" Louis indicated the door as he herded them into the bedroom, ordering the maid in French to have his carriage sent back to the stable.

Alone, the three fell upon each other again.

"Walter! Walter!"

"Clemmie! Louis! When were you married?"

"In January. In London. And where have you been hiding?"

"I haven't been hiding. Papa? Mama?"

"In Edinburgh with Uncle Alec. We've bought a house," burbled Clementina.

"You're going to live there?"

"Yes. It's a lovely town . . . much nicer than Paris. But we thought you would be waiting for us there! When you weren't, we were distressed."

"But Captain Abernethy . . . that rum-runner who got me out of France . . . he said he saw Papa and told him where I was!"

"Yes, but Papa just arrived in Edinburgh and all we knew was that this Strath place. . . "

"Strathblane."

"*C'est ça*. It was somewhere near Glasgow, so we came here and we have been searching for it all week. Only yesterday did we learn where it was and how to get there, and we were just leaving."

"You were going there in that flimsy phaeton?"

"Why not? It's only a few miles."

"You'd have been rattled to pieces on those roads."

"But why did you never come to Edinburgh?"

Walter threw up his hands. "Something always came in the way! Firstly, I was very sick. . . "

"*Oh, mon pauvre petit frère!*"

"Yes! Your wounds!" cried the Vicomte. "Your wrist and shoulder?"

Walter caught his friend's hand in such a strong grip, he cried for mercy. "You see? But . . . before these men come back, I must tell you. . . "

"Yes! How are you mixed up with these peasants?"

"I gave one of them his black eye! In a fight. They work for the Laird of Kirklands . . . the *Seigneur* in Strathblane. He was taking me to jail in Glasgow."

"Why? Did you seduce his wife?"

"He has no wife. Only a sister and I didn't seduce her. I want to marry her . . . but don't mention that to him, please!" cried Walter in alarm.

"You're a naughty boy!" teased Clementina.

"Oh, but I'm not. I behaved like a gentleman to her. But this man . . . her brother . . . thinks I'm a French spy. A *saboteur!*"

Louis was shocked.

"How could he imagine anything so preposterous?"

"He hates all foreigners. He hates the Revolution."

"But so do we all!"

"And . . . he was jealous of me. I worked for a lovely widow that he's sweet on. I was poor! I was tutoring a little boy! I . . . Louis, what are you laughing about?"

The Vicomte gestured at his clothes.

"Your spy disguise! That topcoat!"

"It's a good topcoat! It kept me warm all winter!"

They were back at their lifelong bantering as though they had never been separated. Walter tossed down the valise, which he had clutched throughout and now threw off the offending wrap.

Louis, pointing a finger at his suit, threw up his hands in horror. "*Mais c'est pire!* No one has worn a jacket like that in ten years!"

"And you've cut off your nice curls!" sighed Clementina.

"And all my worldly goods are in that little bag. I have no ring but one watch and only half the money Papa gave me in France. How did you get your millions out, Louis?"

"Millions? I'm a pauper!"

"With a carriage and footmen and your wife in furs! I'm so glad you're married!" He kissed her again.

"All I have is what your father invested for me in Britain before the Revolution made it impossible to transfer funds."

"Well, it seems to be enough to live on."

"It is," interposed Clementina. "But before we tell you our story, you must tell us yours. Before this man comes. . . "

"A good thought. You may be able to convince him that I am who I am."

She threw off her cloak. They sat down and Walter was midway through a confused account of his adventure, interrupted by many questions, when there came a brisk knock on the door.

"*Entrez!*" ordered the Vicomte and it opened to reveal the Laird of Kirklands, flanked by his lackies.

Walter, who had been sprawling on the bed, scrambled off it. Louis advanced on the newcomer, every inch the aristocrat.

"Come in, *monsieur*. We have been expecting you."

Moncrieff stepped forward, looking all three over in

frank astonishment. Then, in his most clipped accent and with a turn of phrase sadly lacking in originality, he said,

"Well, so there you are, Paterson."

Walter bowed.

"Allow me. Clementina, may I present you to Mr Henry Moncrieff of Kirklands House in Strathblane. Sir, my sister, the Vicomtesse de Sincerbeaux."

She swept an elegant curtsey. She was beautiful. She had her brother's blue eyes, fair hair and clean-cut features, and the family resemblance was unmistakeable.

"And my brother-in-law, Monsieur le Vicomte." Trying to see his friend through Moncrieff's xenophobic eyes, Walter observed a good-looking young man, with a direct, myopic gaze, and smooth, straight, light brown hair. He was dressed in impeccable British tailoring and not at all foreign looking.

"Pray be seated, *monsieur*," Louis said courteously. "Do you wish your servants to remain while we . . . converse?"

"Geordie, wait for me in the corridor," ordered Moncrieff a little flustered. When they had withdrawn, he said while looking at Walter. "I . . . don't understand this . . . situation."

"Before we enlighten you," responded Louis, "pray do us the honour of sharing a glass of wine."

"A good idea!" chimed in Walter, starting to enjoy himself. "Do sit down, Mr Moncrieff."

But the Laird remained standing.

"By your leave, there are some matters to straighten out first."

Louis and Clementina both began talking in at once in a mixture of English and French that Walter knew would raise Moncrieff's hackles.

"*C'est mon petit frère* . . . my long lost brother . . . we have been looking for him *partout*. . . "

"*Monsieur, c'est mon ami depuis longtemps* . . . we grew up together . . . he saved my life."

"*Silence! Et parlez anglais!*" Walter cut in. "Forgive us sir, we have just had a very emotional reunion."

Moncrieff glowered.

"I am sorry to cut it short but I must deliver you to the authorities."

Walter quieted his family with a gesture.

"Very good, sir. I have no doubt that whatever authority I am brought before will set me free, for I have not only proof of my own identity, but my friends and family can verify it." He drew the French *laisser-passer* from his pocket, handed it to the Laird and added, "And I believe I can also prove now, that I am not what you think." He picked up his topcoat. "Let us go at once sir, for you have a long journey ahead of you, back to Strathblane."

"No," cried Clementina, throwing her arms around him again. "You're not going to be taken away from us!"

"Then come with me, or at least let Louis come. And I'm not going to the Bastille! You had better ask Mr Moncrieff what I am supposed to have done."

The Laird drew himself up, asserting his dignity. "This man consorts with smugglers. His actions have been suspicious. I believe him to be a foreign agent, a spy. Our country is at war with France."

Louis laughed. "Forgive me *monsieur*, but that is so ridiculous. My friend was chased from the country. He can never go back. They would guillotine him."

"Why?" asked Moncrieff. "What did he do to get into such serious trouble with the law?"

Louis threw up his hands. "There *is* no law there today, *monsieur*. Of the infamy of this Revolution, you cannot conceive! My friend helped me to escape its clutches. And what was *my* offence, you may ask? Simply being born into and old family with extensive possessions. Had they arrested me, they would certainly have found me guilty at my trial and they could then have confiscated all my estates. And to think," he went on histrionically, "that I was once a Liberal! My friend here had more sense!"

"He wasn't a Jacobin then?" queried Moncrieff meaning, as the Scots did, a radical.

"No. He had no interest in politics. He is a poet!" Catching Walter's eye, Louis quickly changed tack. "I myself once waited upon Madame Roland but I was never a member of the Jacobin Club . . . though that is undoubtedly why the Tribunal would have sent me to the Conciergerie had I not been rescued by the courage and resourcefulness of my friend. You look a little pale, *monsieur*. I beg you to be seated."

This time the Laird accepted the invitation.

"I presume you can substantiate your story, sir? Does anyone in Glasgow know you?"

"Certainly. We dined last night with your Lord Provost and met several charming people."

"But . . . had they known you before last night?"

"That banker, Louis," interposed Clementina. "He did business with Papa. My father . . . and Walter's . . . had his own financial house in Paris sir, and the manager of the Bank of Scotland knew him well."

"I know *him* well too." Moncrieff looked reluctantly impressed. "He handled my business when I was in the cotton trade."

"His quarters are close by," said the Vicomte. "I was there this morning, drawing some money because we were actually on our way to . . . to your charming valley, when we met with my . . . my brother. If you would like to step around to the bank with me, I am sure. . . "

"That will not be necessary. But . . . I must still turn

Paterson over to the law. That is my responsibility."

"His uncle in Edinburgh is a judge, *monsieur*. He was recently raised to the bench as Lord Paterson. Does that make any difference?"

"No," said the Laird firmly. "Not unless he can clear his character."

"But surely you will give us time to find him legal counsel? He should not have to defend himself against serious charges without a . . . a solicitor being present."

"Serious charges?" Walter echoed bitterly. "All I did was give Geordie a black eye in self-defence and . . . attack a man who had just shot an innocent old farmer! I hope Melville's in the Tolbooth too!" He let fly at the Laird recklessly.

Moncrieff did not meet his eyes.

"Mr Melville has been . . . dealt with." There was a long moment of silence. Then the Laird asked, "You'll not be going back to your employment in Strathblane then, Mr Paterson?"

Walter hesitated.

"I . . . must see my parents, sir."

"And you will have to spend some time with them, I imagine."

"Oh yes!" cried Clementina, "And he must meet all his cousins and . . . other members of the family! He will be very busy!"

"So let us stop at the Bank of Scotland," said Louis, "for I may have to . . . to . . . *encore, qu'est-ce que je veux dire?* . . . put up bail for Mr Paterson and I have but a hundred pounds on me."

Moncrieff's eyes widened involuntarily but he continued to hold his ground.

"On a charge of treason, he would be kept in jail."

"But . . . treason!" echoed Louis. "I assure you *monsieur*, you will be doing my friend a grave injustice if you persist in such an accusation. He is not even guilty of consorting with smugglers, at least not of his own free will. He has already suffered greatly from the appalling turmoil in France . . . a country I never want to see again! It is finished for people like us." He looked the Laird in the eye and Walter, the banker's son, observed like respond to like through the many generations of landed gentry.

Moncrieff rose and held out his hand to the Frenchman.

"I consider myself a judge of men's qualities, sir. I must, because it is my duty, verify all that you have told me. But if I am satisfied, as I am sure I will be, you will hear no more of the matter. In these times we cannot always choose our associates or . . . er . . . control the course of our actions." He turned to Walter. "I am glad you have found your family and I presume we will no longer be seeing you in Strathblane? So, may I wish you well."

Walter bowed. "I . . . thank you, Mr Moncrieff."

"And perhaps, *monsieur*," suggested Louis, "some time when the weather is more pleasant, we may visit this . . . valley and see your estates?"

"Indeed sir, it would give me great pleasure to show you my improvements." He bowed low to Clementina. "And . . . er . . . yes, I do have a sister who would be happy to make your acquaintance. May I wish you a safe return journey to Edinburgh?"

No sooner was he gone that the three young people broke out again into peals of light-hearted laughter.

"But . . . Scotland!" cried the Vicomte. "What a country! What people! What kind of nobleman is this who works in a trade? And he talks of it openly! And his clothes! Even worse than Walter's! He looks like a farmer!"

"He *is* a farmer. A very good one."

"And what do you know about farming?"

"More than you do! I can milk a cow and muck out a byre and I know about planting." Happiness flooded through him. "Mr Moncrieff is a great landowner, Louis. He does not have as much money as you do but he has built himself a beautiful house. And his sister! Oh, wait until you see her!"

"Yes! You were starting to tell us about her when he arrived! That was why I suggested we visit them. Scottish people are very hospitable."

"I know. I appreciated that! But I hope long before the summer she'll be my wife. We are already secretly betrothed. She has my ring. Do you think you're the only people ever to fall in love?"

PART EIGHT

EDINBURGH AND HOME

Persons of good sense, I have observed, seldom fall into the disputatious turn, except lawyers, university men, and men of all sorts that have been bred in Edinburgh.

Autobiography
Benjamin Franklin

I

DEAR STEWART, Walter wrote. *What is happening in Strathblane? Although I sent letters to Jean, your good self, and several other people as soon as I reached Edinburgh, the only one who replied was Mrs Graham, and all she said was that she was happy I had been reunited with my family, and that she was very busy. Is she marrying the Laird at long last?*

Now almost six weeks have gone past and I am hoping against hope that your silence means no more than an inability to find time for correspondence. And what of the lady for whom I left a message on your desk? I trust her brother thinks more kindly of me now that I am well away from Leddrie Green.

He paused, glanced briefly out of the morning-room window, saw that Charlotte Square was brightening in the sunshine after a brief rain-storm, and wondered how frank he dare to be. The letter might, for all he knew, be seen by more eyes than the doctor's.

I am sure that, in the mysterious way news travels in the country, everyone in the parish now knows that I am not a French spy or even a rum-runner. Mr Moncrieff thought better of his plans to turn me over to the authorities in Glasgow. So, I am now assured of my freedom.

I am indeed 'far ben' with the law for my uncle was just raised to the bench as Lord Paterson. His son, my cousin Peter, follows in his footsteps, holding his own little court daily at the Parliament House, where but for the grace of God and the Revolution in France, would go I too. But that same upheaval which freed the peasants from domination by the nobility also liberated me from the loving stranglehold of my family. My father was so glad to find me alive that he did not press the issue when I told him roundly I had no interest in a legal career.

He has also agreed to invest the money which he would have spent on my further education in a small estate which I can develop. And my brother-in-law, still convinced I saved his life, also wants to contribute to setting me up as an agriculturist. So I have been happily conferring with the Society of Improvers here, and learning as much as I can about modern methods of cultivation, crops and the soil.

Also, to Papa's delight (and my amusement), Louis de Sincerbeaux – now wed to my sister – has decided to study law in my place! He realises he is living in a new world, in which men are more dependent on their own efforts than on inherited wealth. And since he expects to become a father in a few months, he is looking towards the future. His parents remain in Amsterdam, hoping some day to return to France and put the clock back. But he knows this may never be. Moreover, both he and Clementina love Edinburgh with a passion equal to your own.

Shortly after our reunion here, I developed a miserable cold, for which I refused medical aid, remembering your dictum that no doctor could cure this tiresome affliction. My female relatives delighted to fuss over me, which was most agreeable, for I have many pretty cousins. Then my parents took me on a trip to Fife, for some sea air and we stayed with my mother's relatives, who lionized me and showed us around the 'Kingdom'. It is, in parts, so like France that I suspect Papa and Mama will settle there. Our purpose of the trip was to find them a permanent home.

My father has become an old man. In Paris, he was known and respected. Here, he is nobody. But my Uncle Alexander believes that once re-established on his own hearthside, his energies will revive and his vast knowledge of banking, to say nothing of his experience with French landowners, may start him in some new form of business. He even has a degree in Scots law, though his knowledge is rusty. As for my mother, I inherited my love of the land from her and she cannot wait to start planting a new garden.

Since our return from the seaside, I have moved in with my sister and her husband in their Charlotte Square house and now hope to be able to spend more time on my own affairs. At my uncle's, all my leisure was taken up squiring my cousins around the town, and I wearied of the endless dances, concerts, teas, and soirees to which they dragged me, as the latest curiosity from France.

He paused, stood up and stretched, and again looked out of the window. The grey stone symmetry of Charlotte Square left him unmoved. *This is a beautiful city,* he continued. *Indeed, it is lovelier than Paris but how can we tell why one place rather than another touches our heartstrings? You will laugh at me, Stewart – you, who so enjoyed this town – but I would give anything to change places with you and be back in Strathblane. I miss the fresh, moist air of the West, the moorlands, the spacious valley, the mountains and the lochs. The Edinburgh winds are too cold for me. And although the company here is stimulating, it does not compensate for the life I left behind me.*

Bound up in his nostalgia for the West was the thought of Primrose awaiting him by the little loch. He had not dared write to her directly and had often wondered how the doctor might have passed along his message, for he couldn't stop the Laird's sister after church, nor was he likely to encounter her when on a professional call to her brother.

I long to see you again, Walter wrote, *and to complete the Mesmer manuscript. Please let me know what happened between you and Jean, and what of your health?*

Louis came into the morning-room carrying a heavy golf bag. He extracted a putter and started swirling it around, perilously close to the Adam mantlepiece.

"I wish you would take up golf, Walter. It would be

much healthier for you than mooning around the house reading books on agriculture. It is such stimulating exercise."

"I'd rather walk."

"But you walk when you play golf. I tell you, it's just what you need."

Walter's resistance to the Royal and Ancient game was becoming an extended argument. Searching for a new excuse he said,

"I'm afraid all that swinging might strain my shoulder."

Louis was horrified.

"You still have pain in it?"

"No, but such violent exercise. . . "

"Walter," Louis pursued, "I've been meaning to say this to you before. I want you to have that arm examined and if any more treatment is needed for it, you will undergo it at my expense."

"But it's all healed up. . . "

"Yet you are afraid to play golf. Clementina agrees with me," he added.

"*Oh diable.* If you've been discussing it with her, I may as well give in now!"

Louis nodded, grinning.

"And she has picked me out a physician and made an appointment for me? I wouldn't put it past her!"

"No, but she will shortly. You're sure you won't want to go up to the Links with me and try a little game?"

"I have a letter to finish."

Clementina swept into the room in a lacy peignor. Since she found she was pregnant, she had taken to lying in bed most of the morning, saving her energy for her social life. Looking her menfolk over suspiciously, she inquired,

"You're playing this morning?"

"Yes, at Bruntsfield."

"Well, don't keep Walter out long because he is to

escort Betsy and me to a concert this afternoon. It's Mozart.
Your favourite composer."

"And afterwards, do we go to some reception?"

"No. We'll have tea at Aunt Grizell's."

Before Walter could protest, Louis told his wife,

"He's agreed to see a doctor."

"Oh wonderful! I've been so worried about you, *petit
frère*. You're not like yourself. And Mama told me about
those terrible scars on your shoulder."

"They don't hurt . . . but if you insist," Walter went on
quickly, for he knew she would, "I will go and see Dr Tait at
the University. Have you heard of him?"

They had indeed. "He's one of the most eminent men
in Edinburgh. I golf with his assistant," said the Vicomte.

"My *accoucheur* admires him greatly," added
Clementina.

"He trained the Strathblane doctor," Walter explained.
"How do I find him?"

"At the University, I imagine. You could inquire at the
Physicians' Hall on George Street. It's close by."

"I'll do it this morning," said Walter as he jumped up,
folded his letter and pushed it into his pocket. After kissing
his sister, he bounded off upstairs to collect his hat and left
the house before they could ask him what else he planned to
do that day.

It was a small victory but it meant almost as much as his
father's allowing him to decide his own future. They had
been so quietly determined to return him to the role of son
and biddable younger brother. They had even had plans for
Walter and his cousin Betsy. She was a nice pretty girl and
if he had not met Primrose he might well have fallen in love
with her. But now that was impossible. Besides she didn't
appreciate his poetry. Instead of admiring it uncritically as
Primrose had done, Betsy offered suggestions for its

improvement. But, he reflected, what he had written since he had been in Edinburgh had not been as good as his Strathblane compositions. Somehow there was never time for the long mulling over of phrases that he had done while walking around the Blane valley. He wondered frequently where, how and when the successful literary men he had met at his uncle's house did their writing. Edinburgh was so sociable.

Stepping out onto Charlotte Square, there was constant noise and mess from the building of new houses and pavements. The New Town was rising apace and it occurred to Walter as he turned into George Street, that he had had little opportunity to see the older parts of the city. Save for a visit to the Parliament House to see where his uncle and his son administered Scots Law, he had been in the Old Town only at concerts or at parties with his cousins. And they were always conveyed back and forth by carriage.

So as he walked he studied the long backbone of buildings that spread down from the Castle Rock and conceded that even though he didn't want to live there, Edinburgh was as handsome a city as any he had visited in Europe. And Princes Street, the new thoroughfare, had a unique perspective on its historic past as well as the elegant present.

He found the handsome Physicians' Hall without any difficulty and confidently climbed the steps of its classic front. Everyone he talked to knew who Dr Tait was, but none would disclose how or where he might be found. He was possibly at the University. Or he could be making his rounds at the Infirmary. He might even be at home but it was not possible to give out his address.

Walter was storming out of the building completely frustrated by the secretiveness when an old man whom he took to be the concierge called after him.

"Young sir, ye should ask yin o' the caddies. They aye

ken whaur people are."

"*Cadets?*"

"Aye, caddies. And dinnae be feared tae go wi them, sir. They're an honest breed and they'll no overcharge ye." He whistled and a small wizened, ageless person in shabby clothes appeared from the side of the building.

"Ye need a caddie, sir?"

Before Walter could reply, the concierge was issuing instructions. "Jamie, this gentleman wants to find Dr Tait. Ye'll ken whaur he'll be? Tak him there and dinnae charge him mair than tuppence."

The caddy touched a grimy forelock and gave Walter a somewhat gap-toothed grin.

"The Professor will be at the Ordinary the now, sir. He sees his puir patients there afore he goes to the Infirmary. Come wi me and I'll show ye the way."

The other man was nodding reassurance. "Ye gang wi Jamie, sir. He's yin o' the best o' the caddies."

As they set off towards Princes Street, Walter had a vision of Stewart examining the Strathblane indigent at the Kirkhouse Inn and asked,

"How can Dr Tait see patients at an Ordinary?"

"Oftentimes it's just a square meal they puir souls need, sir. He's unco' generous. A grand man. How did ye come to hear about him?"

"Through a doctor who was once his assistant and who is now practising in the West."

"Would that be yon tall laddie wi the limp that ran into trouble last year?

"Dr Douglas Stewart."

"Aye. That's the yin. It was fair terrible what they did to him."

"What . . . er . . . did happen to him?"

"Slapped him in the Tolbooth and gied him the cat o'

nine tails. And just for gettin into a fight, when he was fu', about politics. Yon laddie was nae Radical."

Walter shuddered, *"Dieu!"*

"You're French sir?"

"No. But I grew up in Paris."

They had walked at a brisk pace across Princes Street and across one of the several bridges over the Nor' Loch that connected the New Town with the ancient part of the city. Walter, thinking of Stewart in the forbidding Tolbooth building, shuddered as he listened with only half an ear to the caddy's account of the various people who lived up the dark closes of the Old Town.

"Now here's whaur ye'll find Dr Tait, sir," the man said at last. "That'll be tuppence."

Walter dug some coins out of his pocket and handed them over.

"Naw, naw, sir. I cannae overcharge! Just gang ben," he directed into a building, "and ask whaur Dr Tait is sittin'. Guid day to ye, sir."

Walter entered the hostelry. It was dark, illuminated by a few candles and full of people from various walks of life. When he asked for Dr Tait, he was shown to a booth at the back where he found a large, plump well-dressed gentleman deep in conference with some ragged shivering women and children.

II

The doctor – for it could be no-one else – was listening carefully to lengthy descriptions of aches and pains, asking questions and behaving to his shabby patients as courteously as though they were nobility. To some he handed out pills from his bag; others he directed to a table in the back, where they were given large bowls of soup. One pathetic creature with a hacking cough and a bloody bandage round one leg he told to go to the Infirmary, where she must say she was a patient of his who needed a bed immediately. The woman burst into tears.

"Now, now, lassie, ye're no dying! But I cannae dress yer hurts here and ye need rest. Run along now! I'll tell yer man whaur ye are. He can tak ye back home the morn."

As she was the last of the indigents, he now turned to Walter and his speech changed to English.

"Now what can I do for you, young man? I perceive you're waiting to speak to me, though you look pretty healthy."

Walter stood up and bowed.

"Dr Stewart of Strathblane sir, told me to call upon you. My name is Paterson."

A great smile broke over Dr Tait's benevolent countenance.

"You're Dougie's friend! I've been expecting you. You were an interesting enough case for him to write to me about."

"My family wanted me to see you, to be sure that I was truly recovered."

"If Dougie discharged you, medical science has done everything possible. No need to consult me or anybody else." He held out his hand and Walter shook it. "Now sit ye down and let us have some wine for our stomachs' sakes, as the Good Book recommends." There was a bottle at his elbow from which he refilled his own glass and Walter's. "Now, tell me about this wench Dougie's married!" he said eagerly. "Will she be able to handle him?"

Walter grinned.

"If her name is Jean MacDougal she certainly will!"

"Aye. MacDougal was her name."

"She's a wonderful woman, Dr Tait. I'm . . . so glad!"

"Will she keep him in order?"

"Yes! He even asks her advice."

"That's progress for him, to ask anyone's advice. And to his better health, for he has been very ill."

"I feared so. Is he recovered?"

"Aye, but it sounded like a close call. He sent me some manuscripts of yours, Mr Paterson, scenes of country life and a bundle of poems. He said you would want them."

"I do indeed!"

"They're at my house, and we have just time to walk over there before I'm due at the Infirmary." As they left the hostelry, he continued in a low voice. "It was a tragedy about Dougie. He'd have gone far in Edinburgh. The best assistant I ever had. Conscientious. A reliable diagnostician. The young fellow I have now is pleasant and does things to the best of his ability, but," he shrugged, "his ability's not great. Forbye, he's getting married too, so he'll be moving away and setting up his own practice. If Dougie hadn't been so hotheaded. . . Has he tangled with anyone yet in Strathblane?"

Walter nodded.

"With several people. But fortunately, the Laird, who is his patient, is something of a hypochondriac."

"That should bring him in some money." They had left the street and were approaching a handsome grey stone terraced house. Dr Tait pushed open the big front door and thundered, "Gifford! Where are you?"

A smartly dressed young man materialised, looking harried.

"Here sir. . . "

"My assistant, Dr Gifford, Mr Paterson. Bob, this is Dougie's friend that we've been expecting for this past few weeks." They shook hands and Tait swept him into a library where he pulled a big bundle of papers from a desk drawer.

"Here you are, young Paterson. Your own materials and also a manuscript I suspect you worked on, for parts are in hand much more legible than Dougie's."

"Oh yes, sir! The Mesmer translation! Have you read it?" Tait nodded.

"And what did you think of it, sir?"

"A lot of nonsense. I told him that a long time ago. But," he added with a smile, "the translation is an excellent piece of work and the case histories and notes are well presented. Though as for this animal magnetism or electricity, or whatever you want to call it, there's no scientific basis for that at all."

"But . . . the trances, Dr Tait! He put me into them regularly when he was treating me. It saved me a great deal of pain!"

"Did you ever stop to think maybe it was that magnificent voice of his that calmed your nerves? Dougie was quieting his patients long before he had ever heard of this Viennese quack."

"But . . . he told me that other people could do it too." Walter's eyes went to Dr Gifford, who was looking embarrassed and cut in quickly:

"You were interested in electricity Dr Tait, when that American was here."

"Aye. Franklin. A clever old man. He made a convincing case for the current he'd experimented with. But it was quite different from this magnetic fluid of Mesmer. *There are more things in heaven and in earth* as Shakespeare says. If you want to try to find a publisher for this book, I promise to keep my opinion to myself . . . unless I'm asked for it of course. However, I think you'd be better advised to concentrate on having your own literary efforts printed. Your essays on country life are excellent and my sister enjoyed the verses. I took the liberty of showing them to her. Poetry means little to me. Here," he handed over the papers, "I've suggested some editors. Gifford will tell you where to find them."

He handed over another package of papers – manuscripts that Walter had hidden in the dresser drawer at Puddock Hole. Dr Tait then emptied out of his pocket a sheaf of notes on small scraps of foolscap.

"Take care of these calls and prescriptions for me, Bob. I must be on my way to the Infirmary. Mr Paterson, I hope we meet again soon, but for now I must leave you with Dr Gifford. And you can tell him all the things about Dougie and his bride that maybe you'd hesitate to tell an old man like me!" He slapped Walter paternally on the back and departed in a swirl of energy. It was easy to see on whom Stewart had modelled his professional manner. Walter caught Dr Gifford's eye and they both laughed.

"Did Dr Tait tell you about that other patient of Dougie's," his assistant asked, "the young lady who came here looking for you?"

Walter's heart skipped a beat.

"No! What was her name?"

"It began with an *M* . . . Montgomery?"

"Moncrieff?"

"Yes. Moncrieff. That was it."

"Primrose!"

"I didn't learn her first name. But she's a sister of Mrs John Hamilton's . . . you may know of her. Her husband's a Writer to the Signet."

"She . . . Primrose . . . is in Edinburgh?"

"She was, a couple of weeks ago."

"*Dieu!* That was when I was in Fife!"

"Dougie said in his letter . . . you have it there. Dr Tait wants you to have it . . . that you'd come here, but since we hadn't seen or heard from you we couldn't help the young lady. She was very disappointed."

"But . . . you know where I can find her?"

"You could call on Mrs Hamilton. She lives on George Square and it's not that far from here."

"You can direct me?"

"I'll take you there. I'm going that way myself once I've made up these prescriptions. . . Sit down, Paterson, and read what Dougie has to say. Would you like a therapeutic glass of wine?"

"No, thank you." He found a chair, shaking. "I'll . . . read Stewart's letter. Don't let me disturb you."

He picked up the sheets in the well-known handwriting, as Dr Gifford rifled through his instructions and started taking bottles down from a well-stocked medicine cabinet.

Walter read,

Dear Sir,

I enclose herewith the last instalment of the money you lent me last year so I am now clear of financial debt to you, although for all your other help I can never repay you. I apologise for the tardiness of this final instalment. I was laid low with bronchial pneumonia and have been through such an onslaught of drastic treatment at the hands of my nearest colleague in Killearn, the adjacent parish to Strathblane, that for the past few weeks I have been good for nothing. However, I am now out of his professional clutches and the enforced rest did my weak foot much good, though I fear the leg will always give me some twitches in this confoundedly damp climate.

I have also had a stroke of unparalleled good fortune. I have found the best wife a man could hope for. She comes from an old Strathblane family that owned a poffle of land which she sold after the death of her father immediately prior to our marriage. Her maiden name was Jean MacDougal, and she is not only a good manager, her excellent cooking did far more to speed my recovery than all the pills, purgings and bleedings prescribed by Dr Ogilvy.

(As a result of this experience, I am changing my opinion on the efficiency of these traditional methods of treatment, which seem to lower the body's capacity to fight the disease and restore itself. I would welcome your thought on this matter.)

I now own a milk cow, hens, three dogs, and a cat with kittens, and make my rounds on a sturdy young mare. You will be amused to learn that I also have an apprentice! He was a footman in the Laird's house who had, from time to time, assisted me, and indeed diagnosed my sickness and brought me through its crisis before Dr Ogilvy reached my bedside, for the valley was deep in snow for several days and the roads were impassable.

Since Jock MacLean, for so he is called, had sacrificed his livelihood to care for me, I could not refuse his plea to stay on, particularly after he had borne so patiently with all the disagreeable chores connected with my illness, to say nothing of my ill humour, for I am as you know, a wretched patient.

He is not brilliant but he has good powers of observation, sharpened during my convalescence, by making calls on my patients and reporting back to me their symptoms for diagnosis and treatment. He also made himself useful to my wife and Mrs MacGregor, attending to the garden and the animals. By next year, I hope to send him to Edinburgh for you to transform into a properly qualified medical man. From his training among the gentry, he has acquired beautiful manners and knows how to conduct himself in society.

Mrs MacGregor, who sends you her loving wishes, is still with me. Although she had expressed a desire to return to Edinburgh, she changed her mind during my illness, and she gets on so well with my wife that, upon my recovery, I found myself no longer master in my own house, though the women arrange everything so well for my comfort that I cannot complain.

During my enforced leisure, I completed the enclosed manuscript, which you may remember. The translation of Dr Mesmer's book was made by Mr Walter Paterson, the patient whose case I described to you in a previous letter. I treated him most successfully through utilising animal magnetism. By now you may well have met him, for he was on his way to Edinburgh when last we met. He will tell you the circumstances. I enclose for him some writings of his own, which perforce he left behind him. They seem worthy of publication.

I apologise for such a lengthy epistle but owe you an explanation for my long silence. I trust you continue in your own robust health and that Bob Gifford continues to do well in the position I forfeited so unhappily last year.

I remain, sir,
Your obedient, humble servant,
D E Stewart.

Postscript: You will also be visited shortly by a charming young lady, Miss Primrose Moncrieff, whose brother, the Laird of Kirklands, is a patient of mine. There is nothing wrong with her health. Referring her to you was simply my way of playing Cupid, for she is most anxious to get in touch with Mr Paterson – and he with her! His departure from here was as precipitous as mine from Edinburgh but he left a message for her, and I told him to go to you when he reached the city. So I hope that you will be able to tell Miss Moncrieff how and where she may find him.

III

Bracing himself, Walter lifted the shiny brass door-knocker of the Hamilton house on George Square and let it bang. A tiny maidservant, holding fast to a wriggling little boy, opened it almost at once. Walter took a deep breath.

"Is Miss Primrose Moncrieff in residence?"

Before the girl could answer, the child piped up,

"No, Auntie Primmie's gone home."

"Then . . . may I see Mrs Hamilton?"

"She . . . " the maidservant hesitated. "She isnae 'at home', but . . . who should I tell her is calling?"

"Mr Walter Paterson from Strathblane. Tell her please, that I am a friend of her sister's and . . . and most anxious to have a word with her."

"Come in then, sir." He stepped over the threshold into almost as spacious an interior as in Charlotte Square. The woman took his hat, indicated a chair, then scuttled up a long staircase, dragging the child with her.

In a few minutes she was back.

"Mrs Hamilton's havin' her rest the now sir, but . . . if ye arenae in a hurry, she'll see you."

"Please tell her I do not wish to inconvenience her. Would she prefer me to come some other time?"

"Naw, naw, sir. But she maun get dressed."

To calm his nerves, Walter loosened the string around the bundle of papers, drew some out, and was deep in the rediscovery of his poems when the little maid returned to say her mistress was ready to receive him.

Hastily re-assembling and tying up his manuscripts and trying to keep them together under one arm, he followed her up the staircase and into a spacious drawing-room. In one corner, three pretty children were doing their best to frustrate the efforts of a hawkfaced nursemaid to keep them quietly occupied with some paints and small toys.

Mrs Hamilton reclined on a chaise longue facing the window. She had a blanket thrown over her which did little to hide her advanced state of pregnancy. Older than her brother and sister, she bore a strong family resemblance to both of them, though the regular features that were nondescript in the Laird and delicate in Primrose were, in her case, extremely sharp and clearcut. She also had the Moncrieff family's startling green eyes which were, Walter observed apprehensively, more curious than sympathetic.

He bowed with his Continental grace over the small hand she extended.

"Thank you for receiving me, *Madame*. I would have written and asked for an audience but . . . I heard only this afternoon that your sister had been in town and I came here immediately in hopes that I may be in time to see her."

"She left for Strathblane last Friday, Mr Paterson." Mrs Hamilton's voice was chilly. "She stayed here nearly three weeks, longer than she had anticipated, and she could not remain indefinitely. It was dull for her because I could not take her out in society. My doctor advised quietness for my condition. . . "

She motioned towards a stiff little chair. "Pray be seated, sir. I did not wish my sister here any longer, for childbirth is an unpleasant business and disagreeable for a young unmarried girl to observe. Besides, my brother wished her at home."

"Did . . . did your sister speak of me to you, *Madame*?"

"She did, Mr Paterson."

"And . . . and what . . . I mean . . . " He was blushing like an adolescent, feeling ridiculous. Any moment now he would start talking French. He was encumbered by the manuscripts which he deposited on an inadequate little table, wondering in passing what she might think of them. He was also embarrassed by the uncurbable curiosity of the children behind him.

"You caused my sister a great deal of unhappiness, Mr Paterson," said Mrs Hamilton in a voice like ice.

"That is the last thing I would have wanted, I can assure you."

She fanned herself languidly. "Primrose came to Edinburgh believing she would find you here."

"That should not have been hard. Everyone seems

to know who is in town . . . and who they are . . . and my family, like your husband, are associated with the legal profession. . . "

"Yes, I know. But for a start, she made enquiries through . . . certain people."

"Yes. Dr Tait."

"She went to him because she felt sure he could be trusted not to gossip about her situation."

"Her . . . situation?" he echoed in horror.

"Primrose is very young Mr Paterson, and she has a very tender heart. Your neglect hurt her deeply."

"My . . . neglect . . . ? I never neglected her!"

"When you left Strathblane, Mr Paterson . . . and oh yes, I know all about that. It was only my brother's clemency that saved you from a Glasgow jail! When you left Strathblane, as I was saying, you gave the doctor a message for Primrose, saying you would come back and marry her as soon as ever you could. But," she snapped the fan shut, "after he talked my brother into sending her to Edinburgh . . . for her health ostensibly . . . you were no longer there! You had gone off on holiday. And your cousins were chattering about you and your charms all over town. The gossip was that when you returned you were going to announce your engagement to one of them."

"Oh no . . . no! Such an idea never crossed my mind. We went to Fife because I had been unwell and my parents too and we thought that the sea air would restore us. I know that I should have been in touch with Dr Tait . . . but I didn't know at the time . . . " To add to Walter's confusion, a large soft woolly ball had just rolled towards him and now rested on his feet. Absently, he picked it up and threw it back to the little boy, who of course returned it.

"You could have written to my sister, Mr Paterson."

"But she told me I mustn't! She was terrified that your

brother would find out about us!" He kicked the ball back absently.

"A young girl interprets sudden silence as rejection, Mr Paterson. Your neglect . . . "

"My neglect!" Now he was angry. He didn't like Mrs Hamilton. She reminded him of the Laird at his most xenophobic. "I never neglected her! I was trying to protect her! Protect her reputation, I mean. . . Does Mr Moncrieff know about me now?"

She shook her head. "I think he suspects there is someone, she has been so adamant about not encouraging any of her other suitors." Again Mrs Hamilton fanned herself. "There is a gentleman who has asked for her hand."

"Not Melville!"

"No. Mr Melville is leaving the valley. But he sold his house to a friend of Henry's who has always been fond of Primrose, and now that he has been living in Netherton, they have been seeing a lot of each other."

"Oh, this is too much!" exclaimed Walter. He jumped up, brushing against the manuscript which fell all over the floor and produced an unsuppressable gale of giggles from the children. "I must leave for Strathblane immediately."

"Sit down and calm yourself, Mr Paterson. And leave those papers! Tell me, if you please, how do you feel about my sister?"

"I'm in love with her!" Walter almost shouted, beside himself with confusion.

"That is all very well," said Mrs Hamilton coolly, "but what are your intentions?"

"I intend to marry her . . . if she'll still have me. I gave her my signet ring with my family crest on it, the only thing I had, as a pledge of good faith. But I knew I would have to satisfy your brother that. . . that I could support her properly, and it has taken a little time to put my affairs in order."

"Are you in a position to support her now?"

"Yes, I am. Modestly, but enough. My father and also my brother-in-law, who has far more money than he needs, are both anxious to settle some capital on me, enough to support a small estate." She did not seem impressed. He raised his head proudly. "I can accept their money with a good conscience *Madame*, because I really do not need it . . . save to support a wife like Primrose. I can maintain myself, pay my own way, without help from anyone. I did so this past year after I arrived in Strathblane, destitute and wounded."

"Very commendable I'm sure, Mr Paterson. But what are your plans?"

"My ambition is to return to the Blane valley, buy some property and farm it according to the modern methods your brother uses so successfully. But . . . if I require additional income, I can start up a small educational establishment, teaching languages and social graces that are not taught by the village school. I am a good teacher. I enjoy it. I had several pupils whom I am sure I could continue to instruct."

"Oh yes. I understand you tutored a little boy and that Henry has an 'understanding' with his mother."

"Yes. Mrs Graham. A charming lady." When she said nothing, he floundered on. "We . . . Primrose and I . . . often talked of these things. She too would like to teach painting and music, for she loves children as much as I do. . . "

There was another outburst of mirth from the rear and his flow of words dried up under her gimlet eye. Suddenly he was angry with the whole Moncrieff family.

"Dammit, *Madame*! There is not one day that has passed . . . or one night either . . . that I have not longed for Primrose! I lose sleep every night thinking of her! I have written her many letters but because she told me not to, I have not sent them. If she thinks I neglected her, it's her own fault. She constantly forbade me to do anything that might make your brother suspicious!"

The trace of a dimple appeared on Mrs Hamilton's wan cheek.

"Would you like to join me in a dish of tea, Mr Paterson? I usually have some at this time of day." Before he could refuse, she had rug a little hand bell. "And you might like to be introduced to my children."

"Certainly, *Madame*," though at that moment in his anger and confusion he could with more pleasure have wrung their little necks. But when, like a herd of baby elephants, they rushed out of their corner and surrounded him, scattering his papers again and picking them up with childish glee, he found one of the tiny girls so heartbreakingly like his love, he held out his arms to her smiling, when she jumped up and down and innocently asked,

"Are you the gentleman who's going to marry Auntie Primmy?"

"Yes," he replied spontaneously. "If she'll have me." He shot a glance at Mrs Hamilton who was laughing. "What's your name?" Walter asked the little girl.

"Anne Primrose. I'm called after her."

"And you're almost as beautiful as she is." He bent down to pat her cheek and she threw her little arms around his neck and kissed him.

"That's enough," said her mother, but she did not sound reproving. She motioned to the maid to take the children back to play as another servant appeared with a tea tray and such a lavish assortment of scones and small pastries that Walter suspected the spread had been in preparation ever since his arrival. She poured and handed him a cup.

"Now Mr Paterson," she addressed him as if a bridge had been crossed, "how does Mrs Graham appeal to a man? Tell me about her, for I suspect I am soon to have her for a sister-in-law."

It seemed a good omen, so he did his best to describe his former employer as he sipped the delicate China tea. Possibly due to her condition Mrs Hamilton had a healthy appetite for cakes and as she poured them both second cups, he asked,

"May I hope *Madame*, that you are now more sympathetic to my suit for your sister's hand?"

She nodded. "Truly sir, all I desire is her happiness. She's the youngest of our family. She has had a sad life with our parents dying so young, and her elder brother too. We did talk about you when she was here and I received the impression not only that you were very much in love but you were very compatible with similar interests."

"That is true. Our only disagreements were over how I should approach your brother. She was so afraid he would be angry with her . . . for striking up an acquaintance with me. . . " No need, he thought, to mention the Boards Road and the Gowk Stane. "So . . . may I ask you a great favour? Advise me how to ask the Laird for her hand."

"First you must tell him that you met at Mrs Graham's house." She gave him a conspiratorial smile. "I'll be delighted to help you, Mr Paterson . . . or may I now call you Walter? My name is Catherine . . . Kate for short. Primrose and I spent a lot of time while she was here talking over how you could approach Henry. You had best write to him first, so that he can grow accustomed to the idea."

"How will he take the news . . . that Primrose and I . . . "

She laughed. "He'll have a fit! Not because of you, but because he didn't know! His big complaint is that nobody ever tells him anything."

That, Walter remembered, had been the Laird's reaction when he heard how his sister had sent Walter home from the doctor's in the Kirklands carriage.

"Henry will make a big scene," she went on. "He'll shout and rage. But I've prepared Primrose for that and advised her not to try to reason with him but simply to dissolve into floods of tears, then take to bed and stay there. Henry worries dreadfully about her health. So if he continues to be stubborn, all she need do is send for the doctor. That will frighten him!"

Walter shuddered. He was about to marry into a matriarchy it seemed.

"But I don't believe it will come to that. Probably she'll run crying to her room and Henry will jump on his horse and gallop over to Leddrie Green. And of course Mrs Graham knows all about it."

"And she'll pour oil on troubled waters," put in Walter. "She's good at that."

"So I understand. She'll also point out to him that the chief obstacle in the way of their own marriage is finding a suitable bridegroom for Primrose. And you say you have enough money to support her, so once Henry has calmed down he'll see that. He'll also like the idea of her staying in the valley." She motioned towards a desk. "I see you have plenty of paper with you but if you need something to write with, there are pens and ink over there. And take the other chair, it's more comfortable."

"My concern, Mrs . . . Kate . . . is that I don't think I appeal to your brother. I've tried several times to talk with him and failed. When he was interrogating me, thinking me a spy, I really felt . . . " Abernethy's apt phrase came into his head, "that he didn't like the cut of my jib."

"That was because he felt you were presumptuous. And he was probably jealous. You have two other things that Henry will never have, Walter. Youth and good looks. My poor brother has had a difficult life."

When he looked unimpressed, she explained.

"He was so happy in business in Glasgow but when our elder brother was killed, he had to come home and manage the estates, starting his life all over again."

"He's done a superb job."

"Yes and he likes it. The way to Henry's heart Walter, is through his planting. Primrose says you're fascinated with agriculture too, so you should play on that."

He had by now gathered up his scattered papers and was ready to make notes. Her eyes twinkled and she looked younger and nearly as pretty as her sister.

"I think I could almost dictate what you should write, Walter."

"Then . . . do so please. Just remember, we musn't fail to impress your brother."

"We won't." She flirted her fan. "Henry's very like my father and I observed how my mother handled him. So did Primrose."

He couldn't resist reminding her. "But if she'd listened to me and I'd been able to meet Mr Moncrieff as I wanted, none of these problems would have arisen."

"Maybe not, Walter . . . but remember you weren't as eligible a suitor in those days."

"It all comes down to money, doesn't it?"

"And what's wrong with that?" asked Kate Hamilton. "Wasn't it the lack of it that caused your Revolution in France?"

IV

Walter reigned in his horse on the crest of Craigmaddie and feasted his eyes on the Blane valley, now full of April sunshine. The reflections of plump white clouds drifted flirtatiously across the green Campsie Fells and the air was so clear he could see Ben Lomond's squat protuberance in the distance. He filled his lungs gratefully with the soft air, so moist and gentle after the Edinburgh winds and, as the day was still young, decided to take his time and revisit some old haunts.

He had left his parents at Baldernock where he had spent two days politely listening to a stream of reminiscences about a Scotland that the '45 and the Revolution in France had changed so dramatically, he scarcely recognised it as the country he himself had discovered less than a year before.

Before leaving Edinburgh, he had written to Mrs Graham asking her if she could put his family up briefly. However, he was glad that they had preferred to stay with their old friend Mr Haddow. What had to be done in Strathblane was his own business and so personal he must handle it alone, without his father at his elbow. If, God forbid, the outcome was not what he hoped, he also preferred to cope with his disappointment in the company of his friends in the valley.

Passing the outskirts of Mugdock village, he steered his hired mount down the craggy road which led past Kirklands House. The gates, for once, were wide open but he lacked the courage to go in unannounced. Instead he continued down the well-remembered track to the loch where he had courted Primrose. There was no sign of her on the road as he had faintly hoped. But just before he reached Puddock Hole, he heard a light stampede of feet behind him and turning in the saddle, he found a flock of sheep in his wake. They clustered together as he restrained his horse but then trotted past him fanning out across the fields behind the barn. He had never seen sheep there before and now noticed that little effort had been made to continue the cultivation of Angus MacDougal's crops. The land was rapidly reverting to moor, with weeds and bracken already proliferating.

The farmhouse too looked unkempt and seemed smaller than he remembered. The barn and outbuildings were empty and fast falling into ruins. Someone was living there though, for the collie that had herded the sheep ran out and barked at him. He set spurs to his mount and cantered on down the Boards Road past the Gowk Stane and Mrs Semple's cottage. Far up on the hillside behind her but-an'-ben, he noticed that Wishart's little house was having an addition built. But he was more interested in surveying the valley and observed that in the hamlets of Netherton and Edenkiln there were signs of expansion, particularly around the inkle factory.

There were changes too, outside the doctor's house, *Blaerisk*. Tulips bloomed raggedly in the front garden where a determined assault had been made on the long grass and weeds. The bushes were trimmed and there was a handsome brass tirling pin on the front door.

Walter dismounted and after he had risped the pin up and down, the big panel opened smoothly, revealing Jock MacLean in shirtsleeves. Before they could greet each other, Jean's voice called from upstairs.

"Show the gentleman into the doctor's consulting room and take his horse back to the stables, Jock."

"*C'est moi!*" shouted Walter.

She immediately came rushing down into his arms.

"Lambie! We werenae expecting ye till the morn!"

"Shall I go away and come back?"

"Naw! But Dougie's out on his rounds and I never ken when he'll be here!"

"You and I have plenty to talk about," Walter laughed. "You look very smart."

In a dark wool dress, with shoes and a dainty mob cap, she had left the barefoot farm girl far behind and was now an attractive young matron with an air of authority. But she was also, he noticed, a little wan.

Jean was sizing him up too.

"My, it's you that's so smart! What a lovely coat! And wait till Dougie sees that shirt!"

"I've brought him one just like it."

Jock was bringing in his saddle bags. "Please leave these here. I've gifts to take out. But my horse needs water and oats, if you have them."

"Aye, we've everything nowadays!" exclaimed Mrs MacGregor emerging from the kitchen, beaming. He kissed her too.

"Down Sadie! Down Maisie!" Jean admonished the dogs who were jumping up in welcome. It was, he thought, as warm a homecoming as his reunion with his parents in Edinburgh.

"Oh lambie! Ye maun see ma bonnie wee hoose! I havenae finished reddin it up yet for ye, but . . . "

"Never mind. Let's look it over."

The hall now held Angus MacDougal's grandfather clock and the bleak dining room had been transformed by the handsome table and chairs that he remembered from the farm. The floors were polished to such a high gloss he was almost afraid to walk on them.

"Dougie's havin' his patients come here these days, if they can. It saves his strength. I let them wait in this room unless they've got unco' muddy boots and then they stay in the hall."

"What a grand view of the valley you have from this window! I never noticed it before."

"Naw. He had an auld curtain hangin' there that he got wi the place. I threw it out. Ye can see Ben Lomond." She climbed the steep little staircase, Walter at her heels, and with pride she threw open the door of the master bedroom, now furnished from her old home with a four-poster and the chest of drawers where he had stored his money and Mr Graham's cast-offs.

"I'm weavin' new hangins, Walter. It takes a gey long time but it's goin' to be lovely when it's done. The wee room next door isnae finished yet and Jock's sleepin' there the now."

"Do you have a box bed here?" She nodded. "My French brother-in-law can't believe how comfortable I was in the one at the farm. Where does Mrs MacGregor sleep? And how do you get along with her?"

"She aye had a wee room back o' the kitchen. And there's plenty o' work for the two o' us, I can tell ye! She cleans and washes the clothes but Dougie prefers ma cookin'." She threw her arms around him and kissed him again. "I brought ye up here so we could be private. Ye're a real slyboots, Walter! I never imagined ye were keepin' company wi Miss Moncrieff! No until we got yer letter yesterday and then Dougie telt me a' about it."

"I thought you'd have guessed long ago."

"I'd a feelin' ye had a lassie but I thought it was some yin ye'd met at Mrs Graham's . . . no the Laird's sister!" she added with awe.

"Do you think he'll let me marry her?"

"If ye've enough siller in yer pocket!"

"My father and my brother-in-law are positively pouring money into it. They want me to buy an estate and farm it. Where did those sheep come from, up the Boards Road?"

"Sheep's the Laird's latest. The wool gies a better return than the crops."

The clip-clop of horses' hooves sounded through the open window, accompanying strains of Mozart's *Figaro* in a melodious but free interpretation.

"There's Dougie the now! He maun be hungry. He was out unco early the day. He sings a' the time, Walter! It's to rebuild his lungs after the pneumonia."

"More likely he's just happy."

Her face lit up.

"Aye he is. And so am I and it's a' your doing!"

The singing changed to a shouted inquiry. "Jock, whaur did that horse come from in Maggie's stall?"

"It's mine, Stewart!" Walter clattered downstairs as the front door opened. The friends threw their arms round each other. Douglas slapped his friend on the back then surveyed him as Jean had done.

"Ye look guid but a wee bit pale!"

"I need the country air."

The doctor turned to his wife who had followed downstairs. He took her in his arms and kissed her as though he could never have enough. Then over her shoulder he demanded,

"Mrs MacGregor, did she eat another breakfast?"

"Aye she did, doctor."

"And did it stay down?"

"Aye. . . "

"Good." He grinned at Walter. "She's breedin' already!"

"Dougie," Jean protested, "ye shouldnae blurt it out like that!"

"Why not? I'll wager the whole village kens. And considering my weak state at conception, it's close tae a miracle."

"I've been terrible sick, Walter. Every day. I never thought it would be like that."

"Aweel," her husband consoled, "ye're nearly past that stage now. Ye'll feel fine the rest o' the nine months."

Then turning to his friend, Stewart now exclaimed,

"Paterson, this calls for a celebration. Whaur's the Captain's claret, Jeannie?"

"I thought I'd call on Mrs Graham," said Walter, "To

see how the land lay."

"A guid thought," said Jean, emerging from the dining room with a decanter and glasses on a tray. She led the way into the consulting room. That too, had been transformed. Clean white curtains framed the window. There were no more dusty volumes lying on the floor for sturdy bookshelves lined one wall. The diploma above the mantlepiece was properly framed and hung straight. A bowl of spring flowers decorated the well-polished desk which did however, remain stacked high with papers, pens and other odds and ends.

The doctor's appearance too, had subtly changed. He looked more mature with a streak of grey in his dark hair. And though he would never be handsome, he was beginning to look distinguished. His cheerful manner, which before had occasionally annoyed Walter, was now genuine rather than assumed.

Walter raised his glass, drank and smiled appreciatively.

"Health and happiness to all . . . And how's the Captain? Did he escape the Glasgow jail as he said he would?"

"Oh aye, and the cabin boy too. They came here last week and were asking after ye."

"Are you still . . . ?" Walter asked wondering about the source of the wine he was drinking.

"Naw! A respectable physician's wife cannae be mixed up wi smugglers. Even wi auld Campbell gone."

"He's gone?"

"Aye. Yon raid on the farm was ower much for the Laird. He pulled strings right up the top and had the man removed to anither post. He was banished up North someplace."

"So, who's the Session Clerk?"

Douglas laughed. "Wishart. The biggest supplier o' illicit whisky in the valley!"

"And would ye believe," put in Jean, "he cannae do

enough for Dougie!"

"Aye. Pays ma bills on time and supports a' ma ideas for improvin' the health o' the schoolchildren. Forbye, he keeps me supplied free, wi the Water o' Life which as ye ken, is a useful medicine."

"What about Melville?" Walter asked.

"Gone too," said Jean. "And guess who bought the inkle factory, Walter! Ma cousin, Willie!"

"Is he . . . living here now?"

"No, thank God," said her husband. "He put a manager in. It's ma belief Paterson, that Moncrieff forced Melville's hand and made him sell out and move away as a condition for no turnin' him over to the authorities ower the shootin' o' Jean's faither . . . even though it was a mercy he did."

"And Andra Abernethy comes and goes, just as he used to," Jean put in. "It's as if . . . as if faither died a' for nothing." Tears started in her eyes.

Walter set down his glass and reached for his luggage.

"I've a present for you. Do I have permission Stewart, to give your wife a pair of earrings?"

"It's mair jewelry than she ever got from me."

"I got a wedding ring!"

"Aye, paid for out o' yer ain tocher."

"And for you, my friend . . . " Walter handed over another package. "Dr Gifford steered me to the Edinburgh haberdasher with your measurements."

"Shirts!" Douglas held one up for the inspection of the housekeeper who had appeared in the doorway. "See these, Mrs MacGregor! Now ye can tear up ma auld yins for rags!"

"They're near rags already, doctor . . . and the soup is served."

V

"So when do ye go a-wooing up to Kirklands, Paterson?" Stewart asked over the broth.

"Well, if you got my letter yesterday, the Laird must by now have received my formal request for his sister's hand. I put it in the same post. I told him I'd be staying here. And I've got another letter with me notifying him of my arrival and requesting a meeting."

Jock, who had joined them at the table, spoke up. "I'll take it to Kirklands for ye, Mr Paterson. I'm goin' there this afternoon."

"Ye are, are ye?" said the doctor. "And why, may I ask?"

"I maun deliver a bottle o' that stomach cordial to the Laird. He telt me he was runnin' short o' it after the Service on Sunday."

"Aye. And wi Paterson back to upset his guts, he'll need a double dose."

"They didn't send for you yesterday, did they?" Walter queried apprehensively. Douglas shook his head. "That's hopeful."

"Er . . . If Mr Paterson would like ma room, I could spend the night up at the big house."

Douglas looked at Jock severely. "Only if ye promise to stay away frae Mamie. Ma nerves are no up to anither scare in that quarter."

Walter interposed quickly. "I want to sleep in the box bed."

"We'll sort it a' out later," Jean said. "You be back in time for yer supper, Jock. Did ye know he was goin' to Edinburgh next year, Walter, to the Medical College? Maybe ye can help him find some employment to help pay his way?"

"I can indeed! My sister's always looking for extra footmen. She's got a huge house in Charlotte Square and so many servants I couldn't remember all their names!"

"Charlotte Square! The New Town! The most fashionable part o' the city, Jock. But meanwhile, if ye're goin' up the Board's Road, ye can practice the healin' art on that gamekeeper's family wi' the whoopin' cough," said the doctor.

"You still have that new dominie?" asked Walter.

"Aye." Stewart's tone was less than enthusiastic.

"He's unco' sickly," Jean explained. "Dougie had to lead the singin' at the Kirk in his place on Sunday."

Walter laughed uproariously. "The Kirk has caught you, *mon brave!*"

"Naw! But . . . the man had a fierce case o' laryngitis. If he was to tak his classes during the week, he had to rest his voice on the Sabbath. But he was a' upset, for fear the Session would think he was failin' in his work . . . bein' Precentor is part o' it, ye ken. So I went to Mr Gardner and explained and offered to stand in for him."

"And everyone said ye gied the congregation a better lead."

"That's no sayin' much. D'ye want the horse this afternoon, Jock?"

Walter intercepted a quick exchange of glances between Jean and the young man.

"No thank ye, doctor. Ye'll need her yersel'."

As they rose from the table and returned to the other room, the tirling pin risped on the front door.

"Tak care o' it Mr MacLean, if ye please," said Dougie grandly. "I'm busy the now."

He pushed Walter into the room ahead of him and shut the door. But in a moment his assistant joined them, grinning.

"It's Mrs MacLaren and she maun speak wi' Mrs Stewart."

Jean swept out into the hall.

"Where did Melville go?" Walter asked.

"Back to Glasgow to the import business. And just in time. His workers at the factory were leaving in droves, he was that unpopular. There's as big a social upheaval here as they're havin' in France."

"It's not as bloody."

"Naw. But it's just as radical. A few years ago these raw Heilanders and Irish wouldnae hae been mutterin' aboot yin law fer the rich and anither fer the poor."

Jean came back in, her hands full of coins. She went straight to the desk, took a cash-box and ledger from the drawer and started making notations.

"Don't tell me Mrs MacLaren paid ma bill!"

"She did. And a' in siller."

"No neeps? I've been dunnin' that family ever since I came here, Paterson. This is the first time they've gied me ma money!"

Jean said levelly,

"Them that can afford imported tea and French wine should be able to pay their doctor." She smiled at him fondly, "even when he is a big softie."

"I dinnae hae yer head fer business, that's for sure." He grinned at his friend. "I'm no workin' as long hours. I've twa more mouths tae feed . . . three, if ye count the baby. And yet I'm startin' to make a wee bit o' money. It's a' Jean's daein'."

"Aye, but maist o' the arrears are paid up by now, so there'll no be as much comin' in."

"Courage, lassie! Ogilvy says the whoopin' cough may become an epidemic. That's ma colleague in Killearn, Paterson. A nice man, and strong on public health. Yin o' these days . . . once we learn how to dae it . . . we're goin' tae engraft the whole valley against smallpox. But until then, there's work to do." He picked up his bag.

"I'll come with you . . . at least as far as Leddrie Green." As they were leaving he remarked, "I can't get used to this door opening so smoothly."

"It just needed a wee bit o' adjustin'," said Jock, who had brought around the horses for them.

As they ambled down the Minister's Brae, Walter said, "You'll miss that young fellow when he goes to Edinburgh."

"Aye. He saved ma life wi his prompt treatment. I was taken ill down at the Manse. I near died that Saturday night and when Mr Gardner cried the banns for ma marriage at the Sunday service, he led the congregation in a prayer for ma recovery. Imagine! Jock didnae bide for that. He dashed straight over to ma bedside, examined me, then climbed up here, through a' the snow, for some medicines."

"He knew what to do?"

"Aye. And it was a sobering moment Paterson, when I'd passed the crisis and come out o' a healin' sleep to find ma apprentice at ma bedside, wi ma bag at his feet, and a big tome on respiratory diseases at his elbow. He'd done everything it recommended, which wasnae much, but for me it meant the difference between life and death. . . If only he'd stay away from Mamie!" Douglas exploded, possibly to cover his emotion.

"He got her in the family way?"

"He did but she lost it. I suspect Aunt Semple slipped her some herb while I was carefully looking the other way."

"And how is the good Mrs Semple?"

"Just the same. Enjoyin' her wee bit o' ill health. But she handled a' the lyin'-ins just fine when I was laid up. Hae ye found a publisher for yer poems? They're guid!"

"I think I have, but I've had no luck with your Mesmer manuscript as yet."

"That'll keep. I've anither case history for it . . . that farmer at Milndavie whose wife was so pregnant at Hogmanay. He fell down a gully goin' after a sheep and smashed his leg. Dr Ogilvy was here visiting me when it happened. I was still convalescent. He went around and came back to report that the limb must be amputated immediately and did I feel up to it, for he's no surgeon. Forbye, the man wouldnae consent unless I agreed it was necessary. So Jean bundled me up and we went along the road. And Paterson, Ogilvy was right. The leg was smashed to bits. But . . . I couldnae bring masel' to cut it off. A young fellow livin' off the land wi a growin' family needs his limbs. So . . . I invoked the shade o' Dr Mesmer."

"Successfully?"

"Aye. He went into a trance even quicker than you did. And wi ma sceptical colleague standin' by. When I was sure he felt naethin', I settled down to peace and quiet. And takin' ma time, I put his leg back thegither again. Ogilvy was fair impressed. A guid thing he was there to assist me, for Jock got sick."

"And will the man be all right?"

"Oh aye," said Douglas, as though it was a foregone conclusion. "He doesnae need crutches now. But, he's goin' round the parish sayin' I talked him to sleep! Does that no make me sound like an awfa' bore?"

"Better than being considered a warlock!"

"I suppose so. It was a guid day for me. It saved me from bein' blooded masel', by Ogilvy. He said if I'd the stamina for that long operation, I needed no more care from him. Forbye, he's referring his surgical cases to me instead of sending them to Glasgow. And the farmer was that grateful he gied me Maggie here as a gift, ower and above ma bill.

She's made life a lot easier."

He patted the horse, a huge amiable plodder, scarcely able to keep up with the lively mount Walter had hired in Glasgow.

"So, things are looking up for you, as they are for me?"

"Aye. In every way. I'm glad ye're gettin' married too. It makes a' the difference in the world, when ye wake up in the wee sma' hours, to find someone beside you. Someone ye can talk to. . . . No-one will ever know how lonesome I was until I started comin' up to Puddock Hole to attend you."

"I'm glad I did something for you, after all you did for me!"

"Ye're a catalyst, Paterson. Some people are like that. Wherever they go, they stir things up. It'll be interesting to see what happens when ye settle in Strathblane."

"I'm glad you'll still be here."

"I'll stay until Jock's trained. But . . . then I'm moving on. I'd like to go to London. But Jean has an idea we could emigrate to America. There's a guid medical college in Philadelphia, run by Edinburgh men, who'd welcome me wi open arms."

"But before that, perhaps we can write another book together? Do you know of any estates around here that I may buy?"

"There's Leddrie Green. If Mrs Graham marries the Laird, and I hope she does before he becomes a valetudinarian . . . it'll be up for roup."

"Will Moncrieff accept me as a brother-in-law? And will Primrose still have me?"

"On that last score, set yer mind at rest! Listen! I've been her father-confessor these past weeks, and I assure you she loves you most tenderly. She's a fine girl. And healthy. No consumption or anything like that."

"Her sister says I treated her very badly."

"Naw! Naw! She was terrified ye'd write to her and her brother would find out."

"Is she still afraid of him?"

Douglas laughed. "I can't imagine ony yin bein' afraid o' that man."

Walter refrained from bringing up some past occasions, for by now they were approaching the main gate to Leddrie Green He was about to dismount to open it when there was a joyful shout and it swung back on its hinges.

"Mr Paterson!" Bobby charged onto the road, almost falling under the horses' hooves. "Oh, Mr Paterson!"

"*Robert!*" Walter jumped down and embraced his former pupil. "*Mais tu es déjà un vrai jeune homme!*"

"And what are ye daein' out o' school?" demanded the doctor.

The boy looked sheepish.

"I had a sore throat. But it's gone now."

"Malingering again?" asked Douglas.

Bobby nodded. "I was feared of the Latin test. Are you coming to visit us, Mr Paterson?"

"I am. Why don't you start walking my horse up to the stables?"

As the boy turned up the drive, Walter said,

"You're going to make a stern parent."

"Unless it's a girl, and I eat out o' her hand."

Walter was lingering.

"Are ye scared too, Paterson?"

"Yes. . . "

"Ye've nothin' to fear. Take deep breaths. I'll see ye at suppertime and we'll spend the whole evening drinkin' your health and your bride's."

Catching up with Bobby, Walter asked, "Is your mother at home?"

"Yes. Are you coming back here to live?"

"*J'espère. Tu nás pas oublié ton français?*"

"*Non! Jamais de la vie!*" The boy embarked on a confused bilingual account of his troubles in school and how he couldn't wait to move on to Glasgow University. Walter listened with half an ear, his eyes roaming over the recently planted bushes in the driveway, wondering what else he might grow there, if the property were his. In the stableyard stood a familiar carriage and his heart lurched and sank.

"*Robert*, is Mr Moncrieff visiting your mother?"

"Yes, but he's here all the time. They're getting married. Don't bother about him!"

So much for the powerful Laird, and before Walter could think up some excuse to postpone his visit to another day, the stable boy had appeared, greeted him as an old friend and took his mount. Then Bobby, still chattering, grabbed his arm and propelled him into the house, where he was scarcely given time to rid himself of hat, gloves and riding crop before he was dragged along the passage to the drawing room door.

"*Maman! Voilà Monsieur Paterson qui revient!*"

Hastily smoothing his hair and bracing himself, Walter followed his pupil into the little room which, as on a previous occasion, seemed full of people.

Mrs Graham, the nearest, jumped up with a joyful little scream and threw her arms around his neck.

"Oh, my dear boy! How wonderful! You're here already! Are your parents with you?"

"No *Madame*, I left them in Baldernock." He kissed her, which he now knew was permissible in Scotland. "The minister there is an old friend. . . "

There was a tinkle as a wine glass fell to the floor.

Primrose was sitting on the couch. She was pale, as though she had suffered a long strain but her face was even lovelier then he remembered it. And it had changed. She had grown up, though without losing any of her girlish beauty.

But her green eyes, with their astonishing black lashes met his with a new wariness, though there was joy in them too. And before he could go to her, he found himself face to face with the Laird who was advancing towards him and doing his best to smile.

"Welcome back to Strathblane, Mr Paterson. I received your letter yesterday."

"Sir. . . " Walter took the outstretched hand, "May I call upon you tomorrow?"

"Yes! and come early so that I can show you over my policies." For the first time Moncrieff was looking straight at him, without prejudice, even as though he would like to know him better. "Are you staying with Dr Stewart?"

"Yes. . . "

"Then let me send my carriage for you first thing in the morning."

"You don't need to do that," chimed in Bobby, who was jumping up and down in the rear. "Mr Paterson has his own beautiful horse!"

"Good! Then we can plan on going all around the estate . . . I was most interested in your remarks about improvements to the ground. . . And you mentioned some books you had read in Edinburgh. Did you by any chance bring them with you?"

"Yes. A couple. If you have not read them, I would be glad if you would accept them. . . "

"That is kind of you. Bring them with you . . . What are they?"

"One is on crop rotation. I got it from the Society of Improvers. . . "

It was hard to think about agriculture with all his attention on Primrose. At long last, she was seeing him as he really was. But why was she so apprehensive? Surely she did not doubt his devotion? She was wearing his ring, a good sign, but she was twisting it nervously round her small finger.

"I have had some interesting results, using different crops." The Laird was clearly delighted to have someone to talk to about his favourite projects. "So, I will look forward to some discussion with you. I know Mrs Stewart will want to see you, but I hope you can stay to dinner?"

"Thank you . . . " Walter took a deep breath. He was beginning to blush like a schoolboy, and any minute he might start to stammer, or worse still, revert to French.

"Sir, on the . . . other matter that I wrote to you about. Your sister's hand in marriage. Perhaps this is not the time to bring it up, but . . . May I hope . . . ?"

Primrose jumped to her feet, speaking quickly before her brother could reply.

"Yes! yes, Walter! Henry has agreed. . . Hasn't he, Alison?"

"We were talking about it when you arrived, Mr Paterson. And I for one was so happy that you and dear little Primrose. . . "

The Laird, whom Walter suspected had not been about to concede so readily, interposed,

"If you can satisfy me that you are able to take care of her, as I believe you can. . . "

"Oh, yes, sir. My father will be here shortly. He has documentation of the funds he is settling on me. Instead of sending me to the University . . . when I had already had plenty of education . . . he wishes to establish me on some property of my own that I can farm, as I wish."

There was a brief silence that terrified Walter. Then Moncrieff asked,

"Is your brother-in-law coming with him to Strathblane? I would like to meet him again and he too, wanted to see around my estate."

"He . . . is remaining with my sister at present. She is with child. But . . . he sent you his greetings."

Walter's eyes went to Primrose. Her impish smile had popped out, as though she knew Louis had done nothing of the sort. Their old *rapport* was still there and he took heart, became ready to fight for her.

"Mr Moncrieff, I have admired your sister from the first moment I saw her. You asked me once . . . why I stayed on in Strathblane, why I did not continue to Edinburgh, to my family, after recovering from my wounds last year. It was because I had fallen in love with her, though no-one but she knew it. I couldn't bear to leave her . . . or the Blane Valley either. . . " He mustn't talk too much, mustn't blurt out how they had met at sunset on the Boards Road. "I kept the matter to myself until I was in a position to ask for her hand. I am now, and so, if she is . . . agreeable?"

Primrose turned to her brother.

"You promised our mother you would never make a match for me unless I was willing and knew my own mind in the matter. I do. I have never loved any man but . . . Mr Paterson."

She swept past the Laird straight into Walter's arms.

". . . Henry," said Alison Graham as firmly as though they had been married for years. "These young people should be left alone. . . Besides, we have our own wedding plans to discuss. Perhaps we can have a double celebration. The parish would enjoy that. Let us go and talk in the conservatory. You're coming with us, Bobby!"

"I want to stay and visit with Mr Paterson!"

"Do as your mother says, young man," Moncrieff ordered and taking his future stepson by the arm, he marched from the room in the widow's wake, shutting the door on the lovers.

THE END